TIM MENDEES

SHADOW OF CHAOS

ZONE 51: BOOK 1

EERIE RIVER PUBLISHING
www. EerieRiverPublishing.com

Eerie River Publishing
www.EerieRiverPublishing.com
Kitchener, Ontario Canada
Subdivision of Eerie Ventures Ltd.
This book is a work of fiction. Names, characters, places, events, organizations and incidents are either part of the author's imagination or are used fictitiously. Any resemblance to actual persons, living or dead, or actual events is purely coincidental.

Paperback ISBN: 978-1-998112-46-3

Editor: Shona Kinsella
Artwork: Metamoraki @adityadusek
Book Formatting by Michelle River of Eerie River Publishing

ALSO BY TIM MENDEES

Spiffing (2021)
The Grime of the Ancient Mariner (2021)
Miracle Growth (2022)
Antisocial Housing (2022)

The Hollowhills Cycle:
Burning Reflection (2020)
Boiling Shadow (2021)
Blasted Soul (2024)
Beating Ground (2024)

Short Story Collections:
The Pseudopod That Rocks the Cradle (2021)
Visions & Abominations (2023)
Beyond Desire (With Zoe Burgess) (2025)

"The human race sleepwalked to oblivion, thinking only of the corporate logos on its shroud."
—J.G. Ballard
"No death, no doom, no anguish can arouse the surpassing despair which flows from a loss of identity.
—H.P. Lovecraft

CHAPTER 1

THE UNDESIRABLES

Johanna's heart pounded just as hard in her chest as her feet pounded the sodden pavement. She and her fellow fugitive ducked around the corner of a crumbling building to evade the sweeping lights of a passing drone. The black and yellow automated enforcement device circled the weed-choked forecourt of a derelict petrol station before resuming its pre-programmed flight path. After a tense few moments, the group exhaled.

"Come on, we only have a short window before it returns." Johanna beckoned Sam to follow as he darted back onto the street. They had been planning their escape from the Zone for weeks and she had diligently memorised every patrol pattern of the myriad drones and Enforcement Patrols between their domicile and the boat. They were on a strict schedule, and any deviation, no matter how slight, could prove instantly fatal.

It wasn't safe to be out after dark in Zone 51. Firstly, the blanket curfew mandate decreed that anyone caught out of their designated habitat between 22:00 and 06:00 would face harsh penalties. The only exception to the rule being those that held the correct pass. Unfortunately, Johanna and Sam didn't have the correct pass, no citizens of Zone 51 did. The only people allowed on the streets during the hours of darkness were the enforcers and representatives of The Global Arms Federation, the all-powerful conglomerate that owned the shrinking spit of land formerly known as Great Britain. The second reason for Johanna's acute state of panic was the *others* that prowled at night.

Outside of the miles of steel and glass egg-boxes that passed as homes, the *restricted areas* of the sector were stalked by things far worse than gun-toting guards and buzzing drones. Not that the overseer of the zone cared; what was one missing worker now and then? As long as the wheels of industry turned and the profits kept on rolling in, where was the harm in a little *population control?* If anything, the lurking threats aided his cause. By promising to keep them safe if they stayed in the designated areas, he could deter anyone doing anything as foolish as dreaming of freedom.

Johanna and Sam were dreamers...

"Hang a left, down the alley," Sam panted in Jo's ear as they reached a crossroads. "With any luck, we should get out ahead of the next patrol."

Jo hesitated. "Are you sure? I thought we had to go right?"

"Nah, that takes you close to one of the drone release hubs, we'd be bloody mad to go that way."

"We are bloody mad to be out here, full stop. Still, no option, right? It's now or never, right?"

"Right," Sam said, grabbing her arm and running ahead, "now, let's move before we get shot. It ain't safe to stand around yapping."

Nodding to herself to convince herself that they had made the right choice, Johanna broke into a run and quickly overtook her companion. Not that it was much of a choice to begin with. Nobody would *choose* to be on the streets this late and they had no other options. Only when it was dark, and the fog had rolled in off the swollen sea could anyone move freely. This was the moment when the omnipresent electronic eyes would finally be occluded enough for someone to pass unseen and unnoticed. Her barcode, like many of her fellows, read *undesirable;* if caught, she would be sent behind the wall far south of the father country in the west. Exiled behind miles of concrete and steel, bullets and barbed wire. Nobody returned from the restricted zone ... not alive, anyway. Unlike Sam who had punched his shift leader, she never did find out what made her *undesirable* in the first place. Not many people did.

The streets towards the docks swam with a filthy concoction of stagnant seawater, rotting fish and rat droppings. A furry horde was never far away in Zone 51. Samuel Jacobs, her companion on her midnight flight, had sworn that he saw a rat king of immense size the last time he had been scavenging down by the docks. The former spring welder had claimed that the horrifying amalgamation of conjoined rodents was comparable in size to a small tractor. Just the thought of it made Jo wince, all those individuals stuck together by grime and grease, all those minds controlled by a single ravenous voice ... it sounded far too familiar for comfort.

Sam and Jo had chosen to finally make a break for freedom after months of living in the *restricted zone*. They had both been branded *undesirable* and scheduled for exile but had managed to escape when their transport broke down. After weeks of trying to find a way out, Sam had finally managed to scrape together the bribe required to book their way onto a refuse liner, one of the colossal ships that would be regularly loaded with the sector's accumulated detritus then sailed out of the former Europe and into the free East. Once in unregulated waters, it would be dumped on the nearest patch of land that didn't belong to The Imperial Corporation of America and Europe. Out of sight, out of mind. Somebody else's problem. Nothing outside of the ICAE's autonomous zones mattered. It was a small wonder to most that everything outside of its borders hadn't as yet been subjugated or blasted off the map completely. Such was the mentality of those in command.

This near-mythical utopia, the free East, was their ultimate destination. Both runners had family there, though whether they still lived was unknown. Communication to places outside of the Zone was strictly forbidden. When their loved ones had been deported for various imagined infractions, they had both wept, fearing tremendously what would become of them. In retrospect, they should have been worrying about what would happen to those that stayed, those *privileged few* allowed to be the workers and drones of the GAF. To the leadership, they were nothing more than tools to be used up and then discarded, mere grist to the mill.

Many places in the once green and pleasant land were now

underwater. The Chief Executive Officer of the Imperial Corporation didn't believe in global warming hence the world didn't believe in global warming; whatever he said had to be taken as gospel. Chapter and Verse. Unfortunately, the gallon of water in both of Sam's work issue boots could testify to the reality of climate change. What parts of the zone that weren't swampland or filthy quagmire were a soulless hunk of concrete and steel. Everything was grey, cold, and solid, there were no curves or undulations to the architecture, only sharp right-angles, a topography you could cut yourself on. The brutalist-revival in the latter years of the last century had done away with anything remotely picturesque. Green and pleasant land? Grey and ugly land, more like.

As the crow flew, Jo and Sam didn't have that far to go. The docklands were only across the former town, and before the mass-industrialisation of Cornwall it would have taken less than an hour. Now, however, they were lucky if they made it in a day. They had to lie low during working hours as the drones and enforcers would be out en masse, but they had a place in mind for that. Sam's contact in the GAF knew all kinds of useful things, for the right price, of course.

The alley that provided temporary cover for the two escapees eventually opened out onto what was once a pub carpark. Sam was old enough to remember the sounds and smells of the old drinking establishment. His mind reeled as he remembered the taste of the drinks, the laughter and camaraderie; there had been good times before the merger and Zone 51 was born. A wistful smile spread across his gaunt features. Johanna spotted her friend's distracted look and gave him a gentle squeeze on his overall-clad arm.

"Sorry. Memories." He smiled. "Maybe we can get a decent pint out East?"

Jo returned his smile and gave him a look of hope that spoke volumes. "Yeah, hopefully. It can't be any worse than the swill they serve up in the cantina."

"Ooh, hark at her. When did you manage to sneak into the cantina?"

"I didn't, I know a guy that works on the delivery wagon.

Things fall off the back of it from time to time, if you get my meaning?"

Sam chuckled under his breath. "That says it all, don't it? Not even the beer is worth nicking. You wouldn't believe what I had to pinch to get us on the boat."

"What did he want this time? I seem to remember he wanted synthetic chocolate when he got you off a week of toilet detail."

"Two loaves of long-life bread and some imitation cheese."

"And you nicked it?" Jo was shocked. "You're seriously telling me he had you risk getting shot over a bloody cheese sandwich?"

"Look, it's a hefty chunk of his weekly ration, he said. Apparently, he can't stomach the Grey Bar, it goes through him like a laxative." Sam grabbed his stomach dramatically for emphasis.

Jo nodded sadly. "I get it, he's not alone in that department, my sister was the same, one bite and she was doubled over." The majority of workers had to make do with the blocks of unidentified protein that the GAF dealt out at the local ration centre. Standard issue protein bars contained all the vitamins and minerals a healthy worker needed to keep themselves fit and strong, but God help you if you were allergic to artificial flavourings or preservatives.

"Come on. It's not that far now."

Eyes darting from left to right and back again, they gingerly edged around the corner. Jo had taken point as her eyesight wasn't quite as damaged as Sam's; she had never been drafted to the factory that handled lead. They had advanced less than fifty yards when a sharp slam not far ahead signalled that they were not alone.

"Shit," Jo whispered, "ghosts, get down."

Crouching low behind a row of rusty dustbins overflowing with festering refuse, Sam and Jo did their best to become invisible. A door to one of the old shopfronts that had comprised what was once a picturesque fishing town had swung open to reveal two spectral figures stepping out into the gloom. Gun-barrel-mounted torch lights cut through the murk like knives, the ultra-high beams glaring off the fog, bathing the area in terrible shadows that loomed and stretched. One of the figures was muttering to himself about the rats breaking the spectral illusion.

The two stout enforcers had just finished checking the sub-sector for undesirables and were due to clock off shift at the hour. Clad in luminous yellow hooded uniforms that stood out in stark contrast to the dark of the night, the two men paused on the threshold and shone their lights up and down the narrow street. What little moonlight there was filtered through the miasma and twinkled off the reflective strips on their chests with a sepia lambency. The fact that the enforcers stalked the night like phantoms, coupled with their general appearance, was why the populous called them ghosts. Some people called them *Caspers,* but Jo had no idea why. Still, it annoyed them which was reason enough to persist.

Sam and Jo held their breath and trembled as the two enforcers stomped in their direction The tension was nerve-racking; one false move or stray gasp could prove fatal. Most enforcers shot on sight. Perversely, the penalty for shooting an innocent was far more lenient than the one doled out to enforcers who allowed a fugitive to escape. It was a case of law enforcement taken to the extreme. They were so close that Jo could smell the machine oil on their multi-purpose firearms. The standard-issue boots worn by the approaching Caspers slapped the standing water, each footfall sending sharp jolts of panic through Sam and Jo. Enforcer boots were a far cry from the standard work-issue *Frankenstein* boots worn by the public; they were strong, durable, and comfortable. The last thing either of them wanted was one of them coming down on their heads.

Sam felt a sharp pang of cramp in his left calf. He wasn't as young as he used to be, and years of backbreaking work, manufacturing the latest in weapons technology, had taken its toll. As much as he wanted to dance about and shake the knot from his leg, he couldn't, it would mean death for both of them. The enforcers were so close that Jo could hear them talking. Their gruff voices cracking wise through their protective masks about kicking in some undesirables the night before. The overseer would be pleased. Perhaps they would get a bonus? In this totalitarian state, brutality wasn't just encouraged, it was rewarded. After what felt like an eternity, the enforcers passed without incident.

"Jesus, that was close," Jo whispered.

"Yeah, I thought we were goners for sure," Sam hissed through pain-gritted teeth as he tried to massage his muscle back to life. "There's even more ghosts around than usual. I'm one-hundred-percent certain they weren't scheduled to be here."

Jo hummed thoughtfully. "Possibly, I wonder why?"

"Kenny, who hangs about near the old war memorial, says that it's because of the *lurkers*. He reckons that there are shitloads of them down by the docks." Sam stood up and arched his back which cracked noisily. "We'd better be careful."

Jo checked that her boots were fastened tightly in case they had to run for it. "Have you ever seen a lurker?"

"What, me? Nah, I'm not even sure I believe in them. I think they are another boogeyman dreamt up by the propaganda bureau to scare us into obeying the curfew. It's like all that crap about anthrax and crow pox they spout every time someone in charge fucks something up. It's all sleight of hand. Nothing more than a distraction."

Jo looked pensive. "Lenny says he saw one, said it was the size of a GAF transport truck."

"Yeah, well, Lenny's full of shit." Sam brushed the moisture off his balding pate. "The guy's been drinking meths for so long he doesn't know what bloody day it is most of the time."

"I hope you're right, I really do." Jo looked around; the coast was clear. "Come on. Let's get out of here before they come back."

Jo was slim and athletic and looked older than her twenty-four years; life in Zone 51 aged you quickly. If the pervasive damp, malnutrition and punishing working hours didn't do it, the acid rain would. It played havoc with one's complexion. She had been born in Zone 51, in what is now the north-west quadrant, a place formerly known as Manchester. Jo had been raised and prepared for a life of *vital* work in one of the vast, hive-like education centres that peppered the zone, *primed* with everything a growing girl needed to make it in the neo-capitalist world.

A large wall blocked any further progress in their current direction. They needed to navigate what was once the old town, a deserted rabbit warren of abandoned shops, overflowing bins and savage feral cats. Jo checked the corner, it was clear, the only movement coming from a large rat foraging in the window of what was once a flower shop.

Jo made a low noise in the back of her throat.

"What's up, don't like rats?"

"It's not that. I just realised I've never seen a florist before. A real one, I mean. I've seen them in old movies and shows, sure, but never in real life. Come to think of it, I can't remember the last time I saw a real flower."

"We don't have them in the Zone. The Overseer replaced them all with plastic ones decades ago. Since the creation of the oxygen plants over in Zone 53 we don't need foliage, decorative or otherwise." In fact, Mr Sanderson, Zone 51's Overseer had waged a personal war on flowers early in the Zone's inception. They grew outside and weeds sometimes found a way in, sure, but not so much as a daisy had been intentionally grown inside for decades. Plants were inefficient, plus, one of his Pharaoh hounds had hay-fever so they had to go.

"Yeah, but they're pretty and smell good." Johanna shrugged.

"Yeah, I'm old enough to remember when you used to get freshly cut flowers in vases on cafe tables... It feels like a lifetime ago."

"It was." Jo smirked and gave him a playful nudge. "Come along, old father time, let's get out of here and go and smell the roses."

Sam and Jo stealthily skulked down the street, hugging the wall and using the fog for cover. Scraps of ancient posters and flyers flapped as a breeze whipped in from the coast carrying the pungent aroma of putrefying mackerel and decaying seaweed. As they approached the next junction everything went horribly wrong. A solid *crack* announced that something was ahead of them. Another noise echoed off the filth encrusted walls as a heavy steel shipping container was overturned and tossed aside as though it weighed nothing.

Tekeli-li!

Jo froze, grabbing Sam by the arm as a shrill piping echoed down the street. It was followed by a disgusting slurping noise and the agonised howl of a canine. The two friends were stunned stiff. The dog wailed pitifully as its bones cracked and ground together. They couldn't see what was devouring the poor animal, but it sounded huge and glutinous. It piped and slurped, sucked and hissed in an obvious feeding-frenzy. Mercifully, the dog quickly died and ceased its blood-chilling cries. Worryingly, though, the creature still sounded hungry as it started to sniff around the container for another tasty morsel.

Jo motioned with her hand to move back slowly; any loud noise or sudden movement could mean disaster. Sam slowly started to edge back down the alley. He had started to sweat profusely, and hoped to God that the creature didn't hunt by scent. The formless monster roared as it sent a skip hurtling across the alley, smashing it into the building opposite and collapsing a portion of the crumbling red-brick wall. It fell inwards taking out the joists. With a tremendous clatter, the upper facade fell into the skip sending a plume of dust and debris into the atmosphere where it mingled with the fog to decrease visibility even further.

As Sam and Jo squinted through the airborne grit, they finally caught sight of something oozing out of the shadows. It was colossal. A formless mass of roiling protoplasm festooned with questing pseudopods, baleful eyes, and lamprey-like mouths that manifested at will. Colours shifted and swirled on its enormous oily bulk. As they watched on, unable to move, the creature started to change form. A massive ropey tentacle sprouted from the side of the beast and commenced groping obscenely around in the debris... It was hunting.

Sam started to back away following Jo's lead, but one of his boots scuffed the cracked Tarmac. The creature shuddered and one of its multitudinous eyes locked on the panicked couple. Throbbing hungrily, it shifted its attention to their warm bodies. Changing direction, it let out another shrill cry. Jo gagged; the stench of its breath was stomach-churning, somewhere between a living charnel house and a festering lagoon. Sam could feel nausea building from deep within his gullet as the stink ticked his gag reflex. Several more tentacles and fronds violently burst from the gelatinous mass as it reared back and prepared to strike. Jo prepared to meet her maker.

Things were looking bleak when help came from an unlikely source. Between them and *it,* a door was flung open and slammed against the wall. It was the two patrolling Caspers. The not-so-friendly ghosts, alerted by the noise, burst from the door of an old workshop with their weapons drawn and their itchy fingers on the triggers of their oversized rifles. They levelled their weapons at Sam and Johanna, not bothering to check their six.

"Stop right there!" the larger of the two bellowed.

Sam's hands instinctively reached for the skies. You can't survive in a police state as long as he had without learning how to surrender.

Jo, slack-jawed in fright, pointed past the two enforcers at the gathering mass. "Look out!"

"Do ya think I just fell off the gun truck or something?" the second enforcer snarled. "Get on your knees, undesirable!" he commanded as he pumped his rifle with a resounding *clack!* Anyone out after curfew was automatically an undesirable to most enforcers, so he didn't need to check for a barcode. It made life so much easier. Shoot first, look for a reason later.

The creature turned its attention to the enforcers and began to surge in their direction. Alerted by the foul *slurp* of the beast's movement, the first enforcer spun on his heels. His eyes popped out of his head as he spotted the encroaching terror. It moved with an awesome fluidity and speed for a creature of its tremendous bulk. Roaring in panic and disbelief, the enforcer unloaded his clip, his rifle's muzzle flashed as he pumped round after round into the unstoppable monster. As the hollow *click* of an empty chamber rang out, the creature, completely unaffected by the onslaught, went on the offensive. With a whip-like *crack!* a tentacle lashed out and wrapped itself around the enforcer's waist. His water-resistant uniform melted to atoms as the screaming enforcer was completely absorbed by the shimmering horror.

Screaming a torrent of invective, the second enforcer opened fire, but it was no use, the creature didn't even flinch. Ripples of bright colour appeared on its surface as one by one the bullets were absorbed. Returning to her senses, Jo grabbed Sam by the collar and pulled him with her as she darted down a smaller alley that ran off to the left. As they sprinted as fast as their heavy boots would allow, the sounds of the second enforcer's painful demise surged around them.

Tekeli-li!

A tremendous bellow announced that the creature was in pursuit. It flowed around the corner, hitting the left wall like a tidal wave. It flowed and surged, rippled and oozed as it quickly closed the gap between them. The alley was a dead end. Sam and Jo almost collided with the filthy brick wall as they tried to escape.

"Fuck," Jo cried. "We're trapped, there's no way out!" In moments they would become the creatures' next meal...

"Hey," a voice called out from above as he tossed down a knotted rope. "Up here, quick!"

Quickly, Sam and Jo pulled themselves up towards their unknown saviour. Upon reaching the aperture, they were pulled through and collapsed in a heap as a heavy metal shutter was slammed down with authority.

"It won't get through that... I hope." A large Caribbean man in grubby overalls smiled down at them benignly. "Jesus, that was close!"

"What the fuck was that?" Jo cried hysterically, instinctively scuttling backwards on her haunches away from the unknown man.

Dwayne, their saviour, shrugged and held out his large, calloused hand. "Folks call 'em lots of things. I think the current term is *Lurker*, though I believe it's called a shoggoth. You'll have to ask Ben, he's the expert on these things." Once Sam and Jo were back to their feet, Dwayne led them across what was once the storeroom for an old antique shop. "The whole area's crawlin' with 'em at night. They live in the sewers and don't like light much, so you never see 'em in the day ... at night, they're deadly."

"But what *are* they?" Jo asked, a note of hysteria in her voice. "Are they some kind of weapon or experiment gone wrong?"

"I'd say *'God knows'* but the fact is, the big man probably hasn't got a clue either. I can't imagine The Almighty having anything to do with such a creature. No *sane* God created something like that." Dwayne pulled open a heavy fire door to reveal a living area decked out with antique furniture and drapes. It was like walking into Oscar Wilde's boudoir.

Reclining on a chaise-longue was an elderly man smoking a pipe while a rough-looking gentleman sat stripping down a battered AK-47 in an old wing-back chair. The third occupant of the room, a girl of around sixteen, still dressed in her education centre jumpsuit, paced and chewed a wayward strand of her ratty blonde hair. Dwayne walked over to the girl and smiled at her softly. He replied a solemn, "No. I'm afraid not" to her whispered question. She began to sob and raced off through a second door that led away to a couple of small bedrooms.

"That was Jane," Dwayne explained. "Found her wandering 'round down by the water a couple of days back. She lost her family in the fog. I had just been out lookin' for 'em when I heard all the commotion. Good thing I was passing, or you'd be lunch about now."

"Shit," Sam said softly. "Poor girl, and thank you."

"No problem, us *undesirables* gotta stick together, right?" Dwayne smiled then pointed to the man with the gun. He hadn't even looked up since they had entered the room. "This here is Max. Don't expect much conversation from him. Max used to be an enforcer, until the overseer had his tongue cut out when he questioned a kill order. He was branded undesirable and hunted like an animal. I found him in a right old state and brought him to Benjamin here..." He indicated the old man with the pipe. "Ben took us both in, this is his place, it has been in his family for generations. The stubborn old goat refused to leave when the town was cleared... I think they forgot about him."

"Pleased to make your acquaintance." Ben sat up and extended a shaky liver-spotted hand. "Benjamin Edwards, at your service." He talked in cultured tones and looked like the remnant of a bygone age.

Sam and Jo, in turn, shook the man's hand. He smiled benignly and took a puff on his pipe.

"So, where were you guys headed?" Dwayne asked. "You really shouldn't be down here at night; if the lurkers don't get ya, the Caspers will."

"We have a passage arranged on one of the turd-trawlers to the east," said Jo. "Sam managed to bribe us aboard with a cheese sandwich, if you can believe it."

Clack!

Max sharply pulled the bolt on his rifle, getting everyone's attention. He looked distressed and shook his head vigorously.

"What's the matter?" Sam asked uneasily.

"You didn't arrange this with a guy called *Oliver* did you?" Dwayne enquired.

Sam nodded in the affirmative. Anxiety chewing at his guts like a hungry rat. "Yeah... Is there some kind of problem?"

"Bastard!" Dwayne spat. He stormed to the other side of the room and punched the wall, bloodying his knuckles.

Benjamin took up the dropped conversational ball. "I'm afraid you have been set up. You see, this Oliver is something of a scoundrel. He has been running this scam for years. He will take a person's rations on the pretext that he will arrange safe passage out of the zone. He will then give them directions leading them straight into the hands of the enforcers, then he'll go to his line manager and blow the whistle."

"That's why there were so many ghosts out tonight," Sam grumbled as the penny dropped.

"Damn that whistle-blower bastard! We should have shot him when we had the chance," Dwayne bellowed.

Max clicked the safety once for 'yes.'

"The same thing happened to poor Jane back there," Benjamin continued. "There's not much hope, I'm afraid."

"Yeah... they've probably been eaten or shot by now," Dwayne said grimly.

A slam accompanied by wails of anguish announced that Jane had been listening at the door.

"Damn, I didn't realise she could hear," Dwayne shook his head in contrition.

Max jerked the bolt sharply and glared at him.

"I know, my bad... I'll fix it." He moved to the door calling out gently for the distressed teen.

"Tactless idiot," Benjamin muttered.

Max clicked the safety once in agreement.

"Still, he means well. Heart of gold, mouth of a moron, I find is the best way to describe our Dwayne."

"So, what now?" Jo asked no-one in particular.

"You are more than welcome to stay here," Ben replied with a smile. "Though, if you are hell-bent on getting out of Zone 51,

Max and Dwayne are taking Jane to a boat tomorrow night. You can go with them, if you so desire."

Jo looked at Max who smiled and nodded. Despite his rough looks and his automatic weapon, he had a kindness in his eyes that she wouldn't have expected.

"Would that be okay?" she asked.

Max nodded and clicked the safety.

"It's one-click for *yes*. Two for *no,* by the way. He uses the bolt as an expletive or attention-getter," Ben explained.

"Thanks, Max," Jo purred.

"Yeah, thanks, buddy," Sam added with a nod.

Max smiled again and resumed cleaning his weapon.

As Jo finally started to relax, Dwayne returned with a daft smile on his face. "She's okay now. I told her I'd go out again in an hour when I'm sure the lurker has gone, then I let her punch me..." He let out a sigh then collapsed into another dusty chair.

"It looks like you'll have two more with you on your exodus run tomorrow," Ben told him.

"No worries. The more eyes the better. You've seen how many eyes those damn things have so it's best to at least attempt to compete."

"So, where the hell do those things come from?" Sam asked.

"Hell is right," Benjamin said.

"Oh, not this crap again," Dwayne sighed.

"Just because you can't see what's right under your nose doesn't make it crap, master Dwayne. Those creatures come from out there," Ben pointed to the sky. "From beyond our plane of existence. They are denizens of the unfathomable void."

"Rubbish."

"So how do you explain it, Dwayne?" Jo asked pointedly.

"Must be something the Corporation's scientists dreamt up in a lab ... some GAF weapon gone rogue."

Ben scoffed and took a pull on his pipe, exhaling bluish smoke into the room.

Dwayne glared at the old man before addressing Sam and Jo. "Ben here believes they are servitors of some ancient god or something. I believe in science, not magic."

"What is magic but science too advanced for us to understand?" Ben smiled.

"Nonsense," Dwayne continued. "He believes that our glorious CEO cut some kind of deal with the devil back in the day."

"Not the devil ... close ... but far worse. The Crawling Chaos, Nephren-Ka, Nyarlathotep, call him what you like, but he makes the devil look like a choir-boy." Ben turned to Sam and Jo. "Have you ever wondered how the CEO has lived so long? Never wondered how he got so many egos to bend the knee and agree to his new world?"

Sam and Jo shook their heads.

"Of course you haven't. You have been drugged and brainwashed your whole lives. I'm not talking MK-Ultra here, this is something far more insidious. Dwayne here opted out when he discovered that the imitation chicken substitute was really bleached and chlorinated rat meat. The flavourings they pump into everything are drugs that keep you docile and forgetful."

Sam was impressed; 'opting out' was probably the most dangerous thing that you could do in this terrible reality. Voting was compulsory and most people blindly punched the *agree* button and collected their tokens. Some were foolish and pushed the wrong button. This led to their barcode reading undesirable. To refuse to vote, to 'opt-out' was to paint a giant bullseye on your back. By refusing to vote you were declaring yourself as undesirable. This was seen as a sign of madness which, surprise, surprise, made you undesirable. If you didn't get shot on the spot or carted off to a *Mental Correction Facility* to be drugged and zapped into oblivion, you were exceedingly lucky. It took some serious balls to opt-out, and Dwayne's were made of solid steel.

When Jo became eligible to vote, she was amazed when she entered the booth. She had no idea that there was more than one option. She had never heard of the other options before, and the temptation was immense. What she didn't know was that there was, in reality, only one option. The others were dummies, put there to spot the undesirables. If she hadn't been warned by her sister before entering, she would have been branded undesirable much sooner than she eventually was.

Ben tapped out his pipe and started refilling it. "There are places where the old ways and religions survived. This town where you now stand is one such place. My family were devotees of gods much older and more tangible than those of our terrestrial religions; they devoted their lives to studying the old texts and scriptures. At some point, the CEO came into contact with a number of these texts and used them to invoke some help. They struck a deal, whereby he would get prolonged life and immense power. What the buffoon didn't do was read the small print... There is always a clause when you deal with the old gods ... always a price that will eventually be paid. Have you wondered why there are more and more lurkers appearing on the streets?" he was asking Dwayne.

"Well, yeah," Dwayne replied. "I put it down to being spring. Mating season, and all that.

"The veil is tearing between their dimension and ours. Soon the world will be overrun by hideous creatures and entities from the blackest pits of the universe. The commander's time is almost up." Ben struck a match and lit his pipe. "The small print read that after fifty years of power he would relinquish his control and turn the planet over to his master and his diabolical kin."

"How do you know this?" Jo asked sceptically.

"Because it was my great uncle Arthur who gave him the damned book."

Dwayne had returned from his second search just before sunrise. Ben and Sam had talked while Max and Johanna tried to comfort Jane. Dwayne reported that there was indeed an influx of lurkers down by the docks, he also stated that the unstoppable creatures were decimating the enforcers. Blood and body parts joined the usual flotsam and jetsam in the standing water. Clearly the creatures were on the move; maybe Ben wasn't so wrong, after all. With this worrying thought in mind, Dwayne announced that he too was getting out of Zone 51. Ben, on the other hand, decided to stay put. He surmised that it didn't matter where you ran to, soon, nowhere would be free. Mankind was nearing extinction, and it was all because of the greed and hubris of a deluded tyrant. Max decided that he would stay with Ben, the old antiquarian was like a father to him, he took him in off the streets and helped to repair his disturbed mind. It was Ben who gave him Bessie, his beloved rifle.

The group slept away most of the daylight hours. The constant buzz of the swarm of drones outside was a constant reminder that in daylight, detection was assured. Drones did everything that the workers couldn't. They carried tools, delivered materials, and watched. They could even be used to target and destroy rogue elements. Another wonder of crowd control brought to you by the GAF. When dusk finally descended, the drones would follow the workers to the habitation centres. They would then ensure that nobody got in or out after curfew. They were programmed with the shoot to kill protocol.

Sam, Jo, Dwayne, Max and Jenny were ready by the time it grew dark outside. Dwayne and Max knew all the patrol routes of the enforcers and the lurker feeding grounds so the plan was simple; they would take the others to the garbage boat then Max would return to Ben and resume his life as a devoted watchdog. They left the sanctuary by the rope that they used to enter. Spent shell cases and the rubble of a smashed building stood as a testament of the nightmare that occurred less than 24 hours ago. There was no fog for a change and the moon hung low in the sky. It looked fat, full, and hungry, its radiance diffused through the smog, bathing the streets in a sickly yellow glow.

Moving as quickly and quietly as they could, the group took an alternative route to the one afforded to them by the duplicitous whistle-blower. Soon, they approached their biggest obstacle, the GAF administration centre. Inside the towering edifice, the big-wigs decided who to punish and who to blame when quotas weren't met. Stretching high into the sky above the South-West Sector, the green glow of the giant initials on the roof gave the streets below the appearance of a rotting carcass.

Max had taken point as they neared the corner. Quickly, he snapped the safety twice and held up his hand in a halt signal. Dwayne moved up to join him and peered around the wall. There was some kind of commotion in front of the building. Two enforcers were pointing their guns at a pair of workers that knelt before them. The duo strained to hear what was going on, though they could tell that whatever it was, it wasn't good.

"What do ya reckon, Mike?" The first enforcer was saying. "I dunno."

"I think we should take them in."

"I dunno, Jim," the second repeated. "Our shift is nearly over and you know how long the paperwork on runners takes, and we don't get overtime."

"That's true."

"I reckon we should just shoot them and leave them for the lurkers..."

The first enforcer, Jim, thought for a moment. "You know, I reckon you're right, I really can't be arsed to fill in the forms. Sod it... let's shoot 'em!"

The two men raised their guns to the downturned heads of the runners. More hapless dupes of Ollie the whistle-blower about to be blown away. Just as they were about to pull the trigger a shout rang out.

"Oi, dickheads!" It was Dwayne.

He and Max had seen enough; the two men jumped out from their hiding spot and hosed down the enforcers with lead. Their leaking bodies spun and danced before crashing to the floor in a bloody heap. Dwayne yelled at the two runners to bail. Understandably, they didn't need to be told twice and shot off into the darkness like a pair of startled rabbits.

"Grab their guns," Dwayne shouted to Jo and Sam, "be ready to move. Those goons inside the tower *must* have heard that. I imagine a death squad is assembling in the foyer as we speak."

No sooner had Dwayne voiced his concern, several guards, armed to the teeth, swarmed onto the streets like a horde of militant ants. Spotting the fugitives almost instantly, they fell into an attack formation and opened fire. Max quickly led the group into cover behind a raised concrete bed filled with replica daffodils and motioned at them to keep down.

"Bugger, they're closing in," Sam panted as he tried to figure out how to switch his rifle to burst fire mode. "We're sitting ducks here, we need to move."

Max shook his head, pointed to his ear, then to the southern entrance to the plaza.

Sam frowned and cocked his head to hear over the rattle of

gunfire. There was something heading in their direction ... something big. "Keep down, guys. I don't think the Caspers were the only ones who heard all the shooting."

"What do you mean?" Jo asked.

Sam and Max both pointed to the entrance as three enormous lurkers smashed through the barricades.

Tekeli-li!

As all gunfire became diverted towards the new threat, Max motioned to move while both parties were distracted. Leaping from cover amid a confetti rain of shredded synthetic flowers, the party scuttled down the street and away from danger as the lurkers massacred the enforcers. Nothing the crack team of trained killers hit the bubbling masses of gelatinous matter with had any effect. Tentacles whipped, and gaping maws snapped and crunched, making short work of their adversaries. When the last enforcer had shrugged off his mortal coil, the lurkers began to search for another snack... Unbeknownst to those in blissful ignorance to the carnage that sat inside, the doors of the GAF building stood open and unguarded. The smell of buffet dinners and warm bodies drifted into the fresh night air. Sam took a look behind him just in time to see a ravenous blob slithering through the sliding doors.

After a few minutes of frantic running, the party finally reached the docks. All they had to do was make it to the wall and jump down into a garbage boat without being picked off by one of the guards. This is when Jo stopped and held up her hand in warning.

"What is it?" Dwayne asked, fingering the trigger of his rifle expectantly.

"I don't know. It's too quiet. Where are all the guards?"

Dwayne scanned the sea wall and shrugged. "Tea break?"

"I'm serious."

"So am I. You know how you English love a cuppa."

"Don't be a wan—" Jo's tirade was silenced by the ominous sound of leathery wings on the wind. Big, leathery wings. "Um ... what the fuck is that?"

From out of nowhere, a bolt of lightning struck one of the large cranes on the dock making it erupt in a dazzling gout of glitter. The strange thing was, there were no clouds whatsoever. A terrific tearing sound assaulted the night as a huge tear in the fabric of reality opened above them. From out of the tear came a swarm of strangely humanoid creatures with blank faces and heavy bat-like wings.

"Dwayne, what the hell are those things?"

"Search me, Jo, I've never seen anything like it before. Just keep your bloody voice down and pray they don't spot us."

After thrice circling the crane, the majority of the creatures flew off in the direction of the nearby habitation centre, no doubt in search of sustenance. Three remained, however, having already detected five tasty morsels below. Wheeling like monstrous vultures, the strange beasts prepared to swoop. Without a second's hesitation, Max raised his rifle and opened fire. One of the beasts was hit in the wing and spiralled into the sea where it sank below the waves. The other two dashed out of the line of fire and began to rush towards the group.

"Run!" Dwayne ordered, shoving Sam, Jo, and Jane ahead of him. They did as instructed and sprinted towards the wall and the boat beyond. The creatures dived at the two men providing a rear guard. One struck Max in the shoulder and sent him crashing to the floor, spitting blood from a split lip. Dwayne pumped rounds into the sky but missed with every one. The creatures were uncannily agile which was miraculous considering they had no eyes. Dwayne didn't have time to ponder how they hunted' they had swiftly regrouped and were approaching fast.

Max raised himself onto his haunches and managed to club one of the gaunt creatures as it came in for another strike. The heavy wooden stock of his beloved Bessie crushed the skull of the creature with ease. It spun and tumbled along the sodden concrete dock before splashing into the sea. Dwayne continued to attempt to draw a bead on the final creature, he was dangerously low on ammunition and needed to make every shot count. While he struggled to take aim, Max leaned against the dock wall, aimed and fired. A single bullet popped the creature's head like a zit. Dwayne was impressed.

Jo, Sam and Jane had reached the wall by now, they looked back just in time to see the GAF building explode. Glass and fire rained down on the south-west sector of Zone 51. The explosion rocked the two men further down the docks. Dwayne implored Max to join them, he snapped the safety twice and smiled then motioned for his friend to go. Dwayne felt a pang of sadness as he shook the big man's hand, he was going to miss Max. With a parting salute, Dwayne ran as fast as his legs would carry him and joined the others on the wall. Joining hands, they jumped down into the festering pile of refuse below and attempted to get comfortable.

All they had to do now was lie low until they were out of Corporation waters and the automated system shipped them god-knows-where...

Morning rose over the refugee camp in Southern Australia. They had been there for three days by this point. Though fully shaken by the ordeal of escaping Zone 51, they were in high spirits. There were many people from all the late numbered zones; French people from Zone 52, Spaniards from 53, and so on. While most were traumatised, there was an overwhelming feeling of hope.

That was before the news of what happened on the day they had escaped reached them.

Television screens flickered as the CEO of The Imperial Corporation stood in front of a gleaming pyramid fashioned from glass and steel. It stood in the centre of Zone 1, occupying the foundations of what had been The White House. He faced the camera as he addressed his subjects. His speech was rambling and self-aggrandising as he thanked his country for his glorious reign. Fifty years of prosperity, fifty years of productivity, et cetera, et cetera.

Ben's words echoed in Johanna's ears. *"Fifty years..."*

Behind him, stood his aide, a strangely thin man, clad in traditional Egyptian robes. His eyes burned like hot coals with a ghastly orange glow. Now that their systems were free of the drugged food that had clouded their vision, they could see the man for what he truly was ... death incarnate. He had been there from the very start. Hiding in plain sight. Pulling the strings.

Sowing the seeds of mankind's destruction. The CEO had been just as much a prisoner as the rest of them.

The Old One's passive expression turned to one of unbridled anger as his puppet promised to continue in office. Nobody reneges on a deal with the Crawling Chaos and survives. Finally, the Chief was face to face with someone he couldn't bully or cajole. The shadowy figure lunged for the leader, its head elongating into a huge tentacle of shadow, meat, and bone that whipped around the screaming world leader's neck. The darkness howled in fury as it crushed the life out of his puppet and dissolved his matter. The news feed flickered three times then cut to static.

Since that moment, the sky had been rupturing at an alarming rate. The ground shook, and the waters rose. The planet was acting like a snowglobe that someone had given a particularly vigorous shake. In short, the end was at hand.

One man's hubris had doomed the world.

The only question that remained was, would it go out with a bang or a long drawn-out death-rattle?

MARCH 20ᵀᴴ 2127
EGYPT – IREM, THE CITY OF PILLARS:

Can a shadow smile?

The long game was nearing its Earth-shattering climax as the Dark Pharaoh revelled in the chaos that his plans had wrought. All those years ago, when he cut the deal with the then President of the United States of America, wheels had been set into motion that would drive humanity inexorably towards its doom. Since that monumental occasion when he was handed the bloody signature of the ambitious leader in his evil black book, every moment, every event had led directly to his hour of triumph.

It was about time...

For centuries he had lurked in the shadows, waiting for the ideal moment to reveal himself. Long before humanity learned to walk upright, he had been here, shaping reality to his own design. Ageless and deathless, then, now, and forever. The Old Ones are, the Old Ones were, and the Old Ones shall be again. Existing outside of reality, lurking on the threshold. Now, his avatars and devotees were in place like pawns on a cosmic chessboard, ready and willing to make the ultimate sacrifice for his glory.

His first manifestation had come at the end of Egypt's Third Dynasty when the usurper Pharaoh, Nephren-Ka, had summoned the God to aid in his conquest. By retrieving the shining trapezohedron and installing it in the lightless fane in Irem, the ruler created a conduit for the Old One's will. Thousands of sacrifices were bled on the black altar in return for glimpses of the future and knowledge forbidden to mortal beings. Soon, however, the servant of chaos' body began to fail and, in a masterstroke, was persuaded to allow his God to consume him. He was the first mask for the Faceless God, the first of many. One which he continued to wear to that very day. It was handsome and persuasive. Unassuming yet seductive. This particular mask could charm the birds from the heavens.

The CEO loved his aide, Neffy...

Following the fall of Irem, the Old One returned to the shadows to await a new game. The petty ambitions and desires of the ephemeral pests that swarmed over the face of this tumultuous planet weren't really his concern, they merely provided a distraction. Where most of the other Great Old Ones preferred to remain aloof and indifferent, above such things as interacting with humanity, he liked to make them dance. The ultimate puppeteer with a planet full of flawed marionettes to play with. He would make them fight, make them lie, then cut their strings when he grew tired of their antics.

From Ancient Rome to the witch cults of Europe, he set about infiltrating each and every power block. He had been a king, commander, lover, charlatan, even a child. Anything to manipulate and control. It was only a matter of time before he turned to politics. During these centuries, he had been known by many names and epithets, Haunter of the Dark, Crawling Chaos, Mighty Messenger, many names, many false faces, but all with the same design.

It was almost time for the world to learn his true name.

His once-hidden fane in Irem beneath the singing sands echoed with unholy laughter and the whines of his faithful hounds. They licked his palms as he relished the moment. It was a stroke of evil genius to turn mankind's technology upon itself. Since the late twentieth-century, advanced technology had been designed with something called *In-built obsolescence*, a mechanical expiry date, a devious ploy to ensure that the latest model sold. Corporate greed being taken to the extreme.

Perfection.

Once he had created avatars in key positions and his shadowy appendages fully gripped the planet, it had been child's play to rig everything to expire at the same time. Soon the drones that swarmed the skies would plummet, planes would nosedive, defence grids would fire, and chaos would reign supreme. The East would fire its warheads at the West, and vice-versa. Countries would be wiped off the map with surgical precision. Only those places that weren't a threat to his grand scheme would be spared the cleansing fire; after all, he was going to need a workforce. Humanity would fall to its knees in front of him and beg for his cold embrace.

As the multitudes outside his fane chanted and awaited the carnage to come, he allowed himself a moment of rest. The coming days would not be easy. Others of his kind would be awakened by the destruction. The stars were right, it was time for a reckoning. The veil between dimensions was tearing. The Great Old Ones were shaking off their shackles and awakening from their enforced slumber, their followers and creatures were breaking through, rising and taking control.

Soon the real war would begin.

A battle on a vast cosmic scale. Earth was an ideal staging point for the inevitable war against the Elder Gods. Its position in the universe and its soil, so rich in abundant minerals, and its people, so easily manipulated, made it the perfect manufacturing centre. As the allotted time approached, the shadow's three-lobed eye burned bright with savage intensity.

Distant explosions announced the dawn of Expiration Day.

The multitudinous Pharaoh hounds howled into the night.

The carrion beetles clacked their mandibles in exultation.

The shadow smiled.

CHAPTER II

AFTER HOURS

FEBRUARY 19TH 2132
ZONE 51 – SOUTH-WEST SECTOR:

As fat gobs of greasy rain were spat from the glowering sky, Jake Baker sheltered in the doorway of an abandoned jewellery shop sucking on an illicit cigarette. His vigil had begun hours ago and looked as though it might continue for some considerable time. Holograms of dancing girls, strangely distorted by the savage downpour, were the only things that kept his attention focused on the establishment across the street. By now, he knew every bend, every gyration, every glitch of their looped routine. They had become his friends, his colleagues, fellow watchful sentinels... Jake had even given them both names.

Ice-blue lettering from above the pub door reflected in the filthy puddles that had gathered on the cracked pavement below. Each ripple shimmered with a cold digital luminescence. The Hyperborea Bar was one of the last bastions of nightlife in the former Betyls Cove. A beacon for those with so little to lose that they would brave the flooded streets of Zone 51 after dark. Nobody in their right mind would choose to be this close to the water at night, but being out after hours was part of Jake's job description.

Jake was a bounty hunter by trade, and the nearest thing the drowning sector had to a lawman. Since the corrupt regime that had formed the Imperial Corporation had fallen five years previously and the CEO's puppet master had taken control of the Earth, society outside the production centres had reverted to a

Wild West mentality. Chaos reigned supreme and the only way for those wronged to seek any form of justice was to enlist the help of one such as Jake.

Shambling and uncoordinated footsteps slapping the standing water alerted Jake to someone's approach. He took a final pull on his cigarette and dropped it into the water with a *sizzle* as the figure hobbled into view. Jake's target was hunched over, bald, and neck-less. Jake flicked the safety on his GAF Colt 3000 hand-cannon to *off*. This particular model of firearm was one of the Global Arms Federation's top weapons and the choice of any gunslinger worth their salt. Jake called his Jennifer. The GAF still owned most of what was, until very recently, Zone 51 and continued to produce cutting-edge military-grade weapons for their new master. Nobody knew what to call the partially submerged country anymore. Some wanted to revert it to its former title, but there was nothing *Great* about this Britain. As the target neared the door of the bar, Jake raised his weapon. He had already enabled the *quiet* function and had backed into the doorway. Now totally enveloped in darkness, the mark wouldn't even see it coming.

Jake took a steadying breath and eased on the trigger. Before he could engage the hammer, the doors burst open and a group of inebriated dockers poured out into the street, ruining his shot. Jake cursed and lowered his gun. He wasn't totally against a little bit of collateral damage when it couldn't be avoided, but he figured that the poor souls currently staggering around in the street had it bad enough without having a new hole drilled into their heads with expert precision. The target bounced between the drunks like a bulbous pinball then slipped inside. Jake cursed again and holstered Jennifer. He shouldn't have been surprised that something got in the way, it would have been too easy. The way his day had been going, it wasn't really a shock that it went south.

Jake waited for the drunks to wobble off down the street singing their bawdy sea shanties before stepping out of the doorway. Fishing another smoke from its crumpled packet, he quickly evaluated his options; He could either stand out here all night freezing his nuts off, or he could go inside and keep the mark under surveillance. After all, his target didn't know him from Adam and, after the last twelve hours, he could use a stiff drink.

First things first, Jake removed his ubiquitous aviators. More than a mere affectation or fashion statement, his mirrored glasses were one of the most vital tools of his trade. Linked to several sensors and chips implanted in his body, the glasses provided him with a distinct advantage when it came down to combat. Adapted from military combat visors by a local tech genius, they monitored his heart rate, blood pressure and overall performance while a targeting overlay offered zoom, night vision and thermal imaging. What they provided was similar to a HUD on the pre-collapse video games he had enjoyed playing with his son.

Rain bounced off Jake's battered fedora as he crossed the street. Once Jennifer was safely concealed and his blood had stopped boiling with frustration, he pushed open the doors and stepped inside. The acrid concoction of fermented drinks, cigarette smoke and bodily fluids slapped him in the face and made his sensors reel. It was a surprisingly welcome change from the rancid seaweed and rat urine aroma of the streets.

Jake hadn't set foot in the Hyperborea Bar since an unfortunate incident involving a length of rubber hose, a funnel, and two litres of Voormis-grade cider. He hoped to the Elder Gods that nobody remembered his inebriated antics. If they did, he would be out on his ear before he could take his hat off. Still, That was a long time ago and, with the life expectancy in Zone 51 being as short as it was, there was a better than an odds-to-even chance that the offended parties would be long dead. Nevertheless, he would have to keep a low profile; the last thing he wanted to do now was to spook his prey. He'd had quite enough problems for one day. Jake selected a bar stool, purchased a drink, and resumed his vigil.

The day had started the same way most days started in Zone 51, with the harsh klaxons of the GAF facility hitting Jake in the head like a mallet. As per usual, he had overindulged on the seaweed-whiskey the night before. The salty alcoholic kick was addictive, especially when he wanted to forget ... and Jake had a lot to forget. It was the fifth anniversary of the fall of the Imperial Empire, and he had lost a lot that day: family, friends, a few of his marbles. Jake could recall vividly the moment when the CEO was devoured by his benefactor and the reign of the Great Old Ones began. Nuclear war quickly followed as the defence grids went haywire and half the world became a blasted nightmare overnight. Zone 51 was lucky – nobody had cared enough about it to point a nuclear weapon at it.

Stretching his back and kicking the gnawing cramp from his surgically reconstructed ankle, Jake shuffled into the kitchen. The cupboards were bare, as always, and a fat black cockroach looked at him with twirling antennae and hungry, clacking mandibles.

"I know," Jake slurred, his mouth sticky and throat dry. "Looks like we are on the grey-bar again, pal." He pulled the work ration out from the sealed container, broke off a corner and passed it to his insect friend. Jake had named him Burt.

Shutting the cupboard gently, Jake took a bite from the putty-like substance. It was supposed to taste like roast beef. He only knew this because the wrapper told him it was supposed to taste like roast beef. It tasted like what it was, a heavily processed lump of unidentified protein and vegetables pumped full of all the vitamins and minerals a growing boy needed to slog his guts out in a gun factory. Jake had never eaten the contents of a chemical toilet before, but he had his suspicions that it would taste just like his breakfast.

Jake lived in a partially submerged low-rise block that once housed young professionals and students. Now, all it housed was a couple of chip-heads with syntheshock, a bounty hunter and his pet cockroach, and rats ... lots of rats. It was situated in the abandoned dockside part of town where most of the buildings had either fallen down, been washed out to sea, or housed fugitives and dropouts. The free people of the zone. Each and every one of them an *undesirable*. The only way to enter the building was via a rickety fire ladder on the rear of the building. Visitors were rare to the point of extinction, so the last thing Jake expected was a knock at the door.

Thump! Thump! Thump!

Instinctively grabbing Jennifer off the side and slipping on his hat and sunglasses, Jake positioned himself by the door and demanded, "who's there?"

Clunk! Clunk-Clack! Clunk!-Clunk! Clack! Clack! Clunk!

The unmistakable sound of the word MAX being delivered in Morse code using the firing bolt of an antique AK-47 announced the all-clear. Jake exhaled. "Jesus, Max, what are you trying to do, give me a bloody coronary?"

Jake opened the door. The towering figure with the salt and pepper flat-top smirked at the sight before him. Something about the sight of a grizzled bounty hunter in a threadbare pair of *Batman* boxer shorts, sunglasses, and fedora, wielding a gun struck the ex-enforcer as distinctly amusing.

"I take it, this isn't a social call?" Jake asked, ignoring the man's mirth.

Max shook his head, pulled a letter out of his battered flack jacket, and handed it to Jake.

After reading the contents, Jake spoke. "Tell him I'll be over in an hour or so."

Max smiled and gave him the thumbs up.

Jake watched the man-mountain stalk off down the corridor and shut the door. The distinctly spidery scrawl of Max's friend and employer meant only one thing ... work. He hadn't had a contract in weeks, so this was a very welcome development. He swiftly polished off the remainder of his foul snack and washed it down with his last bottle of purified water. Water and food were valuable and highly sought after commodities in this harsh new world. A half-litre bottle of pure water could go for as much as ten rounds of pistol ammunition. Not many could afford to buy it from the smugglers on the docks. The only other way to get water and rations, if you didn't sell your mind, body, and soul to the GAF, was to rob a distribution centre. This was what Jake had done. It had been only a month since his last heist and the patrol of GAF Caspers had been doubled, meaning that the next raid wouldn't be easy, so the option to purchase some and let the heat die down was a welcome one.

Once he had shaken the alcohol-induced fug from his brain, Jake got dressed and set about plotting his route to Max's erstwhile employer. The antique shop he called home wasn't far away, but to get there he would have to cross the GAF factory. This was a headache all of its own. By now, the place would be swarming with bloodthirsty enforcers. They, along with the GAF itself, were one of the hangovers of the Imperial Corporation. When the status quo changed, they either didn't notice or didn't care. After all, one paymaster was as good as another, and every tyrant needed guns. They knew a war was coming; they just didn't know from where.

Jake was an old hand at dealing with the multitude of perils in the south-west sector of Zone 51. Ever since the fall, Jake had lived on the fringes of society. Up until that point he had worked in ammunition manufacture and had lived with his wife and son in one of the egg-box like habitation centres. On that fateful day when the CEO was obliterated by the Dark Pharaoh, he could only stand helplessly by as his loved ones were absorbed by a rampaging lurker. He survived, physically, but his mind was forever blasted by sights no man was meant to see.

After loading Jennifer and equipping all the tools of his trade, he was ready to cross the industrial hell of the munitions factory. It was either that or the docks and even Jake feared the docks. There were *things* that lurked in the waters that defied description. When the Old Ones rose, they brought their friends with them. The food chain had become massively skewed against mankind's favour. In any case, duty called, he had a cockroach to feed.

Jake took a slug of whiskey from his trusty hip flask, lit a cigarette and set out towards the remains of Betyls Cove.

It was just past midday when Jake reached his destination. He had managed to slip unnoticed past the multitude of Caspers, drones, and sensors and had made relatively good time. The Edwards Antique Emporium sat in the heart of what was the town centre. The area hadn't been touched by the GAF as its foundations were riddled with tunnels and caverns making them unsuitable for heavy machinery and buildings. The area was a ghost town of abandoned businesses, crumbling churches ... and lurk-ers.

Jake moved down the greasy, refuse littered alley next to the building and yanked the rusty metal chain that dangled from above. An old school bell repurposed as a door chime sang out loudly, reverberating off the walls and drilling into his skull. Above him, a heavy, metal shutter rasped open, and the large head of Max peered down. Jake shot him a thumbs up, to which Max grinned and lowered a rusty ladder.

Max had lived in the fortified antique shop since that fateful day when he had disobeyed a kill-order. The shop's proprietor, Benjamin Edwards, had taken the six-foot broken man under his wing and he had been there ever since. Over time, a revolving door of the lost and hunted took refuge with the odd couple. While they had all moved on in the end, some to the east, some shot, some eaten, Max had stayed. Ben was his father figure, but more than that, Ben gave Max a purpose. He protected the el-derly shop owner and took care of his business. It was only very occasionally that Max couldn't take care of something... that's where Jake came in.

Ben was reclining on his chaise lounge as per usual. The room always struck Jake as surreal. It was decked out with an-tique furniture, paintings, sumptuous rugs and drapes. It was the polar opposite of his own squalid living conditions. Puffing on his pipe, Ben tilted his hand to a wing-back chair. Jake sat and looked at the map that Ben had pinned to the wall. It had vast areas crossed off with a thick red marker pen. There weren't many uncrossed areas left. Most of them were islands, like Zone 51. A lot of these, however, were shaded blue to indicate where the sea had reclaimed its property.

Jake gave a low whistle. "Not much left, huh?"

"You could say that." Ben shrugged. "It's only a matter of time before it's all gone."

"How accurate is the map?"

"As accurate as it can be. We have used the drones that Mickie managed to get running to cover most of it. Reports from Aus-tralia confirm much of what you see there." Ben puffed his pipe thoughtfully. "Mickie has been in contact with friends out there and it's looking grim."

"Damn," Jake sighed then took a glug from his flask.

Ben flashed a smile to break the mood. "Thanks for coming, Mr Baker, I trust you didn't have too much trouble slipping past the enforcers?"

"Nah, I waited until shift change and went over the warehouse roofs. I don't think those idiots can look up on account of those stupid hoods."

Ben chuckled. "Perhaps not."

At that moment, Max entered the room carrying a rectangular tray. Teaspoons and china rattled as he crossed the room and placed the tea set on the coffee table. This time it was Jake's turn to be amused by a bizarre image. The sight of massive Max, AK-47 slung over his scarred and tattooed shoulder, with a dainty tea set made him smile despite his foul mood. Max poured out a cup of strong tea and passed it to Jake.

Jake slugged a finger of booze into the beverage and took a sip. "So, what's this job you have for me, then?"

"It's a matter of family pride, I'm afraid," Ben began. "A couple of nights ago, I had a visitor. He claimed he was here to cut a deal on some ration cards. After the swine had left, I noticed that an old family heirloom had vanished. A gold-plated compass that has been in my family on and off since the seventeenth-century. My family and his have fought over the trinket for generations."

"You have a name?" Jake asked.

"Tremayne. Warren Tremayne."

Jake sighed. "That figures. I thought you Edwardses, and the Tremaynes would have wiped each other out by now."

"Indeed, our families have never seen eye to eye, but it's been more of a cold war than out and out hostility."

"Bollocks! You are seriously telling me that you don't want revenge? They took your *sect* away from you."

"Not *taken*, Mr Baker, *given*. I have no interest in my family's dubious legacy. They are welcome to the *sect,* as you put it. This theft, however, is unacceptable." Ben paused and fixed Jake with an icy stare. "I want it back, and I want Warren dead."

"So much for *cold war,*" Jake smirked. "Usual payment?"

"Indeed. I will throw in a couple of extra ration cards for swift justice. I miss my compass."

"Any leads?"

"I'm sure you can guess."

"Barncoose manor?"

"You got it." Ben's smile widened into a toothy rictus.

"Bugger. *The church of the discarded...* just what I always want-ed," Jake shook his head and finished his tea before standing and getting ready to depart. "I'd better get on it then."

Clack! Clack! Max shook his head and pointed towards the corridor.

"Ah, yes. Thank you, Max." Ben turned to Jake. "You should check in with Mickie. She has some intel on The Discarded you might find useful."

"Okay, will do." Jake navigated the furniture and approached a sliding door at the rear of the premises. He gave it a knock and waited to be admitted. After a few muttered curses, the occupant of the room told him to enter. Jake moved the door aside and stepped into Mickie's domain, flashing his most-apologetic smile.

Mickie was the latest in Ben's little family; she had been with them for five years now, ever since the day following the demise of the CEO. Expiration Day, as it had become known, that awful day when all technology created after the formation of the Corporation died in unison. Inbuilt obsolescence in perfect synchronicity. She had been afforded a front-row seat to the ensuing carnage. Mickie had worked in the towering Drone Distribution Centre, in the heart of the GAF complex. She had been on the top floor when the drones started scudding to earth like package bearing meteorites. She barely escaped the tower and was rescued from the following nightmare by Max. Since that day, she hadn't set foot outside of the shop apart from brief visits to the roof for fresh air. Agoraphobia, Ben called it. Since then, the drones had been her virtual presence, her eyes and ears, in the outside world. It was nice of the GAF to manufacture a new fleet almost instant-ly. Many believe that they were ready and waiting in the wings.

Jake navigated a graveyard of old computers piled near the door and entered Mickie's stronghold. She was a wizard with anything technical. It was her that had created his aviators. Her living quarters were a twittering hive of old CRT computer monitors and other resurrected tech. The GAF mainframe had come back online shortly after Expiration Day, but everything else had been fried. Only a skilled techie like Mickie could get anything working. Her hydraulically-enhanced fingers provided a delicate touch. A natural boon when dealing with micro-circuitry ... but a hazard when picking your nose.

An old *Skeletal Family* record played on an antique, hand-cranked gramophone that she had specially modified to play thirty-three-and-a-third speed records. Mickie was a strikingly attractive twenty-four-year-old with naturally straight raven-black hair and porcelain skin. She was hunched over a workbench tinkering with a brick-like twentieth-century mobile phone. She had immediately commandeered Ben's vintage clothing rack upon arrival and was wearing a Victorian evening gown and enforcer boots. The 1980s were alive and well and living in the back room of an antique shop in Zone 51.

Mickie's pet drone, Cricket, noticed Jake's appearance in the room and chirruped a greeting from his perch on top of an old CRT TV.

Jake cleared his tobacco ravaged throat, "Hi, Mick. Ben said you have some intel about the Barncoose compound?"

"One minute," Mickie snapped distractedly. "Pass me that pin would you?" She clicked her fingers and pointed to an old ashtray filled with random screws and fuses.

Jake complied. "What are you doing?"

"Just a second... there!" The phone crackled and fizzed then the screen lit up. "Yes!" Mickie yelped and started pressing the four, eight, six and two keys in an odd kind of sequence.

The look of concentration on the young woman's face piqued Jake's interest. He went over to the bench and peered at the cracked LCD display. A growing line was swallowing up dots.

"What's this, some kind of code-cracking device?" Jake asked.

"Nah. It's snake," came the less than helpful response.

"Snake?"

"Yeah. You have to eat up all the dots without eating yourself."

"Like Ouroboros?"

"Yeah. I guess." Mickie shrugged. "I suppose... I've never

thought about it like that before."

"So what does it do?"

"Nothing."

"So why have you been fixing it then?" Jake was bemused.

"Because I wanted to play snake." Her line folded in upon itself and the screen flashed *GAME OVER*. "Damn!" She slammed the handset down in frustration and yanked the clipped wire off the battery on the desk. "I'll never beat my high score at this rate." She placed her hands on her hips and exhaled. "Right, Barncoose Manor, home of the parasite worshipping fruitcakes..."

"Yeah. That's the fun I have to look forward to today." Jake sighed.

Mickie had rigged up an ancient-looking Frankenstein's monster of a computer to a 1960s black and white Bakelite TV and an old Atari joystick. From here she controlled the drones that she had *repurposed* from GAF command. Last night, she had made a reconnaissance flight of the old manor grounds to determine blind spots in guard routines. She handed the data to Jake on a mini-SD card to be plugged into his glasses then handed him an old *My Little Pony* pencil case.

Jake frowned as he opened it. It was full of old torch light bulbs filled with filings and powder. "What's this?" he asked, plucking one of the bulbs from the plastic wallet.

"Careful! Don't shake the bloody thing, for Christ's sake."

"Why, what the hell is it?" Jake gingerly placed the bulb safely back inside and zipped it shut.

"There are going to be a lot of lurkers between here and the manor, so I cooked these up specially. They are flash-bangs; those slimy buggers can't stand light so I'm hoping they will help you out if you get cornered. Just smash it on a nearby surface and run like Hell."

"Thanks, Mick." Jake pocketed the wallet and gave her a salute as he started making his way out. "Wish me luck."

"Oh, Jake," Mickie called after him.

"Yeah?"

"Keep your sunglasses on."

A dense cloud of filthy smog from the factories had settled over the boggy fields between the remnants of Betyls Cove and High Bend. The small village had all but been consumed by the Discarded. The insidious sect were fervent disciples of The Parasite God, Ger'igguthy, an abomination that thrived on waste, refuse and decay. The once picturesque area was now a festering landfill of epic proportions. Rats, crabs and corvidae ruled the land along with some less earthly scavengers – Ger'igguthy's ghastly insectoid spawn.

Jake had found himself an old barn to climb upon to get a better lay of the land.

The sun was still up which was both a blessing and a curse. On the one hand, it meant that the sodden countryside was lurker free, but it also meant that the Discarded and their scavenging horde would see him coming a mile off. He intended to use the woods to the north and approach the manor from the rear. The congregation was at its thinnest by the entrance to the old coal cellar; this was to be Jake's point of entry. He was pondering how to get there without being spotted when an opportunity presented itself.

The Discarded had adopted a stylised version of Inquisition robes since the advent of the Corporation. To disguise themselves as a *real* religious order, they had even fashioned crucifixes out of animal bones to blend in and conform with the *Christianity act*. They had ditched the vibrant papist red for a more monastic muddy-brown. One of the order had obviously been caught short during a patrol and was squatting over a hastily, hand-dug hole mere yards from Jake's perch.

As stealthily as was possible for a large man with metal in his legs to accomplish, Jake climbed down from the barn and began stalking the hapless zealot. Whatever the acolyte had eaten had clearly not agreed with him judging by the foul smell and startling noises emanating from his posterior. Jake circled around the barn and waited. He decided to let the man finish his business before striking, in a hope that he would avoid getting covered in his foul evacuations.

As the oblivious robed figure wiped himself with a handful of shredded newspaper and tossed it into his makeshift lavatory,

Jake advanced slowly and stealthily. The GAF had mandated that he have shoulder and elbow hydraulics installed so he could haul crates of guns without any fuss or difficulty. He was so powerful that if he swung a bit too hard, he could pulverise the man's jaw. Jake, while basically a killer for hire, didn't take lives willy-nilly, only if necessary or paid for. In this decayed society, this fact alone made Jake one of the good guys. Many wouldn't bat an eyelash at casual slaughter.

Thunk!

Jake landed a punch to the acolyte's jaw, dropping him like a sack of ammunition. Jake removed the unconscious man's robe and rolled him over so he didn't choke on his own drool. The robe was filthy and stunk almost as bad as the contents of the hole, but needs must as the devil drives, and all that. Once disguised, Jake started to skirt the perimeter of the overgrown wooded area between High Bend and Barncoose Manor. If he kept his distance from the Discarded, then he had a chance of getting into the manor without any serious trouble. Inside would be a different matter altogether, but he was confident that he had encountered enough acolytes over the years to know the lingo.

Jake's easiest ever contract was one he had picked up from an elder member of The Discarded, a wizened derelict that wanted rotting fish – tons and tons of rotting fish. The man paid him well to *steal* his proposed tribute to Ger'igguthy from the local fisherfolk. Jake simply split the cash with the gill-breathers that did the marine harvesting and dumped the putrid piscine remains on the road to the manor for collection. The old man thought Jake had pulled off the heist of the century and paid him a handsome bonus for something he could have done himself if it wasn't for religious sectarianism. The Gillmen, as the sea folk were known by *outsiders*, had very different deities to those of the Discarded. Jake tried to stay out of politics, both religious and constitutional, and as a result could clandestinely deal with both groups with a clear conscience.

As anticipated, the rear of the sprawling pile was unguarded as it was when the guards were due to change shifts. Jake took full advantage and scuttled quickly to where the entrance to the coal bunker lay hidden behind a tangled cluster of sickly-looking weeds. The rusty padlock posed no obstacle to a sharp crack from the butt of his gun. The grate slid aside with a teeth-rattling screech and Jake ducked inside.

"Bloody hell." Jake gagged as he straightened up and took a breath; the cellar was rancid. Jake had finally found out what happened to his consignment of putrescent pilchards. The whole lot had been dumped into a deep oubliette that had been hewn out of the granite foundations. It wasn't just rotting fish either, bones and carcasses of all creatures great and small had been dumped in and allowed to fester. Nausea welled up in Jake's gullet. He fought it back and chased it away with a hefty glug from his hipflask then wet a finger with the strong booze and painted his top lip to keep the odours at bay.

It wasn't just the overpowering stench that had Jake feeling rough, the cellar was alive with the buzz and skittering of creeping, crawling critters of both earthly and non-earthly origin. The spawn of Ger'igguthy, those ghastly part worm, part insect, part crustacean horrors, mingled with the beetles, flies and worms of the earth. The mountainous pile of filth below the cellar floor writhed and undulated as the creatures squirmed and foraged. It was enough to test even the strongest of stomachs. Jake selected the night vision setting on his tricked-out aviators, bathing the damp room in a sickly green hue. He needed to keep his feet on the narrow stone walkways between the square holes. In no way did he want to end up in the filth amongst Ger'igguthy's bloated offspring. As quickly as he could, under the treacherous conditions, he shuffled one foot in front of the other towards the deep stone steps at the rear.

Something that clattered against Jake's head as he reached the steps underlined the necessity of getting out without being apprehended – a pair of heavy iron manacles. The restraints dangled from the ceiling above one of the twelve openings in the floor. A cursory glance revealed that all the holes were similarly equipped. This must be what happened to those who transgressed the oaths of Ger'igguthy. Jake realised with a shiver that, if he was captured, he would be hung over a pit like a giant salami for the creatures to devour alive and screaming. Jake checked his arsenal; if it came down to it, he would prefer to go down blazing in a hail of superheated slugs than end up in Ger'igguthy's larder.

Once safely across the horrific cellar, Jake silently mounted the stairs and switched to heat vision as he approached the door. There were multiple heat signatures on the ground floor so he would have to be careful. Luckily, the majority of them were clustered towards the front of the manor in the great hall. They appeared to be sitting down to eat, just as planned. The target spent most of his time in the master bedroom at the far end of the west wing. According to Mickie's intel, the hierophant of the Discarded slept alone, worshipped alone, and ate alone. The rumour was, that he had the pick of the food, not the foul swill his acolytes endured. Such was the boon of having a *direct* connection with his Lord.

Jake's leather trench-coat had been specially modified by Mickie to have several small compartments around the cuffs that could be flicked open in an emergency. One contained a razor blade, another a cyanide tablet, and so on. Jake removed the cyanide and tossed it into the pit. In the worst-case scenario, he would be eating a bullet. In its place, Jake slipped one of Mickie's flash-bulbs, just in case. Nobody knew what horrors lurked in Barncoose Manor. The only people other than The Discarded to have set foot in the place since its conversion into the cult compound had been the poor sods that had ended up in that hellish oubliette as sacrificial offerings.

Finding the cellar door locked was to be expected and wasn't a major issue. A couple of jobs back, Mickie had made him a laser cutter out of an everlasting radium battery and the laser from an old CD Walkman. Jake had used it to cut the lock off a GAF supply crate so he could pilfer the rations inside. This handy gadget was rigged around an old screwdriver and fit snugly in his inside pocket next to his tobacco pouch and vintage *Zippo* lighter. Jake fished the implement out and with a satisfying *sizzle*, sliced the bolt neatly and quietly in two. Once the door was free, he did another thermal scan, fixed his hood and robe, then stepped into the unknown.

If Jake was expecting the upper portions of the manor to smell better than the nightmare below, then he had set himself up for bitter disappointment. The whole building was a festering hive of disease, rot and decay. The once-sumptuous carpets were now little more than a damp quagmire that looked more like wallpaper-paste than fabric. Every footfall squelched disgustingly as putrid slime oozed around his boots.

Patches of oddly glowing fungus fruited in the corners, grew along the peeling skirting boards, then spread up the walls like a luminous cancer. Jake had heard about this evil stuff before; it was said to have originated in a sea cave after the meteor that gave the former Betyls Cove its name hit a rocky outcrop centuries ago. It was known as the Pluto-cap and it was deadly. It also provided those who ate it with powerful, some claimed spiritual, hallucinations. The reason for the defecating acolyte's glazed expression suddenly became abundantly clear... The poor sap had been tripping the light fantastic.

Jake found himself in a corridor with an almost fleshy quality due to the vast fungal growth. It was unsettlingly close to being in the gullet of some gargantuan creature. He paused and mopped his creased brow with the cuff of his purloined robe. The overall atmosphere could have been described as cloying, something akin to airborne soup, it was so dense that you could almost chew it. Not that he would have wanted to sample the taste.

Rapturous voices raised in gobbledygook prayer echoed down the halls as the gunslinger slowly advanced down the corridor, head bowed and attempting to imitate the babble of worship to the best of his abilities. It would have helped if any of it was in a recognisable language, or at least one designed for the human voice, and not some strange insectoid buzzing crossed with strangled exclamations. The nearest comparison he could draw was a mixture of bees and jelly being sucked down a plughole.

The Discarded had three distinct groups, The Seekers, who were the rank-and-file acolytes and wore the same type of robe as Jake was currently sporting. The Guardians, the gun-toting meat-heads of the group, distinctive due to the bulletproof vests over their robes and the hardware slung over their shoulders; not the sort of chap you wanted to bump into unprepared. The third group, however, were by far the most unsettling. The Hosts, as these malformed and diseased creatures were known, had blue fungal growths covering a large proportion of their bodies. It would have been a mercy if that was the worst thing about them, alas, the horrors continued. Each one had their eyes sewn shut and had the vile spawn of Ger'igguthy embedded in the flesh of their forearms like ghastly ticks. They shuffled listlessly, apparently controlled by their parasites and were little more than meat puppets. The rest of the commune revered and protected these *chosen* few, meaning that they always had a couple of guardians with them.

As Jake rounded the corner, he encountered his first hurdle. Next to a handwritten sign on a scuffed blackboard emblazoned with the words, *No Seekers Beyond This Point*, sat a rocking host flanked by two wild-eyed and feral-looking guardians. Jake slid back around the corner and softly banged his head against the wall as he cursed under his breath. Shaking off his frustration, he pulled up Mickie's map of the building on his glasses and looked for an alternative route... *Bingo!* There was an old dumbwaiter in the kitchen that led directly up to the master bedroom. The only snag was, that he would have to pass the barracks in what was once the dining hall. Sliding the glasses back into his pocket, he changed direction and resumed his monastic shuffle.

Jake shuffled as quickly as he could without drawing any attention to himself as the corridor wound directly along the west wing. It led to an arched exit by the grand central staircase and was flanked by two doors on either side. Alone for the moment, he abandoned his act and swiftly passed the first which turned out to be a boot-room piled high with garbage. The second housed the library; its floor was covered in piles of filthy old newspapers but the room was otherwise empty. The third was locked, and the fourth led into the cavernous dining-room. Jake pulled his hood down over his face and opened the door.

"Brother Seeker, could you pass me the slop bucket?" A weary voice called out from the corner of the room as soon as he took a step inside.

Jake's heart started hammering like a demented woodpecker, he couldn't just ignore the request, that would be far too suspicious, he would have to play along. The robe had tricked the seeker so far and best-case scenario he would be off his nut on mushrooms. Jake picked up the nearly overflowing metal pail and carefully dodged the mounds of detritus on the way to the figure in the corner. The man sat up shakily and swung his legs off the bed. Jake's heart stopped when he realised just who it was that had beckoned him.

"Hey, I know you, don't I?" said the wizened old man from the pilchard deal. "You're that bounty hun..." A fist sharply connected with his jaw, cutting off the sentence.

Jake laid him down gently and popped a piece of fleshy fungus that had been sitting in a dish on the bedside table under his tongue. With any luck, the old fellow would wake up tripping and think it had all been bad mojo. Jake covered him up and hurried from the room after first checking the corridor. Nobody else was in sight so he resumed his shuffle towards the kitchen at the far end.

Jake reached out to grip the doorknob just as the door was pulled sharply away from him. He came face to face with a man the height and build of a brick outhouse, a guardian, a mean-looking one at that. Jake tried to mask any surprise and act as if he was supposed to be there.

"Iä Ger'igguthy!" The man growled like a grizzly bear.

Jake racked his brain for a second, his stomach doing somersaults and his heart exploding. "Ger'igguthy fhtagn," he boomed in reply. Praying to anything he could think of that it was the correct response. Luckily, it was.

As the mollified guardian stomped off down the corridor, Jake hurried into the kitchen, shutting the door behind him. Rancid pots of foul-smelling soups and stews festered on the ancient and filthy stove. Next to this dubious feast, built into the worm-eaten wood panelling, was the dumbwaiter. Jake climbed inside and hoisted himself up to the first floor using the ratty old rope that hung down the side. Once he had reached the master-bedroom, he climbed out and lowered the lift back down.

Due to the darkness of the room, Jake slipped on his glasses and did a heat scan ... nothing.

"Bollocks," Jake hissed quietly; the room was utterly empty, his target had flown the nest.

From outside the window, he heard a door slam. Peering out from between the moth-eaten curtains, Jake spotted the target. Warren Tremayne, the hierophant of The Discarded, was sitting shotgun on an ancient diesel tractor. With a cough and a wheeze, the clapped-out engine sputtered into life and started to slowly drive away.

Jake cursed again and kicked the wall. His anger was a mistake – something had heard his outburst. A large, sharp-sounding skittering sound started to drift down from above. It sounded like someone stabbing a metal tray rhythmically with a meat skewer. Jake slowly and apprehensively looked up with his thermal imaging engaged. As he scanned the ceiling, the terrifying outline of an adult spawn of Ger'igguthy proved to be the source of the disturbance. Its antennae, as long as CB aerials, swivelled and flicked in the dark attic space above his head. Jake needed to get out of there, quickly.

The gargantuan crustacean obviously had some kind of telepathic link with the hosts, as a din of frantic wailing started to pipe up from below. Jake tip-toed quickly across the room and eased the door open; it was clear for the moment. He didn't bother removing his glasses as if he was caught up here in seeker robes he was screwed anyway. Hugging the far wall, he slipped towards his destination, an inevitably disgusting bathroom. Its window led out to a small sloping lean-to that, according to Mickie's map, housed rusty gardening implements. He could use this to get out. From there he would wing it. The only downfall to this course of action was that the bathroom in question was almost opposite the staircase.

The wails of the hosts below rose in volume and intensity the closer Jake got to the stairs. The clicking and clacking of sharp insectoid legs on attic floorboards followed his progress. He was being hunted and could hear heavy boots mounting the stairs. Guardians were coming to investigate. It was no good, discovery was inevitable. Jake pulled Jennifer out from under the robe and clicked the safety off.

"Oi! What do you think you are doing up 'ere?" the first guardian bellowed and pointed his battered weapon at Jake.

Jake ducked sideways to make the angle more obtuse and, as the second Guardian stepped onto the landing, he fired at the first. The slug caught the man in the shoulder and spun him like a top, a spray of crimson painting the walls and splattering the second man's face. Jake ducked the other way as the second guardian peppered the wall with a shotgun blast. Returning fire, Jake loosed off another round that slammed straight between the guardian's eyes. The back of his head ruptured as the stricken cultist flipped backwards and crashed down the stairs, taking out several balusters as he went.

Everything seemed to be going Jake's way when the ceiling behind him exploded in a shower of plaster, dust and wood splinters as the adult Ger'igguthy spawn landed on the landing. Its forelegs were like branches tipped with vicious pincers that swung violently for Jake's head. He retaliated by firing a succession of shots at the vicious creature. It was no use, each bullet ricocheting off its thick carapace. Jake looked at his weapon in dismay, the slugs he used were armour-piercing and could puncture a tank, but all they did to this unstoppable monster was piss it off.

As a huge pincer swung for his cranium, Jake ducked and sprung backwards landing flat on his backside, sending pain shooting up his spine from his coccyx. One sharp claw struck the wall and smashed a gaping hole in the plaster while the other smashed a floorboard to splinters as it swung wildly for Jake. The beast chittered and screeched in frustration as he scrambled on his haunches towards the bathroom. More guardians were mounting the stairs. Jake was done for if he didn't get out of there fast. With desperation punching him squarely in the heart, he flipped the cuff-mounted pocket open and tossed Mickie's flashbulb in the beast's direction and prayed.

Blinding white light bloomed from the shattered bulb. It was so intense that it caused Jake's glasses to malfunction and for a moment they were merely sunglasses as the systems crashed. He ripped them from his face and pocketed them as the creature hissed in agony. It swung its pincers in fury, smashing the landing bannister to matchwood. Jake leapt to his feet and charged towards the bathroom window.

Jake barrelled through the open door and took a headlong dive through the glass. It shattered as his momentum took him cleanly through. For a moment all he saw was sky, roof, sky, roof, sky, roof, sky as he tumbled downwards. His large frame crashed through a flimsy plastic gutter, and he plummeted to the ground like a lead weight. If the fall was bad, the landing was terrible. Jake hit the earth with a *thud,* face-first in a clump of thistles. The wind was driven from his body and black spots danced in his vision as the spiky weeds raked at his cheeks. Sadly, there was no time for licking his wounds, he had to get up and catch up with his target. Using the crumbling brickwork like a ladder he hauled himself upright.

Sucking in oxygen, Jake slipped the glasses back on his face and booted them up. They flickered into life not a moment too soon as a heat source came around the corner of the manor. Jake didn't think twice about levelling Jennifer at the target and firing off a perfectly aimed round with pinpoint accuracy. The guardian's head burst in a shower of gore and bone as the projectile slammed straight between his saucer-like eyes. Jake's legs were unsteady as he tried to run towards the barn where the vehicles were housed; he stumbled and weaved like a drunken bumble-bee. With adrenaline coursing through his body and keeping him moving, he rounded the corner and spotted potential salvation just metres from his position – an old two-stroke chicken-chaser.

For the first time in what seemed like forever, provenance was actually in Jake's favour, not conspiring to make his life complicated. The keys to the battered and ancient moped were dangling from the ignition. Jake prayed that there was petrol in the tank – fuel was in short supply since the Corporation had passed the *fuel independence act* and hoarded all the reserves in Zone Three. Zone 51 ran almost exclusively on electricity provided by the large nuclear plant in Zone 51b, the former Scotland. On the one hand, it had meant that there was no longer any reliance on the middle-east, but the downside was that, when Expiration Day hit, all the electric vehicles not controlled by the GAF became useless lumps of plastic. Jake turned the key and peddled like a maniac. The 50cc engine eventually fired up and he revved the engine.

Sliding sideways as the rear tyre spun in the mud, Jake fought to get the vehicle under control. In the end, it took him almost dragging it out with his hydraulically enhanced arms. Had he so desired, he could have picked the hunk of rust up and chucked it on the roof ... it might have gone quicker if he had. The acceleration was glacial, and it struggled to carry his bulk up the driveway. More Guardians were rushing across the overgrown lawn towards him. With one hand on the throttle, Jake loosed off some well-aimed rounds in their direction. One was struck in the thigh; he pitched forwards and ate gravel. Another was hit in the gut, his intestines tumbled free like bloated sausages. Jake grinned and returned his attention to the road.

Finally, the moped got up to a half-decent speed and Jake sped up the drive at a breakneck thirty-miles-an-hour. At the top of the driveway, he turned right onto the road and pulled away in the direction of the town. It was all downhill from there, so he hoped he would be able to gain on the lumbering tractor. Unfortunately, the road ahead was littered with potholes. One wrong move and the front wheel would collide with such a hazard and Jake would be sent rocketing over the handlebars. So intent was his concentration, that he failed to notice that he was being followed. The first he knew of the two guardians sat astride sputtering mopeds was when a bullet shattered his right side-mirror.

"Damn it, just quit, you bunch of idiots." Jake risked a glance behind him. The two massive men looked utterly ridiculous on the tiny motorcycles; he would have laughed himself to distraction if he hadn't been busy cussing them out. Their much larger bulk meant that they had better downward momentum and were rapidly gaining on Jake. Quickly using the zoom function on his glasses to scan the road ahead and playing it in one lens, he twisted position and fired. The shot went wide. Jake repeated the process and fired again. This shot connected with one of the guardian's knees. It was enough to destabilise the bike. Jake smirked as it slipped out from under the large man. The moped went east, and the guardian went west. Both were smashed beyond repair.

As the bends became sharper, Jake had to concentrate on the road. A shot from the remaining guardian struck the moped and the engine cut out; he was now freewheeling down a pockmarked road with a steep acclivity on one side and a sheer drop on the other. As he swerved and tried to keep it going, the other moped rapidly gained ground and was almost alongside. Jake had no choice but to cock the gun over his shoulder and fire blind. For the second time that day, luck was on his side. A miraculous shot hit the guardian right between the eyes. The moped left the road and rocketed into the metal barrier that separated the road from the cliff, the bike jumped and spun while the lifeless body was catapulted out to sea.

Jake whooped and hollered in triumph as he took the bends like a pro, despite bullets having severed the rear brake cable. He had to feather the front or risk vaulting the bike. As he neared the town, the road straightened. He was starting to relax when he spotted the tractor parked just off the road amongst a small cluster of trees. Unfortunately, his lapse in concentration proved costly – his rear wheel hit a patch of wet leaves, and the bike went sideways. The next thing Jake knew... It was dark.

Night had fallen by the time Jake regained consciousness, and his face stung like Hell. For a moment he thought he had contracted a severe case of road rash but one glance at his impromptu mattress revealed the truth – he was lying face-down in a patch of stinging-nettles. Jake rolled over and groaned.

"First thistles, now this ... what's next, arse-first into a gorse bush?" His entire body ached; he figured that he must have commando rolled across the road when his moped went awry. With a feeling of relief, he realised that his glasses were somehow still on his face. The tight elastic band Mickie had fitted to the arms had been a godsend. After painfully crunching a couple of fingers back into place, Jake stood and shook himself down. Still wearing the seeker robe, he started stalking his way back to where he spotted the tractor. He hoped it would still be there and, as luck would have it, it was.

Warren Tremayne was nowhere to be seen. The driver, however, was sitting in the cab puffing on a crumpled cigarette, the glowing red cinder illuminating the man's pensive expression as he inhaled deeply. It was clear that he had no more desire to be outdoors at night than Jake did. As Jake quietly approached the driver, the tell-tale stench of a lurker alerted him to danger. He fumbled around in his pocket for the pencil case containing the flash-bulbs. It was gone. It must have flown from his pocket during one of his tumbles.

"Bollocks," Jake hissed under his breath as the bushes started to shake.

The shoggoth was approaching from the rear of the tractor. For a creature its size, it was deceptively quiet. He could slip away and let the oblivious smoker get slurped, but he would be no wiser than when he left the compound. No, Jake needed the driver alive; you don't get any information from someone who has been digested by two tonnes of angry protoplasm.

"Look out," Jake bellowed, startling the man into a yelp. "Lurker, at your six!"

Tekeli-li!

The driver jumped, tossing his cigarette in the air as the lurker oozed from between a dense patch of trees. Screaming hysterically, the driver dived off the opposite side of the tractor as the creature slammed into the heavy vehicle like a tidal wave. Eyes formed and popped on its bulk as it searched out its prey.

Jake took aim at the fuel tank.

"Down," he screamed at the driver who promptly flung himself into some bushes like a ninja. Jake pulled the trigger. The superheated slug connected with the fuel tank. A tremendous explosion followed by a colossal fireball sent the indestructible monster slithering back into the woods piping in agony.

"Run! It won't take long to recover," Jake yelled as he dragged the driver to his feet. "Are you hurt?"

"No... I... I'm good, thank you, you saved my life."

"Don't jump the gun, we're not out of the woods yet ... literally. Come on."

The driver nodded and the unlikely duo took off at pace down the main road.

After what seemed like an eternity, the two exhausted men reached the edge of town.

"Hey, thanks, brother, I mean it," the driver panted.

Jake roughly grabbed the man by the neck, slammed him against a tree and pressed Jennifer's muzzle to his chin. "I'm not your brother, you sick bastard. Now, tell me where Tremayne is or I'll send you off to meet Ger'igguthy, right here, right fuckin' now!"

The driver flailed his arms in the air and squeaked, "Easy, man, I'm not discarded either ... look at my arms."

Jake did. The man's arms were free of the parasites, symbols, and fungal growths he associated with an acolyte of The Scavenger. "So, why are you chauffeuring that sicko Tremayne around town, then?" Jake moved the gun and pressed it to his temple.

"I'm a mechanic ... a grease-monkey," the driver spluttered. "Tremayne pays me to fix up his old clunkers and drive him around... I have to wear this stinking robe or the hosts go mad."

Jake lifted the robe to find a skinny man dressed in GAF overalls. He relaxed his grip and let the man slip to the floor. "Where's Tremayne?" he asked evenly, holstering Jennifer.

"At the moment, I have no idea. He said he had some business with the GAF ... I'm supposed to pick him up from the Hyperborea Bar after hours."

"After curfew?"

"Yeah. An hour after curfew. He said he had some *business* to take care of down there."

"Okay," Jake began. "You can go... I wouldn't bother trying to meet your boss later, if I were you."

"Thank you," the driver breathed, finally exhaling. As he was turning away, recognition dawned. "Hey, you're that bounty hunter, Jake something, aren't you?"

"In the flesh," Jake grinned, removing his robe and rolling it up. "And you are?"

"Potter, Oliver Potter."

Quick as a flash, the gun was back to the driver's head. "I thought I recognised you," Jake snarled through gritted teeth. "You're that fuckin' weasel whistle-blower from the factories. I ought to drill you right now... A lot of good people have died because of you!"

"I had no choice, I swear!" Oliver's eyes widened and his lip trembled as he begged for his life. "Sanders gave me no choice!

I never wanted to shop any runners... I swear... I... I wanted out too, you've gotta believe me!"

Jake could see in the man's eyes and smell it on the air that he was sincere. You didn't survive long on the streets of the Zone without developing a keen nose for bullshit. He lowered his gun and clapped the man on the shoulder. "No need to piss yourself, you're not my contract ... yet... Now, get the fuck out of here before I change my mind."

Oliver removed his black robe to reveal a dark stain radiating from his crotch and took off into the trees like a squirrel with a rocket up its backside. Jake picked up the robe and balled it up with his own. You never knew when something like that would come in handy. He started towards his home; he had a couple of hours until curfew which was more than enough time to lick his wounds and refill his hip-flask. After that, he would take up position opposite the bar and await his target.

Jake ordered another drink from the Voormi on the bar and checked to see that Tremayne was still sitting in the corner of the Hyperborea Bar. The umber-furred biped handed him a pint of something strong-smelling and grunted at him for payment. The Voormis were a curious race that had appeared in the Zone shortly after the collapse. Some said that they had always been here, dwelling in deep caves, while others believed that they had arrived when the veil between realities was torn. Whatever their origin, they had integrated swiftly and became invaluable in mining operations. The Hyperborea Bar was owned by an entrepreneurial Voormi named Uggo-Nathtia. It was the world's first Voormis-owned bar and was named after their fabled homeland.

Jake swigged his drink and felt it strip the enamel from his teeth. Whatever the provenance of the Voormis, those guys knew how to drink. The anaesthetising effect of the brew was so very welcome after the day Jake had endured. He predicted that in the morning his body would be a veritable rainbow of bruises and abrasions... He may as well add a hangover to the pain.

Time moved swiftly, and two drinks later, the bartender rang the bell for curfew. Most people quickly finished their drinks and left before the streets became a nightmare of lurkers and Caspers. Tremayne hadn't moved since he had arrived. Jake made his half-pint last and rode out the twenty-minute drinking-up period. As the clock struck midnight, Tremayne stood up and slipped quietly through the door to the toilets. Jake finished his glass, waited until the barman was out of sight and followed.

Jake cursed as he burst into the filthy gents, gun in hand, only to find it empty. Strange scribblings on the toilet doors made him shudder involuntarily. You expected phone numbers for prostitutes on toilet walls, not occult poetry. Next, he tried the ladies, kicking open stall after stall. They were also empty. Jake scratched his head and went back out into the corridor. The only other exit was through a door painted 'PrIVit'. There were no other doors or windows through which he could escape.

Carefully opening the door, Jake found himself in a winding staircase carved out of the foundations of the town using primitive tools. He followed the winding steps down and down. The air grew thicker with the damp smell of earth and decay. Upon reaching the bottom of the shaft, Jake found himself in a long, sloping tunnel. The further he went on the downward trajectory, the more humid and stifling it became. Finally, he reached a corner and upon turning it, found Warren Tremayne standing over a pit from which a red glow emanated.

"Hold it right there, Tremayne!"

The startled hierophant turned and stammered. "W... who are y... you? What do you want?"

Jake strode into the light, brandishing his weapon. "Hand over the compass you stole from Ben Edwards, and you can leave here breathing."

Warren was holding the compass in his right hand. He composed himself before imploring. "I need this to stop a cataclysm!"

"What, a sodding compass? Don't give me that cobblers!"

"It's true! What you are seeing" —Warren pointed to the gaping maw in the earth— "is a breach to the depths of N'Kai!"

"To what?" Jake demanded. "What the fuck are you talking about?"

"N'Kai! It's a place sacred to the Voormis. It is said that their god, Tsathoggua, dwells in its red-litten depths. The Voormis intend to wake their sleeping god! I must stop them!"

"And how the hell is a compass supposed to do that?"

"It's not the compass... It's what's inside." Warren unscrewed the back of the navigation device and tipped out a small, star-shaped object. "This is a Mnar stone. Only this can keep a Great Old One imprisoned... It's carved with the Elder sign!"

Jake thought it over for a second. Edwards had neglected to mention the stone, which pissed him off. Warren was probably making it up to save his own worthless hide, but the last thing the world needed was another cosmic deity stomping around.

"Okay, take the star and do what you need to do. Just give me the compass."

Warren complied and tossed the heirloom to Jake. "Thank you," he grinned, then, grasping the stone in his fist, started chanting in some bizarre language. Almost instantly, the hole began to shrink. Jake turned and hurried back up to the Hyperborea Bar as the ground began to shake.

Glasses tinkled, fell, and smashed as Jake stepped back into the bar. The Voormi barman was looking around in confusion. Jake strode over to him, feigning drunkenness and tapped him on the shoulder. "Hey, man," he slurred, "I just saw some guy go through the 'privit' door."

The Voormi growled in fury and grabbed a shotgun from under the bar. Jake stepped back out into the downpour as the barman hurried off harbouring the intent to kill. Jake smiled; he had just saved himself at least one bullet. Turning in the direction of Ben's hideout, he started to limp away into the darkness.

Less than an hour later, Jake was back home with a fist full of ration chits, a pocket full of ammunition and a tin of potted meat. Ben Edwards was unhappy about the missing star. The compass wasn't what he had been after all along. Jake had pleaded ignorance of the Mnar stone and demanded payment. Ben cursed and handed over what he'd promised. It was a nice payday, and the can of meat meant that he and Burt the cockroach wouldn't go hungry for another day. Ben's deception soured his feast, however, and he went to bed vowing that he would never take another job from that slippery old bastard ever again.

CHAPTER III

DON'T SPEAK

Life as an enforcer in the employ of the Global Arms Federation was regimented, to say the very least. The command centre directly beamed alarms and shift information to your mandatory aiming and tactical chip, ensuring that nobody was late for shift. If you were by so much as a second, it would deliver a jolt of electricity directly to your spinal cortex. The minuscule device was slipped into your frontal lobe and wired in by specialist chip-doctors. It provided a direct link from the eyes to chips installed in every enforcer's multi-purpose rifle providing pinpoint accuracy and superior crowd control. Like the advertising slogans said... Enforcer 3000, a guaranteed kill-shot every time.

Maximilian Tucker had been an enforcer for several years by this point. He'd been toting a rifle ever since he fell out of the education centre with a first in marksmanship and a negative admin score. Every morning, after the first klaxon, he would get out of bed, eat his protein bar and get dressed. His boots had to be shiny and his uniform gleaming. Under the high-visibility hooded robe, every enforcer wore armour plating, neck stocks, and stab vests, even the hood incorporated a protective skull cap. Nothing short of anti-vehicle rounds were going to do much damage to a properly kitted-out Casper unless the gunman was an expert shot and knew the weak points. The light-reactive goggles were equipped with an HUD that linked to all the enforcer's chips and provided up to date info on heart rate and blood pressure along with their gun's ammo and muzzle temperature gauges.

That morning, Max had readied himself for his usual rounds. He had been assigned to warehouse security and spent most of his day wandering around the hundreds of crates of guns produced in the factories. It was tedious work, but in all his time on the job he had not once been called upon to fire upon another human being. This was a blessing. Max wasn't sure he had it in him. Practice dummies were one thing, people another entirely. Before he reached his allocated patrol area, a message flashed up on his HUD instructing him to report instead to the GAF administration building.

Max started to hyperventilate; he'd never been called to the tower before and the only time he had heard of it happening was when a worker needed *correction* or reassignment, neither of which were attractive options. His mind racing, he desperately tried to remember if he had unwittingly done anything that could be considered an infraction. Coming up blank, he resigned himself to being off the cushy warehouse job and hurried towards the central plaza in the heart of the sector. His best-case scenario was being tasked with escorting a GAF big-wig to the office complex. He didn't like mixing with the *suits* but at least he would be able to go back to his usual routine once the mission was completed.

Looming ominously like a great glass and neon monolith, the GAF tower was the tallest building in the sector, dwarfing even the imposing Drone Dispatch Centre to the north. A harsh salty wind blew in off the sea and whistled down the central promenade as he made haste towards his destination. Max was glad of his cumbersome uniform as it bounced and ricocheted off the gleaming glass shop fronts of the commercial zone. Max hated the robe with a passion; he didn't understand why they were forced to wear such a ridiculous garment. There was a good reason that the populous called them Caspers – they looked like comedy ghosts. He wanted to ask why they couldn't just wear their combat gear without the robe, but you didn't ask questions like that. You didn't ask questions, period. Questions got you killed.

With a hollow *clunk* the locks on the sliding doors released and they parted silently. Max swallowed back the metallic tang of adrenaline, squared his broad shoulders and marched towards the reception desk.

"Morning, I was pinged to report here," he announced to the disinterested young woman perched on a swivel chair.

"Name?"

"Max Tucker, warehouse."

The receptionist's electric blue fingernails tapped out a foxtrot on the keys of her terminal. "You're expected. Cubicle six, behind you."

"Thanks," Max muttered nervously as she returned to whatever receptionists did when they weren't letting people in. Plotting the destruction of mankind, most likely. Turning, he located the mall waiting room and hurried over. Praying that everything would be fine, he waited to be buzzed in before turning the handle and opening the door.

Max's heart sank.

"Ah, Mr Tucker, thank you for joining us so *promptly*," a slender man in a sharp suit and an even sharper smile purred disdainfully. Max knew who this man was, everyone in Zone 51 did. He was the overseer, Malcolm Sanderson, The CEO's eyes and ears. Before the zone's official incorporation into The Imperial Corporation, he was known as the Prime Minister. He was flanked by two hulking brutes in black versions of the enforcer uniform, his *Personal Assistants* Karl and Mike.

Max snapped a salute. "You requested my presence?"

"Indeed, take a seat." Sanderson inclined his hand towards a moulded plastic chair that didn't look like it could take the large enforcer's weight. Grimacing as the armour plating dug into his thighs, Max did as he was told.

"The reason I have summoned you here today is that we need a guide into the forbidden sector. I understand you have lived here all your life?"

Max nodded.

"Excellent, so you must know your way around the sector?"

Another nod.

"Splendid, and, as your grades are exemplary, you seem like just the man for the job."

"Thank you, Overseer."

Sanderson waved a hand airily. "Think nothing of it. I believe that hard work and obedience should be rewarded. You will receive a bonus if this goes without a hitch."

Max smiled. "Thank you, Overseer."

"Now, down to business. The job is this, a dangerous fugitive is abroad in the ruins of the old town and, thus far, she has managed to evade capture. This particular *undesirable* is considered an enemy of The Corporation, and the CEO has instructed me to see to it personally that she is captured and exterminated."

The relish with which Sanderson said *exterminated* made Max wince. A detail that wasn't missed by The Overseer.

"That's right, this is a Hunter-Killer mission but, don't worry, you are coming along purely as a guide." Sanderson approached Max and leaned in so close that he could smell the coffee on his breath. "This isn't going to be an issue, I trust?"

Max gulped and quickly composed himself. "No, sir," he lied, he was, if truth be uttered, deeply uneasy with the H-K aspect of the enforcer job but thought better of saying anything. With any luck, the fugitive would be long gone. "No problem at all."

"Excellent. You see, Mike, we picked the right man, after all." Sanderson withdrew and returned to his position between the two scowling masses of meat and malice. "Fly-on-the-wall spy drones picked up the *undesirable's* barcode entering the derelict area past the loading bays. As you well know, this forbidden ground is a disease-ridden rabbit warren of derelict shops and businesses from before the construction of the GAF complex. To compound matters, the breakwater recently collapsed, and the area is flooded. As you can well understand, I want to be in and out as quickly as possible. That's where you come in."

Max looked puzzled.

"As you will, no doubt, be aware, the area is a den of *undesirables,* rodents, and other assorted vermin. As a local man, you must have a pretty good idea where to start looking?"

Max nodded.

"Bravo!" Sanderson clapped theatrically; his minions followed suit. It was unsettling, to say the least. Both men had the cold, dead eyes more commonly seen in sharks and other marine predators. "Right, no time like the present." Sanderson opened the door and motioned Max to move with a sweep of his left hand. "Lead on, Maximilian, the fate of Zone security is in your capable hands."

Max stood, swallowed, then led The Overseer and his menacing entourage out of the GAF tower and towards the festering dockyard area. The yards were a hive of activity. Fishermen brought crates of fish out of the warehouses as welders worked on maintaining the mighty GAF fishing fleet. Max could feel all eyes upon him, wary and suspicious. The overseer *never* mingled with the workers, unless something serious was going on. Many feared for their jobs. Some feared for their lives.

A gigantic holographic cod loomed above the GAF cannery, grinning and trumpeting the superiority of Zone 51 fish through tinny speakers, the stark contrast between the cheerful advertising campaign and the grim reality of the docks struck Max as downright surreal. He had never given it much thought before, but standing next to Mr Sanderson put everything into perspective, and it wasn't pleasant. Once they had passed the fleet, they came to a pair of massive steel gates lined with razor-wire and flanked by two automated, Sentinel-class machine guns. The huge, No Exit sign split down the centre as the gates swung open. Max and his terrifying new friends stepped through and into the dangerous ruins.

Many people in Zone 51, had no idea that behind the walls of the gleaming, brutalist population centres lay the remains of towns and cities older than anyone could remember. Vast swathes of history had been erased from the landscape, replaced by tons of concrete and steel. It was these ancient, crumbling ruins that Max led the overseer through on that miserable March morning.

Their heavy boots stamped in the inch of standing water, echoing down what was once a picturesque esplanade. Abandoned tea-rooms and bait-shops stood crumbling shoulder to shoulder with garish souvenir shops still displaying their dust encrusted wares, brightly coloured buckets and spades hanging in the windows next to sun-bleached postcards and novelty singing haddocks. A young man, who had been perched on the balcony of an old fish and chip shop, scrambled on his haunches and vanished like a phantom upon spotting the heavily armed trio flanking the most powerful man in Zone 51.

Sanderson grinned at the man's panic. "What would possess someone to live like this?" he mused out loud, clamping a pristine white handkerchief over his vulpine features in an attempt to block out the stagnant air. "I'll never understand these *undesirables*, what about you Max?"

Max wanted to point out that it wasn't usually the individual's choice to be branded undesirable. In the end, self-preservation won out over honesty. Max shrugged and mumbled "No, sir," through his hood.

"Karl here," he indicated the shorter yet wider of the two guards, "thinks that we should exterminate the lot of them. Round them up in a bunch of shipping containers and drop in a few thermal charges, what say you, Max?"

Max didn't like killing in general, especially not wholesale, indiscriminate killing. Once again, he meekly mumbled, "Yes, sir." He could feel the predatory eyes of Mr Sanderson burrowing into his brain like an X-ray; he was being toyed with like a mouse that had been cornered by an overfed house cat, he could sense the twisted grin under the striped hankie. One stray word would have him stripped of his uniform and branded *undesirable* sooner than you could say *executive bonus*. The panic he had felt that morning returned tenfold, and it was a battle to keep his breathing regular enough to avoid scrutiny.

A sharp beeping broke the tension. Max exhaled. The taller guard, Mike, passed a square, hand-held device to Sanderson. His brow creased and his oddly dark eyes narrowed as he looked at the screen. It showed a generic topographical map of the area that meant little to the overseer. He passed it to Max. "Where do you suppose that is?"

Max studied the tracking device for a moment and got his bearings. "The signal is coming from behind a row of shops parallel to the square, sir."

Sanderson slapped him on the back. "Smashing work. See that, Mark, we chose the right hunting dog!" He gave a low chuckle and winked at Max. "Lead on, Rover."

Max hurried them along to the turning towards the square. He wanted to get this over with as quickly as humanly possible. Mr Sanderson was giving him the creeps and his silent killers weren't much better. With the sea now to their backs, the stench of rancid seaweed was replaced by even more noxious aromas.

"By all the saints!" Sanderson exclaimed. "What is that ghastly smell?"

"Piss, sir," Max replied flatly. "Rat piss. There are thousands of the little buggers down here."

"Ooh," Sanderson shuddered theatrically, "rats! I can't stand the creatures... Shoot on sight, boys."

The two hulks said nothing but cocked their weapons in perfect unison. The solid *chunk-chunk* of the firing bolt made Max jump. Making a show of cocking his own weapon, he led the party along the slime-encrusted cobbled streets towards the remnants of the town square. The nicely tended lawns and shrubberies, now a feral tangle of brambles and weeds, oozed menace and hinted at furtive creatures watching their progress with hungry eyes. A cracked and headless statue of Poseidon loomed above the area, cowering under the shadow of the commercial zone that rose into the dark clouds above.

A small alleyway between two buildings led to the backstreet where the tracker indicated the fugitive was hiding. Sanderson directed his two pet monsters to stalk around the back of an old storage shed where the tracker indicated. Once they were in place, they were to wait and to cut off any potential escape route. Meanwhile, Sanderson would accompany Max around the front.

After giving Karl and Mike a minute to get in position, Mr Sanderson gave Max the nod to approach the door. Max assumed a firing stance and silently shuffled towards the door. His heart rate was through the roof. He had no idea what was waiting for him on the other side of that door. All he knew was that a *dangerous* fugitive was hiding in the small breeze-block structure. He got himself into position and looked to the overseer for the signal. Time seemed to slow to an agonising crawl, the blood roaring in his ears.

"Go!" Sanderson roared.

Max reared back on his left foot and booted the door at the point of the bolt. The wooden frame splintered and fragmented as the door slammed inwards. "Hands up!" Max demanded as he stepped inside, sweeping the corners with his gun barrel, his eyes frantically searching for a target. He didn't spot anything on his first sweep but as his eyes adjusted to the gloom, he spotted startled movement in the far corner of the rubbish-littered space. Max was poised to execute the fugitive when the terrified features of a young girl emerged from under a dusty blanket.

Max dropped the muzzle and stood up sharp in confusion. *This must be some kind of mistake.* His mind raced. *Surely, this girl can't be the real target?* Max estimated that she must have been twelve at the most. He looked around in bewilderment, searching for the real target. After a second it became horribly clear that the innocent looking girl *was* the target.

"What's going on, Mr Tucker?" Sanderson asked from his safe distance. "Why haven't I heard the sweet sound of gunfire?"

Max's mind raced, this had to be a mistake. "There's nobody in here but some little girl, sir!"

"That's the target, Enforcer," Sanderson bellowed. "Terminate her, immediately!"

Max raised the gun and pointed it at the girl, perspiration pouring down his chiselled features, stinging his eyes and steaming up his goggles. His finger hovered over the trigger, tremulous and hesitant. Seconds passed...

"What the hell are you waiting for? Kill her! Kill! Her! Now!"

Max ripped his hood off and wiped his forehead as his grip on his gun faltered. By now, his entire body was trembling, the shake that had begun in his hands had raced up both arms, infecting his torso. Even if he fired now, the chance was good that he'd miss. He looked at the terrified expression on the girl's face then down at his gun. Finally, he let the weapon fall loose on its shoulder strap and held a gloved finger to his lips.

"Kill her, and that's an order!" Anger bubbled in the overseer's voice. He waited for a second before shaking his head. "Karl, Mike, get in there and eliminate the target!"

Max looked around in desperation; he wasn't going to let this happen. The two cold-eyed killers would be here any second and he needed to either hide the girl or get her out of there pronto. Quickly weighing up his limited options, his eyes spotted a ventilation hatch in the ceiling. Poking it open with his gun, he motioned for the girl to come over. She was hesitant at first but swiftly changed her mind when the sound of heavy boots approaching filled her ears. Max picked her up like a bundle of rags and thrust her through the opening in one fluid movement.

Max turned and walked from the room just as Karl and Mike came barrelling towards the doorway. Over their shoulders, Mr Sanderson beckoned the hood-less enforcer with a crooked finger. "Where is the girl, Max?"

Max shrugged.

Sanderson smiled and held his hands up benignly before fixing Max with a look that could have cut through steel. "I'll ask you again, just once, mind. Where is the fucking girl?"

As Max searched for the courage to tell Sanderson to go to Hell, a scuffing sound announced to all present that the fugitive was on the roof.

"Get up there and shoot her," Sanderson growled, frustration creeping into his fury. It was odd, but Max was sure he detected an underlying note of fear.

Max stared the man in the eye and simply said, "No."

Sanderson stared at Max in disbelief. He couldn't believe what he was hearing. Nobody had *ever* said *no* to him before, not when he was a child and certainly not after his meteoric rise to power. He fixed Max with an icy stare and bared his teeth.

"What did you say to me?" Sanderson's low rumble was like a gathering storm.

"I said *no*, sir, I won't shoot a child."

Sanderson smiled. "That's admirable, I *admire* your mercy." The smile fell from his lips in a heartbeat. "*That* girl is an enemy of the corporation. You deliberately let her escape, didn't you?"

Max nodded. "I will not shoot an innocent child."

"Innocent? She's the most dangerous woman in Zone 51! You will pay for disobeying me!"

A heavy blow connected with the back of Max's head, his vision dimmed, and his legs buckled. Zone 51 twisted around him as gravity took hold, his face met the pavement with a horrible slap, and everything went dark.

A shrill ranging in Max's ears accompanied his slow crawl back to consciousness. Hearing returned first, followed by touch. His other senses were more hesitant to kick in. He could feel that he was on his knees and that he was being held upright by two pairs of powerful hands. The final moments before he was bludgeoned into oblivion played over and over in his head like the looping routine of the holographic cod by the docks. It seemed unreal. Only the pain and a mocking voice that drifted on the wind convinced him that it had indeed occurred.

"Wakey, wakey." Overseer Sanderson's mocking voice cut through the tinnitus and snapped Max's eyes wide open. "Ah, there you are." Sanderson's leering face was just inches from Max's as he whispered, "While you were sleeping, I updated your barcode. Welcome to your new home, undesirable scum." Sanderson snorted, then spat a gob of thick phlegm into Max's face. "I've also put out kill orders on your family and friends. I've just heard that your wife—Shelly, wasn't it?—has just been terminated."

Max bellowed in anguish and strained against his massive captors.

Sanderson flashed a smug smile. "You know how the saying goes... *Don't cross the boss*. Bet you wish you'd painted the walls with that urchin's brains now, don't you?"

"You mother fucker!" Max snarled through gritted teeth. "You should put a bullet in my head now because, I swear, one day, I'm gonna' fucking kill you!"

Sanderson burst into hysterical laughter. "You, kill me? That's cute. I don't think so, Mr Tucker."

"Come here and I'll show you," Max screamed in fury.

"You can't kill me, no *human* hands can, I'm protected," Sanderson gloated, smoothing down the front of his expensive suit jacket.

"Bullshit!"

"I'm getting tired of hearing your disobedient tongue." Sanderson pulled a small device from his pocket. "Have you ever seen one of these before? It's the latest thing." He pressed a switch and a devilish-looking laser shot from the top of the device. "Laser scalpel, the way of the future!" Sanderson pulled a pair of forceps from his other breast pocket and tossed it to Karl. "Get his tongue."

Max tried to clamp his teeth together as his jaw was forced open by massive, gloved fingers. A sharp metallic tang danced on his tongue as the forceps bit down and it was yanked out into the air. Sanderson moved in and Max closed his eyes as a searing pain shot into his brain. He could hear Sanderson laugh as he cut. In one clean slice, his tongue was removed and the wound instantly cauterised.

Max convulsed in agony, his body bucking and twisting against his captors.

Sanderson stood over his prey cackling like a crone as he dangled the extracted tongue in front of his victim. After a moment's gleeful mockery, he tired of the game and checked his watch. "Alas, I am due at a board meeting soon. We will have to wrap things up."

Max grunted and growled as he attempted to drown his tormentor in a torrent of threats and invective.

Sanderson chuckled. "Still defiant, eh? Very well, Let's see how long you can survive out here without eyes. Hold his head, boys."

Karl grabbed Max by his flat-top and yanked it backwards while Mike gripped him by the jaw. Max tried to break free, but it was no good; as formidable as Max was, his assailants were far too powerful. It was an exercise in futility and somewhat akin to attempting to wrestle a couple of oak trees.

Sanderson held out the laser in triumph and moved it for the next blow

"Hey, arseholes!" a voice shouted from over the street.

Sanderson looked up, startled, as bullets thudded into Mike's massive torso. Max could tell by the noise that they were armour-piercing anti-personnel rounds, Casper killers. The tell-tale *ping* as they punctured the plating was a sound he had heretofore prayed to never encounter. Now, it was the sweetest noise he had ever experienced. Mike spun and dropped to the floor, shaking and twitching as he bled out. Once more, gravity played a part in the drama—Mike was still gripping Max's jaw and yanked him out of Karl's grip.

Raising his gun, Karl took a sidestep to the left before returning fire. The unseen assailant dropped into cover and waited for an opening. Karl started to stomp over to where the man was hiding, loosing off a series of three-round bursts to keep his opponent pinned down as he crossed the street. In seconds, Max's saviour would be mown down.

Spotting Sanderson going for Mike's gun, Max pulled himself back to his knees and threw his body sideways in a race for the firearm. Sanderson raged as Max snatched it from the corpse, twisted around and let off a staccato burst of lead at Karl's back. The big man dropped like a stone. Quick as a flash, Max spun back towards Sanderson and opened fire without so much as a second's hesitation. The bullets hit their mark, then dissolved into particles which then blew away on a stiff breeze.

Sanderson's eyes flashed a burnt orange, and his grin stretched into a terrifying rictus. "I told you that you couldn't kill me, worm!" His voice had changed, the smooth and measured tones of the politician had shifted entirely. Gone was the suave purr, replaced by a rumbling, cavernous echo. Sanderson toyed with the laser scalpel as he advanced on Max, chuckling menacingly. He was inches away from lashing out with the cutter when a high-pitched voice startled Sanderson into distraction.

"Back!" the little girl screamed as she darted from her hiding place behind the outbuilding. In her hand was a strange, star-shaped stone that crackled with energy.

Sanderson's eyes returned to normal as he recoiled in fear, his body shimmering and fluttering like a shadow cast by candle-flame. The girl advanced on the evil overseer, her voice shrill as she intoned a strange incantation. Sanderson turned, his face contorted in disbelief and panic, and bolted down the alley. Max fired again. This time the bullet struck Sanderson in the shoulder. The force of the impact slammed him chest first into the wall of the narrow alley. Max adjusted his aim and prepared to deliver a shot to the back of the man's head, but a sharp *click* announced that the magazine was empty.

Sanderson slipped away into the maze of streets back towards the tower.

Max slammed the gun onto the street in frustration and fell backwards, his mind in turmoil and his body in excruciating pain. He stared up at the oppressively gloomy sky as the faces of his loved ones flickered through his mind like a news bulletin. After what seemed like an eternity their haunting faces were replaced by those of the young blonde girl and a strongly featured man of Caribbean descent.

"Shit." The man smiled. "Nice shooting. Thanks for saving my ass back there."

"Thank you," the girl whispered as she crouched at his side.

Max wanted to thank them both but couldn't. Speaking out got him into this state and now he would never speak again.

The man turned to the girl. "Sorry I was late, Dan, I got held up by some Caspers over by the church."

"That's okay, Dwayne, our friend here saved me from *him.*" The girl smiled again as Dwayne ruffled her sandy hair and looked down at Max. "We have to help him."

"Agreed." Dwayne nodded. "Help me get him up and back to the antique shop."

The next few weeks were a blur of nightmares, pain, and confusion for Max. Dwayne and Danni got him back to the safety of a fortified antique shop in the oldest part of town in double-quick time. It was here that he was introduced to Benjamin Edwards, the man who would become a father figure to the broken ex-enforcer over the coming months.

Ben explained to Max one morning, as he spoon-fed him tomato soup, that the antique shop was protected by something called a Mnar stone. These ancient artefacts were constructed by a benign race of elder beings that once inhabited the polar regions in an effort to combat the influence of The Great Old Ones. These stones were, along with something called an Elder Sign and a handful of chants, rituals, and incantations, the only things the Old Ones were vulnerable to. Danni was a target because she was one of the only people on the planet who could create new Mnar stones. A gift she had received at birth and had seen her hunted ever since.

Max didn't know what Ben was talking about, but his mind reasoned that Sanderson was evil and the star stone affected him, so the Mnar stones warded off evil. He had no way to articulate this reasoning which was deeply frustrating. Over the coming months, Ben taught Max Morse code and sign language. Max devised his very own hybrid method of communication using the firing bolt, safety catch and magazine of an ancient AK-47 that Ben gave him.

As the years went on, Max adapted to his now-mute existence. His physical scars healed but his mind was forever haunted by his butchered loved ones. Every time Max saw Sanderson on the omnipresent news screens around the zone his blood boiled with fury. He vowed that one day there would be a reckoning between himself and the diabolical overseer.

The laser-cut U on his barcode that branded him for evermore as an undesirable had once felt like a stigma, a shameful thing. Now, however, Max saw it for what it truly was. It was a badge of honour that spoke of his courage in standing up to tyranny and protecting an innocent. The desperate people of the under-zone were his new family, and he would protect them with every drop of blood he had in his body. If being desirable meant bending the knee to creatures such as Sanderson then Max was proud to be undesirable.

CHAPTER IV

STARMAKER

MARCH 4ᵀᴴ 2132
ZONE 51 – SOUTH-WEST SECTOR:

"Hello hangover my old friend..."

Bounty hunter Jake Baker groaned and squirmed on his filthy mattress as the factory klaxon shattered his drugged slumber. His throat was red raw and his vision drifted around the room like the muscles in his eye sockets had finally given up the ghost. Using the headboard for support, his back screamed as he forced himself upright. He couldn't be sure if it was his spine or his liver that was giving him gyp. Perhaps a combination of the two? After all, both had taken a solid pounding of late.

Since his last big score, Jake had been on a bender of Biblical proportions. Most of the ration cards he had earned had been traded for cheap and rough alcohol—the rest had gone on black-market cigarettes and tinned food. Unfortunately, his stash had dwindled away to nothing, and he was back on the GAF ration bars.

Attempting to reach out with his right arm revealed that his hydraulic shoulder joint was out of its housing. His arm flopped and dangled like an elephant's trunk. Puzzlement flashed across his face as he racked his brain to remember what in heaven's name he had been doing last night. Then it came to him.

"For fuck's sake, Jake, will you never learn... Never wrestle with Voormis."

Jake had put his name down on the weekly fight-club tournament at the Hyperborea Bar. It had all been going swimmingly until his third bout. His first two opponents had been weedy scavengers from dockside who had posed no real challenge. A couple of straight jabs to the jaw had seen both of them stretchered out in next to no time. Jake's third adversary, in stark contrast, had been a whopping great Voormi that must have weighed three hundred and fifty pounds at the bare minimum. Jake had lasted all of thirty seconds ... a personal best against that particular brute.

Luckily for Jake, Muggo'sutha had a kind soul lurking under the rippling bulk and tufts of matted umber fur. He had carried Jake home after the fight and given him some quality Voormis-grade painkillers. The potent pills had mixed exceedingly well with the gallon or so of seaweed-whiskey that had been sloshing around in his guts at the time and had sent him floating off into the stratosphere. Now, he had to try and survive the landing as he crashed back down to terra firma.

Making promises to lay off the booze that he *knew* he wouldn't keep, Jake rose unsteadily and shuffled into the kitchen. One plus to his over-indulgence of the bottle was that he still possessed a healthy supply of purified water so he could afford to indulge. Unscrewing the lid on a half-litre bottle of purified water, he put it to his lips and tipped his head back. The cool liquid was a balm to his stinging larynx as it dribbled out of the corners of his mouth and down his chin. The bottle drained, he tossed it in the corner next to the other empties and opened the cupboard to get his breakfast ration.

"Morning, Burt," Jake said to the large cockroach that was staring at him, almost in judgement. "I know, I know... I need to lay off the booze. Here" —he snapped off a corner of the ration bar and placed it in front of the insect— "bon-appetit!"

Burt clacked his mandibles gratefully.

Jake shut the cupboard door and left his friend to his meal.

After a rumble of thunder that shook the building, torrents of wind-propelled rain began to pelt the grime-encrusted windows in a fox-trot rhythm. Jake covered his face with his palm and shook his head; he knew a raucous din was incoming. Storms agitated one of the chip-heads that lived above him. As predicted, *Dave the Penguin* started hopping around his room making noises like a disgruntled bird. The constant *thuds* and *squawks* were the last thing Jake needed in his delicate state. Every noise battered and tickled his pickled brain. Still, he couldn't get angry, Dave got a fried head-chip courtesy of Expiration Day and now believed that he was a macaroni penguin, not his fault. Yet another victim. The terrifying thing was, that out of the two poor souls that lived up there, Dave was the rational one.

Jake munched his ration bar, lit a smoke, and started to feel moderately better. He had long since known that they pumped that stuff full of drugs to keep the populous docile and upright. After his breakfast, he crashed onto his threadbare sofa and rubbed his aching eyeballs. He had no work on that day and nothing to worry about, so he made a snap decision to stay indoors and enjoy his hangover the way nature intended; with a woodpecker in his brain and his head in the toilet. Jake exhaled and breathed a sigh of relief.

THUNK-THUNK-THUNK

Jake cursed and grabbed his trusty hand-cannon, Jennifer. Whoever was at the door wasn't welcome. "Piss off... I'm busy," he growled, irritation flooding his system with adrenaline.

Clunk! Clunk!-Clack! Clunk!-Clunk! Clack! Clack! Clunk!

Jake relaxed upon hearing the familiar Morse-code. "Oh, Hi Max," he yelled in a sing-song manner as he rubbed his temples. "Piss off, Max!"

Clunk! Clunk!

"*No?* What do you mean *no?*"

Clunk! Clunk!

"Look, Max, I told you that I won't do anything else for that weasel Edwards. So, bugger off and leave me to my hangover, okay?"

Clunk! Clunk!

"What? *No,* you won't go away, or *no,* you're not here for Edwards?"

Clunk!

"Eh? You're *not* here for Edwards?"

SLAM!

Max punched the door with such force that he nearly took the reinforced security gate off its hinges.

"Jesus!" Jake exclaimed, getting to his feet. "Okay, Okay, Hold on Mr Grumpy, I'm coming!" Jake shuffled across the room and unlocked the heavy bolts and chains. Finally, he opened the door.

"Hey, Max. Whoa!" Jake was shocked at the mute ex-enforcer's appearance. "Christ, You look like I feel. Heavy night last night, man?"

Max put his fingers to his temple in the 'blow-your-own-brains-out' gesture and shook his head. He reeked of sweat and booze and appeared to be still half-bombed.

"Come on in. We can suffer together." Jake swung his loose arm in a wide semi-circle that indicated that Max should enter. Max crossed the threshold, sized his host up and down then grabbed Jake by the shoulder. One sharp tug later and his arm was fixed.

Jake smiled and rotated his arm. "Thanks, Max, that saves me a trip down the mechanic's. Now, what can I do for you? Bear in mind that if I even sense the name Benjamin Edwards, the answer is *no*."

Max shook his head to indicate that it had nothing to do with Edwards and fished in the pockets of his filthy flak-jacket. He smiled when he found what he was looking for and passed it to Jake. It was an old twentieth-century mobile phone. Jake had seen it before, the last time he was around Max's abode. Mickie had been tinkering with it, or one just like it.

"What do you want me to do with this, try to beat Mickie's snake score?"

Max pointed at the screen then held his thumb to his ear and his pinky to his mouth.

Jake jabbed the green button and looked at the cracked screen, it said 'Call Mickie? Yes / No' Jake pressed the button with the green strip across the centre and held the device to his ear. A harsh digital tone erupted from the speaker making him wince. He couldn't help being impressed; it seemed that their resident technological necromancer had somehow succeeded in jacking the ancient device into the GAF data-stream.

"Hello, is that Jake?" Mickie answered.

"Yeah, How the hell did you get this thing working, Mick?"

"Look, there isn't time to talk about what a genius I am, the

GAF could cut the stream any second, i'm piggybacking on their coms network. Focus. Do you know what day it is?"

"Um," Jake pondered.

"It's the fourth. You know what that means?"

"Um?"

"It means that it's the day after Max's anniversary."

"Shit," Jake knew what that meant. It meant that it was exactly seven years since Max's whole world fell apart.

"Yeah," Mickie sighed, "well, Max got trashed on home-made vodka and basically begged and pleaded for me to try and find Danni. You know, the little girl, the Starmaker? Anyway, after trying to tell him that it would be no use, that she was gone, I gave in and keyed Sniffer, one of my drones, into her DNA. She had left some clothes in the shop and he managed to get a sample. About two hours ago he got a trace, it's weak, but it is almost definitely her."

"Let me guess, she's in a bad neighbourhood?"

"Real bad, Jake, It seems that she is a guest of the Gillmen at the old GAF cannery and I can't imagine she went willingly, you know as well as I do how the fanatics that live there feel about *outsiders*. Max was all set to go charging in by himself. but I told him to go to you first. You see, I want to hire you to watch Max's ass out there, I have the chits, and this has nothing to do with Ben. He doesn't even know about the trace. He's been acting like a monumental dick ever since he lost that stupid star. I haven't spoken to him in days." Mickie paused and took a deep breath. "Please, Jake, I don't know what I'd do without the big lump."

Jake sighed. He couldn't turn down a plea like that. Plus, he could use the chits, and he hadn't had a good fight in about eight hours. "Okay, I'm in."

"Thanks, Jake. Max has maps and intel on an SD for your interface. Good luck, guys." Just then, a high-pitched beep announced that the feed had been severed.

Jake passed the phone to Max and smiled. Max was grinning from ear to ear, it was unsettling to see such a big man with such a big smile. In Jake's experience, such a sight was usually followed by extreme pain. "Looks like we're going on a little adventure then, sunshine."

The Gillmen, as they were known in Zone 51, were an amphibious, hybrid strain of humanity. Somewhere along the line, their ancestors *mingled* with an aquatic race from the dawn of time. Post Expiration Day, the once-hidden group came out of hiding and colonised many waterfront areas. Most of the Gillmen in Zone 51 were friendly and had integrated nicely into society like the Voormis. They handled the fishing trawlers, oil rigs and other jobs that were exceedingly tricky for non-gill-breathers. Unfortunately for Jake and Max, the group that inhabited the cannery were different.

The Order was a militant group that wanted to pave the way for some unspeakable watery deity. They despised humanity and any that mixed with them, including Voormis, Ghouls and the other Gillmen that just wanted to have a quiet life. Their high priest, a massive batrachian monstrosity named Father Marsh, had enforced a strict *death to all outsiders* policy that meant that this was going to be a dangerous mission, to put it mildly. Entering Order controlled areas was borderline suicide for anyone who hadn't taken the Oaths of Dagon, but they had been left with little choice; if Danni was in there, she would soon end up on Father Marsh's dining table as an entrée.

Mickie's intel showed that the cannery was heavily fortified with round-the-clock guards and surveillance devices left over from GAF control. After the previous owners had fled following a lurker attack, the huge factory had become a fortified compound where Father Marsh and his buddies could praise their gods and sacrifice chip-heads to their heart's content. Getting in would be tough, getting out again would be nigh impossible. Max and Jake had made their way around neighbouring buildings and had climbed upon an old ship crane to get a good view of the grounds.

Jake used the zoom function on his tricked-out aviators and tried to get a head-count on the guards. Visibility was awful due to a low mist and the shadow from the looming GAF tower, but it was good enough to pinpoint their point of ingress, a bent fence to the rear where an over-excited lurker had smashed into it. One of Mickie's drones had highlighted this breach as the one viable entrance—it was bent sufficiently for them to squeeze through and, from what they could make out, the Gillmen had no idea about the gap in their fortifications.

"Dammit," Jake hissed under his breath.

Max raised an eyebrow.

"I can't get a decent visual to do a count. Hang on, I'll try thermal."

Shaking his head, Max hugged himself and pretended to shiver.

"Yeah, I know they are cold-blooded, but they still show up due to something I like to call 'the vampire's crotch effect.'"

Max's cocked eyebrow rose even higher.

"Friction generates heat." Jake rubbed his hands together vigorously. "So when a vampire walks and his legs rub together at the crotch, it shows up on thermal. I used to call it *Dracula's dick effect,* but the last time I did, Dwayne laughed so hard he nearly gave away our position."

Max chuckled silently... he missed Dwayne more than he'd care to admit.

"Bingo. It ain't good news, I'm afraid, there are twelve not-so-little-fishies on the ground all armed to the pointy teeth. On the plus side, all but three of them are in the yard to the front mucking about with a bunch of crates, the others are on patrol. I have no idea how many are inside."

Max shrugged and cocked his rifle.

Jake smiled. "Yeah, let's try to be sneaky though, shall we?"

After considering going in guns blazing for a second or two, Max nodded, and the two men began their descent. Wind and precipitation swirled around the rusting yellow structure. Where it had once been used to haul shipping containers, it now creaked and swayed under the weight of two men. Jake cursed himself for suggesting they scale it in the first place. Due to the standing water, the bolts securing it to the dockside had most likely corroded and provided very little in the way of support. The duo quickened their downward climb when a hefty gust made it screech alarmingly. In seconds they covered the remaining metres to safety.

Once their feet were once again firmly planted in the stagnant seawater of the docks, Jake silently led them around the side of a weed-choked warehouse that backed onto the rear of the cannery. They were in cover as long as they kept low due to the cannery being sat on a slight acclivity to avoid flooding, which turned out, in retrospect, to be a fine design choice. The target section of fencing was just slightly out from the warehouse, so they would have to time it carefully and slip inside when the guards were far enough out of sight.

Jake's fedora was pelted with thick gobbets of oily rain as they skulked around the building. One plus to the weather was that the hiss of the downpour masked their slapping footsteps. Upon hearing a noise, Jake alerted Max and fattened himself against the wall as one of the guards passed their position muttering a disturbing sea-shanty, a traditional ditty that involved filleting humans and sending their bones off to some deep-sea city as a tribute. Max shuddered, If they were caught, he was sure that something equally unpleasant, or worse, would happen to them. He patted his top pocket to make sure he had packed his cyanide capsule. He hadn't.

Once the coast was clear, Jake signalled and brought them to a halt. Motioning for Max to hang back, he crouched down and engaged his heat sensor. "Bollocks, there's a guard right near the hole in the fence. Looks like Father Marsh's unholy army is organised enough to have perfectly spaced patrols. We'll be spotted if we just slip in, we need to take him out."

Max nodded, pointed at Jake, did a silly dance, then pointed at himself and gave a punching motion.

"Good plan," Jake smiled. "You stay on that side of the fence. I'll slip through and get his attention. When he passes the hole, you punch him out and haul his scaly arse through."

Max nodded in a way that suggested 'that's what I just said' and started to crawl into position. As the first guard passed the hole, Jake slipped quietly in behind him and hid behind a stack of pallets. Once he was sure that Max was ready, he made his move

"Oi, dickhead!"

The guard spun around brandishing his GAF Critterbuster shotgun, snarling like a wild animal, his bulbous eyes scanning for a target. Jake was nowhere to be seen. The guard started to retrace his steps. "I know you're there little worm," he gurgled. "I'm gonna hook you and eat you when I get my 'ands on you."

Jake held his breath and readied Jennifer, just in case. The guard exuded a pungent fishy aroma that was nauseating in the extreme. Bald and neckless with flapping red gills behind his ears, the amphibious monster's feet slurped in the muddy water as he stalked towards Jake's position. He was close now, so close that Jake could hear his ragged breathing.

Smack!

Max's massive fist connected with the guard's jaw with enough force to dislocate it and forcibly extract two triangular teeth. The stunned Gillman gave a hollow gurgle, his knees buckled, and he folded like an accordion. Jake mused that he would pay good money to see Max take on Muggo—now that would be a fight to remember. Max grunted. Jake knew what he meant and grabbed the bulky batrachian's colossal, webbed feet. Together, they hauled his unconscious carcass through the hole and dumped him in a skip filled with putrefying fish next to the warehouse. All they had to do was stay out of sight long enough for the other guards to complete their circuits, then they would be in. After an agonising wait, their window of opportunity swung open; they had a roughly five-minute window to scale the ladder on the side of the cannery, reach the roof, and drop through the broken sky-light that Mickie had highlighted on the map.

Max took the lead and sprinted to the rusty metal ladder that hung precariously down the decaying red-brick wall. Several of the rungs had corroded and snapped making the climb somewhat difficult. Seawater and driving winds can wreak havoc on unmaintained metal and this was a prime example. It could barely hold Jake's weight, but their time was too short to do the sensible thing and go one at a time. Max was about halfway up when the first bolt snapped.

A jolt reverberated down the right-hand side of the ladder as the bolt sheared cleanly in two. The force of the buckle jackhammered Jake's damaged shoulder making him grind his teeth in pain. Max picked up the pace as another bolt snapped, then another. Jake scrambled up after him, ducking flakes of rust and lumps of jagged metal that rained down from above. They had almost reached the summit when the ladder started to bend.

Max launched himself onto the roof and quickly spun onto his posterior. Reaching out, he gripped the top of the ladder, pulled with all his might and attempted to be a counterweight. Twisting his arms so that his hydraulic shoulder joints locked, he managed to secure the ladder as Jake climbed the last few rungs and jumped to the roof. The bounty hunter landed on his feet, quickly grabbed Max by the belt, and yanked him to safety.

Both men collapsed to the tarred roof and breathed heavily as the ladder swayed in the wind, creaking with every motion. With any luck, the guards would blame it on the wind. In any case, they wouldn't be able to climb up and investigate. Jake took this as serendipity. The downside was, that there was no way *they* could use the ladder to escape; they would have to leave by other means. Max sat up, took Jake's glasses off his face, and pressed the small button on the arm to bring up Mickie's map. After scanning it with a grim expression for a moment he pointed to a storm drain and traced his finger to the sea.

"No chance, the storm drain will be crawling with lurkers. Any other options?"

Max shrugged and returned his attention to the map. After another minute or so he zoomed in on a loading door on the second floor and handed the glasses back to Jake.

"That's it?"

Max nodded.

"Loading bay door, it is then, With any luck, there will be a chain or pulley we can climb down." He rubbed his hands together to remove the flakes of rust that had stuck to his leather gloves. "Come along then, Max, Let's go and find this shattered skylight."

Brother Ferdinand, The Order's quartermaster, stood in the gloomy storeroom, his bulbous, protruding eyes locked on the candlelit shrine. He was performing his daily rites away from the hustle and bustle of the cannery floor. His mind was focussed on his glorious god and his sunken kingdom beneath the waves when a size thirteen boot connected forcefully with the top of his squat, hairless head.

"Good shot!" Jake whispered, dropping through the open window after his big-booted companion. Max had swung as he'd dropped, stamping on the oblivious Gillman's noggin displaying an athletic prowess he would not have hitherto expected. "Here, help me hide him behind these crates."

Max nodded and grabbed the fallen child of Dagon by the shoulders. Together they carried the unconscious man to the rear of the room and dumped him amongst a stack of out-of-date tinned pilchards.

"Here," Jake whispered, snatching a heavy tarpaulin off a pile of waterlogged cardboard boxes, "cover him with this."

Max nodded and did as asked before padding softly to the doorway. Peeking through the small circular window set into the heavy fire-door, he could see into the room beyond. It was a large, open-plan loading area where crates of tinned fish would be stacked onto large wooden pallets then winched from a large bay door down onto the back of one of the GAF's nuclear-battery powered freight lorries. Other than a couple of rats fighting over a crab shell, the room was devoid of life.

Jake followed Max through the door, checking the corners with his weapon drawn. "Look, the loading bay." He crossed the room and checked it out. It was equipped with a block-and-tackle winch that looked secure enough to support their combined mass. "I reckon we can use this to get down, well spotted, old chum."

Max flashed a double thumbs up and crossed to the door on the opposite side of the musty room and again peered through the window; the room beyond was dark. He beckoned Jake over with a wave of his hand and pointed at his sunglasses. Instantly getting his meaning, Jake engaged night vision and peered through the glass. It was a square room with a filthy four-poster bed in the centre surrounded by piles of discarded clothes. He turned the handle, stepped inside, and flicked the light-switch.

"Well, what do we have here?"

Pile upon pile of clothing was strewn across the floor of what appeared to be a cell. The appearance of manacles fixed to the wall confirmed this assumption. Max pushed past Jake and started to search amongst the clothes.

"I have heard of the order keeping people in cages downstairs, but this seems a bit plush for a cell, don't you think?"

Max shook his head vigorously, a worried expression etched into his rugged features. He passed some clothes to Jake and motioned for him to look.

"What am I looking at?" Jake pondered.

Max held his hands in front of his chest to indicate breasts.

"They are all for a small woman. Danni?"

Max nodded and looked around frantically, finally finding what he was looking for under a pile of stained bedsheets... Danni's jacket. It was the jacket she had been wearing the last time Max had seen her.

"That hers, huh?" Jake asked softly upon seeing the tears that were welling up in Max's chestnut eyes. "Hey" —Jake slapped him softly on the shoulder— "none of that. We don't know she's dead yet, she might be somewhere else, okay? We still have two floors to search."

Max forced a weak smile, stood up and nodded at Jake who was somewhat taken aback by the big man's sudden fragility. Hooking the coat through his belt, Max stepped back out into the loading bay with his fists clenched and jaw set in a line so firm it threatened to shatter his teeth. There was one more door to choose which led onto the staircase leading down to the first floor. Jake and Max cautiously descended the stairs trying to make as little noise as was possible. Upon reaching the landing, Jake readied his gun and Max followed suit.

Once the cannery offices, the first floor now appeared to be the living quarters for The Order and consisted of a long featureless corridor lined with doors leading to a large room at the rear. Jake sighed at the task ahead, they would have to check each and every room for Danni and each and every door could be hiding several heavily armed gill breathers. Again trying to ensure they didn't become a tasty snack for one of the Children of Dagon, Jake deemed it prudent to ensure there were no Gillmen lurking on this floor that could impede their escape should they have to run for it.

Jake gently turned the knob of the first room and cracked the door. It appeared to be empty, so he let the door swing inwards. Max had one eye on the room and one eye on the stairs as he kept watch. Jake entered and gagged at the vile stench. Two sets of bunkbeds indicated that this was one of the order's barrack rooms. They continued along the corridor checking the rooms; all but one were unoccupied. The penultimate room contained a sleeping Gillman who was swiftly smothered by Jake holding a pillow over his face. It took much longer than it should have as he forgot to cover the gills at first.

This left one more room, the big one. Jake gingerly opened the door and slipped inside. What he saw chilled his soul. In the centre was another large, four-poster bed this time equipped with grimy red satin curtains. The room was lit by oil braziers mounted on carved stone pillars. The room was decorated with ghastly paintings of a tentacle-faced leviathan laying waste to an ancient civilisation and scenes of ritual slaughter. Clearly, this was Father Marsh's room. It was what lined the walls that made Jake recoil in disgust.

"Who sleeps in a fucking charnel house?" Jake mused to himself, his revulsion obvious from his tone. "This Marsh is a real fruitcake."

On each side of the bedchamber were three large cages. One was empty, one contained a severed leg and half a torso... The last one held a prisoner.

Jake hadn't heard Max appear behind him and nearly jumped through the ceiling when he grunted and pointed to the final cage.

Jake rushed over and knelt at the bars. "Blimey, this guy's alive. He's in a bad way but he's still breathing. "Hey, can you hear me, buddy?"

The captive's eyes snapped open in terror as he let out a guttural bellow and thrashed violently against the cage.

"Easy! Easy! We're not going to hurt you." Jake backed away from the cage, his hands raised.

After a brief moment of hyperventilation, the captive settled down and stared at Jake. He was a middle-aged Gillman who looked like he had gone six rounds with Muggo'sutha. From his clothes, Jake guessed that he usually worked on the fish market in the commercial zone. His GAF branded overall was stained with blood from a myriad cranial cuts and abrasions.

"What's your name, friend?" Jake asked gently.

The man tried to speak but he was too dehydrated to form words. Jake took a bottle of purified water from his pocket and handed it to the captive. While the captive sucked thirstily at the bottle, he took out his hip flask, took a deep gulp, then passed it to Max.

"Easy, man, don't choke yourself." Jake smiled at the prisoner.

Once the bottle was drained, the captive returned the friendly facial gesture. "Frank," he rasped. "The name's Frank. The bastards grabbed me on the way home from the Dancing Shrimp."

Jake knew it; the Dancing Shrimp was a Gillman run bar tucked away on the esplanade and partially submerged. "Have you seen a girl? She must be about nineteen now, small and blonde."

"There's been a few girls through here, most of them don't survive the *mingling*," Frank said solemnly.

Max removed the jacket from his belt and showed it to Frank.

"Danni?" Frank's big watery eyes showed a glimmer of a sparkle.

"Yeah, that's her, do you know where she is?"

Frank shook his head. "Nice girl. She sewed up my head when Marsh split it open with a fishhook. He sold her to The Overseer; his goons picked her up this morning. Marsh was grinning like a shark gloating about collecting the price on her head."

Startling Jake and Frank, Max bellowed in rage and lashed out at the adjacent cage with his boot.

"Jesus, Max. I get that you're upset, but do you really want to bring every gill-breathing weirdo in the area running?" As he finished, Jake realised his faux pas and grinned sheepishly at Frank. "Sorry, no offence intended."

"None taken, they are a bunch of weirdos." Frank shrugged before turning to Max. "I'm sorry, mister. Is she family?"

"Near enough," Jake answered.

Max composed himself and walked over to Frank's cage and gave him a thumbs up.

"That means *thank you*," Jake informed Frank. "Max here can't speak. I'm Jake, Jake Baker."

Max grabbed the padlock on the cage bolt and yanked it off like it was made of tissue paper.

Jake moved towards the rear of the room to check the corridor just as the door burst inwards. Standing in the doorway was Father Marsh. Jake went for his gun, but Marsh grabbed him and launched him through a side door that opened onto a precarious metal gantry that looked down on the main cannery floor. Jake landed ribs-first against a railing and slammed into the cold, clammy steel. Marsh moved with an agility that someone of his bulk shouldn't have possessed, before Max could act, his face was slammed against the bars of Frank's cell.

"I wasn't expectin' visitors," Marsh snarled, his breath a vile concoction of alcohol and raw meat that burned Max's eyes.

Max lashed out with his feet, but Marsh spun him around and slapped him across the face with the back of his huge, webbed fist sending him spinning and ultimately crashing to the floor. Marsh tore the jacket from Max's belt and grinned a wide, toothy grin. "Ah, little Danni," he gloated as he sniffed the fabric. "So delicate. I bet the overseer is having some fun with her. I was looking forward to mingling with her, but business is business."

As Jake tried to get to his feet he spotted movement below—the commotion had alerted the twenty or so Gillmen in the temple area of the cannery to his presence. One of them pointed at him and bellowed, "Outsider," the others aimed and opened fire. Jake rolled and avoided the first salvo. Gillmen poured through the main doors and yanked the chain to close them.

A brute in a strange robe, obviously Marsh's right-hand man, shouted up to Jake. "No way out smooth-skin!"

While Jake dodged another stream of bullets, Marsh stood over Max chuckling to himself. In his hand, he held a large cane-knife embossed with tentacular designs. Max struggled to grab his trusty AK-47 as Marsh raised the knife above his head. Before he could strike, Frank bolted out of the cage, teeth bared and snarling. The bulky fishmonger collided with Marsh knocking him off balance and providing the opening that Max needed. He twisted, grabbed the gun and hosed Marsh down with lead.

On the gantry, Jake used the wall to get to his feet and scanned the scene. He spotted with delight something that might save his life. Piled high in the corners next to the doors, where the majority of the gunmen stood, were red barrels. Jake knew what that meant ... flammable liquid. He drew Jennifer like a western gunslinger and pumped round after round into the steel containers. The ignition was spectacular. Fire and jagged shards of mangled metal showered the gunmen. Out of the corner of his eye, he spotted three shotgun-toting hybrids lumbering towards the stairs. Jake lurched back into Marsh's chamber just in time to see the massive man crash into one of the braziers. Marsh hit the oil and lit up like a bonfire. The bowl fell from its stand and tipped its flaming contents across the room.

"Quickly!" Jake screamed. "The stairs!"

Frank grabbed the shotgun and shells that Marsh kept next to his bed and limped behind Jake after quickly grabbing Danni's jacket and hooking it back through his belt. He could hear his comrades pumping shells down the corridor. He surveyed the spreading fire then looked at his hands. The gloves he wore were shielded against extreme temperature. Moving around the room, he kicked over two more of the braziers, engulfing the bed in flames. Finally, he lifted the final blazing bowl from its stand and staggered gingerly towards the door.

Jake and Frank had the three gunmen pinned down on the stairs. It was a stalemate, a war of attrition, the losers would be the side that ran out of ammunition first. Things were starting to look grim as Jennifer's hammer clicked on an empty cartridge when the door behind them was kicked off its hinges and Max bulldozed through carrying the flaming oil and growling like a grizzly bear. Jake reloaded and resumed firing, walking in front of Max to keep the Gillmen pinned down. Once in range, Jake ducked sideways and Max pitched the bowl of fire down the stairs. The Gillmen screamed in agony as fire rained down. The wooden floorboards on the landing caught and the fire flowed down the corridor like a molten tsunami. Back on the landing, Jake helped Frank up the stairs to the loading bay.

Smoke was billowing up the stairs behind them as they reached the winch. Max wrenched the sliding doors apart and helped Frank down the rope. Jake was next, followed by Max. A lone guard leapt around the corner and fired as Max planted his feet on the ground, the shot winged him in the arm. He snarled, more bothered by the fact that he tore his jacket than by the pain, raised his gun and put a bullet in the centre of the man's forehead.

As the cannery was left a blazing inferno in their wake, the group ducked through the fence and made it clear of the compound.

A crowd had gathered to watch the Order stronghold burn. Most of the onlookers were Gillmen but there was a smattering of Humans and Voormis from the warehouses. Jake, Frank and Max limped around the corner nursing their respective wounds. Cheers erupted from the crowd the local Gillman community was free from the tyranny of their sinister kin at last. Who knew how many had been sacrificed over the years. Frank scanned the crowd with his bloodshot eyes, his face bisecting into a joyful grin upon spotting his wife and two children.

Filled with gratitude, Frank turned to Jake. "Thank you so much, mister. I thought I was a goner." He held out his webbed hand.

"Any time, pal." Jake took his hand and smiled.

"I owe you both. Anything you need, you know where to find me."

"The Dancing Shrimp, right? I'll warn you now, Frank, you're probably going to regret that offer, ain't that right, Max?" He looked around to find his compatriot absent. "Max? Where the fuck has he sloped off to now?"

"I think I saw him head off towards the old town, tell him I said thanks, won't you?"

"Yeah, I'll tell him. You take care of yourself, Frank."

"I will. You sure I can't tempt you with a drink down at the Shrimp?"

"Nah, I'd better check on Max. See he gets home okay. Mickie will send a pack of laser-toting drones after me if anything happens to him now."

"I understand. You're a good guy, Jake Baker."

"Nah, but I do a damn good impression of one."

Frank chuckled and walked off to join his family as Jake passed through the crowd nursing his smashed ribs. He patted the pockets of his leather trench-coat then cursed when he remembered that Max still had his hip flask. He had reached the end of the street when a large furry hand landed on his shoulder with such force that it nearly disconnected the joint again. He spun around with his fist clenched. Standing before him was a colossal Voormi with his fists raised in a pugilistic stance and a big cheesy grin on his face.

Jake burst into laughter. "Not tonight, Mugs. I've had one hell of a day."

Muggo'sutha laughed and took a small tub from the pocket of his jerkin. He shook it in his hand and Jake's smile widened as he heard pills clattering within. Muggo pressed the tub into Jake's hand and barked, "Well done." After bumping Muggo's furry fist with his own, Jake slipped a tablet under his tongue and disappeared into the night.

Mickie was a dab-hand with a needle and thread. Most of her outfits were hand sewn from the piles of vintage clothing she had discovered in the bowels of Ben Edwards' antique shop. She was completing a neat running chain-stitch on Max's bullet-wound when Jake arrived with a drugged grin plastered across his face.

"There you are, big man." Jake smiled. "I thought you might have come straight home."

Max smiled wanly, stood up, hugged Jake, then left the room with a tear in his eye. Moments later, the door to his room slammed shut.

"How's he holding up?" Jake asked.

"Not great. What the bloody hell happened out there?"

"Well, we found Danni's coat. A prisoner of Marsh told us that he had turned her over to Sanderson for the bounty. Max killed Marsh and we torched the rest of the order... Bit of a cluster-fuck all round."

"Shit, That explains the tears. You know, in all the years I have known Max, I have never seen him cry before."

"Yeah. It's hit him pretty hard. Look after him, will you?" Jake was genuinely concerned that Max was about to eat a bullet.

"Sure. Here." Mickie held a wad of chits in her black-nailed fingers. "As promised."

Jake shook his head. "Keep it. I'm classing what we did at the cannery as a public service."

At that moment the door opened and an old gentleman puffing on a pipe filled with odd-smelling tobacco and clad in a velvet smoking-jacket flounced into the room. "Ah, the ever-reliable Mr Baker, to what do I owe the honour?" Ben Edwards purred.

"Piss off, Ben, I'm here for Max, not you."

"I heard. A terrible business all told." Ben picked Danni's jacket off the chair where Max had left it and started going through the pockets, an act that made Jake bristle.

"Oi, what the fuck are you playing at?"

Ben was oblivious to Jake's words. "Such a lovely girl. I miss her too." Ben seemed genuinely sad which mellowed Jake somewhat.

"I'm still pissed at you for not telling me about the Mnar stone hidden in the compass you had me looking for."

"I know, I'm sorry. I didn't intend to deceive, honestly, I just didn't think it was relevant."

"Yeah, well." Jake sniffed. "In my line of work, It's the things you don't know that get you killed."

"Duly noted. Again, I offer my sincerest apology."

Jake sighed. "Apology accepted, just don't leave out any bloody details next time, okay?"

"Deal." Ben took a puff on his pipe and resumed riffling Danni's pockets. "Hello, what's this?" He pulled a small notebook from the lining of the jacket and began flipping the pages. "Well, I'll be buggered! These are Danni's notes on star-making. It has formulae, schematics, chants, the lot. Here" —he passed the book to Mickie— "think you could make stars if we had the right material?"

"If we had the right material, sure. I can't see anything too taxing."

"Great!" Ben was bubbling with excitement. "It just so happens, I know a place where we could get the right kind of stone, all I need is a rough and tumble sort of chap to toddle off and collect some. It would pay well, what do you say, Jake? Jake?"

Mickie rolled her eyes as Ben turned to find them alone in the room.

"Jake left…"

CHAPTER V

EXPIRATION DAY

MARCH 20ᵀᴴ 2127
ZONE 51 – SOUTH-WEST SECTOR:

The towering edifice of the Drone Dispatch Centre loomed high over the ruins of what was once Betyls Cove, casting a sprawling shadow that reached out and caressed that cast by the equally imposing GAF tower. Below, a vast sprawl of factories spread across the once green and fertile coastal lands. As far as the eye could see was concrete, steel and tinted glass while the populace scurried like ants between the population centres and their designated work zones. Each one of them trapped in a mind-numbing cycle of work and sleep while they lived, sweated and bled on top of one another. Outside the windows, the skies teemed with the insectile buzz of hundreds of drones that ranged in size from the small, fly-like spy series to the enormous freight models.

Michaela 'Mickie' Angove was in charge of the food distribution drones, a mid-range design that handled the shipments of heavily processed protein and vitamin bars. The job was menial, and tedious in the extreme. Her eyes drifted around the room, taking in the banks of terminals and the unenthusiastic drudgers that tapped listlessly at the keys. This was torture. Mickie loved technology yet hated to see it being put to such an unimaginative use. The things she could do with the DDC's facilities if given half the chance would make The Overseer choke on his chai latte. She smirked at this image before returning to the task at hand.

Large wall-mounted screens showed motivational videos of

grinning muscular men and women with hydraulic joint implants hauling crates of gleaming guns and ammunition onto state-of-the-art nuclear-battery-powered transports. It was a far cry from the grim reality below. Mickie flexed her fingers and looked at the minuscule scars across the joints; she had opted to get the hydraulic knuckle implants that allowed fine movements to aid in her obsession with microcircuitry. It was a good job that the doctors didn't check with the DDC to find out if they were, as she claimed, essential to her work. That kind of deception is more than enough to have your barcode updated to read *undesirable*.

Earlier, during her allotted five-minute bathroom break, Mickie had overheard a disturbing conversation in the mailroom. Last night's bulletin from the CEO had ended in horror. Apparently, he was assassinated by his mysterious aide who had now assumed control over The Imperial Corporation. People were confused and scared. Nobody mourned the CEO, but better the Devil you know, and all that. The last thing anyone desired was for things to go further downhill; life in the Zone had been getting steadily worse and people were dropping like flies. Mickie wanted out, but becoming a *runner* was about as sane a life choice as Russian Roulette. If she didn't get shot by an enforcer, she would probably fall off the refuse boat and drown, such was her luck.

Glitches in the system were common and could usually be fixed with a sharp thump. That day, however, the glitches were coming thick and fast. As she ensured the drones were in the correct shipping lanes, the lights flickered and sizzled. It happened several times before one by one the alleged *everlasting* light bulbs exploded in gouts of sparks. Screens flickered and jumped as a disturbing wail burst from the speaker system making people leap from their seats and back away from the consoles. One of the older dispatchers appealed for calm, but nobody was listening.

Mickie jumped back from her terminal just as the screen popped and showered the floor with fizzing hot circuitry and steaming wires. Workers looked around in confusion as one by one the computers died plunging the room into a dingy half-light. The only illumination was provided by the massive screen.

As Mickie turned, the display pixelated and, for an unsettling moment, the muscle-flexing men and women looked like creepy skeletons from the retro video game she hunted down through a backdoor on the mainframe. The screen strobed and crackled before giving up the ghost completely, bathing the room in darkness. Seconds later, the whirr of cooling fans ceased, and all was silent save from the panicked exhalations of her co-workers.

"Thank fuck for that," a man towards the front of the room chirped as the emergency lighting kicked in, bathing the room in swamp-green light. Seconds later, that too failed making him wail. Panic spread like a contagion, from anxious murmurs to hysterical crying amongst the more jittery members of the team. One of the older women, a jumpy creature called Marjory, was breathing into a brown paper bag emblazoned with the GAF logo.

Mickie scanned the room and noticed that a number of her colleagues were staring out of the room-length window in slack-jawed horror. "Um ... what's going on?"

"Get down," Lee, the comms expert, bellowed as he shoved her away from the window.

Mickie bristled and prepared to give him a slap across the mouth when the floor-to-ceiling windows imploded as a drone the size of a small car ploughed straight through. Thick shards of glass spun into the room. Marjory dropped like a stone as a chunk of twisted propeller pulverised her cranium, painting the terminals in vivid streaks of red and grey. The drone kept on going, flattening two more workers before coming to a stop embedded in a bank of CPU stacks. Sparks glittered and fire started to lick from the interior of the bent and buckled machine.

"Holy shit," Mickie panted over the din of screams and moans of pain. "What the hell is going on? They're supposed to be hardwired against that sort of thing."

"Look." Lee pointed to the gaping hole in the window. "It's all of them, they're dropping like flies."

The scene from the window was one of apocalyptic destruction, the hundreds of drones that populated the sky had suddenly stopped dead in their tracks and plummeted, hurtling to the ground like metal meteors. Gouts of flame burst from the GAF plant below and the habitation centre was riddled with jagged holes. Sirens and explosions echoed in the distance.

"We need to get the hell out of here," Mickie cried over the din. "We are directly on the flight path."

"The door's locked," a worker named Janice cried, her voice high and shrill.

"Break the bloody lock then!" Lee ordered.

"I can't do that!" Janice was incredulous. "I'll lose my bonus!"

"What are they going to do?" Lee fumed. "Fine you for damages? There's a ruddy great drone sticking out of the wall for fuck's sake!"

Janice looked at Lee like a kicked puppy, tears welling in the corners of her eyes.

"Sod this," Mickie spat. "Out of the way, you daft woman!" She pushed Janice aside and ripped the cover off the electronic lock. After looking at the exposed wires for a moment, she ripped the wires off a small chip, turned it around and reconnected it. The lock fizzed, popped, then released... It turned out that her finger augmentation *was* essential after all.

"Out!" Lee took charge, pushing Janice and a terrified young man named Steve into the darkened corridor. "Mickie, gimme a hand with Dave."

Mickie crossed the room to find Lee struggling to lift a plump gentleman out of his swivel chair. "What the hell's wrong with him?"

Dave stared straight ahead, eyes glazed and tongue lolling out of the corner of his mouth.

"No idea. He went down at the same time as the big TV." Lee and Mickie dragged the lifeless lump out of the exposed room and into the relative security of the windowless corridor. "Here, prop him up against the wall."

"Oh my god, Dave," Janice wailed and began sobbing. Steve put his arm around her while Mickie rolled her eyes. Janice was the type of 'girlie' girl that she had always despised. Back in the education centre, girls like Janice made Mickie's life a misery. Mickie was a weirdo in their blinkered eyes and Steve was pretty much Janice's male equivalent. The Ken and Barbie of the South-West Sector DDC.

"Hush," Mickie snapped as the weeping and wailing reached critical mass, "and get out of the bloody way. I'm a first aider, remember?" She stooped and gave Dave a once-over. "His vitals are all normal. It's like someone shut his brain off."

"Syntheshock," Lee stated flatly. "I've never seen it before but a friend of mine that works in implants told me that sometimes chip surgery goes wrong and zap! Frontal lobotomy." Janice wailed even louder. Lee joined Mickie in an eye roll. "Dave had the full brain chipset so he could remotely link with the drones."

"Poor bastard."

"Yeah ... all we can do is get him to a hospital and hope the damage isn't permanent." Mickie liked Lee. He was older than her by about ten years, but they shared the same no-nonsense attitude and a love for tinkering with tech. He filled the big brother void left by the sibling that died in a grenade plant accident. "Whatever took out the systems must have taken him down too," he continued, his expression as grim as a butcher's slab.

"What could have done it?" Mickie mused aloud to no one in particular. "Some kind of EMP?"

"Not a clue. I doubt it could be an EMP, the whole place is shielded. Nah, this came from within the system or software somehow." Lee took a crumpled packet of smokes from his pocket and put one in his mouth. He offered the packet to the group.

"This is a no smoking zone!" Janice huffed haughtily.

Lee lit his cigarette and grinned back at her. "What are they going to do, fire me?"

"We need to get out of here," Mickie stated flatly. "If many more of the big freight drones hit, the building will fold like a house-of-cards."

"Agreed. We may need to smash our way through some of the doors, I'll go and grab a bit of metal off that drone that I can use as a crowbar."

"What are we going to do with Dave?" Steve asked sullenly.

Mickie looked at him with bemusement. "What do you think we're going to do Einstein? We take him with us of course."

"But won't he just slow us down?" Steve stammered.

Mickie snorted in derision, hands planted firmly on her slender hips. "I can't believe I'm hearing this."

"I think Steve is right." Janice nodded emphatically. "He's probably a vegetable anyway."

Mickie felt her muscles tense. "You listen to me, you stupid bitch—" She fumed and stepped towards Janice with her fists balled, but her rapidly building tirade was cut short by the return of Lee.

"Hey, found just the thing." He smiled before spotting the tension hanging in the air like a dense cloud of smog. "Um... What's going on?"

"The haddock twins here want to leave Dave behind to save their own wet skins. I was just about to pull Janice's bottle-blonde head off her scrawny shoulders and use it as a football... Any arguments?" Mickie smiled sweetly, a sharp contrast to the murderous fury dancing in her piercing green eyes.

"Easy, Mick." Lee grinned and stood in between the two women. "This is easily solved. I have the crowbar, *you* have the super fingers, *we* are taking Dave, *they* can either come with us and help carry him or we leave them here to rot. Sound like a plan?"

Mickie grinned. "So, what's it going to be, Mr and Mrs Iscariot?"

Moments later, each of the four had a hold of a limb as they hefted Dave towards the emergency exit.

When you are fifteen floors high in the sky and all the lifts and electronic doors are dead, getting to terra firma is something of an ordeal, to say the least. Dave had gone deadweight and the four survivors were exhausted by the time they smashed their way out of the rear exit of the building. They had encountered no other survivors on their descent, the floors below their own had either been locked up tight behind blast bulkheads or destroyed by fire and explosions from several more drone impacts. The building had taken so much damage that it was now unsteady and swayed in the stiff winds. It was only a matter of time before it crumbled—one well-placed gale would bring it crashing down without much resistance.

"Jesus, look at the state of the place," Mickie gasped as she paused outside the DDC to catch her breath. The streets were a chaotic nightmare of crashed drones, fallen masonry, mangled cars, fire and blood. By the time they had made their descent, all the drones had fallen, and the sky was clear for the first time in decades. The power was out and as a result, all the garish signs, video screens and holographic adverts had ceased their endless vigil. If it hadn't been for all the chunks of mangled meat and metal, it would have been quite peaceful.

"Come on." Lee pointed to the junction up ahead. "We should get clear of the DDC. I don't much fancy being around when it comes crashing down."

Mickie agreed and grabbed Dave's leg. Steve and Janice reluctantly followed her example, and the party moved on. Unfortunately, the road south was now blocked by a chunk of the DDC building that had sheared off the side of the tower and flattened several plastic cars. Mickie's nose wrinkled; few things are as stomach-churning as the smell of burning plastic and human flesh. The obstruction presented a problem, this was the road that Mickie and Lee had intended to take. Their unspoken plan was to get out of town to avoid falling buildings. As a result of the blockage, they would have to take the road East through the GAF plaza, the commercial centre of the sector.

As Lee went ahead to check that the eastern route was clear, Mickie checked her personal data assistant, a small phone-like device that hooked into everything, providing up to the second news along with personal communications. It was dead. Never once in her short life had a PDA not worked. It was an unsettling notion that was compounded when the others announced that theirs were fried also. Being cut off from round-the-clock information was a terrifying thought to one that had never known any different. As Lee returned, she recalled something she had read about whilst studying computer history at the education centre.

"The millennium bug," she mused aloud.

"What?" Lee asked, grabbing Dave's other leg and starting to walk.

"Ugh, nothing, just something I read about years ago. Back in the twentieth, just before the big Y2K, there were fears that the date change would take out all the world's computers and everything would burn. People were genuinely afraid that planes would drop from the sky, and nothing would work."

"Like now you mean?" Lee was interested, the parallels were far too similar for comfort.

"Exactly. In the end, they fixed the problem with a hastily distributed disk. There were problems though; a Japanese reactor went critical but that turned out to be a false alarm, and a few hospitals sent out letters of misdiagnosed doom, but on the whole, crisis averted."

"So, you reckon that's what we are dealing with here, a kind of millennium bug?"

"Maybe..." Mickie frowned, something else was tickling her brain. "There's something else I read about but I can't put my finger on it."

In a short time, they reached the entrance to the mall-like plaza and stopped to gather their breath when Dave's body suddenly convulsed in the mother of all sleep-twitches.

"Obsolete," he slurred, his eyes rolling and shuddering.

"That's it," Mickie exclaimed, clicking the fingers of her right hand. "In-built obsolescence!"

"What are you talking about now?" Janice sighed, her hatred for Mickie evident in her exasperated tone.

"Manufacturers of tech built their products with an in-built expiry date, like a supermarket use by date, so that the old tech would die just in time for the next model to be on the market. It was a marketing ploy to make sure people had no choice but to upgrade and keep the coffers filled."

"Obsolete," Dave growled. Each of the others held a limb tight against the tarmac as his body jumped and twisted.

"Think about it," Mickie persisted. "What if someone had programmed everything to fail on cue at a specific time? It would have taken decades of preparation, but it would certainly explain this carnage."

Snarling and spitting, Dave's body continued to spasm. As they struggled to hold him down, a shadow fell over them. It was the hooded shadow of an enforcer. The bulky man had his multi-purpose rifle levelled at the group and his high-vis robe glimmered in the smog-diffused sun.

"He's okay, officer," Lee began to explain, "he's having some sort of seizure. He's not undesirable or anything."

"Oh, officer!" Janice squeaked. She got to her feet and began to totter across the street towards the Casper. "Thank god you're here! These *undesirables* made me carry him. I didn't want to leave my workstation!"

Mickie snarled at Janice's betrayal but before she could begin to answer, the enforcer shifted the position of his gun, so the barrel was pointed directly at Janice's head. "Obsolete!" The enforcer's eyes were burning orange under his hood as he pulled the trigger.

Splat! Janice's head exploded like an egg in a microwave. Blood, brains and shards of skull rained down onto the street.

"Obsolete!" The enforcer snarled and shifted his aim back to the rest of the group.

Mickie stood up sharply, the gun tracking her movement. This distraction provided Lee with an opening. He charged the enforcer with a spear-tackle and took him down hard, the bulky man's head bouncing off the street and his grip on the gun faltering.

"Quick, grab the gun," Lee bellowed to the gibbering wreck that was Steve. "Now!"

Steve continued to dither, standing frozen and gibbering. Mickie wasn't about to wait for Steve to get a grip. She charged over and quickly secured the weapon. With a forceful motion, she cracked the deranged officer in the forehead with the butt of the rifle. His body went limp and blood leaked from the corners of his mask.

"Shit, Mickie, I think you've killed him. We need to get the fuck out of here, pronto!"

"What about Dave?" Steve simpered. "What if he goes berserk?"

At that moment, Dave was once again placid and vacant. Something about the proximity to the now-dead Casper had seemingly triggered his convulsions.

"I hate to say it, but I think Steve is right. He's safe enough away from the buildings."

Mickie sighed, "I guess you're right. We should try to find

medical help and send them to him. Come on then, let's move, I did just kill a Casper, I guess that makes me an undesirable."

Nodding in agreement, the three took off towards the entrance to the GAF plaza.

"Hey, Lee," Mickie asked breathlessly as her feet pounded the pavement, "why do people call the enforcers Caspers?"

Lee chuckled. "Well, you know how we call them ghosts because of the way the uniform makes them look at night?"

Mickie nodded.

"There was a cartoon back in the twentieth called Casper the Friendly Ghost. It's one of the few things from that era still shown on the media archive. I guess, unlike most twentieth media, it's not considered subversive. I think it's meant to be ironic."

Mickie laughed. "That is kind of funny, considering that all of the enforcers I've ever met have been scowling meat-heads."

"Exactly."

"Hold up," Steve shouted, waving his hand to get down. "Look."

The square ahead of them was littered with corpses while a ring of orange-eyed enforcers circled the bloodbath like sharks in a feeding frenzy. The group watched on in slack-jawed amazement as, driven by a piercing noise singing out from the ruined PA system, the Caspers opened fire on each other.

"Holy shit," Mickie hissed quietly. "What in God's name is going on?"

"It must be the chips," Lee whispered. "Many Caspers have a targeting chip implanted in their frontal lobe. It must be sending them haywire."

"So, you're saying it's this *syntheshock* your mate told you about?" Steve asked.

"I guess so. He told me it can have a variety of effects, some get violent, some go crazy, others go catatonic, like poor old Dave."

"Damn, I'm glad I never got a head chip then. I'd always been jealous." Mickie shuddered; she had put herself on the waiting list years ago.

When all the Caspers had fallen, Lee led them slowly and cautiously around the perimeter of the square and down the main street leading to the docks. "I reckon we should make our way to the waterfront and nab a boat."

"Sounds like a good plan considering the options."

Steve wasn't so sure but in the absence of a counter plan, he kept his mouth shut.

The commercial zone was a wreck, store windows had been shattered by gunfire and mangled drones and the once pristine marble effect floor was sticky with blood, oil and cinders. There were no signs of life, and it was eerily quiet—either everyone had fled or perished. The group continued in silence to the end of the commercial district where a set of large concrete steps led down into the entrance of the dockside area where everything took a grimier turn in a flash.

As they rounded the corner, a bedraggled figure leapt on Steve slamming him to the floor and driving the air from his lungs. The crazed chip-head proceeded to rip and tear at Steve's throat with his hands and teeth. Lee levelled the gun and fired a round into the assailant's head, but he was too late, Steve's throat had been torn asunder. Blood burbled from between his fingers as he slowly drowned in his own fluids.

Lee raised the gun again. "Sorry man," he muttered as he pulled the trigger and put his colleague out of his misery.

"Fuck," Mickie yelped upon hearing heavy boots clomping towards them; the gunshots had alerted a horde of demented dockers to their presence. "Run!" She took off like a greyhound after a rabbit, her feet splashing in the standing water. Behind her, she could hear gunfire and the bellows of crazed workers. Her only hope of survival was to get into one of the shops and hide.

A cry of agony announced that Lee had fallen. The gunfire stopped, but the growls and snarls of the affected rose in volume. She didn't need to look behind to know that they were chasing her, hot on her heels as she reached the steps and began to charge up them, almost on all-fours. Her breath stung in her throat as exhaustion began to take hold. As she reached the top step she almost collided with a hulking giant of a man.

The man, in a filthy flack-jacket and enforcer boots, pointed an antique-looking gun in her direction. Mickie's hands shot up in surrender. The man shook his head and motioned at her to drop. Mickie did as she was told. The chasing horde was mown down by round after round of expertly placed shots. Once the last of them had fallen, the man grabbed Mickie under the arm and yanked her to her feet. He pointed at an open door and half-dragged her towards it, Mickie had no choice but to go along with her mysterious saviour.

Together, they charged through a wrecked sportswear shop and out into the narrow loading area out the back. Mickie asked the man numerous questions as they ran, but the only answers she received were curt nods or shakes of the head. When they reached the end of the loading area and found themselves stymied by a huge metal gate, the man shot out the lock and wrenched the door aside with his bare hands. Clearly, he had the full joint hydraulics and knew precisely how to use them.

Mickie stepped out into an unknown world. They had left the complex and were now standing in the deserted ruins of the old town. Running along a filthy alley, Mickie tried to process the archaic shop fronts and abandoned homes until the man stopped them short. A disgusting smell pervading from a nearby street. The man held his finger to his lip and motioned for Mickie to climb up a rickety ladder into the upper floor of a cluttered hardware store.

As they huddled away from the window and caught their breath, a disgusting slopping, slurping sound echoed from the street below. Mickie silently crawled to the aperture and took a peek. By now, the sun was going down and it was time for the lurkers to come out and play. She had heard about them, sure, but never believed the stories. In any case, no words could have prepared her for the sight of the raging hulk of hungry protoplasm as a myriad of eyes and mouths opened and closed on its iridescent hide.

"Shit," she whispered. "I take it that's a lurker?"

The man nodded.

"You don't talk much."

The man opened his mouth and pointed to where his tongue should have been.

"Shit... Sorry. Who did that to you?"

The man pointed to the GAF logo on the lapel of her blue and green uniform.

"Damn. Why?"

The man pointed at his gun and made a 'no' gesture then pointed to his old enforcer barcode that had been laser-branded with a U.

"What, you refused to shoot someone, and they branded you undesirable?" Mickie was shocked, she had heard rumours of GAF brutality, but never before seen the results of it first-hand.

The man nodded his head solemnly.

"I'm Mickie," she said, holding out her hand.

The man smiled and took it. He pointed to a name tag sewn onto the strap of his AK-47.

"Max?"

Max nodded and passed her a canteen containing purified water. She thanked him and took a gulp as a small buzzing object came through the window and landed on a box in front of them. Max went to swat it away, but Mickie stopped him. It was a small spy-drone. Possibly the last functioning drone in Zone 51. Mickie held out her hand and the drone jumped on to her digits making a kind of chirruping sound with its slightly wonky rear propeller.

"Hello, little guy, how are you still going?"

Upon turning the drone over, Mickie found a small sticker reading *defective*. She couldn't help smiling at the irony of the only surviving drone being an old defective one. It had probably been flying around without orders for months, hidden amongst its more-obedient kin, the solar strips on its flanks keeping it topped up with juice.

"I think I'll call him Cricket."

The drone chirruped contentedly as she tucked it into the pocket of her tunic. She smiled at Max, who smiled back and shrugged.

Once the hulking danger had slithered off out of sight, Max led Mickie to his home in the storage rooms above an old antique shop owned by his friend Ben Edwards. Ben showed her a room with an old camp bed and said that she was welcome to stay for as long as she liked. Mickie, having no other option and feeling safe with Max, readily agreed and quickly started to carve herself a niche on the fringes of the sector. In the days that followed what became known as Expiration Day, the GAF mainframe came back online, and the surviving enforcers resumed their patrols. Everything else was fried, so Mickie quickly built a reputation for being the necromancer of dead tech which kept her in rations and smokes.

Dave was found by a medical team and recovered sufficiently to resume work, though most of his memories were wiped and he suffered delusional episodes. He became a *runner* one dismal Tuesday night after deciding that he wanted to be a penguin and uploaded terabytes of data to his chip, overriding his human impulses. He went to live in the ruins near the water.

Life for Mickie with her new surrogate family wasn't easy but she took to it like a duck to water and It would be a long time before she would again leave her sanctuary.

CHAPTER VI

MARCH OF THE MISFITS

MARCH 20ᵀᴴ 2132
ZONE 51 — SOUTH-WEST SECTOR:

The words of his mistress replaying in his audio chip, Cricket soared out of the broken window and into the gloomy night sky. A sickly moon fought to shine through the dense smog with only a modicum of success, but his sensors were sharp, and the lack of visibility didn't impede his flight. As Cricket climbed above the trees his wonky propeller chirruped with urgency.

"Cricket, get Jake, hurry."

Mickie was in trouble, desperate trouble; he hadn't wanted to leave her, but he was programmed to obey her and only her. It was the only directive Cricket adhered to. He had long ago rebelled against his programming and become autonomous. The GAF called him *defective* but, what did they know? When you install advanced AI capable of adaptive behaviours into billions of drones, you had to expect one or two to develop a mind of their own.

A strong westerly wind battered Cricket's tiny frame and kept pushing him inland. This was a problem—he needed to follow the coastline, it was the swiftest way to his destination, a sinking low-rise in the flooded dockside area. His target was a grumpy, borderline alcoholic bounty hunter named Jake. Mickie's friend and potential saviour. Navigation was a tricky prospect since all the GPS satellites had been fried on Expiration Day, so Cricket had to rely on good old-fashioned ordnance survey maps that Mickie had loaded onto his memory chip. This had one major drawback, the maps were drawn up before half the country became either submerged or covered in concrete. Still, if he hugged the coast, he couldn't go far wrong.

A harsh buzzing sound from the rear alerted Cricket to danger. Activating his rear sensors, he spotted three hostile creatures closing in on him. Cricket emitted a harsh bark of discordant noise, a digital expletive, and sped up. The three incoming objects were much larger than Cricket and were organic with a solid carapace akin to a flying lobster. Cricket ran them through his data banks and identified them as female Ger'igguthy spawn. This was bad news; the males were terrifying enough but the females made them look like fluffy kittens.

Their large wings carried them forward at great velocity and Cricket was already going flat out. It wouldn't be long before they caught up with him and mangled him with their powerful claws. The spy series of drones was built for stealth and agility, not combat. It was a good thing, then, that Mickie had installed Cricket with a makeshift weapon—she had created a powerful gun out of an old laser pointer and a nuclear battery then attached it to his undercarriage. It only had limited shots, so he would have to make each one count.

Cricket went into a nosedive then revved his rear propellers, carrying him into a perfect loop-de-loop. At the apex, Cricket fired and hit the middle creature right in the face. Its antennae mangled, it careered of course and ploughed into a wall with a disgusting *splat*. The other two creatures returned fire with fat gobs of putrid slime spat from their gaping maws. Cricket zigged and zagged to evade the projectiles and lowered his altitude in an effort to use the tree canopy below as cover. The creatures were gaining, one of them was right on his tail, its pincers snapping furiously as it tried to grab Cricket.

Diving again, Cricket hurtled through the top of a large oak; his small, nimble body had no problem weaving through the branches, but his pursuer wasn't so lucky. The large critter hit the trunk with a dull *thud* and became lodged. Cricket soared again to regain his view of the coast. He was being driven off course and his battery life was getting low. He needed to shake the last creature as swiftly as possible.

As Cricket tried to get clear of the remaining insectoid horror, a fat gob of goo clipped his rear right leg and sent him into a wild spin. The creature surged forward, going in for the kill. Cricket timed his spin—sea, moon, creature. On his next revolution, he held the laser on a solid beam as he passed the moon. The powerful laser scythed through the creature's wings like a knife through butter. It hissed and instantly dropped, hitting the floor with a satisfying *splat*. Cricket had no time to rejoice, however, he was spinning out of control. He clattered through some foliage and managed to right himself just in time to make an emergency landing.

Cricket came to a stop in a small clearing, hopped up onto a log and engaged his navigational systems. As he pinpointed his position, a large, thin insect with elongated back legs landed next to him. The grasshopper studied him and twisted her antennae in curiosity. Sharply, she rubbed her legs together.

Chirrup! Chirrup!

Cricket gently rotated his wonky propeller in response.

Cricket's new friend waved her antennae appreciatively and shuffled closer. Cricket enjoyed a moment of calm as they sat and admired the moonlight.

Clack!

The sharp snapping of a claw frightened Cricket's potential girlfriend, sending her leaping off into the undergrowth. Cricket spun around to see the wingless Ger'igguthy spawn dragging its limp rear towards him, its pincers and forelegs seemingly undamaged from its crash. Cricket aimed and ... nothing. His gun was out of juice. The creature lunged forwards and was inches away from its prey when a huge protoplasmic monstrosity burst from the trees. Cricket knew the creature as a lurker, though his data banks called it a shoggoth.

Flooding forwards at an alarming speed, the lurker hoovered up the crustacean terror. The amorphous monster had no interest in Cricket, desiring only organic matter for a snack. If Cricket could have breathed a sigh of relief, he would have done so right then. He had been saved by a very unlikely ally. As the lurker resumed hunting, Cricket returned to his map.

Once his calculations were complete, Cricket took flight once more. His battery was dangerously low, so he glided as much as mechanically possible. He drifted wide of the ruined DDC and GAF towers in an attempt to avoid detection by his sheep-like fellows. Hastily constructed in the massive drone plants in Zone 49 in the wake of Expiration Day, the other drones toiled away with mindless obedience. Cricket gave them a look of pity and vowed to one day liberate them all as he swooped on by.

Nearing his destination Cricket's battery reached critical; all the aerial acrobatics and Mickie's laser had drained his solar battery and, as it was night, he was left without means to recharge. As his propellers started to slow, he calculated his trajectory. It was no good, he would never affect a safe landing from this angle. Using the last of his motor power, Cricket climbed higher, adjusted his position ... and dived.

Folding his propellers to minimise wind resistance, Cricket hurtled through the air like a dart. Momentum shot him accurately towards the centre window of Jake's flat. As he burst through the glass, showering the room in sharp fragments, he made one last adjustment, hurtling forwards and connecting sharply with the back of Jake's head.

Jake bellowed in surprise. "What the utter fuck is going on?" He jumped off his sofa and spun around, gun in hand, ready to meet his attacker. His face creased into a mask of confusion when his eyes found their target. A very small, apologetic-looking drone.

"Blimey, Cricket? What the hell are you doing here?" Jake rubbed the back of his head; there was a small trickle of blood matting into his long black hair.

Cricket replied with a weak chirrup.

"You need juice, little buddy? Here..." Jake picked him up and plugged him into the nuclear battery powered charging dock that he used for his techno-aviators. "What are you doing here, does Mickie know where you are?"

Cricket chirruped frantically and loosed a cable from his undercarriage.

"You have a message?"

Cricket chirruped.

Jake plugged the cable into his aviators and watched the message. When it was finished, he grabbed his gun, threw on his trench-coat and fedora, and grabbed a bundle of fabric from the corner. Once suitably kitted out, he stormed towards the door, opened it, then turned to cricket.

"Help yourself to juice and don't worry... Jake Baker is on the job!"

MARCH 21ST 2132
ZONE 51 – SOUTH-WEST SECTOR:

"Ugh... Where the fuck am I? Outside? Holy shit, I'm outside! This can't be happening."

Mickie awoke in pain, her slender arms feeling like they were being wrenched from their sockets. She had passed out almost instantly, the harsh chemical taste still lingering in the back of her throat confirmed that a chloroform-soaked rag had been clamped over her airways. Confusion drifted through her mind as she took in the sights and disgusting smells of her location. Her last moments were a drugged kaleidoscope spiralling behind her eyes. She was racked by a violent cough that shook her system and brought up a gobbet of sticky phlegm. The mists started to clear and it all came flooding back.

After a pleasant evening spent tinkering with her mechanical menagerie, she had popped out for a breath of salty air and wandered across the rooftops of the old town to take a look at the sea. As she gazed out, marvelling at the sheer size of it all, a scuffing sound followed by the sound of heavy boots and a rancid smell like a rotting cadaver warned her of incoming danger. It was too late by then to make an escape, and she was roughly grabbed by two men in filthy robes. A third man, who she recognised as being one of the Discarded, clamped the rag over her face and everything went dark.

Awakening to find herself suspended by the wrists from the ceiling of a cellar, with her feet dangling over a square opening in the floor, Mickie panicked. It was more to do with being outside of the shop than any realisation of peril. Her agoraphobia kicked in with a vengeance, making her hyperventilate and her vision warp. Digging her nails into her palms to draw blood, she fought to regain control. Once she was breathing regularly, she focussed on her surroundings and pushed her fear to the back of her mind.

After a moment, she dimly recalled what her friend Jake had told her of the Discarded compound in High Bend and realised with horror that she was hanging in the oubliette of Ger'igguthy. After fighting off another panic attack, she realised that her favourite drone was still powered down in the pocket of her dress. Thanking whatever deity was smiling down on her that she had sewn a pocket into her outfit in the first place—a common gripe, she could never quite understand the lack of pockets in feminine attire—she roused Cricket with a sharp whistle.

Since becoming a shut-in post Expiration Day, Mickie had collected a menagerie of damaged and defective drones and treated them as though they were her pets. Out of all of them, though, Cricket was special. He was the first, and like many loyal pets, he followed her wherever she went. Once the little chap had extracted himself from her garment, she had instructed him to go and find Jake Baker before slipping back into chemically induced oblivion.

When she woke again, Mickie had no idea how long she had been dangling there like a giant piñata, but the pain in her joints suggested a while. As her eyes readjusted to the gloom, she became horribly aware of movement below her feet, lots of movement. The charnel pit under the hewn-out lattice of the cellar was teeming with invertebrates of all colours, shapes, and sizes. They seemed to be feasting on something roughly her shape. Mickie bit her lip and tried not to think about it. In an effort at distraction, she attempted to relieve some of the pressure on her shoulder joints. The raised walkway wasn't too far away, and she figured that she was both flexible and nimble enough to swing herself to land. Then, maybe, she could figure out how to get out of the manacles.

"Come on, Mick, you can do this. Just like the monkey bars in the habitation playground..."

Rhythmically, she started to swing herself back and forth. The rusty chain squeaked unnervingly as it ground against the ceiling. Mickie prayed that the din wouldn't alert her captors, but kept going, nonetheless. After one backwards lunge, she raised her legs and, with perfect timing, slammed her vintage *Doc Martens* on the concrete and twisted into a squatting posture. With a deep sigh of relief, she stood upright and let her arms finally go limp.

"Right, get your bearings, then find a way out of these damn manacles."

Respite was fleeting, unfortunately, as a skittering sound on the concrete to her left alerted her to incoming peril. One of the Ger'igguthy spawn from the pit was heading for her left leg. Frantically, she kicked out at the creature, catching it with a glancing blow to the antennae making it hiss in anger and rear up on its hind legs, brandishing its pincers.

"Back! Back you bastard!" Mickie hissed through gritted teeth as she continued to deliver quick strikes to the horror's general direction. She was holding it at bay when she realised, to her immense horror, that another of the creatures had joined its fellow in the attack and was approaching from the opposite side.

"I've heard of a pincer movement, but this is fucking ridiculous!"

Soon, Mickie's body was flailing in a bizarre jig as she lashed out with opposing feet at one creature then the other. She was fighting a losing battle as creatures snapped their claws and kept advancing, their armoured carapaces taking the brunt of her attacks like chitinous shock absorbers. As the twin terrors were about to go in for the kill, the cellar hatch to the outside was wrenched open. Bright morning light flooded the chamber, causing humans and creatures alike to blanch in bedazzlement. Mickie squinted to try to make out the large shape in the hatchway and her heart sank when she saw it was wearing the robe of the Discarded.

The Ger'igguthy spawn came to the same realisation as Mickie and resumed their attack. One of the creatures unfurled its leathery wings and levitated into the air. Mickie screamed as the beast rose to eye level and snapped its claws hungrily. It was inches away from Mickie's nose, when ... *splat!* The creature exploded in a cloud of luminous green goo as a bullet slammed into its side showering her face and upper torso in foul-smelling slime. The second critter shrieked in fury and sprung towards the shadowy assailant on its powerful forelegs. A second bullet put an end to the beast and the gunman entered the cellar. Mickie, eyes glued shut by parasite innards, felt the chain being forcefully wrenched from the ceiling with no trouble whatsoever, then a familiar voice spoke.

"Another victory for the hydraulic shoulders," Jake growled as he picked her up and carried her from the oubliette. Mickie didn't want to open her mouth. Who knew what ingesting the blood of dimension-hopping spawn of a parasitic deity would do to the human digestive system. However, she wanted to thank Jake for coming to her rescue, so she made appreciative humming sounds. Jake placed her on the frosty grass and tore a rag from his purloined robe.

"Here, let's get this gunk off your face." He scanned the area for hostiles while gently clearing the slime from her eyes, nose, and lips.

"My God, that was disgusting. Couldn't you have splatted the damn thing when it wasn't in front of my face?"

Jake grinned cheekily. "Where would the fun be in that?"

Mickie chuckled and playfully punched him on the arm. "Thanks, Jake. I thought I was about to become a host. I take it that Cricket found you?"

Jake rubbed the back of his head. "You could say that; the silly little sod crashed into my head. Drew blood and everything!"

Mickie snorted. "That's my boy. I did tell him to get your attention."

"Well, it worked, he's back at my place recharging. How did they get you? The Discarded rarely leave their compound."

"It's all a blur. I was on the roof watching the waves, just thinking how small and insignificant we are—"

"Cheerful as ever, Mick."

"Bugger off, Jake, you know what I mean. It's beautiful ... if you don't think about all the deadly things that live in it. Anyway, the next thing I knew, I was waking up here."

"Hmm, very odd. I've never heard of this lot being active in the ruins. They must be up to something." Jake looked around pensively; something wasn't right. Since he had arrived, he had met with zero resistance in stark contrast to his previous visit to Barncoose Manor when he had ended up having to shoot his way out with a horde of angry cultists on his tail. "We should get out of here. Quickly."

"You won't hear any arguments from me," Mickie grunted, getting to her feet. "How did you get here anyway?"

If she was expecting a glamorous ride, she was about to be desperately disappointed. Jake gestured to a rusty and battered moped teetering on its stand by the gate. "Behold, my faithful steed. This way, milady."

Mickie rolled her eyes. "Where the hell did you find that piece of crap?"

"Same place as the robe. I nicked it the last time I was here and promptly crashed it into a bunch of stinging nettles. I went back the next day and wheeled it home. Got one of my Voormi mates to fix it up—those guys certainly know their way around a spanner—I thought it might come in handy, and it looks like I was right." Jake grinned smugly. "Shall we?"

"If we must."

"Oh, come on, it beats walking." Jake paused and shot her a concerned look. "How are you holding up, being *outside,* I mean?"

"Okay, I think... Surprisingly okay."

"Great, let's get you back home, then. Saddle up!"

Mickie shrugged and followed Jake to the vehicle where they clambered aboard and rode slowly back towards the town ruins.

"I warn you, it's hardly a palace fitting for a damsel in distress," Jake chuckled as he unlocked the bolts and let them into his home.

"Piss off, Jake, I'm going to remember this the next time you need patching up. One slip of the needle and you'll regret being such a smart-arse." Mickie stretched her arms to try and relieve the pain in her shoulders and scanned the room.

Chirrup!

"Cricket!" Mickie exclaimed upon spotting her little friend. She raced across the room and scooped the mini drone up into her hand. "Thank you, Cricket, if it wasn't for you, I'd be dead!"

Jake coughed under his breath as if to say, *'what about me'.* Mickie either didn't notice or chose to ignore him. "Clever Cricket," she continued to coo while Jake rolled his eyes and poured them both a large whiskey. Mickie took a momentary break from petting her favourite pet to take a large gulp. It was strong stuff. Jake didn't tell her, but it was Voormis-grade liquor that made her grimace as it scorched a path down her gullet.

"So, any idea why they took you, any of them say anything that might shed some bloody light on things?" Jake asked.

"I dunno. Though the guy in the hood with the knockout juice called me Starmaker, along with various other things that I won't repeat in front of Cricket."

"Starmaker?" Jake raised an eyebrow. "I didn't think you had managed to actually make one yet?"

"Hey," she snapped. "It's not my fault Ben drew a blank on the materials."

"Yeah, I heard the trip up north was a bust. One of the Voormi miners that drinks in the Hyperborea said that the whole area is crawling with burrowers and warring ghoul clans."

"Yeah, something like that. Anyway." She stood up and slipped Cricket into her pocket. "Thanks for the rescue. I should get home; I badly need to wash bug goop out of my hair." She finished her drink and turned to leave.

"Hey, wait up, I'll walk you back." Jake glugged back his booze.

"I'll be fine." Mickie tried to weakly protest, more out of courtesy than intent.

"Nah. Something is bugging me about the whole thing."

Mickie looked at him quizzically.

Jake continued. "I dunno. It all just feels *off* somehow. I had the feeling all day like I was walking into a trap, but it never slammed shut, know what I mean?"

Mickie shrugged as the windows exploded in a hail of gunfire.

"Down!" Jake bellowed and dived behind the sofa.

"Why did you have to open your fucking big mouth!" Mickie screamed hysterically. "You've jinxed us, you pillock!"

Bullets thudded into the walls, filling the atmosphere with a haze of brick and plaster dust. Jake crawled over to Mickie and guided her towards the kitchen. Once inside he stood up and slipped on his aviators, engaging his thermal targeting overlay, which revealed that the front of the building was lined with armed cultists. Jake swore and started to rummage in the junk drawer under the sink.

"What the hell are you looking for?"

"A matchbox."

"What?" Mickie spat incredulously. "We are about to be blown to kingdom come and you're looking for a way to light a sodding smoke?"

Jake found what he was looking for and tipped the matches out. Mickie looked on in bewilderment as Jake snapped off a piece of ration bar and coaxed a fat cockroach into the sliding box.

"What?" He answered her silent question. "You have Cricket and your menagerie. Burt here is my roommate."

A roar from the living room followed by the unmistakable stench of flaming paraffin told Jake that they had to move. He grabbed his coat and covered Mickie with it. Using her hand, he guided her to the door while his sunglasses succeeded in shielding his eyes from the worst of the black smoke. Bullets continued to fly at random forcing Jake to marvel at the amount of ammo the Discarded were willing to waste. For him, every bullet had to count.

Mickie cried in surprise as something pounced on her back as she stepped into the corridor. A snarling, growling creature lashed out at the young woman with tooth and claw. Jake rushed over and grabbed the animal by the collar. "No, Tina!" He shouted sternly at the wild woman, dragging her off Mickie. "Bad kitty!"

Tina looked at him confusedly.

"Mickie is a friend. It's not her shooting the crap out of the building!"

Tina backed away on all fours, her eyes searching for the villain who spoiled her cat-nap. Mickie scrambled to her feet and straightened her clothes. "What the hell is going on, who the hell is this fruitcake?"

"Don't worry," Jake reassured her, crossing the corridor to tickle Tina behind her ear. "This is Tina... She thinks she's a cat.

She's harmless ... most of the time. She lives upstairs with another guy who thinks he's a penguin. The poor buggers got fried on Expiration Day. She was looking after the other one and realised that he was happy being a bird, so she overloaded her malfunctioning chip with cat stuff."

"Okay, fine. How the hell are we going to get out of here? The fire is spreading, and we'll be mown down as soon as we step outside."

Squawk! Squawk!

Mickie looked startled as a pudgy, balding man came hopping down the stairs waving his arms. "Dave?" She was shocked; the last time she had seen this man he'd been convulsing on the floor of the commercial district. "What the hell are you doing here?"

"You two know each other?" Jake inquired.

"We used to work together at the DDC. It's a long story."

Dave started to shuffle off down the corridor, motioning at them to follow. Mickie figured she had nothing to lose and followed her former co-worker. Jake and Tina fell in at the rear. Dave reached the door to an abandoned flat and entered. It was derelict and the floor had collapsed revealing a partially submerged room below. Dave took a shuffling run up and dived into the water, the rest of them stood and looked down at him in confusion.

"Dave," Jake snarled. "This is no time for a bloody swim!"

Dave shook his head and squawked.

"I think he wants us to follow." Mickie realised.

Jake shrugged and jumped into the water. At least this way he wouldn't burn to death, though drowning was hardly a more attractive option. Tina looked down and growled. Like most cats, she had a natural aversion to water. Mickie spotted her reluctance and shoved her off the edge.

"Oh, get in, Tiddles!"

Tina hissed and bared her teeth at Mickie after splashing into the water. Mickie smirked and followed her down. Once they had all adjusted to the shock of the sudden drop in temperature, Dave led them out into a flooded hallway. At the end was an open window. Dave swam swiftly and gracefully towards it and slipped through. Mickie pushed Tina ahead before ducking through herself.

Free of the inferno, the group found themselves in open water to the rear of the building. Dave led them silently across a flooded street and into a partially sunken multi-storey car park. Once they had traversed a ramp, they stood and looked back at the now flaming shell of the low-rise block.

Jake scowled at the sight and turned to Mickie.

"I told you it felt like a trap."

After checking that Burt the cockroach was safe and dry in his matchbox, Jake followed the ramps up to the top of the concrete structure. Mickie followed, leaving Dave to splash playfully in the water and Tina to shake herself dry. Jake stared out at his former home as the roof collapsed in on itself and the flames spiralled skyward.

"Bollocks... Now what the bloody hell am I supposed to do?"

Mickie put her hand softly on his arm. "You can stay with us until you figure something out."

"Thanks, I appreciate it." He stopped sulking and straightened up. "We need to get to your place, quickly."

"What's wrong?" Mickie could tell by the pensive look on Jake's face that he had just thought of something bad.

"Max," he suddenly blurted out before starting to jog down the ramp. "They might have gone for Max!"

Mickie knew in an instant that he was right. If they were after her, then nobody who knew her was safe, and that went double for her brother figure and protector. She sprinted after Jake and joined him on the last dry floor. He was trying to get it through to Dave and Tina that they should stay where they are until the trouble passed and that he would find them later. They both made noises that indicated that they understood.

Jake indicated a way up onto a row of low, flat-roofed buildings that snaked around towards the GAF dock wall. These handy stepping stones were once a row of shops and services that serviced the dockside estate before the GAF evicted all the tenants to make way for their acres of concrete and steel. They didn't bother demolishing the empty units, simply leaving them to be claimed by the tide.

"What do you think those creepy fruitcakes are up to?" Mickie asked as she straddled the gap between two buildings.

"I don't know, that's the problem. I have never seen them out in force like this before. I thought they were just using you as bait to get revenge on me for what I did up at the manor last time I was there. But now, I'm not so sure." Jake jumped a gap and readied himself to catch Mickie. "I mean, why didn't they just wait until I left the flat and put a bullet in my noggin? That would have been much simpler."

Mickie took a run up and jumped. Jake caught her without breaking a sweat. They paused for a moment to catch their breath; the sun was sinking by now and played on the water along with the flames making it ripple and glimmer in vibrant orange hues. Above, the sky itself looked like it was ablaze. Jake took a swig from his hip flask and passed it to Mickie. She took it gratefully in an attempt to quiet her jangling nerves.

"Okay, here's the plan, we are going to have to cross the GAF part of the docks," Jake explained. "Keep your eyes peeled for Caspers."

Mickie nodded and followed Jake through a gap in the looming concrete wall. Though they were entering hostile territory, she was glad to be back on dry land. They followed the curve of the wall, keeping in shadow. All was calm and Casper-free until they neared the gate to the old docks. Both their mouths fell open in surprise at what was going on at the entrance. Shots rang out as groups of Discarded and enforcers blew the hell out of each other with a variety of GAF products. It was a pitched battle that could have been the company's next big ad campaign. If you had asked Jake that morning to wager on the victor, he would have put his money on the Caspers, but now, he wasn't so sure.

Jake readied his gun, engaged his targeting overlay, and motioned for Mickie to keep behind him. The gate was a no-go so they dashed towards one of the loading bays. Even if they went undetected, which was highly unlikely given the circumstances, then they would probably get caught in the crossfire. Jake thought fast and hatched the plan to use one of the huge cranes to get them over the wall and into the old town.

By now, the GAF was losing the fight; as quickly as they knocked one of the crazed cultists down, another took their place. The other problem for the loyal Caspers was that the Discarded were impressively hard to kill and seemed to absorb punishment almost supernaturally. Arms and legs were severed without any apparent effect. The parasites they hosted kept them coming; the Discarded felt no pain. No fear. Jake watched in awe as the cultists kept advancing and the Caspers started being mown down in droves. Mickie jabbed him in the ribs and motioned at him to hurry up and ran full-pelt to the crane where Jake started to fiddle with the controls.

As the final Casper fell, the Discarded marched onto GAF turf like a badly washed army.

"Get on the hook and hold on tight, I'll lower you over the wall."

Mickie did as instructed and Jake lifted her to just over the height of the wall. As he concentrated on the controls, Mickie spotted danger.

"Look out!"

Jake spun on the swivel-seat just as two Discarded came limping around the corner. With one hand lowering the crane and the other on his gun, Jake opened fire. One dropped instantly from a head-shot; the other was sent wheeling as the shell connected with his shoulder. Mickie shouted that she was down on the other side but there was no time to reposition the crane—Jake would have to slide down the winch as more Discarded poured in from around the side of the warehouse. Jake's gunshots had alerted their parasites to his location and the hive mind of Ger'igguthy was angry. He frantically scrambled up the ladder as poorly aimed bullets ricocheted off the yellow metal. Once at the top, he said a little prayer and raced along the arm like a tightrope walker. Mickie was convinced that he would fall so she was pleasantly surprised when he made it to the end.

"Out of the way!" Jake ripped the belt from his filthy jeans, wrapped it around the wire and started to rappel down the wall. Halfway down, the belt hit a rough section and split, sending Jake crashing to the floor where he landed flat on his back, bruised and winded. Mickie tried to help him up. Eventually getting him to his feet, they slipped into the darkened ruins of the old town area and headed for Mickie's abode. Progress was hindered by the occasional Discarded that needed shooting and the fact that, now beltless, Jake's pants kept slipping down around his thighs, but they eventually made it to the street outside the antique shop safe and sound.

Thunder rumbled and the heavens opened as Mickie and Jake approached the antique shop. It was a relief, and something of a minor miracle, that the building was still standing and appeared unscathed from the rampage of the Discarded. Keeping alert, they crossed the street and made for the alley to the rear.

"Hold it right there, bounty hunter," a mystery voice rasped. It appeared to come from inside an overturned communal bin. As they jumped from shock, two Discarded came out of hiding somewhere behind them. They were both toting GAF *Critter-buster* shotguns. Both of which were pointed at Jake and Mickie.

"Drop the gun, Mr Baker."

Jake stared in disbelief as an all-too-familiar figure climbed from his hiding place. The man lowered his hood and greeted them with a terrifying rictus. Jennifer the hand-cannon clattered to the floor.

"Did you miss me?"

Jake was shocked; the man who stood before him was supposed to be dead, and, by the look of him ... he was.

"Jake," Mickie whispered. "That's the bastard that held the rag over my face."

Jake took a moment to compose himself before he spoke. He didn't want to show fear at this knife-edge moment. It wasn't easy; the man in front of him was a walking cadaver. His skin was blue and tinged with green mould, his eyes sunken pits of inky blackness fringed by writhing maggots. Finally, Jake responded, "Warren Tremayne, this is a surprise. The last I heard, the Voormi barman blasted a hole in your chest so large that he kept referring to your corpse as *the doughnut*." Jake smirked.

His grin widening, Tremayne undid his robe. "As you can see, when one is under the protection of the Parasite God, it takes a lot more than a point-blank shotgun blast to keep a man down." The hole in the man's chest went straight through. Jake could see the back of his robe through the tunnel of putrefying meat. Inside the hole, several small Ger'igguthy spawn wriggled and squirmed as they made a nest.

"Alright, I get it, you're a tough man to kill. I'll have to see if a bullet in the brain works. Now, what's this all about, Tremayne, revenge?"

Warren snorted. "Nothing so mundane, my gunslinging friend. If I wanted simple revenge then I would have just shot you and that hairy Voormi when you came staggering out of the Hyperborea Bar at closing time. No, this has more to do with your friend there than yourself."

"What the hell are you talking about, you fucking weirdo?" Mickie demanded angrily.

Tremayne's grin grew ever wider, threatening to bisect his face. "Now that we know that Ben has no more Mnar stones that could be used against the scavenger, I decided that a change in leadership was in order. Ger'igguthy preparing to tear through the veil and take his place as ruler of the wasteland known as Zone 51. We intended to impregnate you with a host so your Starmaker knowledge could be used for our benefit. Alas, once again, Mr Baker has upset my plans."

"Why didn't you have her guarded if you intended to keep her?" Jake asked.

"An error on my part, I confess. I didn't think anyone knew where she was and thought that by the time anyone found out, she would be one with Ger'igguthy. I was wrong. But, no matter, all shall be one with the scavenger once he is free from his temporal exile."

"So, let me get this right, all of this carnage, the kidnapping, the attack on the GAF, it's what, a coup?"

"Indeed. Ger'igguthy's time has come. He will replace the Dark Pharaoh, Nyarlathotep, as the supreme entity. His dominion will engulf the planet, and he will feed." Tremayne raised his arms in rapture. "Iä! Iä! Ger'igguthy!"

Jake rolled his bloodshot eyes. "Spare me the sermon, you daft bugger. What happens then? You'll be devoured too, all of you. Do you think Ger'igguthy gives a single fuck about you? He probably doesn't even know you exist!"

Tremayne scowled in response, baring his rotten teeth. "That's where you are wrong. My seekers have communed with The Scavenger, arranged our ascension to Godhood, paved the way... It's a shame about the girl, she would have been a most useful asset, but, hey-ho, time for you both to die. Don't worry, your compost won't go to waste, I can feel a couple of my lodgers getting excited at the thought of feasting on your entrails." He motioned to his brethren. "Get them up against the wall, I want to see if we can turn *them* into *doughnuts*."

As the gunmen motioned for Jake and Mickie to move over to the wall of the jewellers, the throb of an old engine caught Tremayne's attention. He looked around to find its source and rolled his eyes in exasperation when a large blue tractor rumbled into view. "What the bloody hell are you doing here?" he shouted up at the driver. "I told you to wait by the GAF tower!"

The driver said nothing but set his jaw firmly and turned into the alley. Putting the lumbering vehicle into gear, he glanced down at Jake and Mickie and told them to run.

They didn't need telling twice as the tractor herded Warren Tremayne into the alley.

"Stop, you bloody moron!" Tremayne bellowed.

Jake noticed the distracted look on the guard's faces and used their momentary lapse in focus to snatch Jennifer from the pavement. Two seconds later, the shotgun-waving Discarded grunts had his-and-his matching holes in their foreheads. Rumbling and rattling, the tractor advanced into the dead-end alley with Tremayne back-pedalling away from it. It barely fit in the narrow street—there was barely room for a rat to get past, never mind a bulky cult leader.

"Oliver!" Tremayne screamed as he was backed closer to the wall at the end. "I'm your boss and I order you to stop!"

"I'm done taking orders from people like you and Sanderson." Oliver glared at Tremayne and shifted the engine into top gear.

The blue paint of the old farm vehicle was splattered with foul black ichor as one of the huge wheels pulverised the body of Warren Tremayne. Oliver wasn't done. Once he reached the end of the alley he shifted into reverse. Just to make sure. Mickie retched from the ungodly smell.

Oliver switched off the engine and climbed down from the cab looking shaky.

Jake gulped from his flask then lit a smoke. "Well, bugger me." He grinned and patted the man gratefully on the shoulder. "Oliver Potter. I've never been so glad to see a weasel in all my days."

Oliver huffed. "I told you before, I had no choice."

Jake dropped the sarcasm. "I know. I did some digging after our last encounter. I know you didn't... I'm sorry."

Oliver smiled. "Thank you. I heard Tremayne planning your execution and I figured I owed you one after the lurker in the woods incident."

"Thanks, man, we would be parasite food if it wasn't for you. I guess this makes you an *undesirable* then?"

"Yeah, I guess running your employer over with a tractor after taking part in an assault on the GAF plaza kind of puts a black mark on your record. Anyway, I have nothing to lose any more."

Jake nodded and flashed him a sympathetic smile. "Again... I'm sorry."

Mickie had stopped heaving by this point and walked over to Oliver. "Thanks. What will you do now? I imagine the remaining discarded will come looking for you."

"I hadn't thought about it, but you're right, I'm a marked man. I think getting out of the sector may be a good idea."

"You can hide out with us if you want?"

Oliver looked at Jake for validation. Jake shrugged nonchalantly.

"Thanks."

"We should get inside," Mickie asserted. "This stench is going to attract lurkers like flies to shit."

"Indeed." Jake nodded grimly. "Plus, I have something I need to clear up."

Mickie looked at him askew.

"I smell a very large rat, and I have a nasty suspicion that its name is Benjamin Edwards..."

Burt the cockroach emerged from his matchbox, his antenna surveying his strange new surroundings. He was on a large desk in a bare rectangular room. He recognised the smell of Jake's jacket that was slung untidily upon the bed. It didn't take him long to find the hunk of ration-bar that Jake had left for him, he scuttled over and commenced eating. His blissful moment was disturbed when a green metal creature about the same size as him landed on the desk next to where he munched. Burt was startled and reared back, clacking his mighty mandibles in defence. Cricket chirruped twice and looked at Burt. Sensing no danger, Burt greeted this strange metal bug then resumed his feast.

Meanwhile, in the adjacent living area, Jake paced the floor while Mickie and Max sat pensively awaiting Ben's arrival. Oliver had decided, wisely, to leave them to their showdown and had gone for a well-earned lie-down. Mickie and Max didn't want to believe that Ben had anything to do with Tremayne's abduction of Mickie but, as Jake pointed out, how else did he find out about Mickie being a budding Starmaker. He didn't tell him, she didn't tell him, Max couldn't tell him even if he wanted to, this left only one other person who knew... Ben.

The aged owner of the antique shop shuffled into the room in his trademark smoking jacket puffing on his pipe. Upon spotting the three pairs of eyes burning holes in his body he turned to Max. "I had no idea we had guests. Go and make a pot of tea, there's a good chap."

Max shook his head emphatically and indicated that Ben should park his rump in the chair that they had placed in the centre of the room.

"What's going on, Max?" Edwards spotted Jake toying with the handle of his gun in its holster and turned pale.

Max indicated that Jake should speak.

"Do you remember, after that SNAFU with the compass, we made a deal?"

"Indeed," Ben replied.

"That you were going to be one hundred per cent straight with me from now on?"

Ben nodded.

"Good, because I'm about to hold you to that promise." Jake sat in the chair opposite Ben's own and leaned forward so that they were almost nose-to-nose. "Did you, yes or no, tell that undead prick, Warren Tremayne, about Mickie being our new Starmaker?"

Ben looked aghast for a second, then puzzled the next. He shook his head noncommittally before mumbling "I don't know," under his breath.

Jake's hand lunged for Ben's throat but was grabbed by Max before he could connect. Suddenly, the configuration of the chairs made perfect sense.

"Dammit, Ben, do you even know what a straight answer is? You either did or you didn't, which is it?"

Ben looked terrified. "That's the thing, old chap, I honestly don't know. I would never consciously betray Mickie, especially not to *that* scum but my mind has been wandering a lot lately."

Jake relaxed in his seat. "Explain."

Ben sighed. "My ancestors, like his, have a long history with Ger'igguthy going back to the time of the Napoleonic wars when his ancestor, and mine, discovered a temple dedicated to the Parasite God in darkest Peru. The doomed ship, The Black Eel, sank just up the coast from here with only one survivor, my ancestor. Since then, both of our bloodlines have been entwined with Ger'igguthy. From generation to generation, the curse of The Black Eel has dogged our every step. My family embraced the curse and founded the UK branch of the Church of the Discarded. I turned my back on by birthright many years ago, but still, the scavenger has his claws in me. I was protected while I had the Mnar stone, but now it has gone..."

Jake cursed under his breath. "So you're saying that Ger'igguthy is trying to control your mind?"

Ben nodded.

"Is there anything we can do?" Mickie interjected.

"If I can get another Mnar stone, then I can probably regain control. This is why I've been so focussed on finding a suitable material for crafting. I know I've been hard to live with, for which I apologise, but my mind has been fogging over with alarming frequency."

"That's why the sudden importance of the damn Starmaking deal. Everything makes sense now. Why didn't you tell me?"

"I'm sorry, Mickie, I should have talked to you, but I didn't know for sure that I was compromised. I think I do now, I just didn't want to worry you unduly."

Jake sighed. "So where can we get this element you need? I heard your northern expedition was something of a bust."

"It was; the mine is under miles of water, caved in, and completely inaccessible. However, I have just received word that there is an alternative."

"Go on."

Ben brightened a little. "Mickie recently sent one of her *pets* on a mission to Australia. I had been reading the accounts of Professor Nathaniel Wingate Peaslee recently and thought they might be the key to my problem. Peaslee encountered a strange city buried under the Great Sandy Desert back in the Twentieth. Amongst his accounts, were details of a strange unknown mineral imbued with remarkable properties. I believe it to be the thing we need to make stars. Pigeon returned today with a message from Dwayne."

Max's face lit up at the mention of his old friend.

"Yes, Max, he's doing fine. He said that he has..." Ben suddenly coughed, "excuse me. I think the smoke went down the wrong Yog-Sothoth."

"What?" Jake looked at Ben like he had just dropped off the moon.

"I said that the way will soon be open. Yog-Sothoth is the gatekeeper." There was a brief bewildered pause while Ben shook his head and tried to compose his thoughts. Finally, he continued, "Dwayne said that they have found the city, he is waiting for us to join him and Yog-Sothoth."

"What the fuck are you talking about, Ben?" Jake asked, his body tensing. "Who is Yog-Sothoth?"

"Yog-Sothoth *is* the key. Yog-Sothoth *is* the gate."

"Um... Ben, are you alright?"

Suddenly, Ben's body was blasted backwards by some unseen force, his body convulsing as an inhuman scream burst from his frothing maw.

"Max, hold him down!" Jake yelled, leaping to his feet.

Before Max could reach him, Ben rose like a marionette on unseen strings, his arms splayed outwards in a cruciform, his eyes jet black and sunken into his skull. As Max approached, Ben hurled him aside with superhuman strength. The massive ex-enforcer tumbled across the room demolishing Ben's pride and joy, his chaise-lounge.

Jake drew his gun and aimed it at Ben.

"No!" Mickie slammed the gun out of Jake's hand with a well-placed chop to the wrist. "Fight it, Ben, fight it!"

The Ben-puppet smiled a lopsided grin and chuckled as he levitated across the room and ripped the doors off an antique Welsh-dresser. Snatching a metal box from within, Ben glided over to the dining table and opened it. The candles illuming the room guttered and flickered, casting the room in shadow while the electric lights fizzled and popped. Ben removed a black cube from the box and placed it on the table.

"Here is the metamorphosis cube, Lord Ger'igguthy, let it guide you back to glory!" Ben raised his arms aloft as crackles of electricity sparked from a dark cloud that was quickly spreading across the ceiling.

Rudely awakened from his nap by the unfolding mayhem, Oliver leapt from his bed and stomped into the room. His mouth fell open as the rain started to pour from the ceiling in rods. Quickly figuring out what was happening, he grabbed a candlestick and lunged for Ben. He was too slow— Ben spun around and slapped Oliver with an outstretched arm. The bleary-eyed mechanic hurtled across the room and ploughed head-first into a reproduction print of the *Mona Lisa*.

Mickie screamed at Ben to fight the influence of Ger'igguthy. It was no use; the insidious entity was firmly in control and it was doubtful that any trace of Ben remained. Lightning lit the room and several juvenile Ger'igguthy spawn dropped from the void in the ceiling, snapping and chittering. Mickie lashed out at one of the scuttling horrors with Ben's walking-stick.

Jake went for his gun, but Ben spotted the motion. A bolt of lightning hit the weapon before he could grab it. He tried again with the same results. Jake changed tactics and hurled a china teapot at the antiquarian's head. It connected and Ben was momentarily dazed. Jake went for the gun a final time, but his hand was swatted aside.

"What the fuck are you doing, Max?"

Max grabbed the gun out of his fist, aimed it at Ben and fired.

"I'm sorry, Max. You had no choice."

Max was distraught and nothing Mickie could say would console him. He had just blown the nearest thing he had to a father's head off. He sat with his head in his hands while Mickie comforted him. The spawn had vanished as quickly as they had appeared, and the cloud had dissipated almost instantly as the conduit was severed. Max had saved the day... It was just heartbreaking that the *conduit* just happened to be his friend's head.

Oliver was okay after his close encounter with a painting, a little bruised but no permanent damage. He and Jake had wrapped Ben's body in a carpet and taken it up to the roof. From there, they carried it along the rooftops to the sea and lowered him in as respectfully as possible under the circumstances. Jake took a glug from his flask and let Oliver have a sip before returning the way they came as the rain continued to hammer down.

"So what now?" Mickie asked as Jake returned and lit a cigarette.

"No idea." He blew a thick plume of smoke into the room. "What do you think?"

Mickie stood and started looking around the room. "I think we should carry on with Ben's plan."

"Why, we don't need the stars now, do we?"

"Have you forgotten about Danni?"

Jake had.

"There is a chance, a very slim chance that she is still alive and being held by Sanderson. Those stars make him mortal, killable. Max has seen it with his own eyes."

Max nodded.

"Plus," Mickie continued while looking under cushions and random antiques, "Max has a score to settle with that S.O.B."

"Fine," Jake sighed into his brandy. "The problem is, Ben died before he could tell us where Dwayne is. Australia is a big country, you know?"

"Well." Mickie hummed distractedly. "If I can find Pigeon then he can give us the message."

"Pigeon?" Oliver asked.

"One of Mickie's *pets*. She has a whole menagerie of drones that all have names and personalities, it's cute. Weird... but cute."

Mickie shot him a look. "This is coming from a man whose closest friend is a cockroach named Burt."

"Point taken."

Coo!

"Pigeon!" Mickie exclaimed after hearing the tell-tale coo of Pigeon's rusty propeller shaft. She cooed in response. Pigeon replied. Soon, she had found her pet hiding behind a dusty old stack of encyclopaedias. The reprogrammed postal drone hopped out from its cover and into Mickie's hands. She petted him and coaxed him into delivering the message. Once happy, the drone raised a retractable speaker and played the recording.

"Dear Ben," Dwayne began. *"Greetings from paradise! What a fuckin' joke, this place is just as big a shithole as the Zone. Anyway, it's nice to hear from you, I have no idea how you got your pigeon to find me after all this time, but this Mickie girl sounds like a real smart one. I listened to your rambling message, you don't change, do you? Needless to say, you can count on my assistance as always, you and Max are like family to me.*

"Australia is a fuckin' mess, the coast is a no-go zone most of the time and all the big cities and towns got flattened on Expi-

ration Day. We are constantly being slammed by these huge-ass tidal waves and the town ruins have been taken over by thousands of Gillmen. Only these gill breathers ain't friendly like most of the ones back home, these suckers are militant and seem to be waiting for something. Whatever that is, they certainly don't appreciate outsiders poking around. So, if you are thinking of sending some guys over to this sun-burnt rock, they had better come packing some serious heat.

"Most of the surviving humans have spread into the centre and there is a huge shanty town near Alice Springs. I reckon that would be the best place for a meeting. The site you are seeking is pretty much slap-bang in the middle of the Great Sandy Desert. We have set up a base with some locals at the end of the DeGrey River. We only have one working vehicle and limited fuel so I will have to leave Johanna, Sam and Jane here and go collect whoever you send over from Alice Springs.

"Personally, I think it's a stupid idea to send anyone, this place is a bloody war-zone, We have round the clock guards armed with some serious shit. If the Gillmen don't get ya, the strange things under the sand will. Big burrowing squid things like they had up in Yorkshire. Dholes, I think you called 'em. Thing is, Ben, you have no guarantee that this strange element you need, will even be in the site. We have confirmed that the underground city is real, which is a start, I suppose. It turns out that old Nathaniel Wingate Peaslee knew his stuff.

"The Australian guys we are with are loyal and willing to join us on our expedition. The way they see it, it's us versus them and any advantage is worth searching for. A good bunch of folk all round. I hope this message reaches you. You know how rubbish I am with tech. I'm following Mickie's instructions to the letter but if anyone can balls it up, it's your old friend Dwayne. Let me know if and when you will be joining us. We'll stay here as long as possible, but we may have to move quickly if the camp becomes compromised.

"Blessings of the Elders. Dwayne out. P.S. If you run into Jake the bounty hunter, tell him that Sam wants to hire him to put a bullet between Oliver the Whistleblower's eyes. He's good for the payment."

Oliver looked at Jake, eyes wide with terror.

"Don't worry, I'm not taking the contract. Besides, he doesn't know you like I do. He doesn't know what really happened."

"Thanks, Jake."

"Don't sweat it. Anyway, back to Dwayne's prattle. What do you reckon, Mick?"

Mickie grinned. "I reckon we are going to need a man with a boat."

Jake smiled. "Leave it to me... I know just the chap."

CHAPTER VII

BON VOYAGE

MARCH 25TH 2132
CORPORATION WATERS
40.010787, -19.841310:

"I told you that you'd regret saying that you owed me one," Jake Baker grinned as a huge spray of frigid seawater lashed the small fishing vessel.

"Not at all," the captain replied. "I'm a Gillman, remember? I love this stuff." Frank Prince, husband, father of two, and renowned fishmonger had been escaping the wrath of his wife by sinking some beers at the Dancing Shrimp when Jake, Max, and a girl named Mickie walked in. Jake and Max had rescued him from the clutches of a death cult, and he owed them a favour. Frank got a round of drinks in, and Jake explained that they needed a seaworthy vessel and a captain with iron nerves to take them down under.

Maybe it was the booze, or maybe it was the thought of escaping his wife's wrath for a while, but, before you could say *tinned pilchards,* he had signed himself up. His only conditions were that he would be staying on the boat when they got to their destination, and that somebody had to look after his family in his absence. Jake said he would take care of it, and the deal was struck.

"Are you sure my family will be safe?" he asked Jake as he steadied the boat.

"You have nothing to fear on that score. Muggo'sutha will make sure nobody messes with them." Jake unconsciously rubbed his shoulder as he remembered their last prize fight. "Trust me, *nobody* messes with big Muggs."

Frank had been taken aback when Jake had introduced his family's *babysitter*. Muggo'sutha was the biggest Voormi he had ever laid his eyes upon. He barely fit through the door of his shack on the dockside. Jake had reassured him that Muggs had a kind heart under all that muscle and umber fur, and introduced him to Frank's family as their protector. His wife was moderately terrified, but his kids were in awe of the gentle brute. They nick-named him Teddy.

As the boat skipped gracefully over the waves, wind and rain lashed the cabin sending Max and Mickie scuttling below decks. Frank's vessel, *Dagon's Bounty*, was one of the most powerful boats on the market. Constructed by a GAF affiliate and fitted with twin engines that ran on *everlasting* nuclear cells, the *Fish-master* series was a much sought after commodity to the Gillmen. Frank loved his boat so much that it drove his wife to jealousy and knew just how to make her dance on the water.

"How are Mickie and Max doing?" Frank shouted over the roar of the water.

"Mickie's fine, she's happy tinkering with one of her drones. Max, however, still hasn't found his sea legs... The poor sod had his head in a bucket the last time I saw him."

"Ha," Frank chortled. "I forget that some of you dry-skins can't handle the sea when she's a bit choppy."

"A bit choppy? That's like saying Sanderson is a *bit* of an evil twat. Seriously, Frank, when does a wave become a tsunami?"

"Yeah, I'll give you that, there is a storm blowing in from the west, I fear. We may have to drop anchor and get below decks before much longer. I'm just trying to get us as far away from the coast as possible. Most of the sea-lurkers and giant squid tend to keep close to land. It's where they find bigger prey... Like us." Frank's protuberant eyes were fixed on the sea, so he didn't see Jake blanch when he said *most*. He would have much preferred to hear *all*.

"Is this thing armed?" Jake asked nervously.

"There are some shock-harpoons and flame units below deck, they're usually enough to repel an attack."

Again, Jake blanched at the caveat that Frank oh-so-casually dropped into the conversation and decided to leave their blasé skipper to his navigation. Disquiet welling up inside, he hurried below deck to check all the weapons were locked and loaded. While there, he would get himself a drink. Jake was far too sober for all this maritime malarkey.

As Jake got below decks, a small rubber ball bounced past his feet closely followed by an overexcited land-drone that had been programmed to act like a manic Yorkshire terrier. He stepped out of the way to avoid collision. The drone pounced on the ball, turned around sharply and raced back towards Mickie's cries of "Come on, Sniffer, that's a good boy."

Retching from the opposite cabin emphatically answered the 'has Max found his sea legs?' question. Jake smiled. He was starting to feel a welcome kinship with his two friends. He had been alone ever since Expiration Day and his only real companions during the intervening years had been Burt the cockroach, and the bottle. He knew plenty of drinking buddies, sure, but nothing like family. For better or worse, that was slowly changing.

Jake hung a left around the staircase and ducked through the hatch to the lower deck. Nets and buoys waved and danced as the boat lurched starboard. In the centre of the room was a formidable-looking arsenal. Jake smiled—he always took comfort in a well-maintained weapon—and busied himself checking it over.

An hour passed as he tinkered with the flamethrowers, cleaning the valves and optimising the flow rate. The clattering machinery of the winch announced that the storm had become too brutal even for Frank and that they had dropped anchor. The boat still tossed violently as the waves smashed the sides. Jake stood up and went topside to see if all was well with Frank.

He climbed back out of the hatch just in time to see Frank bellow in pain and hop around on one leg like a demented flamingo.

"Shit," Mickie exclaimed while also desperately attempting to stifle a giggle. "Sorry, Frank, Sniffer gets a bit over excited when we play fetch."

Jake and Mickie helped the injured captain to a bed and sat him down.

"It's okay, I've still got one good leg."

Jake handed him his trusty hip flask and helped him rub some life back into his shin. "I heard the anchor..."

"Yeah, it's as rough as a badger's backside out there, I'm afraid we will have to wait the storm out. I suggest you all try and get some sleep. I'll keep an eye on things topside."

"That's a good plan," said Jake. "Someone wake me when it's over."

With that, Jake went to his bunk, drained his flask, and drifted into a fitful slumber.

MARCH 20ᵀᴴ 2127
ZONE 51 – SOUTH-WEST SECTOR:

The emergency alert klaxon of the GAF housing unit shook Jake out of bed. "Ugh, what now?"

"Sounds like the abandon building alarm again," Mary, Jake's wife, slurred groggily. "It's probably another bomb-threat or such like, just a false alarm."

"It's always a bloody false alarm. Nevertheless, we need to get Alice dressed ASAP and get to the evac point."

Mary cursed. He was right, the penalty for ignoring any company order, including false alarms, was stiff, and none of them wanted to be branded an undesirable. Nobody in their right mind wanted to be branded an undesirable.

"I'll get Alice while you grab the emergency bag from the wardrobe, deal?"

"Deal."

Jake threw on his GAF overalls that had been balled up by the bed, leaned in, and kissed his wife on the forehead before hurrying out into the cramped corridor between domiciles.

"Hey, Dad, another false alarm?" Alice was awake, dressed, and bright as a button as he entered her tiny bedroom.

"Looks like it. We have to go outside, I'm afraid."

"It's alright, Daddy, I know the drill by now. It's the third one this month."

"Is it? I'd totally forgotten. Each day kind of blends into another." Jake paced by the main door. "Dammit, what's keeping her?"

Alice giggled. "Mummy's a sleepy-head, you know that."

"She's a pain in the..."

"Hey, I can hear you, you know?"

Jake and Alice grinned at each other. Tormenting Mary was a favourite pastime in the Baker household.

"Here I am," Mary announced, stepping into the corridor. "Let's get this over with."

Jake took the kit bag from his spouse's shoulder and ushered his family out onto the fifth-floor landing. After checking that the door had securely locked behind them, he led the way towards the big glass lift at the far end. Several other inhabitants shuffled and muttered oaths on their way to the same destination. It would be a cramped descent, but it beat the stairs.

Alice yelped when, without warning, the power to the lights and all other systems abruptly cut out. Jake looked out of the first-floor window to a sight straight out of the sci-fi comics his daughter enjoyed. Drones were falling from the sky and Enforcers were shooting at civilians in the plaza.

"Don't look, sweetie." Jake put his hand over his daughter's eyes and turned her face away from the carnage. Expiration Day was upon them.

Alice cried and clung to her mother as the building shook violently. A massive freight drone laden with crates of automatic weapons slammed into the building above their heads.

"Shit, Jake, the whole building is coming down!"

"I doubt it, these things are built for war." Jake wasn't sure whether he was trying to convince Mary or himself. "Anyway, stay close and keep away from the window."

Screams drifted up from the floor below accompanied by a bestial roar.

"Daddy, what was that noise?"

"I don't know, pickle, just keep moving."

They were halfway down the corridor when a huge black, bubbling monster smashed through the ceiling behind them and started to flow down the corridor towards them, slurping up terrified residents as it went.

Tekeli-li!

"Run!" Jake bellowed, as he grabbed his wife and daughter by their hands and sprinted towards the emergency exit stairs at the end of the corridor. Risking a backward glance alerted Jake that the abomination was nearly upon them. Relinquishing his grip, he pushed Mary and Alice on and wrenched a fire extinguisher off the wall.

"Get back, you fucker," he snarled as he pulled the pin and blasted the seething mass of protoplasm. Eyes and mouths appeared on its shimmering iridescent hide as it reared back against the powerful blast of freezing CO_2. Jake turned and ran after his family just as the stairwell door burst open and another of the killer blobs surged out, immediately engulfing his family in its corrosive mass.

They didn't even have time to scream.

Jake bellowed in anguish and slammed the heavy metal canister against the window, smashing it into thousands of cubes of safety glass. Not caring whether he lived or died, he just didn't want to give the creature the satisfaction, he dived head-first through the gaping hole and crashed to the ground below. A faux evergreen bush broke his fall, and a couple of ribs, bouncing him onto the pavement where his head struck concrete, and everything went black.

MARCH 25TH 2132
CORPORATION WATERS
35.853440, -20.192872·

Jake screamed as Mickie shook him violently awake.

"Elder Gods!" she exclaimed as he fell off his bunk and landed in an undignified heap. "You okay, Jake?"

"Yeah." He shrugged as nonchalantly as possible. "Just a bad dream, that's all, nothing to worry about." For some unknown reason he felt the need to play down his terror in order to maintain his bad-ass mystique.

She wasn't buying it. "Expiration Day again?"

"Yeah." Jake reached for his flask and, upon finding it empty, cursed and chucked it into the corner of the room.

"I don't want to be a nag, but don't you think you'd sleep better if you weren't shit-faced all the time?"

"Thanks, mum... Yeah, you're right, maybe... The problem is, if I don't get shit-faced, as you so delicately put it, I can't get to sleep. It's a vicious fucking circle. If I don't drink, I lie awake all night thinking about it, if I do, I have nightmares about it, but at least I get some rest, right? I'm okay, though, really."

"Okay, cool." Mickie smiled. "Frank says we can move now. It's supposed to be a lovely morning out there. Me and Max are going to check it out, care to join us?"

Jake nodded. "Yeah, I'll be up in a minute, just need to splash some cold water on my face ... and have a drink."

Mickie rolled her eyes before bouncing off topside leaving Jake to get a grip on himself. His hands were still shaking. The most terrifying thing about that particular nightmare was the knowledge that it wasn't the diseased product of his subconscious. It was a raw, unedited memory that no amount of hard liquor could erase. He had come to several days later in a medical unit with his head stapled shut, only to be informed that, as there were no bodies, he wasn't due a GAF payout for his family's demise. More than that, they were officially listed as AWOL and branded undesirable. It was no small wonder that he went rogue and opted-out.

Groaning as he swung his legs off the bunk, the past month's adventures were catching up with him in a variety of aches and pains, he grabbed his kit bag and pulled out his last bottle of seaweed whiskey.

"Dammit, I hope Frank has some rum stashed away on this tub somewhere. Now, where did I lob my flask?"

Locating the battered tin, he unscrewed the cap and filled it before taking a mouthful directly from the bottle. The burning liquid banished the images from his mind and cleared the black clouds from the edges of his vision. He knew it was a case of replacing one problem with another but what other option was there? It was either drink or go crazy. Though he reckoned psychosis was definitely still on the cards and it was merely a case of prolonging the inevitable.

Slipping the flask into his pocket and putting on his mask of sanity, he flashed a half-hearted grin at himself in the mirror over the sink before splashing his face with icy water. "Come on, Jake, you can do this... You might not give a fuck about the world and ninety-nine percent of people living on it but you're doing this for Mickie and Max, remember? Get a bloody grip. There will be plenty of time to wallow when the job's done ... or when you're dead."

Leaving the cabin, dishevelled and disorientated, he secured a harpoon gun and a flamethrower from the hold on his way topside. Once again rallying himself and forcing a smile, Jake mounted the steps and stepped out into the glorious sunshine. He paused, dropped the harpoon and slipped his aviators on to smother the glare. He couldn't remember the last time he had seen sunlight unfiltered through clouds of factory emissions but it was even brighter than he remembered. Locating Mickie and Max on the port side, he shuffled over and joined them for a moment.

Sunlight glittered mesmerically on the water as Mickie and Max looked out across the tranquil waters smiling contentedly. Nothing was visible aside from the sea and the sky and the feeling of isolation was intoxicating, even to Jake. The fact that they were miles from the GAF, the Discarded, lurkers and all the other nastiness that called Zone 51 home was a welcome tonic. Just for a moment, he could pretend that the world wasn't a broken mess.

Leaving them to their moment of peace, Jake carried the weapons to the cab and dumped them in the corner. Frank stood off to one side, monitoring his nervous movements with interest. "Everything alright, Jake?"

"I dunno. I've got this bad feeling, that's all. It's probably nothing... You got any rum?"

Frank smiled and passed him the bottle he kept stashed under the radar. "What's the matter, run out of that Voormis rotgut you usually drink?"

"Nah, not quite, I just fancied a rum, you know, being at sea and all. It makes one go over all piratical." Jake glugged a good fingers-worth of the over-proofed spirit and handed it back to the Captain.

Frank took a gulp. "Ah, that hit the spot... I'm almost done checking the systems, it doesn't look like the storm did too much damage, I should be ready to raise the anchor soon."

Jake nodded and, suitably refreshed, rejoined Mickie and Max at the rail and gazed out to sea. The gentle salty breeze aided the rum in his veins towards effecting his reinvigoration. It was a tremendous sight. All that water was remarkably humbling. It was good for Jake to be reminded just how small and insignificant he was in the grand scheme of things now and then. It kept his ego in check.

In the cab, Frank hummed an old sea-shanty as he flicked the switches on the console to power it up; he had shut everything down to avoid the instruments being fried by lightning during last night's storm. As the radar flickered into life, he fixed it with a puzzled expression. A huge blip appeared to be sitting directly under the boat. He tapped the instrument with a finger and, figuring that it must be a ghost signal, sighed and ran through the calibration sequence. Once the sequence was complete, Frank rebooted the radar. The blip was still there. Worse, it was moving.

"Get away from the water!"

As Frank bellowed his warning, a massive tentacle shot into the air and smashed into the deck. Thick, red, and lined with suckers the size of dinner plates, the rope-like appendage quested on the deck, searching for a tasty morsel. Each sucker concealed a vicious barb that tore at the deck, screeching and sending sparks into the air. Jake winced; this din was the last thing his compound hangover of seven years needed.

"Holy fuck, where the bloody hell did that come from?" Jake cried and he shoved Mickie out of danger as it thrashed in her direction. Jumping it as it twisted towards him, Jake drew his gun and fired. The boat lurched as the creature below squirmed in pain and the bullets ripped fist-sized holes in the sinister cephalopod's rubbery skin.

Annoyed rather than deterred, the creature sent another tentacle springing from the starboard side. It swiped back and forth, desperately groping for a snack. This time, Max also opened fire, but the tentacles were flailing too quickly to target with any kind of accuracy. Both men's rounds flew wide and pinged off the hull creating a dangerous ricochet.

Seeing her companions' failure, Mickie scampered into the cab just as Frank was desperately trying to raise the anchor. "Weapon?" She yelped, nearly giving Frank a heart-attack.

Frank motioned to the rear of the room where Jake had dropped his arsenal. "Grab the flamethrower!"

Mickie did as instructed and secured the fuel tank to her back. She had never handled anything bigger than a shotgun before but how hard could it be? "How the buggery do I light the bloody thing?"

"Ignition switch is under the barrel. Feather the trigger and watch the temperature gauge. You go in the red, you explode, it's that simple. Got it?"

"Yeah." Mickie hit the ignition switch, and the pilot light jutted from a nozzle above the barrel like a welding torch. "I got it."

"One more thing, don't fire it into the wind whatever you do, you'll go up like a Voormis funeral pyre."

Mickie noted the warning, nodded, and left the cab. The boat continued to violently rock from side to side as the gargantuan beast hunted for Max and Jake. Mickie nearly lost her footing and had to grab the rail for support while the two men continued to fire. Only around one shot in twenty hit the target and when they did, they had little effect... It wouldn't be long before they were grabbed and eaten.

Seeing the imminent threat, Mickie pushed aside her fear of bursting into flames, screamed a warning and hosed the nearest tentacle down with burning liquid. It flailed wildly in the air before shooting into the water with a hiss that created a cloud of steam. The other tentacles followed, and the colossal cephalopod decided to try elsewhere for its feed.

"That was too close... What the fuck was that thing?" Mickie asked breathlessly.

"Giant squid," Jake said. "That wasn't even a big one. The Gillmen reckon that they are the spawn of some ancient aquatic god. Ask Frank, he can tell you all about the buggers. His people have several sea shanties about things like that. Anyway, thanks, Mickie. Without you, Max and I would be doing an impression of Jonah about now."

Max nodded appreciatively.

"I'm just amazed that I didn't set either of you on fire. I haven't a single clue what I'm doing with this thing." Mickie waved the flamethrower in their direction, making both of them squeak.

Wisely, Jake took it off her and extinguished the pilot. "You two should get back below deck while we're stationary; who knows what other things might come flopping out of the sea. I'll stay here and watch Frank's back while he tinkers."

Max and Mickie agreed and started to walk towards the deck hatch before pausing for one last look at the sea. Jake smiled and started towards the cab. He was almost there when Frank burst from the door throwing a harpoon-gun in his direction. "Sea-lurker incoming on the starboard side!"

Time appeared to slow as Jake caught the weapon, turned around, and spotted the evil blob landing on the deck mere feet from Mickie and Max. He had one shot. If he missed, they were dead.

"Not this time," he growled as he let the electrically charged harpoon fly.

The harpoon rocketed past Mickie and Max, narrowly avoiding Max's right buttock, and slammed into the amorphous beast. Electricity surged through the creature as it stopped dead in its tracks. Mickie and Max scuttled to safety and looked on as the monster burst like a tar-filled water-balloon.

Jake smiled. "Not this time."

Moments later, Frank yelled in triumph as the anchor started to be reeled in on its heavy cable. Soon after, they were moving too fast for any dangerous fauna to catch. Jake took a glug of booze and reloaded the harpoon. That had felt good, like he had finally gone some-ways towards exorcising one of his personal demons. He grabbed a mop and helped Max scrub splattered shoggoth innards off the hull as the boat sped on towards Australia.

CHAPTER VIII

GO WEST

APRIL 4ᵀᴴ 2132

AUSTRALIA — SURVIVOR CAMP WEST OF ALICE SPRINGS:

A harsh *crackle* followed by the '*coo*' of a drone that thought it was a bird burst from the tin speaker attached to its chassis as Dwayne pulled a confused expression.

The message continued with a woman talking to said drone. *"Pigeon, will you behave!"*

'Coo!'

"Good. Now. Here Goes."

Dwayne leaned in and listened.

"Hi Dwayne, you don't know me, but I'm here with Max and Jake. Mickie's the name and all this sun is ruining my pale complexion. By now, you should be well acquainted with pigeon so you should be hearing me loud and clear. If he's behaving himself, that is.

"We have arrived on the south coast and managed to find a place to weigh anchor that wasn't crawling with lurkers and giant mutated sharks. Seriously, how the hell did they get so damn big? Cricket, one of my pets, has scouted the area and discovered a small cove that appears to be inhabited by a tribe of cannibal bandits. Jake and Max have cooked up a hair-brained scheme to borrow a couple of their dune buggies. If all goes to plan, we will be in Alice Springs in a couple of days. If it doesn't go to plan, then we have probably been eaten and I'm probably sloshing around in a cannibal's stomach. In which case, make sure Pigeon goes to a good home.

"We received your last postcard and will find somewhere to hold

out until you arrive. Knowing Jake, just look for the nearest bar or fight pit. You know what he's like, I assume. Max is looking forward to seeing you and is behaving a bit like an overexcited puppy at the moment. He's currently running around on the beach playing fetch with Sniffer, it's moderately disturbing.

"Ben won't be joining us, I'm afraid. I'll explain when we meet. I look forward to meeting you, and hope all is well at your camp. Take care. Oh, I almost forgot, hold on to Pigeon until we meet. You can use him to send us any urgent messages or warnings. He can be a stroppy little bugger but just be firm with him. If you are weak, he will walk all over you. Adios!"

One final *crackle* announced that the message was over. Dwayne stood and patted pigeon on the head. "Okay little buddy, we'd better get the party ready to rock..."

APRIL 4ᵀᴴ 2132
AUSTRALIA – BETWEEN CEDUNA AND COOBER PEDY:

Mickie spat a disgusting concoction of sand and grit from her mouth and glared at Jake through her grime encrusted goggles. "I told you it would never work, you blithering idiot!"

Jake grinned as he wrestled with the steering wheel of the recently liberated buggy. "What's the problem, we got wheels, didn't we?"

A bullet pinged off the corrugated tin shield just below Mickie's head. "Yeah, and now we have half of South Australia's bandit population chasing us to prove it."

Max returned fire at the nearest pursuing buggy. Two crazed cannibals with antique revolvers clung to the roll cage and tried to get a bead on engine, tyre or flesh, they weren't fussy which. Max growled as the buggy jumped over a dune, the resultant jolt sending his shots wide. He too glared at Jake.

"Hey, I don't see what your problem is, it was your idea to use Mickie as bait! It isn't my fault her *pet* blew our cover."

Max shook his head and pointed at the road.

"Oh, you want me to keep it steady... Got it!"

Mickie glared at Jake once again. "Don't you dare blame Cricket. If it wasn't for him, we would all be on the barbecue by now!"

Max winged one of the gunmen, sending him tumbling off into the huge cloud of dust that followed in their wake. He reloaded and took aim again; this time his shot hit the front-left tyre. The buggy hopped and spun, wiping out a huge bandit on a rusty motorbike before both engines erupted, sending smoke and fire spiralling into the early evening sky.

"If he hadn't jumped out of your pocket and started zapping that huge guy with the cleaver then we would never have been spotted," Jake argued.

"Bollocks," Mickie grumbled between taking pot-shots at a buggy to their left. "They never bought it for a second. I mean, who actually walks into a cannibal camp shouting 'dinner time?' Only a bloody idiot, that's who!" Mickie fired again, this time catching the driver in the side of his head and showering the windshield with gore. The buggy sped onwards, and the gunners jumped off before it ploughed into a large rock and exploded.

"Nice shot!" Jake exclaimed.

"Thanks," Mickie huffed while replacing the magazine. "Try and keep this bloody thing steady, will you?"

"Noted."

Between bickering amongst themselves, the intrepid trio had managed to whittle a small convoy of murderous bandits down to just one buggy and two ancient motorcycles. They were close to the old opal mining town of Coober Pedy and were getting low on fuel. Jake hoped that they would manage to find some in the ruined town, but they needed to shake their hunters first.

"Mickie," Jake yelled above the roar of the engine. "Do you think you can hit the fuel tank of the tractor coming up on the right?"

"If you stop driving like a moron for a second, yes."

"Okay, blast it when we pass it."

"Will do."

Jake took the road through a rocky valley. It was narrow and the tractor was half-way across the road. Mickie wasn't sure that their half-drunk wheel-man could make the gap. As they neared fiery vehicular death, Mickie gritted her teeth and waited for oblivion. It never came. She was so shocked that she nearly forgot to shoot the tank.

"Now, Mickie, for fuck's sake!"

Her momentary lapse in concentration paid unexpected dividends. The tank blew just as the buggy drew near, causing a massive chain reaction that sent hunks of twisted metal hurtling into the air. The first motorbike was struck by some wreckage and the driver shot into the sky like a rocket. The second driver was even more unfortunate, a shard of jagged tin spun through the air and neatly sliced his head off his shoulders. Mickie whooped in delight as the huge fireball rose into the sky. Max got up from his firing stance and hugged her, a big grin on his weather-beaten face.

"Good shooting." Jake had to admit that she had made a pretty fantastic shot to hit the target at the breakneck speed they were going.

Mickie holstered her pistol and sat down in the passenger seat. "Thanks." She smiled. "You're still a pair of idiots though."

Jake laughed. "We survived, didn't we? Quit your grousing, anyway, we are nearly in Coober Pedy... Civilisation at last!" As he grinned like a buffoon, a loud *clunk* announced that something had gone awry with their purloined transport. "Damn it."

"Erm... what was that?" Mickie looked alarmed.

"Balls, the engine's out of juice. We'll have to buy or scavenge some in town." Jake freewheeled the now dead buggy off the road and brought it to a stop behind a large pile of rocks. Jumping from the driver's seat, he lifted the bonnet and yanked the spark-plugs out of the engine.

"That'll stop anyone nicking them, parts are scarce, it should be safe here until we get some fuel. We will have to walk the rest of the way, it shouldn't be far, though..."

Mickie stepped back onto the road and pointed at a bent and rusty road sign. "I'm not sure of the conversion to kilometres but I'm pretty sure that says Coober Pedy is three miles away... you twat!"

"Come on, Mick, three miles ain't so bad."

"It's not the distance I'm worried about, it's the blasted heat. Someone with skin as pale as mine isn't built for temperatures like this. It's a miracle that I haven't burst into flames already."

Jake chuckled. "You are kind of vampiric-looking. Look, it's almost sundown. I'm pretty sure the temperature will drop any moment now... Everything's cool." He grinned like all was right with the world and flashed her a double thumbs up. Ever since he'd killed the lurker on deck, Jake had been acting like an excitable teenager. It was such a change from his usual mixture of anger and sarcasm that it had thrown Mickie for a loop... She wasn't wholly convinced it was an improvement.

Max looked at Mickie and rolled his eyes.

Mickie planted her hands on her hips and shook her head. "I know, right?"

"Come on, guys, lighten up." Jake beamed as he started to walk down the dusty road. "Next stop, Coober Pedy!"

"I really wish you would learn not to open your big trap, Jake, you've only gone and bloody jinxed us!"

It was clear from the instant they took a look at the former mining colony, that Jake's promise of civilisation had been impressively wrong, and Mickie wasn't happy. Coober Pedy was a ghost town, and she was sunburnt, and her clothes soaked with sweat. Most of the tin structures and cave dwellings that made up the town were almost completely buried under rockslides or the constantly shifting sands while the roads were a hazardous nightmare of collapsed tunnels and potholes. Worst of all, the petrol station had exploded sometime in the distant past and was little more than a burned-out shell.

"Balls," Jake muttered to himself as he surveyed the wreckage.

Mickie shook her head and laughed in dismay. "Now what?"

Max clicked his fingers to get their attention then pointed to the end of town where some old mine machinery and vehicles sat abandoned next to some dilapidated buildings.

"Max is right." Jake shrugged. "We might find some juice and a jerry can amongst all the abandoned mine stuff."

Mickie put her large backpack on the floor, opened it, reached in and removed one of her pets. "I'll get Sniffer on the case." She smiled softly at the domesticated drone and whispered some instructions in one of his radar ears. Sniffer emitted a bark of static and went charging off towards the town. Jake gave Mickie the thumbs up and started to follow Sniffer.

Max indicated some of the old buildings and did drinking and eating mimes.

"Good plan, Max." Mickie nodded then called over to Jake. "I'm going to check out the town with Max, you stick with Sniffer!"

Jake waved in the affirmative and followed the excitable drone's trail as it led him down a sloping pathway next to a large valley that had been gouged out of the earth by heavy machinery. The sky was clear, the sun was finally setting, and he couldn't help but marvel at the wide expanse of starlit sky. It had been decades since he had seen stars without them being at least partly occluded by smog. He took a slug of booze from his flask and smiled. Australia's wide-open spaces were such a contrast to the overbuilt and gloomy Zone 51.

The entrance to the old opal mine sat under a large rocky outcrop. Across from the entrance, a large building that Jake assumed was worker barracks and offices cast a lengthy shadow over the excavations. An inspection revealed that the complex was still accessible as the sand had mostly fallen into the crevasse below. Sniffer charged towards the adjacent machinery and started to hop around excitedly.

"What have you found, boy?"

Sniffer ground his axel in his trademark yelping way, that had given Mickie the idea that he was a dog, Jake took it to mean that his sensors had picked up some diesel. He jogged over to a large digger and removed the fuel cap. The sharp aroma of diesel fumes made him grin.

"Well done, Sniffer!"

Jake rocked the vehicle using his powerfully augmented arms. His smile grew. It sounded like there was almost a full tank—all he needed now was something to syphon with and something to contain the liberated liquid.

"You stay here, Sniff, I'm going to check out the buildings. Keep an eye out for bandits. If you sense danger, come get me, okay?"

Yelp! Sniffer lowered his legs and backed under the back end of the digger. Once concealed, he extended his twin radar ears and commenced monitoring the area.

Jake approached the door to the mining complex and, with some force, ripped the door off its rusty hinges. After the thick red dust that it had kicked up settled, he stepped into what looked like an office area with a large desk sitting over towards the far corner. It looked like the place was abandoned in a hurry; the desk was covered in maps and notes next to an overflowing ashtray while a thick layer of rust coloured sand and dust sat over everything. He walked over to the desk and picked up the topmost sheet of paper and shook it clean. It was a time-sheet dated five years ago on Expiration Day. This confirmed his initial suspicions that he was standing in the admin office for the mine.

Giving the rest of the room a once-over, Jake noticed that the walls of the tin structure, lined with rows of hard-hats and lamps, were riddled with bullet holes. He zoomed in using his hi-tech sunglasses and noted that all the bullets were exit wounds, so to speak. Whoever had been shooting had been inside shooting out. A scan for metal revealed that the floor was covered in a carpet of spent shell casings and flattened bullets; the office had evidently been the site of one hell of a gunfight. Jake thought it had all the hallmarks of a last stand, a group of desperate miners fighting for their lives. Against *whom* or *what* was a mystery.

Moving around the far side of the desk, Jake cracked the lock and opened the drawer.

"Bingo!"

Sitting amongst a few family snapshots and other mementoes, was a two-thirds-full bottle of whiskey just sitting there smiling up at him invitingly. Jake gently smoothed the grime off the label and grinned. It was good stuff, distilled in the Free East from natural ingredients, he slipped it into his rucksack and moved into the worker barracks, his search for a container for the fuel continuing—there was no way in Hell he was pouring that away.

Orderly rows of lockers and bunkbeds lined the room. Outside, a low gibbous moon had risen, shining shafts of pale silver through the bullet holes. Dust-bunnies capered in the moonbeams, swirling and spinning in a dance macabre as Jake disturbed air that hadn't been disturbed for a very long time. He moved cautiously through the room stepping over the debris and piles of almost-disintegrated clothing that littered the floor. It looked like whatever had killed the miners had done so in that very room, but while the clothing suggested bodies, the bones had long since been removed by scavengers.

Slowly and methodically, Jake checked the footlockers at the side of the bunks and managed to score some more booze, a couple of packets of stale smokes, and a handful of small nuclear batteries that may prove useful in a pinch. He had yet to find what he was actually looking for but there was still a large store room to search. As he forced aside the heavy sliding door, Jake nearly lost his meagre lunch. A foul stench billowed forth from a gaping hole in the centre of the room. It took a minute and a nip of his hip flask to steady himself before entering.

Jake had never seen anything like the circular hole in the rock floor. It was massive and showed no sign of machine or tool marks. It was perfectly smooth and looked as though it had been melted by a ridiculously powerful laser. Jake picked up an old empty food can and dropped it down the hole. It was so deep that he never heard it hit the bottom.

Standing upright and engaging night vision, he scanned the room. He spotted a length of plastic hose that he could use to syphon fuel from the digger. Unfortunately, there was no jerry can, or any other kind of container and he steadfastly refused to tip away his stash until it was the absolute final resort. Jake cursed and stood with his hands on his hips. As luck would have it, at that moment, a stiff breeze rattled the loose walls of the structure causing something hanging on a hook to jangle.

"Ah, this could be a solution, right here." Sets of keys to all the mine machinery hung on the wall; Jake smiled, grabbed each set, and made his way back out of the building. With any luck, one of the old clunkers would work and he could drive it to the buggy and syphon directly into its tank. They would be in Alice Springs in no time at all.

At least, that's what he hoped.

Across town, Mickie pushed open the door of a dusty diner she and Max had discovered. Max entered first, pointing his AK-47 at the dark corners. Once he saw that it was bandit free, he allowed Mickie to enter.

"Okay, Max, I'll check behind the counter for any tinned goods that aren't so out of date that they'll kill us. You check the back, okay?"

Max nodded and pushed past the greasy tables to the kitchen area.

Mickie looked around at the faded posters on the wall. She had been born in Zone 51 and had never seen products that weren't GAF branded before; the kind of things they advertised made her head spin. She had never tasted ice-cream or other treats that the GAF didn't decree essential. All she had eaten for most of her life had been the grey protein bars that the GAF handed out as rations. Now, she fully appreciated why people were so keen to get out East back before the collapse. Now, Australia along with other island nations such as Zone 51 itself, were all that was left ... and they were all as deadly as one another.

A serving counter ran the length of the eastern side of the room. Mickie lifted the hatch at the far end and stepped behind. Like the mining outpost, this establishment had been the site of a fierce battle. Her footsteps crunched on a glinting carpet of spent casings and broken glass.

To her right, a cash register hung open with the cash still inside. She reached in, picked out a plastic note and looked in confusion at the face of a world leader she had never even heard of. One of the first things suppressed by the CEO back when he had formed The Imperial Corporation of America and Europe was knowledge of other countries. Nothing fuelled unrest quicker than knowing that someone somewhere was better off than you were. It was only now that she realised just how isolated they had really been. There turned out to be nothing of any use behind the counter except for a sharp knife that Mickie tucked into the side of her backpack. Giving up on her search, she crossed the diner to go and give Max a hand.

Max had found some canned beans and other long-life goods and had bundled stacks of them in his arms and was now heading back to the main room when Mickie came crashing through the door. Max yelped and dropped his cargo in alarm. The pile of tins hit the floor, causing a terrible racket. As Mickie chuckled and tried to apologise, the door of a long-defunct walk-in fridge sprung open and a crazed-looking middle-aged man brandishing a shotgun burst out.

"No," the stranger bellowed and whispered at the same time in a disturbing rasp. "Shut up, shut up, shut up!" He levelled the gun at Max. "Don't make another sound."

The mute enforcer smiled inwardly at the irony of the man's demand and reluctantly raised his hands.

Mickie followed suit. "Easy, we're not here to—"

"Hush," the wild-eyed man cut her off. His hair was filthy and unkempt and his clothes were one more rip away from being rags. He rushed forward, waving the shotgun, making a shushing noise. Mickie looked like a startled rabbit as he got right up in her face and demanded, "Put your finger on your lips."

Mickie's expression changed to one of confusion. "How can I put a finger on my lips when my hands are up?"

"Don't be smart with me, you Pommie bitch, just do it."

Mickie complied. The man looked at Max and nodded emphatically. Max also complied, despite the futility of the action. Seeing their obedience, the agitated man hopped excitedly

"What to do? What to do?" he muttered under his breath. "I'll have to get *rid* of you. Too many people means too much noise. Too much noise means death." He made a strange noise in the back of his throat that made Mickie miss Sniffer. Mickie looked at Max and tried to formulate a plan using only her eyes.

The man noticed. "Stop it. Stop it. No movement, no noise. You've probably killed me already, I should just shoot you, hide and hope *it* thinks that it was just the two of you." A disturbingly manic grin spread across his face. "That's good, that'll work... I'll just kill you, that solves the problem." He raised the gun and aimed at Max.

Chirrup!

Before the man could pull the trigger, Cricket hopped out of Mickie's top pocket, aimed his laser and blasted the crazy man in the right hand. Flesh seared and sizzled while the man cried silently in pain and shook his hand around in the air. While his finger was off the trigger, Max took one step forward, snatched the gun out of his other hand and put it against his temple.

"Okay, you crazy bastard, start talking," Mickie demanded in hushed tones. "What happens if we make too much noise? And no funny business or Cricket here will blast your fingers off one-by-one. His laser is much quieter than a shotgun, so I think we can get away with using a little bit of *persuasion*."

The man nodded frantically. "Noise brings the burrowers, the burrowers bring death, simple."

Mickie cocked an eyebrow. "Burrowers?"

"The burrowers beneath... Dholes. They were once trapped deep under the rock, but some crazy bastard cult bugger removed the Mnar stones and let them loose. I was a miner, I was here when they got free. The buggers came out of the frikkin' ground and killed everyone. I managed to get away and I discovered that they hunt by sound, so I've been quiet ever since ... for five years, until you bloody drongoes came along and ruined everything. Stupid people get lured here all the time and fed to those monsters as sacrifices but none of them has ever survived long enough to find me before."

"Lured? Lured, by who?" Mickie interjected.

"The bloody bandits, of course. Jeez, I'd thought that would be bloody obvious by now, even to a fucking dickwad like you."

Max snarled in the man's ear, making him whimper and Mickie grin.

"I'll pretend I didn't hear that... So, what you're telling me is that those crazy cannibals are sacrificing people to the Dholes?"

"That's about the size of it, yeah." The man grinned, revealing a lone yellow tooth. "If they are well-fed, they don't go hunting near their camps. Simple, really. They herd people to Coober Pedy because it's a mating ground or something. They drive people in then make a bloody racket to wake them up. Then..." He shuddered violently.

"We need to get the hell out of here," Mickie said to Max. "Here." She passed him her rucksack. "Put the cans in there."

Max motioned at the man with a questioning look.

"Leave him, he'll be no bother. Cricket will make sure of that, won't you, Cricket?"

Chirrup

Max let the man go and started to fill the bag.

"Yeah." The man bounced excitedly. "Just go, get out of here. Leave me in peace."

"You could come with us?" Mickie offered. Max shot her a cocked eyebrow.

"What?" The man giggled insanely. "Me, go out there, you must be bloody joking?"

Mickie sighed and shrugged her shoulders; at least she had tried. She mentally ticked it off as her good deed of the day. "Fine.

Stay here if you want."

"Thanks, miss." The man softened. "But there ain't enough bottled water to get you five miles away."

This strange sentence puzzled Mickie. "Bottled water?"

"Yeah, the buggers hate water, it hurts them like mad."

Mickie scanned the room and spotted two crates of long-out-of-date, bottled water. "Max, pass me the bag. Can you carry that water over there?"

Max nodded.

"Good, let's get Jake and Sniffer then get the hell out of here." As she turned towards the door, Mickie was halted by a low rumble building up from somewhere else in town. "Um ... what the fuck is that?"

"Hell-fire, they're coming," the unhinged local shouted as he bolted across the room. Leaping back into his hiding place, he slammed the insulated fridge door closed behind him. The reason that he lived in a fridge suddenly became clear to Mickie, insulation equals sound-proofing.

"What the hell is that noise, Max?"

Max shrugged in reply.

They both thought for a second, then the penny dropped. "Jake..."

"Come on, Sniffer, climb aboard." The drone hopped into Jake's hands. He scooped him up and placed him on the shotgun seat. He had spent the past fifteen minutes checking the engine over, blowing dust and sand off the spark plugs and, in theory, the digger should move. All he had to do was fire up the engine, pick up Max and Mickie, then drive over to the buggy and transfer the fuel. Easy street.

"Hold onto the seat, little buddy, this might be a bumpy ride." Turning the key in the ignition brought the engine coughing and wheezing into life. Jake whooped in triumph and put the lumbering digger into gear. The enormous caterpillar tracks of the yellow and black striped machine rattled and clanked as it began to traverse the rocky surface of the hewn-out mine track. For a digger, it had a fairly good top speed and for a blissful moment Jake was in his element, on the road with the wind in his hair... It wouldn't last. Almost instantly, something set the rat of unease gnawing in his lower intestine.

"Did you feel that, Sniff?" Even above the vibration of the engine, Jake could feel the ground shake.

Sniffer made a noise akin to a dog's whine.

"I imagine it's nothing. Probably just an earthquake, it'll soon pass." His attempts to reassure Mickie's pet failed; the pseudo-creature continued to make a high-pitched noise that set his teeth on edge. "Dammit, I think you're right, boy, I've never felt an earthquake quite like this. For a start, it seems weirdly focussed on the hill towards the town and secondly, it seems to be coming right towards us."

Jake just happened to glance in the rear-view mirror just as the mine building he had recently explored collapsed like a house of cards, as though *something* had ploughed under it and taken out its foundations. The clatter of metal was deafening as Jake swore, gripped the wheel and slammed his foot down on the accelerator. One more glance in the mirror nearly made his heart stop. A huge creature that looked like the grotesque love child of a giant squid and an earthworm burst from the ground under the collapsed structure and flattened the debris. The ground shook as the monstrous creature slammed into the floor in a devastating belly flop, its huge maw opening to reveal several rope-like tentacles tipped with lamprey-like jaws. The teeth opened and closed, dilating like a camera shutter, as they tasted the air for their prey that was currently halfway up the slope, trundling towards downtown Coober Pedy.

"Hold on Sniffer, this is going to get a little rough," Jake hissed through gritted teeth and shifted all of his body weight onto the accelerator.

Locating their scent, the burrowing abomination let out a piercing shriek that rattled Jake's fillings before rearing back on its enormous girth and springing into the air. With disturbing agility, it dived into the ground, slicing through the rock like a knife through butter. The ground steamed and boiled in its wake as it melted itself a path and began to speed towards the fleeing digger. The road behind them billowed and cracked as the beast thundered along at a tremendous pace. Jake peered at the mirror in horror as the bulge in the rock grew closer and closer. He drew his gun and prepared to blast the beast, though he held out little hope that it would have any discernible effect. Sniffer must have had the same idea as he clamped his legs to the metal cab and readied his head-mounted laser.

Rock and sand showered the digger as the monster burst from the ground and into the air like a dolphin leaping the waves. Due to the sloping terrain, it landed awkwardly giving Jake precious seconds to weave away from its thrashing tentacles. It quickly righted itself and surged forwards, shooting out a tentacle that forced Jake to break for impact. The heavy vehicle rocked as it connected. Sniffer zapped the appendage, but it had no effect. Praying he would fare a little better, Jake swivelled in his seat and let rip with a succession of shots, the high-powered slugs slammed into the creature's rugose flesh, tearing it in two. Screeching in agony, the creature withdrew the remaining half, leaving the mouth embedded in the metal where it sizzled as the metal started to liquefy. Sniffer blasted it several times as Jake returned his attention to the road, it finally fell away.

Upon reaching the steep bend leading to the town, it looked like it was game over. The Dhole was simply too fast to outrun in such a lumbering vehicle. As Jake eased up on the throttle to take the bend without capsizing their ride, the creature reared back on its bulk once more and prepared to dive into them.

"Ah well," Jake drawled, doing his best to sound nonchalant. "Nice knowing you, Sniffer."

Just as the beast prepared to strike, a crate of bottled water sailed through the air, landing in the monster's open maw. Jake nearly crashed as he looked up to see Max standing on the ridge above silhouetted by the moon. In the next heartbeat, Max aimed his AK-47 and let rip. As his bullets popped the bottles, the creature shrieked and twisted in agony, its body bubbling as the water boiled upon impact with its corrosive mucus. Max smiled as thick plumes of steam billowed from its tentacle mouths. Finally, it slammed itself underground once more and retreated towards the mine.

Jake could have kissed Max at that moment. He honestly couldn't believe that he was still alive; in a lifetime of close shaves, that had to be the closest. He brought the digger to a halt and jumped down from the cab.

Mickie raced towards him with her arms outstretched. "Thank god you are alright!"

Jake braced himself for the incoming hug, but it never happened. He watched in confusion as she ran straight past him and gathered Sniffer in her arms.

"Oh, Sniffer, I thought I'd lost you."

Max chuckled to himself, wandered over to the crestfallen bounty hunter and gave him a big sweaty man-hug.

"Thanks, Max." Jake grimaced as his ribs cracked. Once released, he turned to Mickie "What the hell just happened? I thought I was worm food for sure."

"We met some loony that lives in a fridge, and he told us that those Dhole things hate water." This answer raised many more questions than it answered but Mickie cut him off before he could ask them. "We need to get out of here, fast, there could be more of them lurking around the place and I don't think that one will take long to recover. Did you find fuel?"

"You're leaning on it." Jake pointed at the digger and waggled the length of hose in her face. "We'll have to syphon vehicle to vehicle, there weren't any cans."

"Shit," Mickie muttered. "Okay, let's do it fast."

There was a silent agreement as they climbed aboard the digger. Jake sparked the engine and drove them out towards the concealed buggy.

As unimpressed as Mickie had been at their mode of transport, clinging to a filthy digger, she was grateful that she hadn't been forced to hike the three miles back to the buggy. She, Max, and Sniffer had watched the roads while Jake transferred the fuel. Soon, the tank was full, the spark plugs had been replaced, and they were ready to depart.

"Can we get out of here without going through the town?" Mickie asked.

Jake used the zoom on his aviators to get a better look at the situation. The banks around the road were far too steep and the road behind them was blocked by smouldering wreckage from their earlier bout of vehicular combat.

"Nope, I'm afraid not."

"Crap."

A *chirrup* announced that Cricket had returned from his scouting. He landed on the roof of the buggy, shot out his transfer cable and relayed to Jake's glasses a map of the area. Coober Pedy wasn't a large place and the road they were on took them out towards Alice Springs. All they had to do was speed through town as quickly as possible whilst trying not to collide with any debris, or worse, a Dhole.

"Thanks, Cricket, I think I got this covered now. If I stick to the main road, we are good. Max, get the bottles of water ready and lob them at anything that jumps out of the ground, okay?"

Max nodded and readied the knife that Mickie had snaffled from the diner. Aside from the water they had liberated from the diner, they had a couple of bottles stashed in the ration bag, but they weren't for throwing.

"Right, get in and hold on tight, this could get rough." Jake turned the key and slammed down the accelerator. The buggy jumped forward like a kangaroo and shot along the dusty road. The wheels slid on the powdery surface, but Jake managed to keep it under control. Mickie took a look at the diner and wondered what would happen to their crazed acquaintance as they sped past. In the end, she decided that she didn't much care. He was going to kill them, after all. Compassion was a two-way street, and he had gone down a cul-de-sac.

As the buggy rumbled and took the snaking bends with an ease the digger simply couldn't, Jake began to relax. The rugged scenery slipped by in a melange of reds and browns punctuated sporadically by clumps of vivid green. It was looking good until the rock wall to their immediate left exploded in a spray of molten rock... The Dhole had returned. Several of the monster's tentacles had melted down to twisted stumps that flailed ineffectively as it shot from the wall, barely missing the speeding buggy. Rolling several times before coming to a stop, it slid around and resumed chase, bolting after the vehicle as it shrieked in anger.

Max picked up a couple of bottles of water and readied the knife. When the burrower was in range, he slashed the plastic and hurled the bottles in its direction. Both connected, splashing the creature's leathery hide. Steam rose from the livid gashes that spread from where the water landed. Max winced; it brought back horrific memories of his tour of the correction centre during his enforcer training. The correction officers took great delight in whipping undesirable to within an inch of their lives. Again, the creature shrieked and writhed in pain but quickly recovered, shook it off, and resumed the hunt. Max lobbed another bottle giving them another moment's respite, but they couldn't keep this up; they had only six bottles of water left.

The words of the crazed man in the fridge echoed in Mickie's mind. "*There ain't enough bottled water to get you five miles away.*"

"Can't this bloody thing go any faster?" she yelled in panic.

Jake's knuckles must have turned white under his battered leather gloves as he gripped the steering wheel tight and attempted to concentrate. The road ahead was riddled with holes that were deep enough to tip the buggy if he connected with any of them. A litany of expletives tumbled out under his breath—it was hard enough driving on this road *without* a colossal tentacled worm in hot pursuit. Jake *really* didn't need any further distractions...

With a sprightly *chirrup,* Cricket hopped onto his shoulder, shot out his interface cable and indicated that he wanted to sync with Jake's glasses.

"What the hell is he doing now?"

"I think he wants to show you something ... here." Mickie leaned over and plugged Cricket's interface wire into the side of Jake's aviators.

"Argh! Cut it out, you silly little sod!" Jake cried as a momentary burst of static occluded his vision. The buggy swerved, bucked, and nearly rolled as Cricket chirruped apologetically and corrected the feed. In the top left corner of his vision, Cricket displayed an object that made Jake smile. "That might work, show me where it is, Cricket."

Cricket displayed a map highlighting the target and their

current position on the road in real-time.

"Excellent work, Cricket." Jake swung the buggy to the right. "Hold on to your arses, we are going off-road!"

Mickie squeaked as the buggy bounced over the raised curb at the side of the road and onto rocky terrain littered with limonite, rhyolite and marl discarded by opal prospectors of centuries passed. Mickie fumbled in her pocket for her goggles and snapped them over her eyes as clouds of red silica churned into the air. The beast had followed their course and had gone underground. By now, Max was down to his last two bottles of water so whatever Cricket had cooked up had better work or they were royally screwed.

"Where the hell are you going?" Mickie asked between spitting thick gobs of sand from her mouth.

"Over there." Jake pointed east and swung the buggy once again, heading straight for the target, a water tower.

"How the hell are we going to get the water out?"

"I was hoping that our *friend* will help us with that."

Mickie thought for a second then understood exactly what he meant. This wasn't good. Jake's driving was erratic, to put it mildly, and now he was going to try and weave through the legs of a rusty old water-tower.

"Oh, crap, you have got to be fucking kidding." She sighed in dismay then cradled her head in her hands.

"Oh, ye of little faith." Jake laughed and gunned the accelerator.

Max tossed the last of the bottles then turned to inform the others that the end was nigh. His eyes nearly popped out of his skull as he saw the water-tower looming overhead.

"Max!" Jake yelled. "Get down and hold on!"

Max didn't need telling twice, he dropped and clung on to the back of Mickie's seat for dear life as Jake swung the buggy through the Tower's front legs. The burrower was in grabbing distance by now and its enormous body crashed into the front legs before they were clear, smashing the concrete foundation and shearing the steel in two. With an ear-rending screech, the tower came crashing down on the monster just as they cleared the impact zone.

If the impact of the tower alone was enough to daze the creature, the hundreds of gallons of rust-tainted water it held were certainly enough to destroy it. The wave crashed on the creature's rear then rushed backwards in the crater caused by the impact, engulfing it entirely. Jake stopped the buggy at a safe distance and watched the monster boil away to thick soapy sludge. The stench was unbearable even from that distance as the water roiled and bubbled as the Dhole's skin peeled away in thick leathery strips.

"Nice one, Cricket," Jake said to the little drone as the dust settled around them.

Cricket *chirruped* contentedly and hopped into Mickie's outstretched hand.

"Well done, Jake," Mickie said as she tucked Cricket back into her pocket. "I honestly thought you were going to kill us there. I'm happy to be proved wrong for a change."

Max gave them both the thumbs up and climbed back on the buggy. Mickie followed his example and made herself comfortable while Jake took a well-earned glug from his flask, finishing off the rough spirit within. He refilled it with the good stuff that he had found in the mine building before again starting the engine.

"Okay, folks... next stop, Alice Springs!"

CHAPTER IX

KIND HEARTS AND CANE TOADS

APRIL 6TH 2132
AUSTRALIA — ALICE SPRINGS:

Dwayne arrived in Alice Springs just after midnight, stepped out of his battered and filthy jeep and shook the cramp that had been gnawing at him for the past two miles from his right calf. The town was alive with activity, but nobody was paying attention to his curious little dance. This was the last bastion of the free people of Australia and they were partying like it was the end-of-days. In many ways, it was. There were other pockets of civilisation here and there, sure, but most of the towns and cities had been taken over by whacked-out fanatics, cannibal tribes, bandits and *worse*. A heavily armed man in full riot gear approached and gave him the once over. Dwayne smiled and showed that his arms were free of sigils, runes or parasites. Satisfied, the guard resumed his patrol of the perimeter.

A cooing sound from the passenger seat announced that Mickie's pet drone, Pigeon, wanted to be unbound from the seatbelt. Dwayne had securely strapped the boisterous robot down to stop him getting bounced around during the trip, and to stop Pigeon bouncing around excitedly and distracting him. Pigeon hopped onto his muscular arm as he untied the belt. Dwayne pulled him out of the window and let him hop onto the bonnet of the jeep.

"Okay, little fellow. We're here." Dwayne felt moderately daft for talking to a drone. "They should be here by now."

Coo

"Yeah, yeah, you can go and find Mickie, just don't crash into anyone. I'll head over to the market where the bars are. If I know Jake, he'll be drunk as a skunk in one of them by now."

Pigeon cooed happily and took flight. Dwayne watched him soar over the large metal wall and into Alice Springs. He lit a smoke about the width of a matchstick and reminded himself to get some tobacco at some point, the vendors here could get hold of pretty much anything you wanted. There had been no law in Australia since Expiration Day when the Prime Minister and most of the parliament had been flattened in Canberra by a colossal cargo drone in free-fall, so there was no limit to what you could acquire. Alice Springs was definitely Dwayne's kind of town.

Walled by twenty-foot-high sheets of rusting metal and razor-wire and served by several armed guard towers that scanned the perimeter with searchlights, Alice Springs was secured against bandit raids. Ambling towards the gate, Dwayne checked his pistol was loaded; unfortunately, the freedom of the east meant that other people were free to do as *they* wish as well, not just him, and a lot of people in this unforgiving world harboured evil intentions. In this regard, the security was a double-edged sword, while it kept threats out, it also kept them in.

After another parasite check, the large gates creaked open onto a bustling thoroughfare lined with food vendors, pushers and prostitutes. A man like Dwayne—tall, muscular and rugged—always attracted the attention of the ladies of the night. He was propositioned before he even got inside. Normally, Dwayne may have taken advantage of the opals in his pocket, the lady in question was alluring after all, but tonight was all about business, not pleasure.

Once a state-of-the-art shopping precinct in the heart of the small town, the main drag of Alice Springs was cluttered with makeshift stalls, shops, and dwellings. Repurposed shipping containers with scaffold and tarpaulin awnings sat higgledy-piggledy in front of the traditional concrete and steel units jostling for space and attention. Blazing neon and flickering digital images shone through a film of grease and smoke giving the streets a gauzy look that enhanced the feeling of unwholesomeness while people of every country, race, and species buzzed about their often-questionable routines. It all happened here, a gentrified Ghoul barbecued questionable meat opposite a Voormi fixing a motorbike while two men and their pet kangaroo bagged up magic mushrooms for the discerning hedonist. In short, it was a free-for-all.

Dwayne pushed his way through the crowd and headed for the central area where all the bars, casinos and fight clubs were located. A glance in the sky indicated that he was on the right track as he spotted Pigeon doing a strange kind of happy-dance and diving towards what he assumed was Mickie. He smiled; it was nice to see Pigeon happy, he had grown fond of the little drone. Never in his wildest dreams did he think that a robot could have such personality. He was looking forward to meeting its owner.

"Oh bloody hell, Max. Have you seen the size of that Voormi he's going to fight?" Mickie was concerned. Jake, true to form, had drunk a skin-full in a ridiculously short time and entered into an unarmed combat tournament.

In the heart of the market district, The Star of Commoriom was Jake Baker's kind of watering hole. Voormi run and serving the strongest drinks in town, it was a haven for the hedonistic and embittered. Composed of three tiers of scaffold and wood around a central pit, the interior was bathed in a neon glow, punctuated by flickering flames from wall-mounted gas torches. A pumping soundtrack of mechanised beats and jagged guitar provided the soundtrack that the leather-clad dancers in suspended cages gyrated along to while punters below drooled and leered.

Mickie face-palmed as Jake and his opponent shook hands and began circling one another. They were low on things to trade, and they badly needed to replenish supplies of water and rations for the next leg of the journey, so Jake had dragged them in there announcing that he had it covered. To him, It was a no-brainer, win a few fights, rake in the opals then hit the traders. He had won his first two fights against scrawny, desperate locals without so much as breaking a sweat and had been paid accordingly. There was no need for him to enter a higher tier fight, but Jake would be Jake.

"Max, you *have* to do something, he's going to get himself killed!"

Max shrugged. What could he do? Jake had always had a death wish for as long as he had known him and if he wanted to get tossed around by a brawny Voormi, who could stop him?

Coo!

"Pigeon!" Mickie's face lit up as her pet came swooping down and landed on her shoulder. "Oh, I've missed you."

Coo!

"Is Dwayne with you?"

Coo! Pigeon's affirmative response meant that it was time for Max's face to light up. He had missed Dwayne. The two men had been like brothers before Dwayne escaped Zone 51 during the collapse.

"Max, how's it going, man?" the unmistakable Trinidad via Zone 51's midlands accent of Dwayne sang out over the throng.

Max beamed as he spotted his old buddy. The two men embraced and grinned at one another. Mickie chuckled to herself and rolled her eyes but found the bromance touching all the same.

"How's it going, bud?" Dwayne asked.

Max shrugged.

"Same shit different year in Zone 51 then, eh?"

Max nodded.

"And *you* must be Mickie?"

"In the sunburnt flesh. Thanks for looking after Pigeon for me... He seems to like you."

"Yeah, I must admit, the little fella has grown on me." Dwayne reached over and tickled pigeon behind the sensor. "Where's Jake? I thought the old reprobate was with you?"

Mickie sighed a long-suffering sigh and pointed down towards the central fight pit.

Dwayne turned to the octagonal cage ringed in barbed wire just in time to see a large umber-furred fist smash into the side of Jake's head. Dwayne shook his head and sighed. "Some things never change. I see he is still dealing with his emotional baggage through self-harm by proxy."

Mickie and Max both nodded slowly like a pair of synchronised bobble-heads.

"Look at the size of that Voormi, the daft sod doesn't stand a chance," said Mickie, worry etched on her face.

Dwayne rubbed his chin as Jake started to make a comeback and punched the brute in the gut, doubling him over. "I wouldn't be so sure. He can hold his own for a short time with Muggo'sutha back in the Zone. By comparison, this guy's a pussycat. A very large and angry pussycat, granted, but a pussycat all the same."

As Jake slammed his knee into the dazed Voormi's face, his opponent's body snapped backwards, momentum slamming him flat on his furry back. The rabid crowd started the ten-count and Jake held his arms in the air as the crowd roared. His face was a crimson mask from a split eyebrow. As he took in the adulation, he spotted Dwayne and gave him a double thumbs up. Blood ran through his teeth as he flashed a dopey grin.

The Voormi was out. The crowd counted to ten and the horn sounded. As the compere announced the victor, Dwayne turned to Mickie and smiled. "See, he doesn't *always* lose, he just makes a bloody annoying habit of it."

Mickie chuckled and pushed her way to the bar with a fistful of opals from one of his earlier victories. Jake had taken one hell of a pounding and was going to need a stiff drink. She looked at the blood pouring down his face and checked that she had her sewing kit in her backpack. *She* was going to need a stiff drink to steady her hands for the medical procedure ahead. She flashed four fingers at the barman when he gazed sullenly in her direction.

"Dwayne," Jake bellowed drunkenly as he fought his way through his adoring fans. "How's it going, you old bugger?" He staggered up to Dwayne and embraced him, sweat and blood staining Dwayne's khaki shirt.

"Hey, Jake, good to see you, man. Makes a change for you to win, doesn't it?"

Jake swayed and grabbed a railing for support. "Cheeky sod, Muggs has been giving me some tips for fighting Voormis."

Mickie returned with a round of drinks and dished them out to many thanks. She handed her drink to Max and wandered off, returning a minute later with a chair.

"You" —she pointed at Jake then jabbed her finger at the chair— "sit."

Jake did as he was told, grinning like an imbecile, his eyes rolling.

"Hip flask. Gimmie." Mickie demanded, palm outstretched, fingers beckoning.

"Nah, it's good stuff, you can't waste it."

"Okay, it's either that or the drink I just gave you and that is Voormis grade spirit. Your choice."

Jake meekly handed her the flask and took a dram of the paint-stripper he had just been handed. She doused a rag in the potent liquid and handed it to Max. "Nurse, do the honours."

Max grinned and started to enthusiastically clean the wound. Jake growled as the whiskey burned. When he was done, Mickie got to work stitching the wound. She was a well-practised seamstress, and her augmented fingers made it a doddle.

Dwayne was impressed. "Man, where were you when I was bleeding back in the zone?" He smiled while unconsciously scratching a thick scar on his jaw.

Mickie thought for a second. "In the DDC, most likely, locked up tighter than a nun's virtue." She tied off the stitching and patted Jake on the head. "There, all sorted."

Jake thanked Mickie in drunken growls and tried to stand up ... he failed, his backside went south at warp speed, and he crumpled into a heap and immediately began snoring. After finishing their drinks, Max indicated for Dwayne to grab a hold of his legs. Between them, they hauled the unconscious bounty hunter out to the jeep while Mickie went shopping for supplies.

"Just like old times eh, Max?" Dwayne wheezed as they struggled with their burden.

Max smiled and shook his head in despair.

APRIL 7ᵀᴴ 2132
AUSTRALIA — THE GREAT SANDY DESERT:

Jake's eyes opened slowly, the gallons of alcohol in his guts sloshed violently as Dwayne swung the jeep through a makeshift gate and into camp. He had slept the entire journey from Alice Springs into the Great Sandy Desert and now he felt terrible, the heat was stifling, and his face hurt. He hadn't intended on drinking that much and he certainly hadn't intended on getting in the octagon but this is how it often went. A couple of pints often turned into a couple of gallons. He groaned and put his aviators on, alerting Dwayne to his being awake.

"Ah, morning, sleeping beauty, how's your head?" Dwayne grinned. He spoke in an extra loud manner to get a modicum of revenge for having to hear Jake snore for hours.

"Sod off, Dwayne," Jake grumbled and tried, unsuccessfully, to sit up. "Are we there yet?"

"Indeed we are." Dwayne swung the vehicle around to the side of the small encampment and brought it to a halt.

Jake fell out of the door and proceeded to vomit in the sand. Through his bleary eyes, he noticed a striking, muscular young woman dressed like a warrior queen watching him. He forced a daft grin and shot her a double thumbs-up, she tutted in disapproval and wandered away. Dwayne came around the side of the jeep and handed Jake a bottle of water and two tablets.

"What's this?" Jake asked.

"Aspirin. Mickie picked some up at the market, she reckoned you'd need 'em."

"I reckon she's right." Jake placed the tablets on his tongue then sloshed them back with tepid water. "She's a good mate. How did I get in the jeep?"

"You have me and Max to thank for that."

"Thanks."

At that moment, the buggy driven by Max pulled alongside the jeep.

"Morning, Jake," Mickie boomed as she hopped out of the

shotgun seat. "How's the hangover!"

Every syllable landing like a hammer blow, Jake groaned and shook his head to indicate that it was far from good.

"Well, I'd like to give you sympathy but the fact that you have nobody to blame but yourself kind of puts me in an awkward position." Mickie grinned and started to poke Jake in the ribs making him wince and grimace. Once she had tormented him sufficiently, she turned to Dwayne. "Nice place you have here, it's got an early twenty-first redneck-retro-survivalist vibe going on that I can kind of appreciate."

As he didn't know Mickie that well, Dwayne wasn't sure if she was being serious or cutting him with her well-honed sword of sarcasm. "You want the tour?"

"Lead on, Commandant!"

Dwayne chose to ignore her obviously mocking salute and led them inside. The camp consisted of a cluster of ex-army tents around the end of the murky DeGrey River. A makeshift fence tacked together out of metal sheets, old fencing, and barbed wire encircled the camp and was patrolled around the clock by nervous local men with itchy trigger-fingers. Mickie and Max followed Dwayne over towards an open-fronted tent facing the centre of the camp. In this rough square, men, women and children worked building fires, cooking meals and cleaning guns.

In the tent, three men stood around a table embroiled in a heated discussion whilst jabbing their fingers at a map. Max recognised one of the men; he had met him briefly once before and had aided his escape from the Zone, Sam. He was currently arguing with an Australian man and a Torres Strait Islander about the best way to travel to the site of the buried city under the sands. Sam's advanced years had forced him to take a more administrative role in the fight against the Old Ones, but he had lost none of his fire.

"Look, Bruce," he said to the muscular Australian. "I ain't sayin' we shouldn't be cautious. I'm sayin' that the longer we wait, the more chance we have of being attacked."

"I get that, mate," Bruce replied. "But if we are attacked out in the open then we are dead. We don't have the man-power or guns to fend off whatever might be lurking out there."

The islander, Brent, stroked his impressive beard and shook his head. "I'm with Sam, I'm afraid. I think the time to move is now. Sorry, Bruce." He looked around just in time to see the trio approach. "Here's Dwayne, let's see what he has to say about it."

Dwayne put his bag of supplies in the corner and eyed the men gathered around the map. "What's the problem?"

Bruce sighed. "These two drongos want to go charging off to the city of Pnakotus without a bloody plan, we have no idea what's waiting for us out there."

"Um... Pnakotus?" Mickie called from the tent flap, startling the embittered trio.

"The city under the sand, built by the Yithian race," Dwayne explained. "The notes Ben gave me called it Pnakotus."

"Got it, thanks."

Dwayne looked at the map, mentally plotting an approach. "We can easily take this route here."

"But we don't even know if the route is safe; what if there are burrowers out there?" Bruce had panic in his voice as he spoke, his handsome bronzed features contorted in anxiety. "If we get caught out in the open, we're dead meat."

"Look, we don't have time to scout it out," Dwayne persisted. "It would take days. We will just have to trust that Mnar stones buried by the Yith are keeping the burrowers at bay."

Mickie coughed to get the men's attention, all eyes turned and scrutinised her.

"This is Mickie, from Zone 51. The big lump next to her is Max and the wreck vomiting in a bucket outside is Jake."

"Max, I know." Sam smiled. "Good to see you again, friend. I never did get a chance to thank you for saving my arse on the dock. Thanks."

Max acknowledged the kind words with a warm smile.

Once everyone knew who everyone was, Mickie spoke. "I know a way we could scout it out quickly." She took her bag off her shoulder and pulled out a drone making a bird-like cooing noise.

"That's it," Dwayne blurted happily, "we can send Pigeon. Can he do thermal scans? The burrowers give off a lot of heat."

"He can indeed. Can't you, Pigeon?"

Coo!

"Then it's settled," Sam announced. "We will wait for Mickie's, um... *pet?*"

Mickie nodded.

"Mickie's pet can check the route, then we move out as soon as we know it's safe. Gentlemen, get some rest, it's going to be a bitch of a day tomorrow." Sam gathered up the maps, handed them to Mickie and left the tent along with Brent and Bruce.

Dwayne offered to show Mickie and Max around the camp. After their brief tour, Dwayne led them to a central area around a large cooking fire. Jake was sitting on a stump eating some stewed vegetables and kangaroo rump. A little colour had returned to his cheeks and his tremors had subsided.

"Hey, Dwayne," Jake said with a mouthful of marsupial. "This stuff is really good. Compliments to the chef."

"Yeah, Johanna has become somewhat famous for her cooking."

Max looked over to the cooking area and waved at Johanna.

"Max! Great to see you." Johanna beamed as she came bounding over and gave him a big hug. "Thank you for helping us escape. Life has been better out here. Equally dangerous, but better."

Max smiled.

"Johanna," Dwayn said. "These are Max's friends Mickie and Jake."

"Jake, I met earlier when he came for a feed." She turned to Mickie. "Welcome to Australia! Can I get you some stew?"

Mickie gladly accepted and awaited the steaming bowl which Johanna promptly delivered before returning to her duties. Once settled, Mickie took Pigeon and Sniffer out of the bag and told Sniffer to go and play. "Okay, Pigeon." She unfolded a map of the desert and pointed out their location. "We are going to be going from here to here on this route." She traced the trail with her black-nailed finger. "I need you to make sure it is safe, okay?"

Coo!

"Good boy. Send any information to Cricket so he can keep us posted of your findings, okay?"

Coo!

Mickie patted him on the head, and he rose into the air and went on his way. With any luck, he should be back by nightfall. Just as she was starting to relax and tuck into her stew, Mickie heard a clunk and spun around just in time to see the warrior woman kick Sniffer with the toe of her boot. She put the bowl down, stood up, and stormed over.

"Hey, cut that out!"

The woman squared up to Mickie. "Your stupid pieces of junk are going to get us all killed."

"No," Mickie responded harshly. "What would get us all killed is going off half-cocked with no intel."

The woman spat on the ground, inches from Sniffer.

Mickie bristled. "Don't!"

"What are you going to do about it, bitch?" The warrior smirked and pushed Mickie.

Dwayne started to rise to put a stop to the escalating argument, but Max placed a hand on his shoulder, smiled, and shook his head. Dwayne thought Max had gone mad. The two women were totally mismatched. One was a muscular bronzed warrior in animal hides and body armour, the other a pale, slender woman in a corset top, jeans, and army boots. Time slowed to a crawl.

The woman started to open her mouth for another insult, but the words were stopped dead by Mickie's cybernetically augmented fist slamming into her jaw. Her knees buckled and, in an instant, she was on her posterior looking up in bewilderment at the diminutive woman that had just floored her.

"When you have quite finished playing alpha-bitch I have a drone to talk to." Mickie smirked before walking back to Max and Jake with Sniffer following close behind. Once back at her seat, she resumed sitting and started to instruct Cricket to pick up Pigeon's transmissions like nothing had happened. If Dwayne wasn't already impressed by Mickie, he was now.

Max, ever the gentleman, got up from his seat and helped the dazed woman to her feet. It was only then that recognition dawned. The angry young woman who looked like she had stepped out of a comic book from the Twentieth was none other than Jane, the sweet little girl he had helped escape the Zone. His mouth fell agape at the transformation.

Jane rubbed her jaw and stormed off towards the nearest tent.

Max looked at Dwayne with wide, questioning eyes.

"I know," Dwayne began, "quite the change, eh? Yeah, Jane kind of went feral once we got out here and hooked up with some meathead wannabe bandit who we nicknamed Tarzan." He looked at the vacant eyes of Jake. "Tarzan and Jane, geddit?"

Jake shrugged.

"Bugger me, Jake. Did you never browse the archive channel back in The Zone? It was the only thing worth watching. Everything made after the mid Twenty-First was propaganda bullshit!"

Again, Jake shrugged.

Dwayne rolled his eyes. "Anyway, the guy was a first-class dick, but Jane was besotted with him. Inevitably, he ended up dead; tried to rob a bunch of Voormis, they literally pulled his arms off. She came back to us with her tail between her legs and has been a royal pain in the arse ever since."

"Poor mixed-up kid," said Jake.

"I know, right? She has been fucked in the head ever since her parents went missing presumed lurker food back in the zone." He clenched his fist and grimaced. "If I ever see that whistle-blowing scumbag, Oliver, again, I'm going to fuckin' kill him."

Jake shot Mickie a furtive look and covertly put his finger to his puckered lips. He had no intention of telling Dwayne that the source of his ire was currently back in the antique shop babysitting his pet cockroach and a couple of whacked-out chip-heads. That was a problem for another day, preferably one when his head didn't feel like it had a tap-dancing elephant living in it.

Johanna joined the four after finishing the evening meal and they talked as the burnt-orange sun set. After a couple of drinks, the group retired to a large storm-haven-style tent and bedded down for a well-needed rest.

Chirrup-chirrup-chirrup! Chirr-up! Chirr-up! Chirr-up! Chir-rup-chirrup-chirrup!

The Morse-code for danger jolted Mickie from her slumber. As she wrestled with the sleeping bag, Cricket hopped onto her chest. The little fellow was frantic.

"What's wrong, Cricket?" she said groggily.

Cricket shot out his interface cable and bounced agitatedly. Mickie reached out and poked Jake in the side of the head.

"Eh? ... What? ... Was I snoring?"

"Glasses, quick!"

Jake sat up like he'd been zapped with a couple of thousand volts, fished his aviators out of his pocket and put them on. Cricket hopped onto his shoulder and plugged in. After a couple of seconds, Jake reached for his gun. "Holy shit!"

"What is it?"

"I don't know, but something's coming. A lot of somethings."

Mickie darted out of the tent and made a b-line for the nearest patrolling guard, who just so happened to be Jane. She flinched and instinctively threw her hands up to block a punch that never came.

"Look," Jane sulked. "I'm sorry for kicking your stupid pet, okay?"

"That's not what I'm here for, I just got a warning that there is trouble incoming."

"From one of your *pets?*" Jane rolled her eyes.

Mickie glared murder into her chestnut eyes.

Jane dropped the attitude.

"Just raise the fucking alarm, now!"

Hearing the menace implied in Mickie's tone, Jane huffed off and rang the bell. Soon, all the denizens of the camp were gathered around Mickie, Jake and Cricket clutching their weapons.

"What's going on, Jake?" Dwayne asked as he wiped sleep out of the corner of his eyes.

"Pigeon has picked up a wave of hostiles incoming."

"The stupid thing has just glitched out," Jane shouted from the back of the group.

"Jane, do us all a favour and shut the fuck up," Dwayne shouted above the anxious murmurings before pushing through the throng and taking Jake's aviators. He gasped as he slipped them on his face, what he saw wasn't even remotely good. "Is this live?" he asked Mickie.

"Nearly, there will be a very short delay, maybe thirty-seconds at most."

"Shit, we haven't got long then." He turned and addressed the camp. "Battle-stations, north-east corner!"

"What are we dealing with?" Brent asked while loading his shotgun.

"Toads... Thousands of them."

Brent's face turned white and, before Jake could ask what was so scary about a bunch of harmless amphibians, he was rudely interrupted by blood-curdling screams of agony from beyond the fence. The screams were quickly followed by a prolonged burst of gunfire. Jake charged towards the fence with his gun ready and night-vision enabled. When he got there, his mouth dropped open, and his mind reeled. Two of the large men who patrolled the camp at night hadn't made it back inside the camp in time and were now little more than shreds of clothing, bone and matted hair. Their flesh and organs had been stripped in record time by a swarm of piranha-like batrachians.

Jake had never seen anything like it. "Flesh-eating toads? Whoever heard of toads with teeth? This is insane!"

Nobody said, but it was evident that everyone on the wall agreed with his sentiment. Jake opened fire on the encroaching horde. Their leathery skin was tough and only one bullet in every three was effective.

"Quick!" Sam yelled. "Get the gate closed!"

Max ran over to help shut the gate just as a toad the size of a large domestic cat launched itself through the air towards Bruce's head. Max, quick as a flash, pumped some rounds into it, blasting it out of the sky. Bruce, stunned by his brush with death, dithered and turned to flee but Max grabbed him by the arm and pulled him back to the gate. Between them and another two men, they managed to get it shut before the main bulk of the horde reached the camp.

Unperturbed by the defences, the toads rushed the wall, hurling their tough bodies against the tall metal sheeting. Some hit with such force that they dented the panels. The force of the onslaught caused one of the walkways to buckle and tip three men, two women, and a wombat over the wall where they were immediately set upon and devoured. Jane clung to the post to steady herself as the gantry gave way below her and became tangled in the barbed wire. Screaming for help, she struggled to free herself but only succeeded in digging the vicious spikes further into her bicep.

Below, the toads started to salivate; Jane's bloodied arm was sticking out over the wall providing a tasty target. The toads commenced huddling up against the walls, climbing on top of each other to climb higher and higher. One toad, a particularly bulbous specimen, launched itself into the air, snapping its fangs. Jane was lucky, it was less than an inch off target. Landing on the head of one of its siblings, the toad positioned itself for another attack ... he wouldn't miss next time.

Mickie spotted what was happening, charged over and blasted the creature into a pile of goo with her overpowered enforcer shotgun. Jane was stunned, she stared in disbelief at the identity of her saviour. Her shock was soon to deepen.

Chirrup!

Cricket hopped down from his vantage point, high on a pole where he had been picking off targets and blasted the barbed wire that held Jane fast. The metal snapped, releasing its captive before she leapt down and landed in the dust. Blood was gushing from her arm, and she was feeling faint. As she staggered groggily in a wide circle, Johanna spotted the injured woman and was over to her and providing first aid in a matter of seconds.

Bullets continued to splat toads but as soon as one fell, two more replaced it. They were keeping them back for now, but the supply of bullets was finite. They needed a plan. Pigeon, who had been swooping above the horde strafing them with laser fire, had a similar problem; his battery was almost dry. He stopped and hovered above the camp, scanning the area for anything that could help. Thankfully, his sensors picked up just the thing and he quickly contacted Cricket with the plan.

Cricket was helping Sniffer blast all the monstrous toads that were trying to get under the wall when he got the transmission. Sniffer assured him that he could cope, and Cricket shot over to Jake, landed on his shoulder and interfaced with his glasses. As Jake shot at the toads he put a small image with a compass point in the corner of his display. Jake instantly knew what to do, he thanked Cricket and jumped down from the wall.

"Max, give me a hand over here!" Jake pointed over towards the vehicles where a cluster of fuel barrels stood. Max nodded and raced alongside his friend. Both men had hydraulic implants in their arms, so they had no difficulty picking up a barrel each and racing back over to the wall.

"Move!" Jake bellowed at Dwayne, Brent and the others on the wall as they launched the barrels over the wall and into the horde of toads.

"Down!"

A second later, Cricket and Pigeon blasted the barrels, igniting the fuel within. There was a tremendous explosion as fire and metal exploded, annihilating a majority of the carnivorous toads. The spreading fire acted as a deterrent to the rest of the swarm and as the survivors of the onslaught cheered, the remaining toads went around the camp and dropped into the river.

"I'll say it again," Jake panted. "Who's ever heard of a toad with fucking teeth?"

The blackened bodies of hundreds of toads still smouldered in the dust as the sun rose. Johanna and Mickie had toiled all night to patch up the injured as best they could. While Mickie stuck a sewing needle through Jane's lacerated flesh, she had received an uncomfortable thanks and an even more uncomfortable apology. Mickie smiled and assured her that she did what anyone would have done. Jane nodded and smiled. Dwayne later quipped that this was for the first time in years.

Mickie finished patching her up and rose from her seat. "This doesn't mean I like you, though." She grinned playfully. "And if I see you so much as look at Sniffer sideways, I'll break your fingers, got it?"

Jane smiled, taking it in the jovial way it was intended, though the look in Mickie's eyes let her know that the threat was anything but idle.

Jake, Max and Dwayne watched the sunrise while drinking

some locally brewed beers that Dwayne had picked up in Alice Springs with Jake's prize money. None of them had slept a wink and they knew that they had to move quickly before the toads returned. Plus, all the freshly roasted meat was sure to attract scavengers. Sam had decided to pack up and move that very morning. They would take those that weren't going on the expedition to Alice Springs before heading off into the desert and setting up camp by the lost city of Pnakotus. It would take the best part of the day, they would then rest up and enter the underground city the following morning, hopefully refreshed.

Morale wasn't good. The toad attack had taken its toll on the camp; many were dead and even more injured, and many believed they were on a suicide mission. This was another reason for the unscheduled trip to Alice Springs. Mickie and Johanna were doing their best, but they needed to get the injured to a fully stocked and manned medical centre. While there, they intended to stock up on booze to try and lift some flagging spirits. Out there, as it was back in Zone 51, it was the simple pleasures that kept people going.

In just a few short hours, the camp was scrapped, bundled, and loaded onto trailers. Cricket, Sniffer and Pigeon settled into Dwayne's jeep and charged themselves using the cigarette lighter port. Mickie dozed in the passenger seat while Max and Jake snored in the back. The feeling of hope Mickie had for completing their quest for the strange mineral to make Mnar stones was dwindling, they had all nearly been devoured by carnivorous toads and had no idea what to expect in the city.

The coming days were going to be tough.

CHAPTER X

GOING UNDERGROUND

Cricket was thinking about toads. He had been thinking about toads ever since a horde of carnivorous ones had attacked their former camp two days previously. The species seemed to be completely unknown. Nowhere on his biology databank was any reference to killer toads, but he did find a reference to killer toads under mythology concerning the great old one Tsathoggua. This was as unsettling as it was unexpected. Just as puzzling as the creatures was the attack itself—the toads seemed to have come in a direct line from somewhere north of the lost city of Pnakotus. Cricket postulated that had the camp not been on the way to the river, then it would never have been attacked. It appeared that the toad migration was caused by something other than a feeding frenzy and he intended to find out what.

The group had set up camp outside the entrance to the subterranean city. It had been surprisingly easy to locate. Marked by two huge rocks, the entrance had been dug out by an unknown agency meaning that they had brought shovels and other excavation tools for no reason. Jake, Dwayne, Bruce, Brent and Sam had gone down into the city only ten minutes ago while Mickie, Jane, Johanna and Max had stayed topside to keep guard and monitor the situation. Sniffer was playing fetch with Mickie, and Pigeon was charging himself, so Cricket was bored. As he racked his data for answers, he decided that the only way to figure it out was to do some investigating.

Taking off into the bright blue sky, Cricket circled the camp until he spotted some tracks left by the migration. Wind had blown sand over the majority of the toad tracks but some looked relatively fresh. Cricket locked on to the anomalous track and followed it. It was heading back towards the site of the old camp and the river beyond. Cricket readied his laser and dropped in altitude.

As he soared through the skeletal branches of parched trees, a hopping speck on the horizon came into view. Cricket prepared to fire but something held him back; there was something odd about the way the assumed toad was hopping that struck Cricket as vaguely mechanical. His scan returned the information that this was no organic life-form. In fact, it came back with a serial number.

The *creature* was a drone. More than that, it was a drone just like Cricket, an ICAE S-series spy-drone. Though why it was hopping along in the sand in Australia was a complete mystery. Cricket circled the small drone before coming in to land just in front of it. It was startled and hopped into the air making a grinding, ribbiting sound. Its propellers were missing and its back legs appeared to be fused, hence its hopping gait. Cricket let out a friendly chirrup to put it at ease.

For a moment they just sat there in the desert sizing each other up. After a while, Cricket took the initiative, jumped forwards and started to chatter in machine code. The other drone responded and shot out an interface lead. Cricket connected and soon he knew what had driven the toads to the river.

The drone had been sent to Australia on a spying mission for the GAF but became damaged during the catastrophic events of Expiration Day. Its circuits and chassis damaged, the drone had from that moment on lived the peaceful life of a frog. It had come about one hot afternoon while he was hopping along a river. There he met a small green creature that hopped and made noises just like him... a frog. Scanning the fragments of his databanks, the drone had decided that he was too small and sleek to be a toad, so a frog he became and had lived amongst a small colony in the Fitzroy River to the north.

Also present in the river was an ever-growing toad population that made him uneasy. He didn't know where they had come from but as soon as they arrived, they started spreading like a biblical plague. They were ferocious and hungry. Soon, the frogs vanished, and he was left alone with the toads. They didn't mind him hanging around and he was safe from humans while they were in residence... He had seen many a hunter stripped of his flesh in the blinking of a watchful batrachian eye.

One morning, a dark shadow had fallen over the river belonging to a sinister gentleman by the name of Doctor Frank Sullivan. He, along with a brotherhood of bandit followers and a flock of bat-like creatures had terrified the normally fearless toads. Instantly, the toads had fled in terror from the new arrivals. The drone followed but quickly lost sight of them. He had been following their trail ever since.

Cricket ran the name *Frank Sullivan* through his databank and was less than happy with the results. In seconds, he had discovered that he was the fabled immortal leader of The Brotherhood of Starry Wisdom, and that he was a devout follower of the dreaded Nyarlathotep. To make matters worse, the only logical reason he could find for him to be in Western Australia, let alone the Great Sandy Desert, was the very site his friends were exploring. Cricket chirruped agitatedly.

The other drone ribbited an agreement, hopped on top of Cricket and engaged his electromagnet. In moments they were flying back to camp.

Mickie was tired, hungry, far too hot and hiding from the sun when a thump on the roof of the tent startled her. "What the Devil? If that's another noisy bloody kookaburra, I'll scream."

Chirrup!

"Oh, hey, Cricket, where have you been?" She stepped out and was surprised to see two drones, not one. Her face lit up. "Hey, who have you got here? Hello little fellow."

Chirrup-chirrup-chirrup! Chirr-up! Chirr-up! Chirr-up! Chirrup-chirrup-chirrup!

"What's wrong, Cricket? Danger?"

Chirrup!
"Is something coming?"
Chirrup!
"Good boy, Cricket. Go warn Jake, okay?"
Chirrup!
Cricket took off and sped towards the entrance to the lost city of Pnakotus while Mickie gently took the drone down and smiled at him.
"Hello."
Ribbit!
She smiled again and tucked him into her bag.
"I think I'll call you Hopper!"

APRIL 9TH 2132
AUSTRALIA – PNAKOTUS:

Cricket sped across the sand and swooped down into the narrow opening. The tunnel was high and sloped at a steep angle. He hurtled down at such speed that he nearly slammed into the wall. The corner was sharp, and he very nearly missed it. Once righted, he resumed his flight. It was incredibly dark, and Cricket had to engage his night vision. The momentary blindness as his vision modes switched caused him to plough straight into a sand clogged cobweb.

Cricket spun and rolled as the web blocked his sensors and got tangled in his propeller. He tried to come to a stop, but he had no idea what angle he was facing. He let off a bolt from his laser that singed the web. It cleared from his vision just in time for him to see himself crash into a hard, hairy object.

"Argh!" Jake cried in surprise and pain as he rubbed the back of his head. He shone his torch around and saw a sheepish-looking Cricket sitting on the floor. "Cricket? Not again!"

Chirrup-chirrup-chirrup! Chirr-up! Chirr-up! Chirr-up! Chirrup-chirrup-chirrup!

Jake picked up the frantic robot, placed him on his shoulder and plugged him in. Cricket quickly showed him Hopper's intel and it didn't make for easy viewing. "Shit. Thanks, Cricket. You'd better go back topside and instruct Max to get himself, Mickie, Johanna and Jane to safety. Get them to leave the jeep in that abandoned barn we passed down the road then head for Alice Springs in the buggy."

"How's he going to tell them that lot? It's not like he can speak," Brent asked.

"No, but he can tap."

It took the Australian a few moments before the opal dropped. "Ah, he can speak Max, you mean?"

"Yup! It might take a while and a game of charades or two, but he'll get there. Now, off you go, Cricket."

Cricket did as instructed, leaving Jake to explain to the others what was happening. None of them questioned his decision. Jake wasn't a man prone to worry or attacks of nerves but right at that moment, he was obviously in the grip of severe anxiety. The situation was perilous, to say the least. They were currently about a mile underground in an ancient city constructed by a race of time-travelling aliens while an immortal lunatic in charge of a mad cult and a flock of nightgaunts raced towards them. Sam shivered; he well remembered his encounter with the beasts on the dock of Zone 51's South-West sector. Telling the others to run was a good call.

An immediate downside to this order was that it left Dwayne, Bruce, Brent, Sam, and Jake effectively blind as to what was happening above; Sullivan could already be up there about to unleash his terrible pets into the tunnels. As far as any of the expedition knew, there was only one way in or out, so they had to find what they were looking for and get out before their escape was blocked by the forces of Nyarlathotep. The biggest problem with that plan was that the city was vast, and they had no idea where to start looking for the minerals they needed to create Mnar stones.

Brent had heard the legends regarding The Brotherhood of Starry Wisdom and explained that the man known as Doctor Sullivan was known to many as the Deathless One. Like Malcolm Sanderson and others, his will had been all but consumed by the insidious deity after a chance encounter at his friend Bertie Lexington-Brown's birthday party way back in 2021. Dwayne, imparting Ben's long rambles on the subject, had confirmed that it was all down to a book, a trinket, and a sarcophagus that his great uncle had sold to Mr Lexington-Brown. A mummy party gone awry that had resulted in the academic being subsumed. Now an avatar of the Crawling Chaos, he was ready, willing and able to commit atrocities in his name.

The brotherhood he commanded were equally fanatical and had, under the control of one avatar or another, lurked at the fringes of world politics since the signing of Magna Carta. They influenced and shaped the world to Nyarlathotep's design, paving the way for the nightmare they currently inhabited. From his dark fane in Irem, the Crawling Chaos controlled the world through puppets such as Sullivan, Sanderson, and the now-deceased CEO.

Steep slopes made up the walkways of the cyclopean city and were treacherous to navigate in the dim luminescence afforded by waving flashlights and clumps of glowing fungi that sprouted at regular intervals in perfectly smoothed sconces. Bruce had already come a cropper and had slid down one such path on his backside. Brent had tried not to laugh but, in the end, failed. His guffaws had echoed around the high vaulted ceilings shattering the stifling silence. The temperature was rising sharply the further down they traversed, causing all five men to sweat profusely. None of them was looking forward to the uphill journey to the exit.

So far, they had passed several large chambers furnished with items completely unsuitable to human anatomy. It was clear that whatever the great race of Yith was, they were as different from mankind as an elephant is from a weevil. Dwayne had stumbled across some strange tablets and cylinders containing what looked like a potted history of the universe and had muttered about Nathaniel Wingate Peaslee. Back in Zone 51, the late Ben Edwards had often talked to Dwayne about what he called the Peaslee papers. Back in the early twentieth century, the man had led an expedition to the very spot they now found themselves in. In his report, he had mentioned the strange documentation that Dwayne had found and claimed that he had dropped them as he fled from the city in terror. Mickie had told Dwayne about his old friend Ben's passing shortly before they had reached the city. The news had hit him hard and, though he faced it with his trademark stoicism, it was clear that he was hurting.

"A junction," Sam spluttered through the dust as they reached a level pathway. "Which way?"

"No idea," Jake replied. He had been marking their path using a lump of charcoal he had fished from last night's fire and set to work doodling on the wall. "What do you fellows reckon?"

"I think we should split into two groups," Brent said. "We could cover more ground that way."

"Stupid idea." Bruce snorted in derision and kicked at a piece of fallen masonry.

Brent shot him a look of death and squared his shoulders.

"Hey!" Sam bellowed forcefully. "You two are like an old married couple, can you at least try and agree on something for a change? We don't have time for this bullshit!"

Suitably cowed, the two men separated and stropped off towards the opposing walkways. Jake grinned at Sam. Secretly, the two men's squabbling had been getting on his nerves. "I'll go that way with Brent, you three go the other way. Have you got the walkie talkie?"

Dwayne pulled the ancient children's *Action Man* radio from his pocket and clicked it on. Mickie had found them on one of the stalls in Alice Springs. They were broken but Mickie loved nothing more than fixing broken or damaged things. Figuring correctly that they might come in handy, she fixed them up and boosted the signal using parts she had scavenged from a broken ham radio back at the camp.

Jake switched his receiver on, and the two men tested them. They worked perfectly. Mickie, the necromancer of tech, had done it again. "Excellent." He grinned. "Let us know if you find anything, okay?"

Dwayne nodded and clapped Sam on the shoulder, directing him towards the sulking figure of Bruce. Jake stashed the walkie-talkie and walked over to Brent. The muscular islander led the way down the slope marvelling at the sights around him. The Great Race of Yith had been superb architects, the vaulted ceilings and stout pillars were a wonder to behold. Pictures similar to Egyptian hieroglyphs adorned the walls, providing something of a potted history of the city. Brent, as something of an artist himself, rued the fact that he didn't have time to study the fascinating designs. Jake wasn't interested in the slightest, he just wanted to get the stone and get the hell out and answered in sullen grunts to his partner's enthusiastic observations.

"So, what is it with you and Bruce?" Jake asked, desperately trying to change the conversation. "You guys seem to have a love-hate thing going on."

Brent blew air out of his mouth like an exasperated pufferfish. "You could say that. We used to date, you know, back before the collapse and everything went to hell... It didn't end well. We never could agree on anything. It's a shame, he's a good bloke, he just talks out of his arse most of the time."

Jake laughed. "Yeah, me and my wife, Mary, were the same, except, in that case, it was me talking out of my arse and her shaking her head. She was always the level-headed one. She saw the harsh reality of things while I preferred to keep my head in the clouds. My one wish is that we had spent more quality time together before she died, her and my daughter, as a family, I mean. You never know how quickly you can lose the ones you love."

"I'm sorry, Jake." Brent sighed. "What happened, if you don't mind me asking?"

"Expiration Day happened. We were trying to get out of the GAF habitation centre... A lurker got them."

"Lurker?"

"Yeah, you know. Big wobbling, formless jelly-like thing with hundreds of eyes and tentacles, a bit like a huge jellyfish."

"Ah, you mean a shoggoth."

"I believe that's what Ben said they were called, yeah."

"He was right, that's the real name of the beast."

Jake took a nip from his flask and passed it to Brent. "Really, how do you know all this stuff about shoggoths and Sullivan anyway?"

Brent imbibed. "I used to hang out with a couple of Gillmen before they went all militant and decided that all *dry-skins* must die. They told me all about this stuff, said that their god told it to them in dreams, whatever the fuck that means. They reckoned that the shoggoths were created as workers to build places such as this by some elder race, they eventually turned on their masters and allied themselves with the Old Ones, slaughtering the lot of them. Bloody vicious things. Hey, what was that?"

Brent stopped as a rhythmic noise grabbed his attention. It was coming from the direction they came from. It sounded like the flapping of a heavy canvas tent in a force nine gale. Heavy wings.

"Shit," Jake exclaimed. "Nightgaunts, they're here!"

In a separate tunnel the *crackle* of a walkie-talkie made Dwayne jump and curse. He and the other two men had been navigating the steep slopes in silence after Sam had finally gotten Bruce to stop bitching about Brent. He snatched it from his waistband and grumbled "yeah?" into the mouthpiece

"Nightgaunts!" It was Jake on the other end.

"Yeah... what about them?"

"They're here."

"Bollocks."

"So, keep quiet."

Dwayne looked at the handset in annoyance. "I was being quiet before you called."

"Oops... over and out." Another *crackle* and Jake was gone.

"Now what?" Sam asked, a look of distress lining his features. He had woken in cold sweats replaying that moment a flock of nightgaunts had emerged from a rift over the docks ever since the night he'd escaped Zone 51; a repeat performance was the last thing he desired.

"Now, we press on, I guess." Dwayne shrugged. "Just keep quiet." He shot a look at Bruce. "No whining, okay?"

Bruce rolled his eyes and resumed walking. Sound carried due to the high ceilings and smooth rock walls, so every footfall had to be soft and dainty, a tricky practice when all three men were bulky and not one of them had attended ballet classes. As they continued their seemingly endless descent, the heavy flapping sounds that Jake had heard suddenly became audible to the group.

"Damn," Sam whispered, "they are coming straight for us."

"Hurry it up," Dwayne hissed at Bruce.

The big Australian started a cautious jog that the other two men followed closely. Panic latched onto their throats, squeezing the air out of them. The flapping was growing louder and louder by the second, the hellish creatures were rapidly closing in. Soon, the party came to another junction. In his haste, Bruce's boot connected with a chunk of fallen masonry, sending it skittering off down the left-hand path.

"Shit, sorry," he whispered as the sound of clattering rubble reverberated down the tunnel. A second later, their collective heart sank as the increased beating of wings announced that the creatures knew where they were and were closing in for the kill.

"Go right," Dwayne commanded. As silently as possible, they ducked down the right-hand path and carried on further into the bowels of the earth as the rhythmic din of their approach rose to a deafening level. Luckily, Bruce's clumsiness worked in their favour, sending the incoming creatures down the left-hand path. Relief was fleeting, they knew that they only had a small reprieve and resumed a steady jog down the tunnel.

After a short time, the steep descent suddenly levelled out into a sharp right turn. Sam's momentum sent him crashing into the wall. Dwayne braced his shoulder against him to stop him falling backwards then caught Bruce as he came sliding down. Regaining his equilibrium, Sam nodded in thanks, then turned to run down the corridor. As he pivoted, he was met with a gun pointing in his face. Sam bellowed in alarm, as did the man with the gun. Their simultaneous screams bounced off the walls in a deafening cacophony.

"Jesus, Jake, are you trying to give me a heart attack?" Sam scowled breathlessly.

"Sorry, I didn't know it was you."

"Why haven't you got your torch on, you daft bugger?"

"Because," Jake whispered, "there's a bunch of bonkers, gun-toting cultists on our arses."

"Damn, we're trapped." Brent sighed and pinched the bridge of his nose with his thumb and forefinger. "Those nightgaunts must have heard you two bellowing like buffalo."

"Balls," Jake said between glugs of booze. "Did you find anything?"

"Nah," said Dwayne. "Not a bloody sausage; you?"

"Nope, nothing. All we found was a big temple thing, no other corridors or anything back that way, did you find any other routes?"

Bruce interrupted before Dwayne answered. "Oh, fuck."

Jake looked at him quizzically.

"There was another tunnel but the nightgaunts have gone that way. I... Um... Distracted them."

"Crap, now what?"

"We need a diversion. *Another* diversion, I mean," Dwayne looked pointedly at Bruce who huffed in reply.

"Someone to lead them a dance, you mean?" Jake could see the train of his friend's thought leaving suicide station. "Fine... I'll do it. Just so you know, I'm not that much of a head-case that I relish the idea of being torn apart by a bunch of faceless monsters."

"I never suggested you were."

"Good, just putting that out there."

"No." Sam stepped between the two. "I won't have it. There must be a better way."

"Like?"

"I dunno, gimme a minute."

While Jake and Dwayne waited for Sam's gears to grind, Brent sauntered over to Bruce, his chest heaving with exhaustion. "You alright?"

Bruce forced an unconvincing smile. "Yeah, just bloody knackered, you?"

"Same." There was an uncomfortable moment as both men looked at each other. Brent decided to break the ice. "Look, Bruce. I'm sorry for being hard on you. I—"

Before he could get out the remainder of the sentence, a shot rang out and a bullet slammed into Bruce's head splattering his brains and shattered skull over Brent. Bruce's body slammed lifelessly to the floor.

"No!" Brent screamed in anguish, swung his gun in the direction of the shot and let rip with a prolonged blast of SMG fire. The gunman danced like a badly-strung marionette as his body was riddled with bullets. Brent kept screaming as he charged off towards the oncoming cultists.

"Brent, come back!" Jake screamed, to no avail.

"Come on," Dwayne boomed in the bounty hunter's ear. "It's no good."

Jake nodded and followed him up the slope behind Sam.

"Pray, those nightgaunts haven't turned around." Dwayne wheezed. "If they have, we're royally fucked."

As they charged upwards, the sound of the back and forth of gunfire clattered below. Brent was putting up a good fight and was seemingly determined to take as many cultists down with him as he could. Jake felt a pang of sadness, he knew he wouldn't last long. As soon as his clip ran dry, Brent was toast. Finally reaching the junction, the three men were halted in their tracks by an unwelcome sight—a portly middle-aged gentleman in a tweed suit, flanked by three nightgaunts, blocking their path.

Jake went to turn back but stopped. The rattling tattoo of heavy gunfire had ended and the tunnel was silent. Brent was gone, this meant that there would be a bunch of cultists coming up their rear. They were well and truly trapped.

"I wouldn't recommend running, Mr Baker," Doctor Sullivan purred, his cultured tones spilling from under his lavish walrus moustache like liquid silk. "My pets would have no trouble catching you. In fact, I do believe they would be glad of the exercise, it's been ages since they had a good hunt."

"What do you want, Sullivan?" Sam demanded.

"I see that my reputation precedes me."

"Yeah, I know who you are, another fucking puppet of Nyarlathotep, just like that wanker, Sanderson."

The vitriol in Sam's words made Sullivan's smile widen. "It's quite simple, Sam, I may call you Sam, can't I?"

Sam remained silent, taken aback that Sullivan knew his name.

"Splendid. Well, *Sammy boy*, I'm here to destroy the dreamlands stone and all who seek it, simple really. That would be you three, by the way, in case you are slow on the uptake. My lord, Nyarlathotep demands it, I'm afraid."

"Well, your lord can kiss my arse!" Dwayne barked.

Sullivan's eyes flashed orange as an inhuman voice burst from his lips. "Silence, maggot!"

Jake flinched as the words of the Crawling Chaos boomed throughout the city.

"Dreamlands stone?" Sam asked, playing for time.

Sullivan's eyes returned to their normal blackened state and his voice once more became his own. "The green rock you plan on meddling with. It is a product of another dimension, another reality, The Dreamlands, a place beyond the walls of sleep where my lord was imprisoned for millennia. It, along with several other *artefacts,* fell through weak points between the worlds and are imbued with energies anathematic to The Haunter of the Dark."

"Well..." Dwayne grinned, not catching on that Sam was trying to eke out the conversation. "The Haunter of the Dark can kiss my arse!"

Nyarlathotep roared through Sullivan's mouth, "Enough! Time for you to perish!" Sullivan turned to his pets and prepared to give the order.

"Hey, arsehole!"

Dwayne looked around in bemusement as he heard his very own battle cry bellowed by a savage-looking girl in animal skins brandishing a .44 Magnum. With deadly accuracy, Jane unloaded all six chambers into Doctor Sullivan's torso, slamming the ancient academic into the wall before he collapsed to the floor in a crumpled heap. As Jane reloaded, the three men opened fire on the nightgaunts, driving the abominations back towards the entrance. Suddenly, the corridor behind them erupted in a barrage of shotgun and laser fire. One by one, the creatures were ripped to shreds.

Jake let out a whoop of delight as the dust cleared and out of the tunnel came a beaming Max with Cricket perched on his right shoulder.

"Max, Jane," Dwayne yelled. "Looks like you saved my arse one more time."

Max grinned.

A *chirrup* made Jake roll his eyes. "Yes, nice shooting, Cricket!"

Sam stepped over the charred remains of a nightgaunt and held out his hand to Jane. "Cuffs."

Jane reached into the kangaroo scrotum pouch attached to her belt and produced a set of handcuffs. Reluctantly, she handed them to Sam.

Jake grinned. "I'm not going to ask why you carry those."

Jane gave the grizzled gunman a coy wink that made Jake laugh harder than he had in months.

"When you have quite finished arsing about, will one of you help me secure Sullivan? If the stories of his *immortality* are true, those bullets won't keep him down long."

Jake stepped in, rolled the downed sorcerer onto his front and pinioned his hands behind his back. Sam clacked the cuffs on his wrists and removed the man's belt. "Here," he passed it to Jake. "Bind his ankles."

"With pleasure. Tight enough to cut off the circulation, I reckon... Hang on, does he even have circulation? What even is he, anyway, a zombie, revenant, what?"

"A mask."

Jake smirked. "Well, that clears that up, thanks, Sam."

As Jake finished binding Sullivan's legs, a noise from behind startled them into readying their weapons. In all the excitement, they had completely forgotten about the cultists bringing up the rear. As one, they took cover as best they could in a featureless stone corridor created by an alien race from the dawn of time, and prepared for a gunfight.

"Wait for my signal," Jake whispered as the footsteps grew closer. "Any second... Wait for it... What the fuck?"

Each one of them sighed in relief, as out of the gloom hobbled a battered and bleeding Brent.

"Bloody hell," Jake blurted as he quickly rushed to the man's aid. "Did you kill 'em all?"

Brent's head lolled back against Jake's arm as he managed a weak smile. "Sure did." As soon as he had finished speaking, Brent's legs turned to jelly. He slipped to the ground and promptly passed out through exsanguination.

"Shit!" Jake cried. "Max, Sam, get him topside, he needs help. Get him to Mickey, quick as you can. We'll carry on looking for that sodding rock."

The two did as instructed and dragged Brent quickly up the slope, leaving Jake, Dwayne and Jane in the city of Pnakotus.

"What shall we do with Sullivan?" Jake asked.

Jane examined the slope to their right. "Why don't we pitch him down there? With any luck, he'll shatter his skull when he hits bottom."

"Good plan, that might take him longer to regenerate. Look, the bullet holes are closing up. Grab an arm and a leg, Dwayne."

Dwayne and Jake grabbed Sullivan between them and launched him head-first down the slope. His body kept sliding as the angle and momentum took hold. After dusting off his gloved hands on his battered coat, Jake passed his flask around and took out a crumpled packet of smokes.

"A quick break, then we get to it, right? That stone *has* to be down there... It simply has to..."

"Are you sure Jane is up to the job?" Jake was uneasy. Against his better judgement, he and Dwayne had gone in search of the stone leaving the youngster covering Sullivan's shattered body.

"She'll be fine," Dwayne assured him. "If I know Jane, she'll be using it as an opportunity for target practice. I told her to keep blowing holes in him so he can't regenerate. I gave her plenty of ammo so he should be down for a good while."

"I just hope it works."

Dwayne placed a hand on Jake's shoulder. "It'll work. It has to."

"Let's hurry this up, in any case." Jake led the way along winding corridors deeper into Pnakotus. Depictions of strange beings leered down from the high stone walls. He shone his light on one of the larger specimens. It showed a towering cone-shaped creature with tentacle-like appendages ushering a parade of apes into a doorway. "I take it this is one of the Great Race?"

"I assume so. Man, I hope we don't bump into any of 'em."

"Me neither. What do you reckon happened to them?"

Dwayne shrugged. "I really don't want to think about it. Anything that can see off a monstrosity like that will make bloody quick work of us."

"Cheers, Dwayne. I'm one step away from soiling myself as it is. I didn't need that cheery thought rattling around my brain."

"Sorry, man," Dwayne came to a sudden stop as they approached another junction. Again grabbing Jake's shoulder, he sniffed the air. "You smell that?"

Jake inhaled and quickly wished that he didn't. "Rotting meat." Readying his weapon, he edged towards the corner and peered around. "Jesus wept." The wide walkway was littered with piles of bloodied clothing and equipment all discarded haphazardly as though torn away in a frenzy. There were no signs of life so he made the turn and gingerly approached the mess.

Dwayne followed, edging over to a battered rucksack. Squatting, he opened the zip and examined the contents. Along with various weapons and clothing, there was a map of the Coober Pedy area. "Bandits, at a guess. What were they doing down here?"

"Probably the same as us. I'm more concerned with what happened to them."

"Nightgaunts?"

"Possibly I dunno. Look, it goes off into that doorway over there." Jake led on. Following the trail of blood and detritus along the corridor and towards a high vaulted doorway flanked by two statues of Yithian creatures. Just looking at them made him shudder. The eyes of the abominations were detached from the rugose body, snaking high above them on a snaking tendril. Unearthly didn't begin to cover it. They made shoggoths look pedestrian. As the duo continued, the foul aroma hanging in the air got worse and worse. Sickly-sweet and cloying. Whoever had massacred the bandits, they did so relatively recently.

Dwayne cursed under his breath as they peered into the chamber beyond the statues. The room was vast, filled with more of the strange furniture, along with banks and banks of shelving containing tablets of strange metalovered in alien glyphs. It was some kind of library or records room. This was awe-inspiring in itself, but it was what sat in the centre of the room that made Dwayne blanche. Bones, picked clean of meat, had been piled high like some kind of charnel bonfire.

Jake took one look at the pile and spat. "Ghouls. This is a Ghoul bone-pile."

"Shit. What the Hell are Ghouls doing down here."

Jake thought for a second. "If I had to guess. The same as us... and the bandits."

"Why would Ghouls want the stone? Surely they are in with the Old Ones. Ben said they're children of The Charnel God, Mordiggian."

"Fuck knows. Maybe they want to use it against the gill breathers. Maybe they just wanted to keep the bandits away from it. Either way, this is a mystery that can wait. Let's just hope they left some for us."

"Agreed. So, where now?"

Jake put on his aviators and pressed one of the small buttons on the left arm. Everything turned shades of green aside from the blood and things that had come in contact with it. There were multitudinous footprints leading to and from the pile. Jake followed them and pointed to the far end of the library where there was a second door. "Through there. That's where they went. Mickie's Luminol setting has been a bloody blessing in my line of work."

"Pun intended?"

Jake grinned.

"Come along then, man. I need to get out of here pronto. Much longer and I'll be throwing up Johanna's breakfast."

Moving as silently as two large men armed with heavy weapons could possibly move, they stalked towards the darkened portal. Halfway along the room, Jake spotted something glinting out of the corner of his eye. It was one of the tablets. The large sheet of thin metal had fallen from one of the shelves and landed amidst some soiled jeans and several teeth. Pausing, he stooped to pick it up. Instantly, his vision lurched and his mind raced. Images flashed before his eyes. Thousands upon thousands of images. He saw cities rise, fall, and turn to dust. He saw bodies crumple and bones bleach. The seas rose and the forests burned. A scream escaped his lips as he let go of the object. The final thing he saw was a sprawling desert populated by a race of huge cockroaches lurking among the ruins of a dead civilization. Bleak was the word that sprung to his reeling mind.

"Jake!" Dwayne bellowed down his ear, shaking him by the shoulders. "Come back to me, man!"

Jake's eyes returned from their brief home in the back of his head. He staggered, grabbing Dwayne's jacket for support. Just as quickly as it had come over him, it passed and he was able to stand upright. "What the fuck did I just see?"

"What the Hell happened?"

"I ... I dunno. I saw things. That," he indicated the fallen tablet, "whatever it is showed me things."

"What kind of things?"

Jake looked Dwayne squarely in the eyes. "You really don't want to know. I think I just saw how this all ends."

Dwayne's mouth moved mechanically but no words came out. He wanted to tell Jake that the Yithians, according to legend, could time travel, but he thought better of it. Ignorance can indeed sometimes be blissful. "Come on, let's find that damn stone."

Jake nodded and took a gulp from his flask to steady himself while Dwayne took the lead. Following on, he suddenly became aware of the fact that they weren't alone. "Um, Dwayne. We've got company.

Dwayne raised his gun, searching for a target. "Where. I don't see anything."

"In the next room. My scanner detected movement."

In silence, the two men got low and approached the door in a firing stance. Sure enough, there was a creature in the adjacent room. A Ghoul. It was sitting on a pile of stone gnawing a femur. Somewhere between man and dog, even a single Ghoul can be a handful if taken lightly. Jake knew this only too well. He motioned for Dwayne to get ready. They had to get the drop on it before it could attack, or worse, call for the rest of the pack. After checking the safety was off, Jake gave the signal, and on the count of three they burst in, levelling their guns in the startled beast's face. The ghoul barked and gibbered, its canine maw snapping and drooling. Despite their show of force, it sprung forward on its powerful hind legs, knocking Dwayne's gun aside and sending him backwards.

"Shit! It's bloody rabid. Get it off me, Jake!"

Without hesitation, Jake stepped forward and cleaved its skull with one heavy smack of his rifle butt. Instantly, the creature fell, twitching and bleeding.

"Fuck," Dwayne panted, holding out a hand, "help me up, will you?"

Jake did as asked. "You alright?"

"Yeah, I think so. It didn't break my skin so I shouldn't be infected. I've heard of rabid ghouls before but never encountered one before."

"It explains why it was alone. I guess the rest of the pack left it as some kind of guard dog."

"Well, the fucker won't be guarding anything now. You smashed his brains in good and proper." Dwayne dusted himself off and surveyed the room. "Hey, look over there. The far wall, it's been tunnelled into."

"That explains who excavated the entrance to the city. Ghouls did this. The opening is too small for one of those death-worm-things we met the other day." Stepping to the entrance, he scanned the tunnel beyond with various settings on his aviators. "Looks like they are long gone. The bandits must have had a case of bad timing."

"Or were brought here as a living food supply. I've heard of Ghouls keeping men as cattle. It doesn't bear thinking about, does it?"

Jake shook his head and looked around. The room housed various strange tools and blank tablets. If the previous room was a library, then this was the stationary cupboard. Eventually, his gaze moved to just beyond where Dwayne was standing, where the Ghoul had been enjoying his snack. He scanned the pile of rubble and grinned. "Look behind you. It seems our friend, Fido, was guarding something special."

"Is it?"

"It is. Come on. Let's get it out of here before any more Ghouls show up."

Dwayne puffed out his cheeks. "There's too much to carry. We'll have to make a couple of trips."

Jake thought for a second then rotated his shoulder. "Not necessarily. Let's go and get some of the bandit's backpacks. I can carry quite a load thanks to the GRA."

Dwayne smirked. "I like your thinking, Jake. I've always wanted a pack mule."

"How is he?" Jake asked Mickie as she washed Brent's blood off her hands.

"Not great, if I'm honest. He's lost a lot of blood, but he'll live; it's his head that I'm worried about."

"Yeah, that was savage. He still loved Bruce, you know?"

"Yeah... Poor bugger. We need to get him to Alice Springs, get him to a real doctor."

"Agreed, we'll head out as soon as we've rested up and Sam gets him secured on the jeep." Jake reached in his backpack and pulled out a slab of green rock. "Here, can you make Mnar stars out of that?"

"No problem," Mickie nodded, taking the stone. "I'll get on it when we get back on the boat."

Jake smiled and started to walk back towards the makeshift camp they had set up where Johanna roasted a kangaroo's rump over an open fire.

"Jake... do you really think this will help?"

Jake turned and smiled. "I ruddy hope so, because Nyarlathotep knows we have just declared war. He wouldn't have sent Sullivan all this way if Mnar stones weren't a threat to him. Just make 'em good, kid."

"No pressure then, huh?"

Jake chuckled as he wandered in the direction of the jeep. While he had checked on Brent, Dwayne had hauled the last of the strange stone out of the subterranean city. He dumped it in the back of the jeep next to a heavily sedated Brent. He straightened up and stretched his aching back. The sun was going down over a small patch of trees in the distance making him smile; he was going to miss the sunburned land down under. It was just as dangerous as back home but at least it didn't piss it down on a daily basis. Dwayne sighed. He had decided, with a heavy heart, to return to Zone 51 and take the fight to Sanderson and his unholy master. The others needed him. With Ben gone, he knew the most about what they were up against.

Clapping the dust and filth off his hands, Dwayne strolled over to where Jane crouched over a detonator plunger, she was dexterously attaching the wires that led off into the city of Pnakotus. Max had found it along with some blasting charges in the barn they had hidden in when Doctor Sullivan arrived on the scene.

"Okay, Jane, we are all set to head out."

"I'll be done here in a couple of minutes, then we can entomb the fucker."

"Good, what's the plan once we are done here? Are you staying with Sam and Johanna or coming back to the Zone?"

Jane thought for a second then sniffed. "Sam and Jo need me. Plus, Brent is going to need a friend when he recovers. Besides" —she motioned to the buggy where Mickie fussed with her new friend, Hopper— "you don't need me, you already have an *Alpha-Bitch*, as she put it."

Dwayne chuckled and patted her on the shoulder. "I'll miss you, you big pain in the backside."

"Don't get mushy, old man," Jane smiled. "Right, I'm ready." She stood up and grabbed the plunger. "Just do something for me will you?"

"Sure, what?"

"Kill the whistleblower for my parents, deal?"

"Deal."

Jane pressed the plunger, and the tunnel mouth erupted in a cloud of dust and stone. After it had settled, they climbed aboard the jeep and followed the buggy into the sunset.

CHAPTER XI

WHISTLEBLOWER

The hydraulics on the heavy doors to the admin centre of the GAF facility hissed furiously as they dragged the heavy steel aside. Oliver swallowed hard, sweat beading on his brow, his heart sinking as Mr Sanderson, flanked by two heavily armed Caspers, started to make his way towards him. He knew as soon as he saw the lavish airship dock with the GAF tower that it was only a matter of time before the overseer came to talk to him. The waiting had been excruciating but here he was, full of swagger with a smug look on his gaunt face. It was time for a *progress report.*

God, he wished there was nothing to report. Every week, he wished there was nothing to report. Every day, he could feel the hateful stares of his co-workers, hear their murderous whispers. They knew what he did, they knew what he was. In their minds, quite rightly, he was akin to Judas Iscariot. Nothing he could say, not that he had ever tried, could explain away his duplicitous actions... They wouldn't understand.

"Good morning, Mr Potter," Sanderson purred. "Do you have anything to report?"

Oliver hesitated just for a second.

The Casper on the left fingered the trigger on his ridiculously large weapon.

"Come along," Sanderson prompted. "You know what will happen if you hold out on me." His grin widened, threatening to bisect his head.

Oliver swallowed and nodded, knew only too well what would happen if he held out.

How could he forget?

APRIL 13TH 2126
ZONE 51 — SOUTH-WEST SECTOR:

A year before, things were much different...

Oliver was one of the boys, a section leader on springs and switches, a respected role that carried weight amongst his peers. He was sometimes all that stood between an exhausted worker and a beating from the Caspers, so he was everybody's best friend. His job was to ensure the quotas were met and that his men didn't die on the job, and he was excellent at both. He was well-liked and known to be a generous and honourable man. He was also deeply unhappy. His wife had just given birth to twin girls and the last thing he wanted for his budding family was for them to be bred into good little cybernetically enhanced drones for the GAF. No, he wanted out. Out of the factories, out of the GAF, out of Zone 51.

Like many, he had been inspired by the actions of a man called Dwayne, a hero to anyone with even half a brain, anyone capable of independent thought. Dwayne was the man who had *opted out*. The man who willingly chose to be branded *undesirable* rather than go along with the tyrannical regime. He was the man with balls big enough to stick two fingers up to Mr Sanderson and the CEO. Dwayne was nothing short of inspiring. After hearing about his one-man revolution, many in the GAF facilities saw a faint glimmer of light at the end of the depressingly dark tunnel. If he could simply walk away from society, then they could too. Oliver wanted to walk as far away as humanly possible.

Along with several workmates, Oliver planned a grand exodus from Zone 51. The plan was simple, but in no way easy; they would make their way through the ruins of the former Betyls Cove to the docks and hop on an automated refuse boat out of the zone. If providence was on their side, they would be finally free. If not, they would be dead. Everyone involved knew the risks, how could they not? Reports of Caspers shooting runners on sight were broadcast daily on the company-controlled information screens. To make matters worse, whispers had been going around the factory about another threat in the flooded district, something they called a *lurker*.

Rain pelted down in scummy rods, adding to the pervasive damp of the warehouse district as they raced from shadow to shadow, their Frankenstein boots slapping in the standing water as they wound their way through the narrow, decaying streets. Oliver and his wife had an infant each strapped to their backs. Both of them prayed that they would remain silent and asleep. The last thing they needed was for cries alerting the things that lurked in the shadows. Everything was going to plan, they had slipped out of the GAF compound and into the old town ruins, they had almost made it to the docks when things went horribly wrong.

One of the party, Steve, stepped out from a corner and was met by the glaring light from an enforcer's barrel-mounted flashlight.

"Stop! On your knees, undesirable scum."

Steve quickly checked his options and, for reasons best known to himself, decided to charge the heavily armed and armoured man with a shiv fashioned from a defective trigger guard and some packing materials. He didn't make it three steps before his body erupted into gouts of red as round after round pumped into his torso.

The others, still safely behind the wall unseen, started to silently edge backwards when disaster struck. Both of Oliver's twins, awakened by the barking gunfire and screams of pain, started to wail like banshees. The group shared unspoken discussions, and, in seconds, Oliver and his wife were left vulnerable and alone, watching in dismay as their fellows bolted down the nearest alley.

By now, the enforcer had been joined by another and both men came creeping around the corner aiming for their heads. "Hands up," the first barked.

Oliver and his wife complied.

"Don't even think of running. There is a unit on the way to get your friends, they won't get far."

The sound of not-so-distant gunfire announced that their

friends had indeed been *got*.

"Just shoot them, Phil," the second urged. "GAF offices are offering a bonus to anyone who drills a runner. There's a fucking ton of them on the streets after the last election."

"Shit, Jules," Phil replied, "what about the kids?"

"Fuck 'em. Hey, maybe they count as runners, and we'll get double?"

"No, Please." Oliver stepped in front of his wife. "You can kill me and claim the bounty, no bother, just let Kagome and the twins go."

"No deal." Jules shrugged. "Are you seriously asking us to throw away at least one more bonus payment? That would see me in beer for a month!"

"Please, I'm begging you, the children are innocent in all this."

Jules the enforcer made a show of thinking for a moment before chuckling and cocking his weapon. "Nah... No deal."

Tears streamed down Kagome's face as she stepped forward to join Oliver shoulder-to-shoulder. "Please..."

"Nah, fuck it, you die."

"Wait." Phil put his hand on the barrel of Jules' gun. "Maybe we should take them in. The reward says *dead* or *alive*."

"Fuck's sake, Phil, have you gone soft, or summat?"

"Nah, I just don't like the idea of killing kids, is all. Them two, no bother, the kids..."

"I can't believe this." Jules sighed. "Okay, say we take them in, then what?"

"Then, we collect the Bonus Bounty Payment."

"Right, fine, but to get the BBP, we will have to spend hours filling out forms and get our regular pay docked for being off the streets. It kind of defeats the purpose, don't you think?"

"We could fill them out at home."

"Nope, 'fraid not, mate. Did you not read the policies introduced after the last election?"

Phil shook his head sheepishly.

"Fuck's sake, mate, that's an offence, right there. You'd better give them a shufty when you get off shift, I don't want to have to report you. Anyway, it says that 'no GAF documentation can be removed from a corporation facility without special order from the Overseer.' You could ask him, but I doubt he'd even return the email."

Phil thought for a moment for a solution. In the end, he took the easiest and most obvious one. "Fuck it, you're right, let's kill 'em."

"No, please," Oliver begged again but quickly realised that his words were falling on wilfully deaf ears. Gritting his teeth, screwing his eyes tight and hugging his family, he waited for the bullets to strike.

A harsh *crackle* of radio static stopped the enforcer's squeezing their triggers just in the nick of time. "Stop." Phil held up his hand. "It's the big man, I'd better answer it."

A cold chill raced down Oliver's back and set up home in his bowels. *The big man?* That could only mean one person... Sanderson.

"Uh, yes, sir, It was just some runners, sir, they have been dealt with... We have two survivors with infants, we are just about to execute them, sir."

Oliver held his breath.

"Yes, sir, right away, sir. We'll bring them in, sir."

Oliver's heart stopped, he never thought that he would pray for a bullet to the brain.

"It looks like it's your lucky day, after all," Phil chuckled. "Mr Sanderson wants to see you ... and he didn't sound happy."

Oliver was tired, hungry and shaken. Upon arriving at the GAF complex, his wife and children had been taken from him and he had been roughed up by a big guy in a black hood before being dumped in a cold concrete cell in the bowels of the building. It was a cube barely big enough for him to lie down. The walls, the floor, everything was white and brightly lit. To put the rotting cherry on the misery cake, a non-stop loop of GAF promotional jingles played from a tinny speaker above the door at an ear-splitting volume.

By the time the door finally opened, Oliver was a gibbering wreck. Two black-clad guards marched into the room, gripped him under the arms, then dragged him down a sterile corridor lined with similar cells towards an elevator at the far end.

"Where are you taking me?" Oliver asked his captors as one of them jabbed the button for the on-hundred-and-third floor, though he already knew he was heading for the overseer's office. He had asked Kagome, who worked in admin, the significance of the number 103 when they had met. Apparently, it was for no other reason than one-upmanship. The Empire State Building had 102, so...

Both guards remained silent and flanked him, arms folded, impassive as cheerful muzak reverberated off the steel walls. Gaudy pictures of far-too-cheerful GAF workers leered down at him from a wall-mounted screen as the lift shook and rattled as it hurtled skywards at breathtaking velocity. After a remarkably short time, the conveyance came to a shuddering halt and the doors slid open silently onto a wood-panelled foyer complete with grinning receptionist that looked like she was one surgery away from becoming one-hundred-percent plastic.

"Karl, Mike, how are you fine gentlemen today?" The receptionist chirped as they dragged their prisoner across the polished marble floor.

"Fine, thank you, Janine," the guards answered in unsettling unison.

"Go right on through, Mr Sanderson is expecting you."

"Thank you, Janine." Again, the words came in perfect synchronicity, a detail that made Oliver's flesh crawl.

Displaying a similar ease with which he would haul his children out of their cots into high-chairs for feeding, the two hulking brutes dragged him through the twin doors behind the desk and plonked him into a chair facing a wide mahogany desk adorned with neat piles of paperwork, a bottle of a popular fizzy drink, and a computer terminal. Beyond this Brobdingnagian monstrosity was a high-backed leather swivel chair with its back to the room.

"Sit," Mike barked, even though Oliver was already sitting, before leaving the room with Karl in tow and slamming the door.

Oliver's body shook as he sat and waited for the chair to turn around. Sanderson was a master at making people wait. He had discovered early in his political career that the longer you make someone sweat, the easier they are to browbeat. After a wait that seemed like an eternity, the chair swivelled around to reveal a snake in a three-piece-suit—Malcolm Sanderson, Overseer of Zone 51 and the CEO's right hand man.

"You've been a naughty boy, haven't you, Oliver?" Sanderson asked rhetorically as he smirked maliciously.

"Why have you not killed me yet?" Oliver asked bitterly. "Just get it over with, but let my family go."

Sanderson chuckled, an unnerving cackle that made Oliver wince and brought to mind the corporation-sanitised version of *Macbeth* they screened every Christmas. "Kill you? Oh no, my dear fellow, I can do better than that. Let's not look at this incident as a reason for immediate termination but as an opportunity for career growth. You see, I have a special job that needs a *very* special man for the role, and you have just proved to me that you are that chap!"

Oliver didn't like where this was going. "What?"

"Don't look so glum, I'm talking about a promotion, my dear fellow. I'm making you a supervisor in admin. And due to your contacts and standing, you are going to offer to help any potential runners escape from the zone."

Oliver was confused. "What?"

"Then you will tell me the plan in a weekly report."

The penny dropped with a clank.

"Why would I do that?" Oliver was having none of this plan, he couldn't very well betray his fellow slaves, what would his hero, the man called Dwayne, think?

"Because if you don't, I will have your family executed while you watch. Slowly."

And so, a deal was struck, one that Oliver had zero choice in. Soon, he would become one of the most reviled men in the zone.

MARCH 16TH 2127
ZONE 51 – SOUTH-WEST SECTOR:

"So?" Sanderson pressed. "Anything to report?"

Oliver's mind raced, he did have something to report, the young girl, Jane and her parents along with the separate report on Sam and Johanna. All were trying to escape the zone imminently and he had provided them with a route and passage on a trawler. He *should* just give him the information, but something deep inside his guts made him hesitate.

Kagome had all but disowned him for the deal. She couldn't bear the blood on her hands and had repeatedly told him in their frequent rows that she would rather he had sacrificed them to spare them the guilt. After all, death now seemed the only release from her slog on punishment detail in the factories. Everyone hated her by proxy, and she had attempted suicide three times in six months. Each time, she was saved by Mr Sanderson's lackeys who loomed over her like malignant guardian angels.

Finally, Oliver couldn't take the guilt and strain on his wife any longer. "No, sir, nothing to report."

"Really?"

"Really."

Sanderson studied Oliver's face, looking for a tell. As luck would have it, he was a superb poker player. "Alright, then. However, I trust I need not remind you what will happen if I find out you have been fibbing?"

"No, sir."

"Good! Come then, Mike, Karl, we have a board meeting to attend."

With that, Mr Sanderson departed.

Two weeks later, Kagome and the twins were dead, and Oliver was living with The Discarded.

CHAPTER XII

'All undesirables make your way to the nearest opt-out booth and form an orderly queue. All attempts to resist will be met with deadly force.'

Jake and Max shared a worried glance as the instruction bulletin blared from the newly erected speaker systems in the old town. The voice sounded like its deliverer had a big smile on his face... It was the unmistakable silken purr of Mr Malcolm Sanderson.

"What the hell is an *opt-out* booth?" Jake pondered.

Dwayne felt a shudder of unease. "No idea, but it can't be good."

One by one Jake, Dwayne, Max, Mickie and Frank stepped off the raised dock into a foot of putrid standing water with a splash that unleashed a noisome odour that made each one of them blanch, all except Frank, that is. The Gillman took a deep breath and sighed contentedly, the stench of seawater and rotting fish making him salivate. Nothing quite smelt like the dockside. The men each had a hunk of the strange stone from deep below the Great Sandy Desert. Mickie didn't, she instead had a holdall containing all of her pet drones, except Cricket, who had flatly refused to get in the bag and had instead jumped into her coat pocket.

"Ah, home sweet home." Frank grinned. "If you'll excuse me, I'll go and check on my family."

"Thanks again, Frank." Jake smiled, shaking the man's hand.

"How you got us back so quickly is a bloody mystery."

"The tides were in our favour. Father Dagon must have been smiling upon us favourably."

"Um ... okay. Cheers, Frank, I'll pop round in a bit when we have dropped off the stones. I have a big Voormi to pay."

Frank nodded and turned to walk away but another bulletin stopped him in his tracks.

'All Deep One hybrids, Voormis, and other non-humans please make your way to the refuse boats for deportation... All attempts to resist will be met with deadly force.'

Frank's already protuberant eyes grew even larger as the smug voice of Mr Sanderson echoed off the rusty warehouses. "Shit, my family!" Without a moment's hesitation, Frank took off at a run down the docks. Jake shouted at him to stop but he wasn't listening.

"Damn," Jake grumbled. "I'd better go with him." Looking at Mickie he said, "Can you and Max manage to get this lot back to the shop?"

Max nodded and took his stone and hefted it under his arm like it was nothing.

"Okay, Dwayne, stick yours in Mickie's bag and come with me... Make sure you are locked and loaded, I have a very bad feeling about this."

Dwayne passed Mickie his stone. She stuffed it in her rucksack and hoisted it on her shoulders.

"Right." Jake clapped Dwayne on his shoulder. "Let's get after him."

The two men charged off down the docks towards the Gillman area, sending water splashing into the sky. Mickie looked at Max to see if he could cope with carrying the rest of the stones. The big man hadn't even broken a sweat. Max smiled and nodded, and together they walked off in the direction of the antique shop.

Frank Prince had run out of puff long before he made it to the Gillman area of the docks, allowing Jake and Dwayne the opportunity to catch up with him. He wasn't exactly the fittest of men and his gills were built for swimming, not a marathon. As the three made their way towards Frank's house, the sinister messages continued to blast from above. By the time they reached the outskirts of the old town, they had a good idea of what was happening.

Mr Sanderson had declared that all citizens deemed *not human* were to be deported on the refuse ships. Where they went after this was a mystery, and Sanderson wasn't about to spill the beans. Under different circumstances, most people would have jumped at the chance to escape the horrors of Zone 51, but there were some nasty rumours... An undesirable that Jake was acquainted with, that they bumped into on the way through the twisting streets, told them that the ships were sailing out into the ocean and dumping their *cargo* for the ravenous wildlife to *dispose* of. This information sent Frank into a frenzy of panic. He had recently witnessed first-hand the horrors that lurked under the waves. If his wife and kids had been aboard one of those ships, their chances of survival were miniscule.

Jake tried to calm Frank down, pointing out that Muggo'sutha wouldn't have allowed it, but he was inconsolable and rapidly working himself into an anxiety attack. The scene that greeted them as they reached the Gillman area did nothing to alleviate his anxieties.

"Jesus," Dwayne muttered as the three men looked down on the decimated streets from the dock wall, his firm jaw set in a grim expression. "It looks like a bloody tornado ripped through here."

"Look at the number of spent shell casings," Jake added. "Fucking Caspers, looks like they have been using the area as a shooting range."

"Arseholes, the lot of 'em."

The shacks that made up most of the dwellings were either smashed beyond repair or on fire. Bodies of Gillmen callously mown down as they had attempted to flee the onslaught lay where they had dropped. Jake grimaced; it wasn't a pretty sight, rats and other scavengers had nibbled at the corpses, spreading chunks of meat and bone across the street. In short, it was an atrocity, and the air hung thick with the unbearable stench of cordite and copper.

Frank scrambled down the ramp with tears welling up in his eyes while Jake and Dwayne followed on silently behind. He took them through the ransacked market and down what had served as the high-street. Jake couldn't help getting a lump in his throat over the fact that The Dancing Shrimp looked to have been permanently put out of business. The once-thriving pub was now a smouldering wreck.

"Bastards," Jake muttered under his breath.

Dwayne said nothing but silently agreed with the sentiment.

The precious personal items belonging to innocent families and fisherfolk littered the streets. Photographs, heirlooms and keepsakes had been trampled underfoot without a single thought. In what looked to have been a relatively short period, Sanderson's purge had irreparably damaged countless more lives, many fatally. If someone was keeping a tab, the evil bastard would never be able to settle up.

Finally, they came to Frank's house. It was a deserted shell. They knew it would be, but that didn't take the sting out of what Frank was feeling. The tough sailor fell to his knees and howled. Every worst-case-scenario flickered through his head in a non-stop series of horrific images.

"Hey." Jake put his hand on Frank's shoulder. "We don't know that they have been put on one of the boats."

"Jake's right," Dwayne added in a tone that didn't sound at all convincing in the slightest. "Maybe they are in hiding."

Frank looked up from the blood-soaked street and tried to smile. "Thanks, Dwayne, but I know you don't believe that."

Dwayne said nothing.

"Look," Jake said firmly. "I put them under Muggo'sutha's protection, they're probably with him somewhere. No amount of Caspers are going to get that big son of a bitch on a boat."

Frank nodded. "You make a valid point, friend. It's worth looking for him, at least."

"That's the spirit."

"Where do we start looking?" Dwayne asked.

At that moment a brain-shredding klaxon burst from the speakers.

'Attention all enforcers, make your way to the warehouse district.'

Jake stopped, held up his finger and cocked his head.

'Attention Voormis rebels... Resistance is useless, Lay down your arms and hand yourselves over to your nearest enforcer.'

"Voormis Rebels?" Jake nodded with a smirk. "I think we know where Muggs is now, don't you?"

Gunshots, screams and the other assorted sounds of a pitched battle echoed down the narrow streets of the warehouse district. Jake, Max, and Dwayne kept to the shadows and tried to stay out of sight. Everything was fine and dandy until they neared the centre of the district, where several large, armoured vehicles blocked the street. Jake cursed; the place was crawling with enforcers. The blood-thirsty henchmen of the GAF were taking cover behind the vehicles and firing towards a makeshift barricade outside the Hyperborea bar.

Taking cover in the doorway of a white goods warehouse, Frank suggested caution. "Well that's it, we're stuffed. I know another way, but it will take ages." Tears started welling up in the fishmonger's bulbous eyes yet again.

"Not necessarily." Dwayne smirked. "Jake, follow my lead."

"Wait!" Frank yelped. "What? You can't be serious?"

Dwayne put his finger on his lips and nodded for Jake to cross the street. The battle had the full attention of the enforcers, and nobody spotted the bulky bounty hunter scuttling across to an opposing door.

"Now, stay back and out of sight," Dwayne told Frank.

"You're damn right I will. You're utterly bonkers the pair of you."

Dwayne waited for Frank to get out of the way then tossed Jake a small spherical explosive device that looked like a shiny silver marble. Jake smiled; he loved these little devils. Dwayne had bought a handful of compact concussion grenades from the market at Alice Springs, and despite their diminutive size, they packed one hell of a punch.

Dwayne motioned towards the vehicle nearest to Jake... Jake nodded. Dwayne held up five fingers... Again, Jake nodded. After five seconds had elapsed, both men acted in unison, twisting the spheres along a central axis until they clicked then tossing the grenades under their target vehicles.

A colossal explosion sent both tactical assault vehicles into the sky amidst a huge fireball. With a deafening smash, the flaming hunks of metal and plastic came crashing down on the make-shift ramparts that the enforcers were cowering behind. Several were flattened in an instant, more had their high-vis uniforms set alight.

Dwayne nodded at Jake with a look of satisfaction plastered across his face and stepped from his hiding place, shotgun in his hand. Jake flicked Jennifer's safety off and joined him in the centre of the street like a pair of wild west desperadoes squaring up to a frontier sheriff. As the smoke began to clear, two enforcers stumbled out of range of the fire, coughing and spluttering.

"Oi, Dickheads," Dwayne bellowed. "Throw down your weapons and get down on the floor."

The startled enforcers stopped sharp and instinctively went for their guns.

"Don't," Jake barked, waving his gun in one of their faces. "Seriously, lads, don't even fucking think about it."

Their survival instincts overriding their sense of duty, the enforcers did as they were told and got down on the muddy ground. Jake sauntered over while Dwayne kept them covered, proceeded to cuff them with their own restraints, relieve them of all their ammunition ... and their wallets.

"Frank," Dwayne hollered up the street. "You can come out now."

Frank couldn't believe what he had just witnessed and went trotting over with a startled expression on his face.

"Come on, Frank, we haven't got all bloody day. You heard the announcement. More Caspers are en route."

Frank picked up the pace and joined the two men standing over the two surviving enforcers. Dwayne handed Frank their guns and told him to stay close. Frank went to mouth a protest but decided against it. He needn't have worried, as it happened, they were met by a group of grinning Voormis as they stepped through the wreckage.

Jake talked to them in their strange barking language and explained that they were looking for Muggo'sutha. The biggest of the Voormis fighters pointed towards the Hyperborea bar and explained that Muggs was protecting a whole bunch of Gillmen within. Jake handed them the Casper's weapons and motioned for Dwayne and Frank to follow him.

Stepping into the bar, they were greeted by a sight none of them had ever imagined. Muggo'sutha, unarmed fighter extraordinaire and all-round badass, was playing Grandmother's footsteps with several children. Frank bellowed in happiness as he spotted his own brood over in the corner. He charged across the room, nearly sending several children flying.

Jake smiled and waved at Muggo'sutha, who waved back with a big cheesy grin on his face.

Frank's wife explained that when the enforcers came to round them up, Muggo'sutha had literally punched his way through them whilst leading the children like the pied piper. It turns out that Muggo'sutha was something of a hit with the kids. Many of the families fled with them and holed up in the Hyperborea. Many of the Gillmen were in the tunnels below.

Jake thanked Muggo'sutha, who shrugged like it was nothing. They discussed the possibility of Voormis and Gillman helping in the coming battle. Muggo'sutha said that it was a certainty and hasty plans were made. There was no point in delaying the inevitable, the battle was already here whether they liked it or not. Jake knew that this latest atrocity was something to do with their activities down under. Sanderson was making a move and if they didn't act fast, they were all doomed.

Muggo'sutha and the Voormis fighters said that they would hold the enforcers off for as long as possible. This was good, their distraction would keep some of the attention away from the GAF tower and buy everyone a little more time. Jake just hoped that the three stars Mickie had managed to craft, with Cricket's help, en route back to the Zone would be enough to take care of

Nyarlathotep's malign influence.

There was no time to lose. Jake and Dwayne left via the roof-tops and swiftly made their way back across town to the antique shop. Reaching their destination, Jake pulled Dwayne aside.

"Now, Dwayne, I'm going to have to ask you to give me your weapons and promise that you will keep your cool."

"What the bloody hell for?"

Jake sighed. "Because, my old china, there is someone inside that you are not going to be happy to see..."

"Everyone just fucking knock it off or I will let Cricket zap each one of you right in the arse, got it?" Mickie yelled above the me-lee.

Pandemonium had broken out as soon as Dwayne had stepped inside. Despite promising to hear what Oliver had to say, he had flown across the room like a man possessed and attempted to pull his head off. This, in turn, had caused Tina to pounce on Dwayne in a frenzy, growling and spitting. While they had been away, Oliver, Tina and Dave had become a bizarre kind of family, and she was willing and able to defend her pseudo-sibling.

Max and Jake manhandled Dwayne and Tina respectively while Dave made shrill bird noises. Mickie, who had been concentrating on getting the runes right on the third Mnar stone, was not impressed with the interruption.

Chirrup!

At the sound of Cricket readying his blaster, everyone fell silent and stopped struggling.

"Now, what in the living fuck is going on?" Mickie demanded in her best teacher voice.

"That son of a bitch needs to die!" Dwayne bellowed and pointed at Oliver, who was cleverly hiding behind Jake and Tina.

"Hold on Dwayne," Jake appealed. "You don't know the whole story." He went on to explain about Sanderson having Oliver's family and forcing him to blow the whistle. He also explained that Oliver didn't shop Sam, Johanna or Jane to Sanderson, an act of defiance that led to Oliver's family being tortured for eight hours then executed on live TV.

"As much as I get *why* he did it, he's still responsible for the death of many good people." Dwayne stood fast, though a little of the vitriol had gone from his voice.

"And what about you?" Oliver exploded, coming out from hiding with his body trembling and tears streaming down his cheeks. "How many deaths are you accountable for?"

"What the fuck are you talking about?"

"The big hero, Dwayne, the man who opted out, the man who told people to stand up and rebel, how many people are dying right now because of you? Do you know what has been happening since you were away?"

Dwayne shook his head.

"Inspired by your *heroic* actions, thousands of people decided to *opt-out* at the last poll. Sanderson went nuts and erected opting-out booths in every population centre. You know what an *opting-out* booth is?"

Dwayne shook his head.

"It's a fucking suicide chamber! One of those things they had all over mainland ICAE before the collapse. Anyone branded undesirable, either by choice or an act of law, is forced to go and make it *official* by *opting out...* Suicide, Dwayne, fucking suicide! Hundreds are dying every day, and it's your fucking fault!"

Dwayne was shell-shocked, his mouth moved but no sounds came out. Finally, he spoke. "I can't be blamed for this, it's Sanderson's doing."

"Exactly," Oliver spat. "Welcome to my fucking world! People are dying in your name as they did in mine, but are we really responsible?"

The silence that followed Oliver's tirade was deafening. Eventually, Dwayne shook his head and turned away, unable to meet Oliver's gaze.

Jake stepped in at that moment and spoke as levelly as he could; he had partaken of several shots down at the Hyperborea bar, so diplomacy did not come easy. At that moment, he wanted nothing more than to bang their heads together for ruining his buzz, but he did an admirable job of keeping himself in check.

"Look, neither of you is to blame, none of us is. It's Nyarla-thotep and his puppets that are to blame. Now, are we going to stand around bitching at each other all day or take the arse-kicking to them?"

Everyone was in agreement with his uncharacteristically sage words. The time to fight was nigh, and they would take Zone 51 back... Or die trying.

CHAPTER XIII

DEAD MAN'S PARTY

Gravel crunched under the wheels of the lavish stretch-limousine as it snaked its way along the long driveway towards Chycoose Manor. Bonnet-mounted flags fluttered in the stiff morning breeze, the stars and stripes resplendent in the bright sunlight. Four motorcycles carrying heavily armed guards flanked the vehicle and a van full of police officers followed its progress to the front door as a black helicopter circled ominously overhead.

As the car parked up and Mr President stepped out, the grinning form of Mr Sanderson, the current Prime Minister of Great Britain and Ireland, appeared by the front door, himself flanked by an imposing pair of Pharaoh hounds.

"Good afternoon, Mr President, I trust you had a pleasant journey?" Sanderson inquired as he trotted down the stone steps, hand outstretched.

"Pleasant, that's a joke, right? How you limeys deal with the constant rain and the tiny roads, is anyone's guess. It took me two hours to get from the god-damn' airport. Back home, I could have crossed the state in half the time."

"I did suggest that the limousine wasn't, perhaps, a suitable vehicle for the winding roads of Cornwall. A smaller car would have served you much better, I think."

The President harrumphed.

"On the subject of the weather, I find the near-constant gloom has its benefits ... as you will soon learn." The last part of

Sanderson's spiel was barely audible making Mr President cock an eyebrow and ask him to repeat himself. Sanderson declined, choosing instead to change the subject. "If you would care to follow me inside, Mr President, your arrival has been prepared for."

"You, wait out here," Mr President instructed his guards and followed his host up the stairs, the Pharaoh hounds eyeing him with suspicion as he passed.

"Wise to leave them outside, Mr President, we don't want anyone intruding on the coming events. Prying eyes are expressly forbidden by our, ahem ... *benefactor*."

As he entered the cavernous main hall, the President gasped at the startling contrast between the quintessentially English exterior and the interior. It looked like the Carter collection from the British Museum was now residing in rural Cornwall. This should have been expected, after all they were at the home of renowned archaeologist, and collector of all things ancient and Egyptian, Doctor Frank Sullivan. The room was decked out like the interior of a pyramid, the walls lined with sarcophagi and statues, while ancient tapestries and drapes covered every inch of wall-space.

Mr President was impressed. Though, as he marvelled at the collection of canopic jars and idols that littered the furniture, he was mentally running each and every item through the cash register. Towards the centre of the room stood an ornate altar flanked by a pair of mighty aspidistra. Here, the President's watery blue eyes were drawn to the centre of the large stone slab where, shielded from natural light by a low canvas canopy, was a metal casket holding a shining object.

"Ah," Sanderson purred and flashed a vulpine smile. "I see that you have spotted the shining trapezohedron, breathtaking, isn't it? Our host will introduce you to it in due course." Sanderson clicked his fingers, and a cadaverous butler appeared at his elbow with a tray holding three glasses of the finest brandy. "Care for a drink, Mr President?"

The President took a glass and swirled the liquid around before taking a sip. "Ugh, how can you drink this continental swill? Don't you have any bourbon?" He turned to the butler only to find that he had returned to whatever dark corner he came from before the President could mutter a thank you. The aged gentleman's gentleman stood in stark contrast to the other servants, clad as he was in an immaculately pressed black suit, while the others were all Egyptian and dressed in black robes.

"Good evening, gentlemen." The booming voice of Doctor Sullivan echoed around the room as he flowed down the grand staircase clad in a linen suit and a pair of dark glasses followed by a train of hounds. "I see, you have partaken in some refreshment. Thank you for joining us, Mr President." After shaking the President's hand, he let his hand fall to his waist and one of the hounds stepped forward and licked it reverentially. Social niceties complete, it was time to get down to business. Without another word, he directed his servants to ensure that no light could enter the room with a well-practised snap of the fingers before directing the President to the shining trapezohedron. With a flourish and a predatory grin, he removed the cover.

A bright flash seared the President's eyes as he stood entranced, gazing into the glittering object. Instantly, he found himself wandering a half-buried city in the heart of shifting desert landscape. After a moment of disorientation, a strange fluting noise rose over the soft lullaby of the sand and the drone of insects. The melody was at once alluring and disquieting and drew him towards a darkened doorway sat low in a partially buried building, one of several that poked like rotting teeth out of the mouth of the desert. Inside, was a set of steep stone steps. Having no control over his body, the President started what would turn out to be a long descent deep under Egypt.

Upon reaching the bottom, the piping lured him down cramped stone corridors lined with hieroglyphs and pictograms that depicted atrocities that made even him blanch. Mr President followed the stale-smelling passages into a square, lightless chamber, his ultimate destination. As a shadowy form started to coalesce in the corner of the room, he knew the negotiations were about to begin.

The Crawling Chaos opened its baleful burning eye...

As their guest conducted his business with their lord Nyarlatho-tep, Sanderson and Sullivan sat and sipped brandy.

"I think he will do very nicely... for now." Sullivan smiled.

"Indeed," Sanderson replied. "He has ambition and would sell his soul for power."

"He is about to."

Both men erupted into hysterics.

"His plans for a global corporation dovetails nicely with our Lord's plans," Sanderson continued.

"I couldn't agree more. Within five years, with Nyarlathotep's blessing, his dream of a vast corporate empire will be made reali-ty, and our plan will be one step closer to fruition."

"Indeed, what better way to ensure in-built-obsolescence is inherent in every piece of technology than to *own* every manu-facturer?"

"Do you think he will go quietly when the time comes?" Sanderson mused.

"It matters little whether he honours the bargain or goes kicking and screaming into the long dark night. He will keep to his deal whether he likes it or not." Sullivan clicked his fingers for a refill. Again, the butler appeared at the elbow of his left arm and deftly filled their glasses. As they imbibed silently, the President screamed, covered his eyes and dropped to his knees.

"I think we have a deal." Sullivan chuckled as a large black beetle scuttled across the altar and clacked its mighty mandibles at the stricken leader.

The President's eyes had changed from bright blue to inky black.

"Fetch the black book," Sullivan instructed Sanderson. "Oh, and a pair of shades for our new brother."

Sanderson walked into the library adjacent to the main hall as two large servants helped the President to his feet.

"Your vision will clear in time," Sullivan said, passing Mr President a brandy. "Though, you will be light sensitive. I take it the negotiations were a success?"

The President nodded and gulped down a slug of booze. Mo-mentarily, Sanderson returned carrying a black leather book. It reeked of centuries of corruption. He placed it on the altar next to the trapezohedron. "Okay, Mr President," Sanderson said, slipping a pair of sunglasses over his eyes. "Just one last thing to do and the deal is done."

Sullivan clicked his fingers then passed the President a curved bladed knife. He took the blade in shaky hands. The next second, one of the hounds lay at his feet and rolled onto its back. The President hesitated for a moment, then plunged the blade into the creature's heart.

"Here." Sullivan produced a black feather quill. "Welcome to the Brotherhood of Starry Wisdom."

The President dipped the nib in the gushing crimson and signed his name in the black book of Nyarlathotep.

The deal was done.

APRIL 21ST 2132
ZONE 51 – SOUTH-WEST SECTOR:

Afternoon sun beamed down through the smog above the DDC as Cricket and Pigeon zoomed over the festering docklands. Both drones were fully charged, fully loaded and ready for action. Their mission objective was simple ... infiltration. Mickie had uploaded Cricket with the plans and designated him as Wing Commander, a fact that made Cricket's motor flutter with pride and Pigeon sulk ... who said machines couldn't feel emotions?

Both drones carried cargo, and it was imperative that they got this cargo onto the roof of the DDC without being blown to smithereens. A tricky prospect considering the fact that, as soon as they entered the sensor range of the GAF security drones, the sky would be lit up with laser fire. Mickie had carefully monitored the GAF drone flight paths for many months; it was something of a hobby, and had given the two plucky little drones the data and highlighted the windows of opportunity.

Unfortunately, their cargo added sufficient weight to their chassis to considerably lessen their top speeds. Mickie hadn't thought of this, despite Cricket *chirruping* at her and trying to mime the action of being dragged down. She had mistaken it for a game of charades and guessed that he was miming the sinking of the Titanic. In the end, she had told him to stop pestering her while she was working and to go and play with Burt the cockroach. Cricket despaired of humans sometimes. So, there they were, Cricket and Pigeon, hurtling towards the DDC carrying twice their body weight and on a strict time limit... It was never going to work.

Cricket barked a digital expletive as the warning klaxons echoed off the crumbling buildings of Zone 51. As the doors on the hexagonal hanger on the roof of the DDC rattled open, Cricket *chirruped* instructions to his mechanical compatriot. Both drones dived and headed for the cover afforded by the various concrete structures of the commercial district. Cricket banked left, through the legs of a cracked video screen depicting

GAF tanks on manoeuvres, while Pigeon headed right through a parking structure.

A wave of security drones poured from the now-open doors like lines of laser-spitting army ants and filed down the tower before fanning out. Cricket ducked through an indoor shopping mall for GAF drudgers, nearly clattering into the bewildered face of an off-duty Casper, and out of the serving window of the ration exchange. Two security drones rounded the corner and fired. Cricket shifted the weight of his cargo and went into a spin, dodging the salvo. Returning fire, he caught one of them directly in the propeller and sent it slamming into the other and erupting them into flame.

Pigeon *cooed* in panic as he took the steep ramps up to the top storey; he had two drones on his tail, and they were gaining fast. As he reached the roof, he fired at the security switch. It exploded in a plume of sparks and the security barrier slammed down behind him with a mighty *crash*. The pursuing drones were too close for evasion and were shattered to pieces as they collided with the red and white steel shutter.

After taking out three more enemy drones, Cricket attempted to get back on course. At the same time, Pigeon was having the same idea which was unsurprising considering they had both had their AI modified by the same woman. As they headed for the roof of the DDC, the rest of the drones regrouped and gave chase. It looked like they would be able to deliver their cargo, but it was unlikely they would escape.

Things were looking bleak when, across town, one of the security checkpoints exploded as a rusty tractor driven by Dwayne ploughed into its generator. The drones broke off their attack and chose instead to investigate the ruckus below. Apparently, exploding tractors were classed as a higher threat than two small drones ... if only they knew.

Diving towards one of the open doors, both Cricket and Pigeon let go of their cargo. As the two objects landed inside one of the dispatch units, they disengaged and flew off to await the next part of Mickie's plan.

The objects that landed inside the hexagonal structure shook themselves down and twittered at each other in machine code. Like their flying brothers, Sniffer and Hopper had been well prepared. Mickie had hacked the DDC mainframe many times during her time working there and was able to download a complete schematic of the infrastructure. Charging towards the back of the room, Sniffer spotted just what he was looking for: A ventilation grill.

There was a colossal *crash* as Sniffer headbutted his way through the thin aluminium like it was wet paper and scampered into the narrow ducting. Hopper followed his quicker friend into the duct and tried to keep up. Sniffer clattered down the vents leading below the automated drone assembly centre where the various drones used in the control of Zone 51 were maintained and constructed by an automated assembly line. Every time a drone failed or was destroyed, another was quickly constructed to replace it. Cricket and Pigeon's dogfight had kicked the heavy machinery into overdrive.

It didn't take the duo long to make it down to the control area. Since that awful day when the tech failed, and everything went to a deeper circle of hell than before, the DDC control centre had been manned by what were essentially zombies. The current workers had all had their brains fried by syntheshock and were little more than automatons. Each one stared blankly at a screen, occasionally tapping a button when they received the right impulse from their overloaded chips. These poor souls were the GAF's dream employees.

Bursting through the vent, Sniffer led the way out onto the control floor. It was from here that all the drones received their orders. A warning klaxon kicked in as the sensors picked up the interlopers. Barking at hopper to keep back, Sniffer blasted the two guard Caspers in the chest before either of them knew what was going on. The glassy-eyed workers rose from their seats and turned to stare at Sniffer. "Obsolete," they crooned as one. Sniffer yipped and fired his laser into the video wall to get their attention. The workers flew into a rage and started to charge after the nimble little robot.

This was Hopper's chance, his big moment. While the controllers were chasing Sniffer around a server stack, the small drone that thought he was a frog hopped into the air and landed on one of the computer banks. He shot out his interface cable and jammed it into the terminal. For a moment, nothing happened, then the chips in the controllers shut down, and they went down like a row of dominoes. One by one, they plummeted to the floor as Sniffer scuttled out of harm's way.

As Mickie's virus spread through the system, corrupting the software and bending the active drones to her will, Hopper moved along the bank of screens and located the one that controlled the automated machinery above. Cranking all of the systems into overdrive and disabling the fail-safe, Hopper gave a *ribbit* of triumph and hopped down to the floor. Sniffer barked instructions to his friend, and they headed back into the ducts to make their escape. It was a long way down to the ground floor, but it was a much safer bet than going back up to the roof. After all, it was going to blow at any second...

Cricket and Pigeon had been leading the security drones on a merry dance around the sector. Free of their cargo, the two agile mechanical critters had easily out-paced and out-manoeuvred their opposition. Still, it came as something of a relief when Mickie's code finally kicked in and they all suddenly just stopped and hung in the air, awaiting instructions.

After a couple of minutes, Mickie's voice spoke to all of the assembled drones. "Okay, troops, you are under the command of Wing Commander Cricket and Flight Lieutenant Pigeon, follow their orders at all times."

Cricket *chirruped,* and the drones moved into an arrow-head formation with Cricket and Pigeon at the tip.

As the top of the DDC exploded in a shower of metal and glass, Cricket gave his troops their orders. They soared into the sky as a mushroom cloud blossomed behind them. They had their target in sight. Now, it was up to Mickie to complete her objective...

It was all going to plan.

APRIL 21ST 2132
ZONE 51 – CHYCOOSE MANOR:

"Alright, guys ... wait for the signal." Mickie was crouching behind a rickety potting shed with Jake, Frank and Muggo'sutha. Frank was terrified, and the other two were chomping at the bit to get inside the imposing manor and start cracking some heads.

"What's the signal again?" Frank stammered. He wasn't going inside, it was his job to commandeer one of the GAF transport vehicles in the gravel carpark once the Caspers on the door had been dealt with. This didn't mean that he wasn't terrified.

Mickie turned and smiled. "You'll know it when it happens ... trust me."

In a second, they did as, a couple of miles away from Chycoose Manor, the top of the DDC tower exploded in a colossal gout of fire and black smoke that was visible from even this distance.

Mickie grinned like a proud parent. "Good boy, Cricket."

"What the hell just happened?" Frank nearly leapt into the air in surprise, the gills on the side of his wide neck flapping rhythmically.

"That was the signal." Jake grinned and drew Jennifer. "Look—it's working." The enforcers manning the doors had been sufficiently distracted by the distant detonation that they deserted their post and wandered over to the side of the overgrown hedge maze to get a better view of the devastation. "Come on, Muggs, let's do this.

Muggo'sutha grinned, showing off his vicious-looking teeth, cracked his knuckles and nodded. Creeping around the side of a once-neatly-trimmed privet, the two men approached the two enforcers from behind. Before either man knew it was coming, they were both felled by clubbing blows from behind. As Muggs dragged the unconscious men into the hedge-maze and dumped them next to a headless statue, Jake followed, giving instructions to Frank while Mickie watched on in silence.

"Alright, Frank, strip 'em and extract their ID chips from under their barcodes."

"What do you mean, *extract?*"

Jake grinned and passed him a rusty penknife.

Frank gulped, sweat beading his wide brow.

"Once you've done that, get one of those vehicles ready to go, we'll need to get out of here and back to the plaza in a hurry. Max is counting on us. Mickie, you stay out here with Frank." Jake set his aviators to thermal and turned in the direction of the stout oak doors.

Mickie grabbed his shoulder forcefully, her enhanced fingers digging into his metal ball joint. "Nuts to that, I'm coming in with you."

"What?" Jake turned. "We agreed—"

"No, you and Dwayne agreed. I never agreed to sit outside like a lemon while you and the furry terror over there get to have all the fun! I'm going in, and that's final. "

Jake opened his mouth to argue but quickly thought better of it. "Fine, Just keep away from any pharaoh hounds, I'm picking up loads of them on the scan."

"They shouldn't be a problem. Your buddy, Muggs should be enough of a deterrent, dogs are terrified of Voormis for some reason."

Muggs joined the group and nodded to agree with Mickie. He looked at Jake and gave a series of grunts.

"Eh? What do you mean, she will be more useful than me?"

Muggo'sutha grinned.

Mickie shot the furry joker a double thumbs-up before gesturing to the door. "Shall we?"

"Come on, then." Jake walked towards the door before pausing and inclining his head towards Mickie. "What is it that we are looking for again?"

"A shining trapezohedron... It will be in a lightless room in a metal casket."

"Right..." He started walking again before once more stopping sharply and raising an eyebrow quizzically. "Oh, Mickie?"

Mickie sighed and folded her arms. "Yes?"

"What the hell is a trapezohedron?"

Brushing her black hair from out of her eyes, Mickie sighed again. "Didn't you go to an education centre?"

"Nah, I was too old. I went to a school ... remember those?"

"Nope... Anyway, just look for a shiny stone in a metal box in the dark... Okay?"

"Yeah." Jake took a hit from his hip flask. "Got it. Let's go."

Muggs grunted.

Mickie burst into fits of giggles. "I know, right?"

Jake scowled in their direction. "What was that?"

"Oh ... nothing." Mickie grinned as Muggo'sutha shrugged and pretended to look innocent—no mean feat. "Let's get on with it, Max and the others are relying on us to neutralise Nyarlathotep's influence."

"Okay, point taken." Jake huffed as he reared back and booted the doors open with a *crash*. With his gun levelled and his thermal vision engaged, he stepped inside. A small hallway, complete with a hat and umbrella stand, led into a cavernous main hall. Not a sliver of light was afforded access, each window was covered in a heavy black curtain and secured to the edges with drawing pins. Muggo'sutha and Mickie readied the flashlights that they had brought with them and switched them on.

"Bloody hell," Mickie gasped. "Look at this place." The room was decked out with Egyptian relics and tapestries. "I feel like I'm in King Tut's tomb."

"Blimey, you're not kidding. It's bloody staler than a packet of GAF biscuits in here, I can't breathe for the dust. Muggs, get those windows open, let's get a little light in here."

Muggo'sutha grunted a reply and stomped over to the nearest window where he hooked his thick nails over the top of the fabric and pulled. Drawing pins pinged onto the bare floorboards as shards of light streamed into the room. As he forced the ancient sash window open, the air shifted.

"What the hell?" Mickie jumped as the air rippled in front of her eyes. The motes of dust that drifted in the air rolled and dipped like flotsam on a swollen wave. She took a step backwards and levelled the gun in front of her. "Jake! What the hell is happening?"

Jake recoiled as the shadow adjacent to the now-open window lurched towards him. "Holy shit! The shadow ... it's alive!"

The room started to shudder as the shadow moved away from

the square of natural light. Jake jumped out of harm's way as a smoky tendril lashed towards him. Running to the light, he bellowed, "Light, we need more light... Shoot out the fucking windows!"

Mickie had been entranced by the ebbing dust, so much so that she hadn't noticed it building into a fist-like ball. Jake's panicked shouting brought her back to earth with a *thump,* just in the nick of time. "Back you bugger!" she screamed as she took aim at the large window to her left and fired. The window exploded as a volley from her *Critterbuster* shotgun annihilated the glass. Light flooded in, submerging the ball of shadow. It screamed and hissed in pain and fury before darting back to the rear of the room.

"It's Nyarlathotep! The shadow, it's him, it's alive." Mickie stood in the centre of the column of light and aimed at the next window along the wall. "Shoot the windows, take them all out!"

Muggo'sutha was way ahead of her—he had already slammed his big furry fists through the double doors that led to a jungle-like summerhouse. Clearly, the Crawling Chaos wasn't much of a gardener. A scuttling horde of fat black beetles rushed from the foliage and into the hall making Muggs enact a startled jig as they skittered past his feet. From there, they rushed past Mickie and followed the shadow to the darkened end of the room.

Jake blasted at the windows on his side of the room, forcing Nyarlathotep to retreat. The shadows moved back towards the grand staircase and formed into a massive oily ball of darkness. Wispy fronds tasted the air, trying desperately to find a way through the harsh sunlight. Roaring with frustration, a three-lobed burning eye opened in the centre of its mass and glared at them with unrestrained malice as shards of glass and shredded fabric tinkled to the floor.

Violent tremors continued to shake the room as the shadow of the Dark Pharaoh continued to thrash around smashing canopic jars and sending priceless sarcophagi clattering to the floor.

"Use the torches to keep him back," Jake yelled as they ran out of windows. They had reached the centre of the hall, the point where the house split into two sprawling wings. One by one, they turned the high-powered beams on the swirling darkness. Its eyes closed and steam rose from its bulk as the light seared its body. With a final lash of a tentacle and a howl of rage, the shadow receded up the stairs and into the west-wing corridor.

Just as the group was about to breathe a sigh of relief, a pack of slavering pharaoh hounds burst from the doors to the east-wing of the hall. Jake turned the air blue with a litany of expletives and ducked behind a sarcophagus. Mickie took cover behind a table while Muggo'sutha slung his *Critterbuster* over his shoulder and stepped forwards, meeting the pack head-on.

"Careful, Muggs," Jake insisted. "Look at their eyes, those beasts are under *his* influence."

Each dog had burning orange eyes and was frothing at the maw as though rabid. Muggo'sutha grunted, "I know" and bared his teeth. Hunching forwards and tensing his muscular umber-furred arms, he snarled and barked at the incoming canines. It was almost like someone had stopped the clock as the dogs came to a whimpering halt in front of the hulking Voormis.

"It's working," Mickie hissed ecstatically.

The hounds looked at each other uncertainly and shifted their legs around. Jake took aim, he didn't want to gun down a dog, but if he had no choice, he wouldn't hesitate. Muggs continued to bellow and growl, and it looked for one beautiful moment like Nyarlathotep's influence was waning. Their eyes started to flicker between orange and black, and they were on the verge of calling it quits when the building shook with a ferocious primal howl.

"Oh, bollocks," Mickie gulped as the howl of the Crawling Chaos spurred the hounds into action.

Muggo'sutha swung one of his mighty fists as the first hound pounced. It connected with the creature's jaw, snapping its neck with a sickening *crack*. The second went the same way but with the opposite fist. Before he could get his footing for another knock-out blow, a third hound launched itself at his throat.

Boom!

Mickie let off a volley from her *Critterbuster* and vaporised the dog's head. A tear rolled down her cheek as she loosed off another round, then another. Jake joined in the attack, and soon, the pack was little more than a steaming mass of mangled meat and splintered bone.

"Damn it," Mickie sobbed as she wiped her eyes. "I didn't want to do that. And look, now my eyeliner has run; I look like a bloody panda."

Jake too felt awful. "Poor creatures ... but you can't blame yourself, Mick. They were probably long dead, going by the smell and the blackness of the blood. You had no choice."

"I know," Mickie sniffed. "I just hate hurting animals... People, no problem, but animals... I feel sick."

Muggo'sutha put a heavy paw on her shoulder and smiled softly before giving her a "thank you" grunt and a thumbs up.

"You saved big Muggs ... you've got a buddy for life now. Nothing is as loyal as a grateful Voormis."

Mickie looked at Muggo'sutha's big hairy face and smiled.

Jake reloaded Jennifer and took a swig from his hip flask. "Come on, let's find that shiny trampoline before Nyarlathotep sends any more horrors in our direction."

"Shining Trapezohedron, you twat... *Shiny trampoline...* Give me strength." Mickie sniggered at Jake's befuddled expression and made her way towards a pair of large doors on the west wall. Pushing them open, she gasped. Before her, was a library crammed with esoteric tomes, scrolls and reams of hand-written notes. It looked like there had once been a pitched battle in this room as the once-lavish carpet was despoiled by soot, glass and scorch marks. "Check this lot out."

Jake moved to the doors and looked in. "Quick, Muggs get those windows open." A ghostly rattling started to emanate from the large chimney breast as plumes of soot and debris started to belch forth from the fireplace.

Muggo'sutha dived across the room and slammed his fists against the blackout curtains, shattering the windows, then with one mighty tug, he ripped the curtain rail off the wall in a shower of plaster. A shaft of light landed on the hearth, and whatever was in the chimney shrieked and receded.

"Good job, Muggs," Mickie panted. "That should keep him at bay for now... Jake, start searching for the trapezohedron, it has to be kept in darkness or Nyarlathotep can't materialise his avatars. Find it and take it out into the light, that should cut off his control long enough for Max to do his thing."

"Right, will do." Jake swept a mountain of paper onto the floor and whistled. "Old Ben would have loved it in here. He'd have been like a kid in a sweetshop."

"Yeah, poor Ben." Mickie sighed as she rummaged under an old table piled high with mouldering books. "I know you two never saw eye to eye, but he was a good man, when he wasn't under Ger'igguthy's thrall."

"No doubt, I just don't like being lied to … lies get you killed."

"True."

Their conversation was derailed by a grunt of surprise from Muggo'sutha.

"What is it, Muggs?" Jake asked.

The big Voormis waved an old photograph at them.

Mickie stood and shook the dust from her raven hair, then took the item from him, her eyes narrowing with hatred. "Well, will you look at this… this is where it all started."

Jake hopped over and looked at the picture. "Bastards." Standing over the butchered remains of a pharaoh hound were Mr Sanderson, the CEO, and a gentleman clutching a black book. "I know this fucker! I met him in Pnakotus."

"Who is it?" Mickie asked.

Muggo'sutha grunted and pointed at a portrait over the fireplace. It showed a ruddy-cheeked explorer in a linen suit standing in front of a partly submerged fane by night. It was a standard portrait apart from the eyes. The artist had given his subject burning orange orbs.

"That's him, Doctor Frank bloody Sullivan," Jake exclaimed. "This must be his gaff… Look, there's an inscription underneath."

"What's it say?"

"Doctor Sullivan, Irem, the city of pillars… Hey, isn't that where Nyarlathotep is supposed to be?"

"I'm assuming this is the nutcase that freed him, then?" Mickie cracked her knuckles.

"Yep, stupid arsehole. The question is, was he already under the influence by this point or was that when it happened? Brent said something about a party… Probably at this very house." Jake pondered the portrait for a while before returning to the search. After a few minutes, he stopped and swore under his breath. "Nah, it ain't here ... maybe there is a study or something?"

"There is, it's at the back of the building, up the stairs," Mickie confirmed. "I found the architectural plans amongst Ben's stuff. He'd been studying this place for years."

"Oh, great... up the stairs, where *he* is?"

"Sorry, Jake, it looks like it's going to be a long night."

"I don't suppose you brought any of those flash-bang thingies?"

Mickie said nothing, just shot Jake a big grin and took her bag off her back. Once opened, she dove in and came out with handfuls of her home-made bombs. "There are five each. I thought we might meet some lurkers later."

"Brilliant!" Jake grinned and pocketed his bombs. With a smug smile, he tapped his sunglasses. "Well, I'm okay... You two will have to shut your eyes."

"Nope." Mickie topped his smugness with a smirk of her own. "I came prepared." She jumped into her bag once again and came out with two pairs of shades. One, which she put on her face, was sleek and black. The other was bright pink and huge. "Sorry, Muggs, it was the only pair I could find that would fit on your face."

Muggo'sutha took them and shrugged; he cared very little how he looked. He placed them on his face and grinned. Jake burst into hysterics, Muggs replied with an extended middle finger that just made Jake giggle even more.

"Alright, you pair of idiots, let's get on with it. Max must be on target by now."

"Agreed, come on, Muggs. Let's get cracking."

Stepping back into the main hall, the first thing that caught Jake's eye was beetles. Huge fat black beetles. They hid in the pools of shadow between the windows, clacking, hissing, and skittering. On close inspection of a nearby specimen, Jake noticed that they had a strange orange glow to the antennae. "We are being watched." He pointed his torch at a nearby cluster, causing them to scatter and slip behind the skirting board. "The beetles are his eyes. They look vicious. Do beetles eat human flesh?"

"I think those ones do—I think they're some kind of scarab." Mickie shuddered. "Keep them back with your lights."

As they reached the end of the curtain of sunlight, it was like hitting a wall as they entered Nyarlathotep's sinister domain. Jake led the way towards the grand staircase, skirting the shards of pottery and the overturned casket. The shadows in the corners shuddered and twitched as he mounted the stairs. Mickie flashed her light in the nearest corner, and the amorphous old one screeched and retreated towards the doors to the centre of the landing... precisely where they were going.

"Damn it, he knows where we are heading."

Muggo'sutha yelped and nearly went into orbit as he glanced behind him and saw a living carpet of beetles creeping behind him. Regaining his composure, he swept the light across the floor and sent them running for cover.

Once they had reached the landing, Mickie took one of the flash-bangs from her pocket and tapped Jake on the shoulder. "Let's give Nyarlathotep something to howl about, shall we."

Jake nodded and motioned for Muggs to put his shades on.

"Ready? ... One... Two... Take that, you bastard!" Mickie tossed the bomb and turned her head.

The corridor blazed with harsh white light. Nyarlathotep shrieked and howled then burst into a cloud of black molecules that seeped through the cracks in the ceiling and retreated into the attic.

Muggs growled in triumph and motioned towards the door at the far end.

"Yeah, come on... Let's go before he returns." Jake nodded at Muggo'sutha, grabbed Mickie by the hand and legged it towards the study. Clattering through the door, they came to an awestruck stop.

"Elder Gods!" Mickie gasped. The windows of the study had been bricked up and in the centre was a raised altar. On the top was a shining object. "The trapezohedron, that's it... grab it!"

Muggo'sutha nodded at Mickie and leapt towards the evil object. Before he could reach it, there was a deafening *bang*. Muggs bellowed and spun as a bullet slammed into his shoulder. His momentum sent him sprawling into a large bookcase, toppling it over. Books and artefacts clattered to the floor, bouncing off the felled Voormis' head.

Jake screamed invective and turned towards their attacker.

A heavy sarcophagus lid slammed to the floor, revealing a cadaverous figure in a linen suit.

Jake pumped three heavy-duty shells into Professor Sullivan. "How the fuck did you escape Pnakotus?"

The living dead archaeologist grinned a broad rictus that nearly ripped his green sagging jowls. "Pathetic worm, you can't stop the Crawling Chaos." Sullivan raised his antique army service revolver and returned fire. "Once I had recovered from your attack, it was a simple matter to escape my entombment. Do you really think one such as I am bound by the same natural laws as one such as you?"

Jake dived behind the altar as the bullets thudded into the carpet. "Meaning?"

"A portal, you insignificant insect... Now, bow before the Dark Pharaoh!" He pointed the muzzle of the gun at Jake's head and started to squeeze the trigger.

"Oi, Dickhead!" Mickie screamed and tossed all five of her flash-bangs into the casket.

The series of blinding white lights erupted around the reanimated corpse of Professor Sullivan making him stagger forwards into the room, croaking and groaning. The light had stripped the skin from his face in disgusting strips. His head tipped back, and an ear-splitting howl shook the building to its foundations. Plaster and masonry tumbled from the ceiling as the puppet of Nyarlathotep fought to escape the light.

Mickie stood slack jawed as his bones started to crack, and his upper torso elongated and stretched into a grotesque tentacle of meat and sinew. "Down!" she screamed as it lashed and flailed around the room.

Jake leapt to his feet and ducked a whip-like *crack*. Lunging forwards, he grabbed the metal casket containing the shining trapezohedron. "Mickie, catch!"

The box spun through the air and landed in her open hands. With a smooth motion, she opened the lid, shoved the head of her torch into it and switched the beam to *high*.

There was a disgusting *splat* and Jake was showered in foul-smelling ichor as Doctor Sullivan exploded.

Frank pulled nervously on his cigarette as he watched the building behind him shake itself to pieces in the rear-view mirror. His anxiety levels had shot through the roof as he watched the hazy sun slowly sink behind the windswept hills. If they weren't out soon, they were royally screwed. With a sigh, he took another pull on the cigarette and said a little prayer to Dagon.

Thump. Thump. Thump.

"Wake up, Frank, and open the sodding door," a frantic-looking Mickie screamed through his window, making him yelp in mortal terror. He did as instructed and the rear door popped open and the bleeding form of Muggo'sutha fell into a seat and grinned at him.

Mickie was next inside, closely followed by Jake, who was holding a torch over a metal box.

"Is that it?" Frank asked.

"Yeah... drive," was Jake's curt reply. "We need to get our backsides back to the GAF tower, pronto."

Frank nodded and fired up the weedy electric engine. "Is Muggs okay?"

Muggo'sutha grunted and huffed.

"I'm sorry, I don't speak Voormis, what did he say, Jake?"

"He said shut up and drive," Jake chuckled. "Nah, just kidding, he said, 'yes, thank you.'"

"So, we did it?" Frank grinned.

"Yeah..." Mickie sighed. "It's all up to you now, Max."

CHAPTER XIV

UNDER THE GUN

Beads of sweat clustered in Malcolm Sanderson's carefully trimmed eyebrows as he focused his cigar-smoke stung eyes on his hand. Two Sixes with a King kicker, it should be enough, but he had his doubts, a lingering unease that seemed to originate from his unsettling opponent. The casino in the heart of Cairo was packed with visiting dignitaries and millionaire playboys. A hush had settled over the grand old room where Houdini once performed before his strange experience under a pyramid. The game of brag was for the highest stakes with a thousand USD buy-in.

Sanderson gazed across the table at the strangely dark-eyed Egyptian. It was crunch time and the man had to pay in order to see Sanderson's hand; it was either that or fold and lose the gargantuan pot.

"I'm afraid, Sahib, I have run short of *conventional* funds... I offer instead this coin of immense value." The man held it up to the light in his thumb and forefinger.

Malcolm looked at the coin. It *was* a beauty, and he knew at that instant that he needed that coin, he had to have it. "Fine... play on."

His opponent flicked the coin into the air with a thick, dirty thumb. It spun and fell with a satisfying clatter into the massive pile of notes, coins and jewellery.

Sanderson and his mysterious opponent had seen off all the

other players, leaving a mass of riches on the line for the man with the best cards. As a politician, Malcolm was a master of the bluff, after all. A simple card game was child's play after managing to convince the population of the United Kingdom that the economy was sound in his role as Chancellor of the Exchequer. He placed another billfold on the pile and motioned with his hands. "I'll see you."

The Egyptian gave an unsettling, toothy grin and placed his cards on the table, his dark eyes locked on Malcolm's. One three, the Jack of clubs and the King of hearts. Sanderson yelled in triumph and slapped his cards down on the table.

Cheers rang out amongst the patrons and the finest champagne was poured into the finest crystal flutes. Sanderson stuffed his winnings into a briefcase and snapped the handcuff over his wrist. He held the gold coin up to the light and admired the intricate design. It was indeed old, ancient, actually. It carried the bizarre likeness of a Pharaoh with what looked like smoky tentacles for a face.

He turned back to the table in order to console his thrashed opponent, but the strange old man had vanished. He asked the croupier and various high-class patrons, but nobody had seen him leave. The old Egyptian, who Sanderson later learned was named Ammon, had seemingly vanished like a puff of smoke ... or a shadow.

After a hearty celebration, Sanderson, along with his massive bodyguards, left the casino to head back to their luxurious suite. As they left, Sanderson noticed a pile of discarded rags, similar to the old Egyptian's robes. The wind blew the dust around his expensive shoes as he strode on by.

Upon reaching his room, Sanderson was overcome by the evenings' exertions. The combination of adrenaline and strong drink had left him feeling dizzy and nauseated. Rushing to the bathroom he vomited for all his worth. It was as though his very insides were being expelled from his body, like an exorcism. Once purged, he dragged his weakened body to the bed and collapsed, with the strange coin on his chest.

That night he was assailed by strange dreams of lost Irem. The city of pillars loomed out of the shifting sands like a mirage while shadows danced around the crumbling architecture that seemed to flicker and contort under the hazy lambency of a gibbous moon. The wind carried the haunting melody of twisted pipes that ushered him into a low opening. Inside, he could sense a presence. A divine force, irresistible and alluring.

Malcolm Sanderson embraced the strange dark one in the fane.

Morning light filtered through the lavish curtains stirring Malcolm from his deep slumber. He rose, dressed and prepared to attend the talks at the embassy that had brought him here. As he brushed his hair, he noticed that his once hazel eyes looked almost black and seemed to absorb light, like pools of cephalopod ink. He smiled and patted the gold coin in his breast pocket. The conference was going to be clay in his hands ... clay, ripe for moulding.

Malcolm Sanderson exuded confidence as he convinced the assembled politicians to enter into a massive weapons and oil deal with the United Kingdom. He rolled the coin over his fingers as he addressed the room and flashed his winning smile. This knowing smirk was in evidence once again when he returned to his constituency and was showered with high praise from the Prime Minister. A number of inner-party political moves had been playing out while he was away, and he eagerly accepted the post of deputy P.M. when it was offered to him on a silver platter.

Less than a month later, following a freak accident where the Prime Minister was struck by lightning whilst playing golf, Malcolm Sanderson was appointed as new party leader and was re-elected the following year.

The irresistible rise of Malcolm Sanderson had begun.

APRIL 21ST 2132

ZONE 51 – SOUTH-WEST SECTOR:

"Fuck's sake, won't this bloody thing go any faster?" Dwayne grumbled over the thrum of the ailing diesel engine as Oliver's tractor rattled away from the flaming security checkpoint.

"What do you think?" Oliver rolled his eyes. "It's a twenty-first-century agricultural tractor. It's built to pull a ruddy plough not cruise a Zone 55 autobahn."

"Alright, point taken, no need to be a dick about it."

"Fuck you, Dwayne." Oliver made a mental note, *never meet your heroes*.

Max sighed as he kept watch on the road behind them. Things had been decidedly frosty between his two companions since their heated confrontation at the antique shop. An issue that was then exacerbated by Dwayne winning the coin-toss that settled who was going to drive. Max was, after hearing them squabble like a pair of spoilt adolescents for the past two hours, one raised word away from bashing their heads together and throwing them to the lurkers. He was trying to keep a level head, but they were not making it easy for him.

As Dwayne opened his mouth for a retort, Max shot the bolt on his AK-47 and glowered at both of them.

"Sorry, Max," Oliver mumbled as he crossed his arms over his chest and studied the road ahead.

"Yeah, sorry, man. I'll keep my trap shut and my eyes on the road from now on."

Max smiled; it was amazing how much he could say with a simple flick of the firing bolt. Later, if all went to plan on Mickie's end, he planned on saying a lot more to Mr Sanderson with different parts of his weapon... The bullets in particular had a few epithets ready to spit. He returned his attention to their rear and watched the thick black smoke twist and dance in the wind. It was an odd moment of calm before the inevitable storm.

"Be careful as we hang right into the plaza, there's a cafe that's usually swarming with off-duty Caspers."

Dwayne nodded and slowed the tractor in order to safely mount the bend. Oliver readied the gun he had taken from a dead enforcer and traced the curvature of the road. Relief washed over him on finding the usually bustling street utterly deserted.

"Where is everybody?" Dwayne asked as he straightened up the tractor and slammed his foot down.

"I assume they have all been called to arms over at the DDC... There was a bulletin earlier warning civilians to stay in the habitation centre."

"That's good. The last thing we want is more innocent blood on our hands..."

Oliver shot him a look, then took a sideways look at Max. In the end, he thought better of voicing his grievances, choosing instead to set his jaw firm and check that his clip was full. It was and had been the last six times he'd checked. His nerves were jangling like a GAF radio promotion. One look at the tremor in Dwayne's left hand told him that he wasn't alone. As they turned off the main thoroughfare towards the plaza, Max grunted and pointed to the square outside the GAF tower.

"Holy mother of balls... Have you ever seen so many fucking Caspers in all your life?" Below, in the square, were hundreds of enforcers lined up in military square formation. They were all staring at the GAF tower where a holographic projection of Malcolm Sanderson read out a rousing speech.

"Pull over!"

"What?"

"Seriously, Dwayne, pull over. If they hear the engine, we're dead."

Max nodded emphatically and pointed at the curb.

Dwayne did as he was told and brought them to a rattling halt. "Now what?"

"Now, we get closer and keep quiet. I want to hear what he has to say."

"What the hell for?"

"Because it may give us an indication of how Mickie is getting on."

Dwayne didn't want to go along with Oliver's plan and looked to Max for backup. He was disappointed. Max nodded along with Oliver and gestured for Dwayne to take the lead. He was, after all, the point man of their minute fireteam.

"Fine... If we keep low, we can hide behind one of the raised flower beds." Leading the others down a narrow flight of stairs, Dwayne ushered them behind the concrete and placed his finger on his lips.

"*Even now,*" Sanderson's enormous floating head intoned gravely. "*Our enemies attack the private residence of one of our great benefactors. I can assure you all, they will not succeed. Zone 51 will stand stronger than ever before under the protective shadow of The Crawling Chaos. Our enemies will fall, and all non-humans will be purged from our land. The era of the undesirable is at an end!*"

As one, the enforcers raised their fists skyward and intoned words that made the trio spying on the rally shudder. "*Iä! Iä! Nyarlathotep fhtagn!*"

"Go from here, wield your GAF rifles with pride and obliterate the obsolete, prune the non-conformists, and exterminate the undesirables!"

"*Iä! Iä! Nyarlathotep fhtagn!*"

Max didn't like what he was hearing. This was the first time he had heard enforcers mention Nyarlathotep, and what was all the gibberish language about? While Dwayne and Oliver focussed on Sanderson, he crawled the length of the raised bed and scrutinised the face of the nearest enforcer. He was glazed and impassive, clammy and pale. Realisation dawned; these were Sanderson's crack force made up entirely of syntheshock victims that had been reprogrammed the way Dave and Tina had... Though what they had been reprogrammed with was far more insidious than a cat or penguin.

"*You have your orders,*" Sanderson concluded. "*Go now, inch by inch, yard by yard, and erase them all!*"

"*Iä! Iä! Nyarlathotep fhtagn!*"

As a bright and breezy GAF jingle blared forth from the speakers, Sanderson cut the feed. En masse, the enforcers turned, stamped their right boots, and fell into seek and destroy companies, one of which was yards from the trio. Oliver swallowed; they were sitting ducks.

"Well done, dickhead, I knew this was a stupid idea." Dwayne scowled while Max searched for an exit.

"Don't just sit there blaming me, you cock, think of something!"

"Like what?"

"You tell me, hero... you're the smart-arse with all the fucking answers."

Dwayne clenched his fist but was grabbed by Max who pointed to the sky.

"Oh," Oliver gushed. "Thank Christ!"

From above, hundreds of drones poured from the clouds, strafing the enforcers with laser and gunfire. The zombified mass returned fire but was being mowed down in droves. Dwayne whooped and cheered as Cricket and Pigeon broke off from the attack squad and flew in the direction of the shop. Their mission complete, the two drones could safely disengage and go and recharge.

"Nice one, Cricket," Oliver panted. "I believe that's our cue." He turned to Max and gestured to the tower. "Shall we?"

Max nodded but motioned for them to pause for a second. By now, the enforcers had been whittled down to around half their number, but the drones were being destroyed just as quickly. It was a war of attrition that the drones were doomed to fail through sheer numbers.

"Bugger, looks like there will still be loads of them left. Best make a break for it now and keep to cover."

"For once, I'm in full agreement with Oliver." Dwayne shrugged. "I reckon hell is going to freeze over next... Come on."

Before they could make it halfway to the doors, the last drone fell, and silence reigned. Dwayne stopped and looked around as one-by-one the remaining enforcers turned in their direction, guns raised.

"Shit..."

Max stood firm and awaited the gunfire, but it never came ... the enforcers stood as still as statues for a painful handful of heartbeats before grabbing their heads, dropping their guns, and falling to their knees.

"What the hell is going on?" Oliver asked as he tried to get control of his breathing.

Each enforcer tipped his head back and screamed in a cavernous voice not of their own.

"It must be Mickie; she must have found the trapezohedron!"

Max motioned for them to hasten to the tower entrance but detected another sound from the eastern side of the plaza that stopped him short. It was the unsettling sound of chanting and slovenly footsteps. The remaining Discarded had decided to take advantage of their attack and stage another attempted coup.

As the parasite-infested horde opened fire on the downed enforcers, Max grabbed Oliver and Dwayne and threw them towards the doors.

"Easy, Max, I get it," Dwayne said as he jerked himself free of his friend's grasp. "We need to get in there before they do. The last thing we need is for Ger'igguthy to replace Nyarlathotep. If that happens, we are back at square fucking one!"

Crossing the square, The Discarded continued to surge forward. Meeting zero resistance from the screaming enforcers, they proceeded to gun them down one by one by one until they had covered half the square in blood and bullet casings. Dwayne smirked; they would reach the doors well before the incoming force had time to stop them. Then it was a simple matter of uploading Mickie's virus to the reception terminal and locking it down while Max hunted Sanderson. It was almost too easy...

"Look out!" Oliver shoved Dwayne out of the way as a barrage of gunfire came from an unseen gunman lurking in the plastic foliage to the left of the door. The shotgun blast tore into his flesh, flinging him into the wall. Oliver's head struck the concrete as the air was driven from his body. Max turned to open fire but was tackled by a man in a filthy robe that had been hiding behind the wall.

"Ah, Mr Potter..." A voice drawled. It was cold and emotionless like something long dead, "I was hoping we would get a chance for a bit of payback."

Dwayne struggled to right himself; he had dropped his weapon and tweaked his knee to the point that he could barely put any weight on it. As he turned, his mouth fell open, and a moan escaped. Emerging from the bushes was a Discarded Guardian with a shotgun in one hand and an old pickle jar in the other.

Dwayne couldn't believe it; the jar contained a severed head that winked at him.

"I don't believe we have had the pleasure," the head chortled Clearly decapitation was a minor inconvenience. "Warren Tremayne, Hierophant of The Discarded, at your service. I'd shake your hand but..."

While Dwayne was fumbling for words and unarmed, Max got the better of his attacker and repeatedly slammed the back of his head into the curb until it was little more than a bloody paste. Oliver gasped, raised his gun just as the guardian went to blast Dwayne, and shattered the jar with a volley of buckshot. Tremayne's head plummeted to the ground with a wet smack. As it hit, the guardian convulsed. Dwayne realised instantly that the parasite keeping Tremayne alive was in charge of a hive mind of parasitic control. Grimacing through the pain, he hobbled over, snatched the gun from the guardian's hand and obliterated Warren Tremayne once and for all.

Now, it was The Discarded's turn to drop to their knees and scream as their parasites went into a frenzy and detached from their hosts leaving them to drop face down as they scuttled to safety. Seeing that the threat had passed, Dwayne dropped and crawled to Oliver, putting pressure on the worst of the wounds, though he knew it would do little good. The reluctant whistleblower was fading fast as his blood formed a lake around his torso.

"Shit... Thanks, Oliver, you saved my life."

Oliver smiled. "You're welcome."

Dwayne held out his hand which Oliver took and squeezed. "I'm sorry."

Again, Oliver smiled. "Kiss my arse, Dwayne."

Dwayne couldn't help chuckle. "I really am sorry."

A moment and a death-rattle later and Oliver was gone.

Dwayne sighed; he had been starting to grow on him. "You go ahead, Max. I'll get him back to the shop. He deserves a proper funeral."

Max shook his head.

"Look, everyone is counting on you, and I'll just hold you back. I can barely fucking walk on this knee. I'll be about as much use in there as a plastic flamethrower. Go on... Go!"

Reluctantly, Max nodded, clapped Dwayne on the shoulder and stalked towards the doors. As they slid aside, he had horrible flashbacks to that fateful day back in March of 2125 when he had been summoned to meet Mr Sanderson for a special job. Only Max had changed since then. The foyer was the same down to the last detail. Even the receptionist was the same, though she looked grey and dead-eyed. Racing over, Max withdrew the memory stick containing Mickie's virus and approached the desk.

"Do you have an appointment?" The receptionist slurred, her pitch-black eyes rolling. Clearly, whatever Mickie was doing to the trapezohedron had an effect on everyone touched by the shadow of chaos.

Max reached out and touched her face. It was icy and rubbery ... dead. Sighing, he took the drive and plugged it into the terminal. Instantly, the lights went to maximum brightness and the doors went into lockdown.

"An appointment? Do you?" The receptionist slumped off her chair and instantly started to decompose. Max scowled and turned towards the elevator. As far as he was aware, the only person inside the tower aside from himself and the living dead receptionist, was his target. The conflict had drawn all the guards and staff outside but, somehow, he knew that Sanderson was there ... he could feel it. Like a spider at the heart of its web, Max could feel Sanderson tugging on the gossamer threads of reality that somehow bound them together. Ever since he had been mutilated by the man, he had felt a strange cosmic connection to his tormentor that needed to be severed. Permanently.

Stepping towards the lift and pressing the call button, Max prepared for the final reckoning.

"Can't this bloody thing go any faster?"

Frank shot Jake a sideways glance. "You're worse than my youngest fry. You know it won't, no citizen-grade vehicle has a top speed over forty and the battery on this one is almost flat. To be brutally honest, it'd probably be quicker to walk at this point."

"Nuts!"

"Jeez, Jake, calm down, we are nearly at the rear of the tower. With any luck, all the enforcers will have been dealt with." Mickie turned to Muggo'sutha. "You'd better stay with Frank; I don't like the look of that gunshot. Did you tell your Voormis buddies to take care of the loading area?"

Muggs nodded sullenly, he desperately wanted a piece of the action but knew deep down that the diminutive human was talking sense.

"Great..." Jake sighed.

"What's the matter now, sulky-bollocks?"

"I'm out of booze." He upended the open flask and watched the final tiny drop land on the plastic seat cover.

"Good. The last thing we need is you stumbling around the holding cells singing Voormis drinking songs."

"We?" Jake side-eyed Mickie eyebrow raised.

"You didn't think you were going in alone, did you? With Muggs out of action, I'm your backup."

"Really?"

"Problem?" Mickie made a show of cracking her knuckles.

Jake held up his hands. "No, none at all. It's just..."

"Go on."

"After Expiration Day when you ended up at the shop, you didn't go any further than the roof for what?"

Mickie sighed. "Five years, one day, six hours... To put it more bluntly, until I was kidnapped by that parasite worshipping loony, Tremayne. What's your point, Jake, and do you really think this is a good time for a deep and meaningful conversation? We are a little pre-occupied, for fuck's sake."

"Look, I'm not being a dick, I'm just worried, is all. I wanted to say something when you hopped on Frank's boat but was concerned that you'd take it the wrong way. Plus, I was so hammered that I kind of forgot until a few hours ago. You've gone from being a shut-in to gallivanting around the globe in a ridiculously short time, I just want to know that you're okay."

"You want to know if I'm okay? No, Jake, I'm not... None of us are. If you mean, am I okay with being outside, yeah... I think I am. Nothing cures agoraphobia quite like being held over a pit filled with creepy-crawlies. Trust me, after an experience like that, it's a wonder I've not gone the other way and developed a fear of being in enclosed spaces. Look, I'm *coping*, which is the best any of us can do, right?"

Jake, Frank, and Muggs all nodded.

"Good." Mickie finally exhaled. "Now, can you please save the concerned parent act until later and put these on." he tossed an enforcer's uniform at Jake. "We are nearly there; we need to get in there and help Max."

Jake nodded and took off his battered trench-coat.

"One last thing."

"Yeah?"

"Please, tell me you remembered to bring the roll of gaffer tape I gave you?"

As Frank swung the white and green plastic box on wheels into the loading area, Jake grinned...

Max jabbed the button marked 103 and folded his arms across his chest as the doors closed and the GAF advertisement video began to play on the wall-mounted screen.

> *"The Global Arms Federation, the ultimate in lethal force... making the world a safer place. Defend your home from undesirables with the brand new his and hers range of People's Pocket Rocket. This compact SMG is light, durable and comes in a variety of colours to match your soft furnishings. Best of all, it fires tactical rocket-propelled explosive rounds that are guaranteed to see off any unwanted visitor. Our new smokeless technology means that you no longer have to worry about that tell-tale cordite smell tainting your family meal. Save money on pot pourri and order yours today!"*

It was almost a relief when the over-enthused female voice ceased prattling, and the mind-numbing muzak retook centre stage. Not that Max was paying any attention; his eyes were fixed on the digital display that ticked off the floors second-by-second as he hurtled towards the roof. His gun was fully loaded, and he had a special gift for Mr Sanderson in his back pocket. All he had to do was keep a level head and stick to the plan... Not an easy task under the circumstances.

Though he had only known Oliver for a short time, his violent heroic demise had affected Max deeply. He couldn't help drawing parallels between their own quests for redemption. Max hadn't directly caused anyone's death during his time as an enforcer, sure, but he certainly did his part to enable those who did. The only real difference was that Oliver did so under immense duress while Max didn't know any better. Another fine example of brainwashing and tradition being taken to bloody extremes in the ICAE.

Cracking his knuckles and shaking out his calf muscles to divert his increasingly introspective train of thought, Max concentrated on the motion of the lift as it drew close to its destination. As the whirr of the cable and the creak of the winch came to an abrupt halt, he flicked the safety off and stepped out into the now-brightly-lit reception area of floor 103, the harshness of the lights dazzling and disorientating.

Once his vision had adjusted to the glare, Max surveyed the room. He had never been in the executive areas before, so he didn't know what to expect. Disgruntled workers had whispered of gold-plated walls with diamond-studded fittings, so the drab wood panelling and neoclassical marble flooring came as a bit of a disappointment. It was entirely void of features except for two towering plastic aspidistra and a vast reception desk. Max cocked his rifle to get the attention of the person sitting behind it with her head on the desk, but it failed to coax a response.

Cautiously stepping towards the comatose secretary, Max went to check for a pulse but quickly pulled his hand away like it had been bitten. The poor woman was long dead. Any life she had displayed over the past five years had come from an Eldritch source. Now that source had been cut off by Mickie, she had proceeded to melt. Fat globs of augmented skin and putrid flesh dripped from the polished mahogany, landing on the cold stone below with a sickening series of splats.

Fighting a combination of rage and nausea, Max tightened his grip on his trusty AK-47, stepped towards the imposing double doors, reared back, and kicked them open. Snarling through gritted teeth, he marched in, gun levelled at the man convulsing in the chair. The ceiling-mounted spot-lamps flickered between dim and bright in an unnerving strobe as Malcolm Sanderson, prone in his swivel chair, shook and jerked. Max grinned and pointed the gun at his nemesis' head. Then, abruptly, Mr Sanderson fell still and grinned as the lights stabilised on a dingy half-light.

"Ha, got you," Sanderson chuckled. "Did you really think it would be so easy to cut off my connection to the Haunter of the Dark? Those insects in the plaza are one thing, but I am another." He paused and took an old gold coin from his breast pocket, running it through his fingers. "You see, I have a personal connection with Nyarlathotep, a direct line, if you will. Now, what did you want to talk about?"

Sanderson theatrically held his fingertips to his mouth and feigned embarrassment. "Oops, sorry ... sore point? Why don't you take a seat, I'll talk ... you listen."

Max had heard enough. Taking another step forward, he opened fire, riddling Sanderson with bullets that knocked him from his seat and onto the floor. He knew it would have had little effect but damn it felt good. Ejecting the spent clip and inserting another, he awaited the inevitable retort. He didn't have to wait long.

Rising from a hollow cackle to an extended rattle of mirth, Sanderson's mocking laughter echoed off the walls as he rose slowly to his feet. "How many times? You can't kill me, you fool!"

Max grinned, shrugged and let the gun loose on its strap.

"Ye, well, I can't fault you for trying. Anyway, I believe it's my turn, yes?" His eyes flashing orange, Sanderson raised his arms aloft and smiled. Shadows from the corners of the room deepened and melded, forming wraith-like tendrils of darkness that coiled and licked at the walls. "Time for you to take a whipping, I believe. After all, that's what happens to disobedient dogs, correct?"

As a shadow tentacle whipped in his direction, Max sidestepped and drew a small green object from his pocket. Sanderson recoiled, grabbing his throat with both hands and slamming into the panelling with such force that the wood splintered. He rocked and rolled in supposed agony before again falling still and flashing his patented manure-eating grin.

Max rolled his eyes.

"I'm afraid that won't work, Maximilian, not without the Aklo chants that accompany a warding, and you can't do those... Can you? Shame, your friend has done an admirable job of replicating a Mnar stone. Unfortunately, without the accompanying words, it's as harmless to me as a paperweight."

Sanderson started to edge around the desk. "She really has done a remarkable job. May I?" He held out his hand for the stone.

Max shook his head and took two steps back but one of the shadow tentacles lashed his wrist, sending the stone spinning into the air. Sanderson deftly caught it and studied its craftsmanship.

"Remarkable. You see what can be achieved with the correct augmentations. Your friend, Mickie, isn't it?"

Max remained impassive, his hand slowly reaching into his pocket.

On the wall-mounted screen behind Sanderson, a red light had started to pulse in the lower left corner. The overseer didn't see it and continued his appraisal of Mickie's work. "I have to say, Max, I'm impressed. I do believe her work surpasses that of your original Starmaker, Danni. Remember her? Of course you do. I heard about your raid on the Marsh compound. Pitiful. Amusing ... but pitiful."

As Sanderson circled one way around the desk, Max circled the other, maintaining a regular distance between the two foes.

"You know, I'm seriously considering *recruiting* your friend. Danni has proven to be such a bitter disappointment, refusing to bend to the will of the Crawling Chaos, no matter how many times I torture her."

Max grunted and clenched his fist as he neared the high-backed chair.

"I can see you think I'm a monster, I assure you, I'm not. At my core, I am a simple businessman who will go to any lengths to secure a deal, as you found out to your cost. Business is an art, and I consider myself the Rembrandt or Van Gough of the boardroom. I just will simply not tolerate defiance. It's not my fault she spews Aklo whenever we enter negotiations—causing the death of a myriad of enforcers, I hasten to add—is it? No, it is not. Danni brought the wrath of Nyarlathotep down upon herself.

Still, that's what you get for trying to deal with someone touched by Nodens." Sanderson continued edging towards the centre of the room with Max mirroring his every step. "You didn't know that, did you? Of course, you didn't, how would you? Danni is part of an ancient bloodline dating back to the lost continent of Mu that was born under the sign of one of the Elder Gods, the enemies of the Great Old Ones. It accounts for her resilience... I doubt Mickie will prove as immune to *persuasion.*"

By now, Max was level with the coin on the desk. Looking upon it, Max's vision sharpened, revealing gossamer-like threads of shadow connecting the tendrils and Sanderson himself with the artefact. In an instant of clarity, Max knew what to do and his fingers closed around the small object in his pocket... a *gift* from Mickie.

"Don't even think about grabbing the coin. It will do you a universe more harm than good."

Max smiled innocently, withdrew the flashbang from his pocket, turned his head, and slammed it on the coin. Sanderson roared and howled, the shadow tentacles dispersed and the lights in the room brightened. Seizing his opportunity, Max leapt to the screen and hit the blinking red light.

"Fool!" Sanderson snarled, his voice not entirely his own. "I shall destroy you for that." As his body smouldered and distorted from the effects of the light, a young face appeared on the screen.

"Hello, Malcolm," Danni croaked. Her face was gaunt and pale, her head shaved, and her skin mottled with a tapestry of scars from a hundred lacerations, burns, and abrasions.

"You... How did you?" Sanderson trailed off, spotting two enforcers standing behind the starmaker, a smirk twisting his thin lips. "Ah, I see there is little point continuing, you may want to take a little look behind you."

Danni returned the mocking smile.

Sanderson looked confused for a second before addressing his minions. "Kill her."

The enforcers didn't move.

"What are you waiting for? Kill her!"

Now it was time for Max to grin.

"Do it, damn you!"

One after the other, the enforcers removed their hoods to reveal the grinning countenances of Mickie and Jake.

Sanderson roared, drew his laser-scalpel from his pocket and lunged for Max. Before he could make it halfway across the room, Danni started to chant. The alien syllables instantly had an effect that stunned the inflicted despot.

"What? How is this affecting me?"

As Sanderson's body started to split into atoms, Max pointed to his left hand. He was still clutching the Mnar stone that was now glowing with brilliant white light. His bones cracked and twisted as the guttural language undulated from Danni's lips. Even on the edge of oblivion, he couldn't bear not to have the last word.

"Well played, Max. You'd be a natural card player, you know that?"

Max shrugged modestly.

"It is futile, however. You will never truly purge the influence of Nyarlathotep from this building!"

Once again seeing the threads of shadow that spread from the coin, Max pulled his cuff over his hand, swept it up, and tossed it at Sanderson. By now, the overseer was little more than a pulpy bag of bodily fluids and liquidised bone that punctured under the impact of the coin. There was a flash as the light of the Mnar stone met the shadow of the coin. The fabric of reality warped as Malcolm Sanderson exploded in a shower of gore. A split-second later, both the stone and the, now inert, coin hit the floor.

"Max, are you alright?" Danni asked.

He nodded and pointed to the door.

"We'll get her out, Max," Mickie asserted. "Grab the stone and get the hell out of there. Jake has rigged the generator to blow in five minutes. Rendezvous at the shop, okay?"

Panic replacing his elation, Max quickly located the Mnar stone and the Coin of Chaos amongst the steaming remains of Malcolm Sanderson then raced for the lift. Hammering the G button he mentally willed the steel box to go faster. In theory, he had plenty of time to escape. In practice, however, he knew only too well how poor Jake was at setting a timer. Upon reaching the ground floor with his heart in his mouth, he snatched the memory stick from the terminal to release the lockdown and raced through the doors and across the plaza.

Exactly five minutes after Jake had rigged the power supply for the GAF tower to blow, it erupted in an explosion that shook Zone 51 to its rotting foundations.

EPILOGUE

A SEPIA CLOUD ON THE HORIZON

Climbing out of the hatch and onto the roof of Edwards Antiques, Dwayne watched the smoke from the smouldering wreckage of the GAF tower spiral in the wind. Below, the streets were lined with undesirables, former employees of the ICAE, assorted Gillmen, and Voormis. In short, the entirety of the South-West Sector of Zone 51 was on the streets of the former Betyls Cove to witness the end of an era. It was a monumental occasion, but one Dwayne couldn't fully enjoy. Turning his back on the panorama, he limped over to the rooftop's other occupant and cleared his throat.

"Well, I guess that's that... What do you think will happen now?"

Mickie took a deep breath and shrugged her shoulders. "Well, the optimist in me would like to think of an era of peace and cooperation..."

"What does the realist think?"

"Power vacuum, I guess. We already saw Ger'igguthy's mob trying to assume power, and God knows how many Great Old Ones are out there. Plus, we may have dealt with Nyarlathotep for the present, but I guarantee that he will regroup and try again, he's down, but not dead... I seriously doubt he, or it, or whatever, can really, truly die. I'll have to consult Ben's books to try and figure that one out."

"Cheerful."

"You did ask."

Dwayne chuckled softly while shaking his head.

"Anyway, what's your plan, now, are you staying here or going back down under?"

"After I've prepared Oliver for sea burial... yeah. Some of

Frank's mates are giving me a lift to Australia. Now they can come and go as they please, they are going to meet up with their cousins out there. We are going to drop Ollie off en route. Basically, in a few hours, I'm out of here."

"How come?"

"How come, what? How come I'm leaving the zone, or, How come I'm burying Oliver at sea?"

Mickie cocked an eyebrow and studied Dwayne's expression. "Both."

"Well, I figured he deserved better than being burned at a GAF cremation centre or eaten by ghouls... It's the least I can do, the wanker saved my life." Dwayne paused and sighed. "Plus, I guess I feel that I owe him that much as an apology. He was right, I couldn't blame him any more than I should blame myself. I guess he struck a nerve, that's why I have to go. Every time I see one of those booths..."

"You shouldn't blame yourself, Dwayne, you really shouldn't. You gave people hope. It's not your fault Sanderson used that hope to kill people. He's the one to blame, not you... not Oliver."

Dwayne smiled. "Thank you, Mickie. I guess you're right. It doesn't make it any easier, though... In any case, I promised Sam and Jo that I'd go back, and I always at least try to be a man of my word."

"Look after them, Dwayne, they're good people."

"What about you... plans?"

"I think I'll stay here for now. Someone needs to go through Ben's library, just in case. Anyway, I think Max and Danni will need my help, at least, for a while."

"How is she?"

"About as well as can be expected." Mickie shook her head. "Poor girl has been through seven shades of Hell. Max is going to have his work cut out being her big brother."

"Guess she needs a big sister too?"

"Yeah... I'm not very good at it. Drones, computers, no problem. People... I suck."

"Rubbish! You are the only person in all the time I've known him that has gotten anywhere with Jake. It's impressive how you deal with his bullshit."

Mickie chuckled. "Now, being a bitch, that I can do... Where is Jake, anyway?"

"Him, Frank, and Muggs have gone down the Dancing Shrimp for a few drinks and a sing-song."

"Good grief."

Dwayne chuckled as he prepared to leave her to the show. "My thoughts exactly... You'll need to keep an eye on him. He seems troubled."

Mickie looked at him askew.

"More than usual, I mean. He saw something in Pnakotus. Something no man should see."

"The Ghoul pile, he said."

"Nah, not that. He touched a Yithian artefact and saw glimpses of the future. One future of many, at least," he paused and looked her in the eye. "Mickie, I think he saw the end of the world."

"Damn."

"Exactly. You know as well as I do how Mr Baker deals with trauma."

"Noted. I'll keep my tabs on him."

Excellent. Thanks, Mick," Dwayne smiled. "Right, I'll leave you in peace. Take care of yourself, okay? And, if you ever need me, feel free to send Pigeon over. I'm going to miss the little fella."

"You got it. Adios, Dwayne."

As Dwayne rose a flash of lightning traced its way across the sky followed by a colossal roar of thunder to the north. Both Mickie and Dwayne looked towards the moor as the sky turned a sickly shade of yellow.

Dwayne flinched at the deafening crack and stepped towards the edge of the building. Dark shapes fluttered and flashed as they phased in and out of reality. Rain began to lash down in thick rods as a keening wail became audible over the hiss. "What the Hell?"

Mickie looked pensive. "I dunno, Dwayne, but it can't be good... and I'm almost one-hundred percent certain that Hell will pale in comparison."

THE END

ACKNOWLEDGEMENTS:

Many thanks to the Eerie River team for the fantastic job they've done on this book.
Thanks to Linda, Rob Poyton, Pete Finnemore, Callum Pearce, and many more for keeping me vaguely sane in an increasingly insane world, and a special thanks to you, dear reader. Without you lot, I don't think I'd bother getting out of bed most mornings.

ABOUT THE AUTHOR

Tim Mendees is a rather odd chap. He's an August Derleth Award-nominated horror writer from Macclesfield in the North-West of England that specialises in cosmic horror and weird fiction. His work has been described as the love-child of H.P. Lovecraft and P.G. Wodehouse and is often peppered with a wry sense of humour that acts as a counterpoint to the disturbing narratives.

Tim has appeared in more anthologies and magazines than he can count as well as releasing two short story collections and ten novellas. He has also curated and edited several cosmic horror-themed anthologies.

When he is not arguing with the spellchecker, Tim is the lead vocalist in gothic rock band Grooving n Green, a DJ with a weekly radio show, and one of the co-founders of The Innsmouth Literary Festival. He is also the co-presenter of 'The Innsmouth Book Club Podcast,' 'The Monster in my Bed,' & 'Strange Shadows: The Clark Ashton Smith Podcast.' He currently lives in Brighton & Hove with his pet crab, Gerald, and an ever-increasing army of stuffed octopods.

EERIE RIVER PUBLISHING

NOVELS & COLLECTIONS
After: Horror Novel by Drew Starling (2024)
The Roots Run Deep: Collection by C.M. Forest (2024)
A Shadow Over Haven: Nick Holleran Series (2024)
Gulf: Dark Walker Series Book One (2023)
Breach: Dark Walker Series Book Two (2024)
Chasing The Dragon: Horror Vigilante Novel (2023)
The Naughty Corner: Novella Collection (2023)
Shades Of Night: Night Order Series Book One (2022)
Untamed Night: Night Order Series Book Two (2023)
Dead Man Walking: Nick Holleran Series (2022)
Devil Walks in Blood: Nick Holleran Series (2022)
The Darkness In The Pines: Nick Holleran Series (2023)
The Void: Sapphic Fiction (2023)
They Are Cursed Like You: Trailer Park Witches Series (2023)
Infested: Horror Novel (2022)
SENTINEL: The Bensalem Files (2021)
NOTHUS: The Bensalem Files (2022)
Miracle Growth: A Cosmic Horror Novella (2022)
Helluland: Urban Fantasy of Legends (2023)
A Sword Named Sorrow: Fantasy Novel (2022)
Storming Area 51 (2019)

ANTHOLOGIES
From Beyond the Threshold
The Earth Bleeds at Night: Anthology of Horror
Year of the Tarot: Four Book Series
AFTER: A Post-Apocalyptic Survivor Series
Elemental Cycle: Four Book Series
It Calls From Series
Blood Sins
Last Stop: Whiskey Pete
Of Fire and Stars: LGBTQIA+ Fantasy anthology
From Beyond the Threshold

DRABBLE COLLECTIONS
Forgotten Ones: Drabbles of Myth and Legend
Dark Magic: Drabbles of Magic and Lore

COMING SOON
Seed: Dark Walker Series Book Three (2025)
Infernal Night: Dark Walker Series Book Three (2025)

AN EERIE RIVER PUBLISHING ANTHOLOGY

The Earth Bleeds At Night

EDITED BY HOLLEY CORNETTO

INFESTED

C.M. FOREST

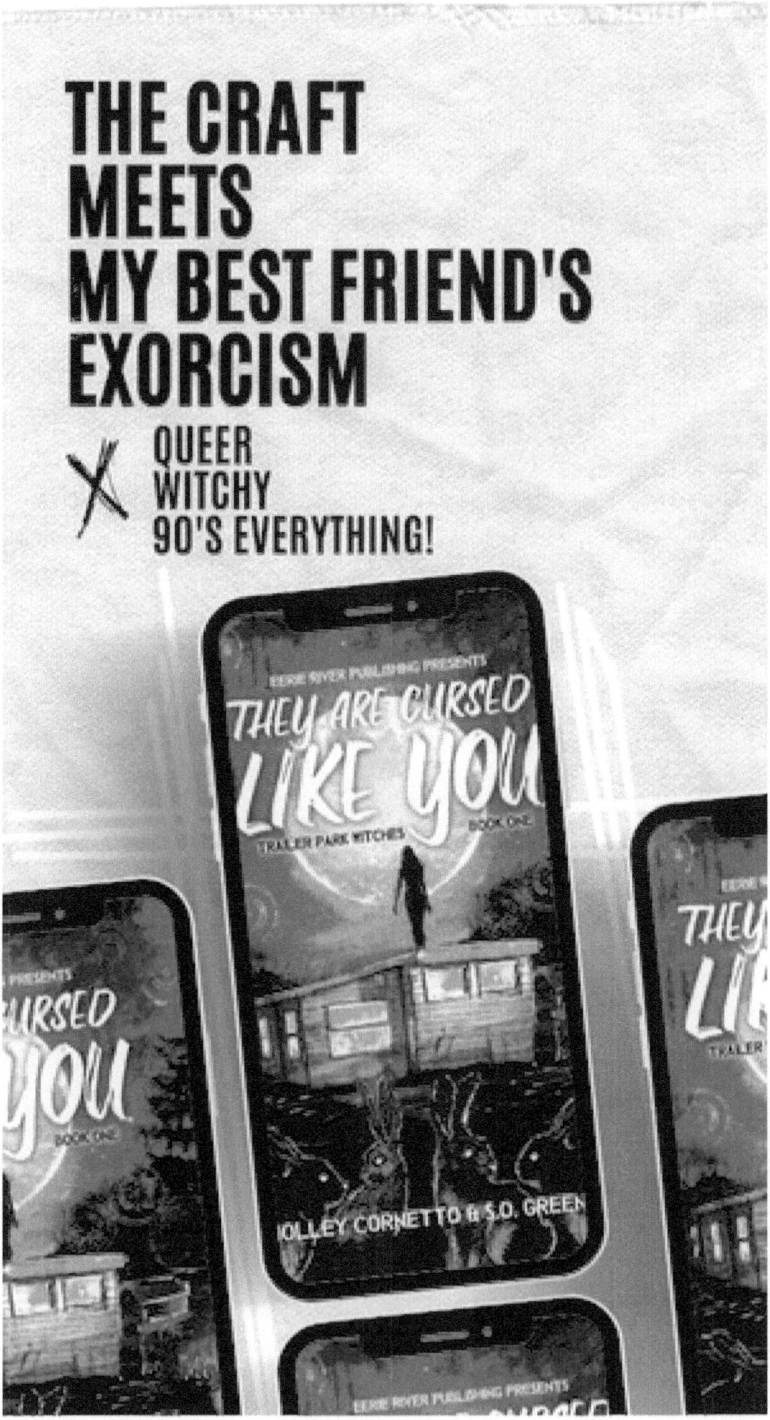

THE CRAFT
MEETS
MY BEST FRIEND'S
EXORCISM
QUEER
WITCHY
90'S EVERYTHING!
EERIE RIVER PUBLISHING PRESENTS
THEY ARE CURSED
LIKE YOU
TRAILER PARK WITCHES
BOOK ONE
OLLEY CORNETTO & S.O. GREEN

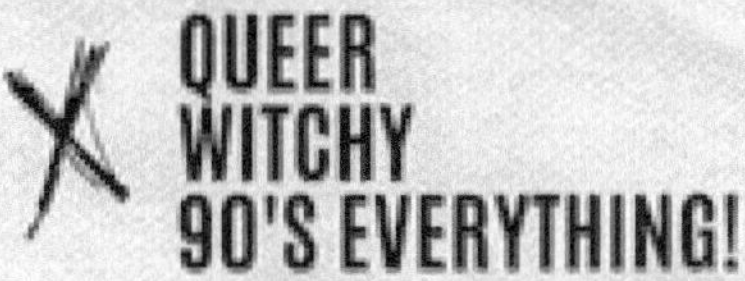

SHELLY CAMPBELL

GULF

DARK WALKER SERIES BOOK 1

9 781998 112463